THE MEN WHO ROBBED

THE

GREAT TRAIN ROBBERS

ALSO AVAILABLE BY THIS AUTHOR:

Scream If You Want To Go Faster (2004)

Discover more titles by Mick Lee at www.micklee-theauthor.com

THE MEN WHO ROBBED

THE

GREAT TRAIN ROBBERS

MICK LEE

Matador
9 Priory Business Park
Kibworth Beauchamp
Leicestershire LE8 0RX, UK
Tel: (+44) 116 279 2299
Fax: (+44) 116 279 2277
Email: books@troubador.co.uk
Web: www.troubador.co.uk/matador

ISBN 978 1783062 485

British Library Cataloguing in Publication Data.
A catalogue record for this book is available from the British Library.

Typeset in 11pt Aldine401 BT Roman by Troubador Publishing Ltd

Matador is an imprint of Troubador Publishing Ltd

For Jackie and Peggy

The Main Cast

The robbers
Gordon Goody, Hairdresser
Bruce Reynolds, Antique dealer
Ronald 'Buster' Edwards, Florist
Ronald Biggs, Builder
Roger Cordrey, Florist
John Daly, Antique dealer
James Hussey, Painter and decorator
Roy James, Silversmith
Danny Pembroke, Builder
Harry Smith, Decorator
Robert Welch, Club owner
Jimmy White, Café owner
Charlie Wilson, Greengrocer
Tommy Wisbey, Bookmaker
William Boal, Engineer
Brian Field, Solicitor's Clerk
Lennie Field, Seaman
John Wheater, Solicitor

The men who robbed the robbers (all fictional)
Eddie Maloney, IRA Fundraiser (a.k.a. 'The Ulsterman')
Tommy Lavery, Career criminal
Jack Armstrong, Lavery's right hand man (and train robber)
Mickey Griffin, Lavery employee (and train robber)
George Parlane, Lavery employee

The men who caught the robbers

Detective Sergeant Joe Watson, Flying Squad (fictional)

Detective Inspector Cliff Barclay, Forensics & Flying Squad (fictional)

Detective Inspector Frank Williams, Flying Squad

Commander George Hatherill, Head of C Division and New Scotland Yard

Detective Chief Superintendent Ernie Millen, initial Head of the Flying Squad

Detective Chief Superintendent Tommy Butler, Head of the Robbery Squad (Head of the Flying Squad from September 1963)

Detective Chief Inspector Peter Vibart, Flying Squad

Detective Sergeant Steve Moore, Flying Squad

Detective Sergeant Jim Nevill, Flying Squad

Detective Sergeant Jack Slipper, Flying Squad

Detective Superintendent Malcolm Fewtrell, Bucks CID

1

'You've found some mugs for this train robbery, then?'

'Oh yeah, they're just what we need.'

The hierarchy had insisted that this man was their ideal partner on the British mainland. Eddie Maloney, the best fundraiser in the business, pressed him again, the northern accent already grating.

'How do you mean?'

'I mean, they're thieves. Decent ones.'

'They'll be able to pull off this sort of job?'

'I reckon so.' Tommy Lavery paused to drag on his cigarette. 'Look, they're villains, but they're not from one of the big London firms. That was supposed to be important, wasn't it?'

'Yes, it was.'

'They're professionals, don't get me wrong. We can't do this with a bunch of idiots.'

'Precisely.'

'But they're not the sort to run around with guns.'

'Good.'

The plan felt perfect, right down to fitting up the men they were hiring to do the job. The Irish Republican Army was keen to avoid the attention that using the likes of the Krays or the Richardsons would attract. It was also important that nobody got shot, because guns made the English police mad.

Eddie huddled into his overcoat to stay warm, as he tried to

1

keep pace with his new business partner. He reminded himself that it was all for the cause, that this was the big operation that would deliver cash for back home. His speed through Green Park was driven by Lavery's lengthy gait, and he tried to focus on the man's face. He was a renowned Manchester villain, known, apparently, as the 'Beast of the North'.

Lavery stopped to light Maloney another cigarette, which he did with ease, despite the wind. Steady hands, useful in a crisis. Not that he envisaged any problems. All they needed were a bunch of gullible thieves to do the hard work for them, to rob a train. He returned to quizzing Lavery.

'How did you find these men?'

'You don't need to know, Eddie.'

'I think I'm entitled. I do have all the inside information.'

'And I have all the contacts.'

Lavery cast his match away and laughed. Eddie looked around the park, and spotted two men standing under a tree, staring in their direction. They had been by the gates five minutes ago when they walked into the park.

'Tommy, you know those two over there?'

Lavery didn't even glance over. 'Yeah, they're my boys.'

Eddie was alone with no back up, at least for now. What was Ger Whelan setting him up for?

'How many men you got? For the job?' Eddie asked.

Lavery carried on walking, pulling on his cigarette enthusiastically. 'I don't know yet.'

'What?'

'We've got the ringleaders hooked. They're dying to meet you.'

'Set it up, then.' This suited Eddie. Lavery's word meant nothing until he saw them in person.

'It already is. Gordon Goody wants to meet the man with all the inside information,' Tommy said, smiling.

'That's me.'

'Indeed.'

'And, how did you find him?'

'Oh, through a bent clerk who works for a bent brief I know. Name of Brian Field. He's represented Goody and some of his pals before. He slips them inside information on his richer clients. You know, then they go and rob them.' Lavery laughed.

'Sounds a liability to me.'

'No, he's solid, is Brian.' Lavery returned to his business-like face. 'Done some work for people I know. We can rely on him, and this lot, they trust him too. Goody and his associates, they know a few faces round South London.'

'Do they know you?'

'They might by reputation. But, to be honest, most of them have no idea the North even exists. Their world begins and ends in London.'

'I don't mind that.'

Maloney thought about his instructions. They needed money for the struggle. There was no problem sourcing all the equipment for the fight, there were plenty of places to get your hands on bombs, bullets and guns. What they lacked at that moment was the finance, which was where Eddie came in. His links to the organisation went back to before the war, when his father fought alongside Ger's dad, Terry Whelan. A conflict never mentioned in British history books. Since the surrender of the 1922 agreement, they would always be struggling for true freedom.

'Can we agree how we're going to work together first, before you talk to Goody?' Lavery enquired.

'That would make sense. You know what we want from it. Our share.'

'Yeah, I do.'

Eddie glanced across at Lavery. How much could he be trusted? He had little choice; this was the pre-selected partner, instruction coming from above. There was no way he could pull off a heist like this alone, and the organisation had confidence in Lavery. The hierarchy were keen to set up links with organised crime in England outside of London, where there was less police attention. All the smuggling going on down at Liverpool docks was, apparently, Tommy's doing. Who was he to judge when Ger Whelan told him otherwise?

Maloney's attention was drawn to a man in a sharp suit sitting on a bench about twenty yards ahead of them, studying a newspaper. Who was he working for? The police? This Lavery? Or was he just an innocent businessman, thumbing through *The Times*? He had a right to be paranoid, given what he knew, and what they were planning. Lavery exuded calm and confidence.

'As we discussed, we take a million off the top, regardless of what they steal,' Lavery stated coldly.

'Yes.' Maloney accepted that this was their opening gambit.

'And we split that fifty-fifty.'

'Straight down the middle, yes.'

'So, regardless of what they take, that's what we're getting.'

'Yeah, we need to motivate our new friends, don't we?'

'Suppose so.'

They would owe the crew they hired to do the job, nothing. Without their set up there would be no robbery, no fortune for whoever carried out the raid on their behalf.

'Look, we know there's going to be at least two million on that train, possibly more if we pick the right one.' Maloney tried to exude authority, an expert on moving substantial amounts of money about.

'And, that's what we're gonna tell them?' Lavery asked.

'Let's say it could be up to four million.'

'Four million?' Lavery's eyes widened. Imagine the reaction of the everyday thieves. Eddie was comfortable with an easy five hundred grand and minimal risk. Would Tommy be tempted to ask for more?

'Well, let's let them think that. Truth is, it doesn't really have the capacity to carry more than about three, so our man tells me.'

'And he's reliable, is he?'

'Totally. You could say he's like family,' Eddie said.

'How'd you get a man on the inside?'

'That's my business, I'm afraid, Tommy.'

Maloney was still keen to play what cards he had close to his chest, knew Lavery would do the same in his position. Without accurate inside knowledge, no self-respecting thief would raise a finger. The secret to any successful heist was to know what was going to happen in advance, and be ready for it. As soon as you started guessing, you got caught.

'We need to persuade this lot that we don't exist. Neither of us,' Maloney carried on, desperate to protect his inside source.

'Oh, don't worry, I know ways of making sure these thieves we hire know exactly where we stand.'

The two men stopped underneath a tree towards the corner of the park. A young couple walked past, arm in arm, kissing as they went. Maloney eyed them with distaste. There was a time and a place for everything, but not that in public. He scanned the area and spotted the two men who were following them, leaning against a set of railings, about fifty yards away. One of them appeared to nod in their direction. Eddie looked around but saw no sign of recognition in Lavery's eyes.

His new partner had something else to suggest. 'I want to have a couple of my boys in on the job. On the inside, you know, just to keep an eye on it.'

'What, to join in, you mean?'

'Yeah. That way we can both know what's going on. I don't want them to double cross us, whoever they are. This way we can feel more secure.'

'Those two you mean?' Eddie asked, indicating the men watching.

'Maybe. Certainly one of them.'

Eddie pondered this for a moment. The idea of watching the men they hired from the inside struck him as a sensible one. There was a lot at stake. 'Fine by me.'

'Good.' Lavery rubbed his hands together, and headed for the park exit. 'Eddie, I'll let you know through Brian Field when and where to meet Gordon Goody.'

'I want to get going straight away.'

'You'll hear by tomorrow, I'm sure. Shall we meet up afterwards?'

'Yeah. I know a place,' Eddie replied. There were cafés the Irish community used that were definitely safe. The two men who had been watching them loomed up at Lavery's shoulder.

'Good. Through Brian?' Lavery asked.

Eddie nodded, and they shook hands. Maloney then sat on a bench and watched the three men leave the park together. He toyed with following Tommy, but knew he was an isolated force. He worked alone on the British mainland, only called up extra manpower when there was a deal going down. The organisation had already told him to call upon Lavery's help if he needed it. How did you keep a watch on your guardian without raising suspicion?

2

Gordon Goody studied the man on the park bench, whose face was hidden behind a newspaper, then scanned the commuters walking past. His escort had disappeared, having steered him in the direction of the mysterious seated figure. He cleared his throat.

'My name's Gordon. You wanted to meet me.'

The man dropped the paper a few inches, and looked up, then peered left and right down the pathway, examining passers by. Gordon followed his gaze and when he looked back, the figure was staring into his eyes. There was no sign of recognition. He was dressed like an accountant or a solicitor, in a suit and overcoat, and appeared rather ordinary. Was this really the high flyer with an incredible tip-off that Brian Field had mentioned?

Brian had been scant with the details over the phone, other than the fact somebody wanted to meet Gordon with a view to using him and his friends on a massive heist. Brian had played a significant role in helping he and Charlie Wilson get off the Heathrow robbery charges earlier in the year. His share of that sixty odd grand had been pretty useful for a while, but was already running out. There was no harm in checking out this vague possibility.

Gordon was already sick of playing games by the time he reached the bench. He met a go-between called 'Mark' at Field's office, was then driven around North London to Finsbury Park and led to this stranger. He cast around looking for Russian spies. There had to be easier ways to be introduced to people.

The man cleared his throat and then stood up, leaving the newspaper meticulously folded on the bench, as if it was a form of signal. Gordon looked around again, all he saw were commuters, minding their own business.

'You can call me Jock. Let's go for a walk, shall we?' The accent certainly didn't sound Scottish; it had a familiar ring to it.

They shook hands and Gordon eyed the man in front of him. He was short and round, balding, hardly looked like a master criminal. He set off walking, forcing Gordon to step into line alongside. The pace was deliberate and purposeful. The man placed his trilby hat on his head, and waddled slightly as he moved.

'Brian Field tells me you and some friends of yours might be able to handle a big job.'

The question came as no surprise to Gordon, matching the message Brian had passed on. He decided to play along and listen. The man smiled across at him, and Goody began to relax. He wasn't in any danger, not if Field had set this up. The police had nothing on him. If they wanted to lift him for the Heathrow robbery there had been many opportunities to do so in the past few weeks, they wouldn't need to lure him to somewhere like this. He had no enemies, only friends in this game.

'He did mention it was big, yeah,' Gordon replied, watchfully.

'I want to talk to you about something in confidence.'

'Fine.'

'We'll only have one chance with this plan, we need the right men, and we need to time it just right.' Jock paused to allow a woman pushing a pram to pass in the opposite direction. 'We're looking for men with a talent for thievery.'

'I know some people,' Gordon replied.

'Gordon, I have an exciting opportunity to discuss with you. You come well recommended by Mister Field.'

The accent had a definite Ulster twang to it, distant, perhaps educated out. His own had been overpowered by thirty years in London.

'I know him, yeah.'

'You don't recognise me at all?'

'No. Should I?'

Goody studied the face. It didn't ring any bells. He just looked bland, utterly normal.

'I watched you, in court. The Barclays trial.'

Goody said nothing, just stared at the side of the man's face. His subject was looking straight ahead, avoiding eye contact.

'Yes, I was there for just a couple of days. We were casting around, you know, looking for people.'

'People?'

'Yes, for this job.'

'How big is it?'

'The biggest, by far.' The man sounded extremely matter-of-fact.

'Tell me more.' Gordon was glad Buster wasn't there, he would have gone mental with the waiting games, probably have smashed him one by now.

'Do you know anything about mail trains?'

'A little bit, yeah.'

'Oh? What do you know?'

'Well, it is possible to hold up trains.' Gordon looked around him. That nagging thought about the police on his tail was there again. They wanted to set him up, annoyed at his acquittal after the Heathrow bank job. They were desperate for anything to nail him, Charlie and Bruce too. 'Look, are you recording this somehow?'

The man stopped and turned to look at Gordon. His eyes narrowed in annoyance.

'Fine. If you don't want any part of this, I'll go somewhere else.'

He set off again, leaving Gordon behind; although it didn't take him long to catch up. They were only talking. What the hell would that prove? As long as he didn't say anything about any previous jobs he would be fine. Jock took a right turn down another path, steering them away from pedestrian traffic. After he caught up along side the little man, Gordon decided to apologise.

'Sorry. But, the heat has been on me for a while. I mean, it's backed off now, but you never know.'

'I'm told you won't have any more problems over that.'

Gordon was surprised, and failed to hide it in his voice. 'What do you mean, problems? What are you saying?'

'Just that I have reason to believe you're not being followed any more.'

'How d'you know?'

'I know. That's all you need to know.' The man smiled, and it looked genuine.

Gordon had felt the observation drop off in the previous couple of weeks. Buster mentioned it too. For some reason, this man also knew. He would carry on listening for a while.

'Go on, tell me more.'

'Right. Mail trains. Let me tell you about one that runs regularly.' The man took another turn, left this time, away from the oncoming traffic of two men with briefcases. 'It runs daily down from Glasgow all the way to Euston, stopping off at several points. Then it runs back up again. The one coming down from Scotland is the interesting one. It's called the 'Up train'. It makes no sense, I know, but there you go. Cigarette?'

Gordon took one. So far, only relatively interesting. Who wanted to steal mail? Too much work sorting it out for the financial return, everybody knew that. There had been chatter for a while about big train jobs, ones to blow your mind, large quantities of money, but nothing more specific. Anyone who had done time in the past few years would have heard a whisper, or been told about it by someone. All this was a myth, as far as Gordon was concerned.

The man calling himself Jock lit for both of them, and walked on again.

'This train contains normal mail; you know, letters, that sort of thing. But it also pulls something called a High Value Package coach. This coach is always the first one on the train after the engine. It contains dozens of bags containing used money, and it stops off to pick up even more money on the way. Thing is, this money is either being transported for depositing at London banks, or due to be destroyed when it gets to London.'

'Destroyed?' The very idea was crazy. Who would want to get rid of money? It always had a use.

'Yes, some of it. Old notes, even Scottish and Irish ones sometimes. Anyway, thing is, it's all unmarked. It's all insured as well, so stealing it, nobody loses out.'

Gordon wasn't bothered about the morality of lifting a large amount of money, had no concerns about where it was going, or what was meant to be done with it. If there was loads of it, he knew people who would also be interested in stealing it.

'Right, how much, then?'

'Well, it does vary. There can be as many as sixty or seventy bags on a typical 'Up' run.'

'Yeah, but how much money is that?'

'Normally, up to a million pounds. But on some trains there's a load more. On a Bank Holiday train for example, it could be as much as four million.'

Gordon tried to avoid breaking stride. Four million? Jesus Christ! That was beyond any thief's wildest dreams. Four Million? It was time for the obvious question.

'How come you know all this?'

'We have inside information. It's very reliable. This is a huge opportunity, and we're looking for someone to take up that opportunity.'

'Four million you say?' Gordon's legs trembled, but he managed to keep up with the squatter man, who just kept on walking as if they were discussing the weather.

'If we pick the right day, it'll be a minimum of two million, and could be as high as four, yes.'

'Jesus.'

'I know. That's why we're looking for someone who is capable of pulling off a logistical challenge. There's not only stopping the train, but then the operation to remove it all.'

A thought flashed through Gordon's mind. 'Wait. You keep saying, 'we'. Who's this we?'

'Me and my business partner.'

'Who?'

'Oh, come now, Gordon. These are early stages. I can't tell you any more than that. What I want to know is, do you think you and your friends could carry off such a job? Are you interested?'

'Who wouldn't be?' Gordon heard this come out of his mouth, and it was true. Four million quid? It was staggering. Even if they had to use a large crew there would be a massive payout for everyone. He could retire for good to somewhere hot, spend the rest of his life living like a king.

'I'll have to put this to my associates,' he said, hoping he was covering up the nerves.

'I just wanted to run it by you first.'

'Have you asked anyone else to do this?'

'No.' Jock was looking straight ahead again, avoiding eye contact. This could still be a set up, of course, designed to get them for something at last. He would have to tread carefully.

'Why don't you do this yourself?' If this man knew Brian Field, the bent solicitor's clerk, then he must be a crook. Surely he would have the manpower to pull it off? Why trust anybody else to do it?

'I have people I work with, as does my partner. But they are slightly indisposed at the moment, and time is pressing. This job has to be done this summer and it will take a degree of planning. It was clear from the Barclays job you fellows know what you're doing, and can plan properly.'

Gordon thought about the lack of ideas that were currently kicking around. The Heathrow bank robbery worked pretty well until a tip-off came. Nowhere near as much money as they thought there would be, but their elaborately constructed alibis worked well. He had to smile at the switch that was made to the evidence that looked to be damning him, a bowler hat that he was supposed to have worn on the job, when they dressed up as city gents. DCI Vibart's face was a picture when Gordon comically pulled a hat several sizes too large over his head on the witness stand. Bruce Reynolds's hand behind the job was crucial. He would have to be involved, as would Buster Edwards, if it was this big he wouldn't be forgiven for leaving him out. Charlie Wilson would provide part of the muscle, but they would need more men than their immediate circle.

'D'you have any more information about the task?' Gordon asked.

'I can tell you if you confirm you can handle the job.'

'Yeah, but I need a bit more, there will be questions to answer and it would be good to give my colleagues more detail. For instance, how well is the train guarded? How big a team will we need?'

'That sort of thing, I'll leave to you.'

Gordon thought about the amount again. It was unimaginable. They would be thankful to him for the rest of their lives. Bruce would love to get his teeth into a project like this.

'Okay, I understand. I shall talk to my associates,' he said as calmly as possible.

'Good. And please, only a small number to begin with. We need to keep this as tight as possible, keep a lid on it.'

'I will.' Gordon thought again of all the rumours that flew around. The man was right.

'You think you can pull off a job of this size?' Jock asked.

'Yeah. No problem at all,' Gordon replied, trying to sound confident. In truth you never knew until you got down to the details.

'Can we meet next week?'

'Sure.'

13

'I'll arrange it through Brian Field.'

'Good.' At least Gordon wouldn't have to go through all the spy routine again. The man offered his hand and they shook to cement a plot that would shape his future.

'And Gordon. One last thing. If anything happens to you in the next week, you know, anybody pays you a visit, this meeting didn't take place.'

'Of course not.' He must mean the police. Not much chance of him letting this little secret out.

'Goodbye.'

The squat man with the familiar accent walked off to the right, down the path and disappeared into a small group of trees. Gordon stood wondering if this had really happened. It was always possible it was a set up, but the amount of money was mind-boggling, way beyond anything the Met would dream up. He couldn't wait to tell the boys.

3

Jack Armstrong stirred his coffee in the quiet café on Seven Sisters Road, and studied Tommy Lavery as he walked in. His boss looked annoyed, and he was probably going to be the one who copped the flak again. Lavery approached the counter and ordered himself a coffee, wisely avoiding the food. The place was empty bar a woman in the corner, poring over a newspaper, eating a sandwich. She was taking her life into her own hands, judging by his discarded bacon roll.

The food kept him busy while he waited for Lavery to arrive. He instructed Mickey Griffin to stay outside; these types of discussions were out of his league. The application of muscle was his strength, not brains. Lavery said he didn't want to overpower the Irishman when he arrived later. Jack assumed he meant both literally and metaphorically.

He blew on his drink to cool it, and his boss sat down next to him. Receiving a mug of coffee seemed to have calmed him down. Maybe he just hated London.

'Fuck. No sign of him yet?' Tommy asked.

'No.'

'Good. I want you to follow him when he leaves.'

'Shall I take Mickey with me?'

'No. Do it yourself. I'll take Griff with me.'

'Fine.' Jack was used to following orders. You questioned

nothing with his boss, not if you valued your limbs. Even if you were one of the limb-breakers yourself.

'I want to know who his bloody insider is. See what you can find out.'

'How long you want me to follow him?'

'Use your judgment.'

This was a phrase Tommy employed a lot, usually as a test. Archie and Bex had used their own judgment over that post office raid in Moss Side the month before, and they were looking at a ten stretch.

'We can't give him an inkling,' Lavery continued. 'He thinks we're splitting the million between us. Stupid little Mick.' Lavery chuckled quietly. Jack looked at the woman in the corner who was still examining her newspaper. The counter area was empty.

'How we gonna hit him?' Jack asked his boss.

'We can work that out later, wait to see what he wants to do with his share.'

'Good.'

'Then we fuck him over.'

Jack studied Tommy. There wasn't a drop of excitement in his face. This was purely business. They were going to rip off a whole organisation, pretty much an entire bloody country. Lavery looked like he was discussing the composition of the England cricket team.

Their eyes were drawn to the door of the café, and the object of their discussion walked in without looking across. He waited at the counter for the owner to appear from out back, and ordered himself a cup of tea. He was sensible in avoiding the food. Maloney walked over and ignored Jack Armstrong completely, focusing his attention on Lavery.

'Afternoon.'

Maloney sat down opposite his boss and Jack smiled inwardly. He needed to slip under the radar. This Mick was oblivious to the set up. He would front everything for them, and end up with nothing. Such was life.

'Were you followed?' Lavery asked.

'No. I've done a few turns and a double back. Definitely not.'

'Good.'

'He's interested. The amount excited him. He nearly came in his pants.'

Lavery nearly choked on his drink and Jack was grateful he had nothing in his mouth at the time. It wouldn't do to spit at a business partner.

'Well, it is a huge opportunity,' Lavery replied, rather obviously. It certainly was from the way Jack saw it, but not for these Irishmen.

His boss was already making plans for the men who would be on the raid, men they didn't even know the identities of yet. Jack was glad he would be there at the sharp end, part of a gang, preparing to turn them over. His boss insisted that he and Mickey ensure they didn't bugger off with all the money, but his chief instruction was to gain the trust of all the thieves. That way they would be well placed for the subsequent parts of the operation.

Lavery seemed to be surprised that Maloney would let him pick off the spoils, rob the robbers. The Mick was too honourable. They were close to finding a group of mugs to do all the dirty work, and Jack was going to be central to taking the whole bloody lot. It would be like stealing from a class of sticky fingered children.

'I reckon they'll bite,' Maloney offered, slurping at his drink.

'Good.'

'And we're going to meet them next week.'

'We?' As Lavery responded, Armstrong thought about how his boss had no need to come out into the open yet.

'Yes, I think you should meet them.'

'I thought we agreed you were going to be the front man?' Jack's boss was turning purple again. Lavery didn't lose it too often, but when he did you had to be in a different county.

'I am. I just think it might give them some reassurance,' Maloney insisted.

'I'm not convinced. I quite like being in the background, you know, driving people here and there, making everyone think I'm a go-between.' Lavery smiled at the subterfuge, and Jack joined in. He was probably getting a small kick from having already met this Goody without him knowing. Staying hidden would also help with the dirty work they had planned for later.

'Oh well, have it your way.' Maloney backed down. Most people did when they were confronted with an angry Beast of the North.

'When will you meet them?' Lavery asked.

'Next week. I'm sure it's on.'

'Good.' Lavery wiped his hands on a napkin and stood up to leave. 'Keep me posted.'

Jack rose to join his boss. They scraped their chairs as they got up, attracting the attention of the woman in the corner. There were no female undercover cops; everyone knew that, she was just an innocent. Don't stare too hard at the tall northerner, Jack thought. They turned their backs on her instinctively as they left, leaving a stunned looking Maloney sitting there, nursing his mug. Jack gave him a little wave as they passed by the café window. He really had no idea what was coming.

He had heard stories about what the Irish did to the people who double-crossed them, probably all bollocks. This time Maloney's mob were dealing with a force that reached further than they could ever imagine, deeper into the establishment than the bloody Russians, and that was saying something. They conducted business the right way, evenly dispensing justice and fairness. Jack Armstrong was convinced he was working for the good guys, the winning team.

4

The three men stood on the platform at Euston Station, eyeing the heavy bags being unloaded. Even though Gordon Goody had suggested the visit, Bruce Reynolds still saw himself as their leader. Buster Edwards was the first to interrogate Gordon.

'So, is this why you brought us here? You taken up bloody train spottin'?'

'Look for yourselves.' Goody nodded towards the train.

They watched half a dozen men throwing bags off, escorted by loads of uniform. Bruce switched his attention to Buster's face. He looked like a schoolboy in the biggest sweetshop in the world.

'Fuck me, they look stuffed,' he exclaimed excitedly.

Buster's observation was correct. There were about forty bags on the platform, all from the front coach. The police were all over it. They couldn't hit the train there because security was too tight. Bruce was buzzing, felt alive again, that gnawing pull of the challenge was bringing him to life. His brain whirred, and still they knew little of the details. But watching the packages come off the train at four in the morning was a beautiful sight.

'That's the High Value Package coach,' Gordon whispered. Bruce was suddenly aware they might look conspicuous, three grown men clutching platform tickets, watching tons of money being unloaded off a train.

'Come on, let's take a walk about.'

Bruce led them out on to the main concourse. They had seen what they needed to see. Gordon's informant was right. The train was loaded with money.

'Don't forget, this is just a normal run. Our friend said sometimes it's two or three times as much as that on board.' The two men listened to Gordon, Bruce already focusing on logistics. He was intrigued about the informant.

'How did he say he got this inside knowledge?' Bruce asked.

They were all fully aware that the secret to any job was information. Knowing what moved where and when, and how much it was guarded. It was clear that they would have to stop the train on the move.

'He wouldn't say. Only that he seems to have a lot of information about the trains and when the right time might be to hold one up.'

'I guess we need to see the whites of his eyes, test him out,' Bruce said.

'Don't you think we could just rob the fuckin' thing anyway, not tell this bloke?' Buster seemed to be keen on going it alone, now they knew the job was possible. Until they saw the train in front of them, this had been another of Gordon's tall tales.

'What, say "no" and then do it anyway?' Gordon asked, and Buster laughed.

'Yeah. Why not?'

'But how do we know when it's worthwhile?' Bruce interjected.

'Looks fuckin' worthwhile to me,' Buster exclaimed, looking back over his shoulder to the packages that were piled up on the platform, ready to be bundled into vans.

'Who is this bloke, anyway?' Bruce asked Gordon.

'I dunno his real name. He called himself Jock, but I reckon he's an Ulsterman.'

'Ulsterman?' Buster asked.

'Yeah. He might have been trying to hide it, but he's definitely from there.'

Bruce didn't give a monkeys where he was from. What mattered was the quality of his information.

'We should meet him,' Bruce said.

'He wants to do the same. He wants to check if we're up to it.'

Buster snorted. 'Course we're fuckin' up to it. Four million quid? Jesus.'

Bruce thought more about the mail train. Moving objects were always problematic. Often it was the intellectual tease that drew him into a job, and his colleagues knew it. Other thieves were stopping trains, he had heard about it on the London to Brighton line, but with limited success.

'How does he know how much it's going to be?' Bruce thought about the massive sacks. They looked full, but they could all be fifty bob notes.

'You can ask him yourself.' Gordon sounded miffed.

'You didn't take notes?' Buster asked. He was a right one for stirring it.

'Course I fuckin' didn't.' Goody was on the defensive. Bruce smiled because he had no need to be. Buster was just winding him up. Gordon calmed down a touch. 'We was walking through a park. He was just going on about money and trains. My head was spinning.'

Bruce wondered how he would have reacted. Buster would probably have pinned him up against a tree.

'How come nobody's done this job before?' Buster asked.

'I dunno. I think he has people he works with, but it sounds like they're a few men down. If you know what I mean?'

Men inside, Bruce thought. They were dealing with a gang who were lacking manpower, and his group were stepping into the breach. He didn't care if they were second choice. Four million quid ironed out a lot of problems. There was an obvious possibility they couldn't ignore.

'You think this could be a set up?' he asked.

'I thought about it. Because of Heathrow.'

'Yeah.'

'It's a bit elaborate for the Old Bill, ain't it?' Buster threw in.

Bruce had to agree. If they wanted to dangle a carrot, it wouldn't need to be this massive. 'Look, it can't do us any harm to meet this bloke, can it?' he reasoned.

'No, you're right,' Gordon said. 'Buster?'

'Yeah. Fuck. Four million quid.'

Bruce studied his colleagues. They had all served time; all paid their dues with shitty jobs that paid back bugger all. Even the Heathrow takings were a fraction of what they expected. You had to take any figure with a pinch of salt.

'We need to talk to a few others,' Bruce reasoned.

'Yeah. We'll need a few hands, looking at that thing. Let's think about who we might need,' Buster said.

'Roy and Charlie, maybe Harry?' Gordon threw in.

Bruce wanted to start with the most important addition. 'Let's give Charlie a ring.'

The three men left the station with a spring in their step. After a barren few months, things were looking up. Judging by those sacks on the station platform, they were going to attempt one of the biggest robberies the country had ever seen.

5

*16th May 1963: The White Hart pub, Brick Street,
Piccadilly, London*

Lavery swept into the deserted saloon bar and swore immediately.

'Fuck me, Eddie, I'm sorry. Had to take a piss in the park.'

'Nice.' Maloney wondered why he couldn't wait to use the one
in the pub, but decided to drop it.

'Well, anyway. I know for certain they're not tailing you. There
was just the three of them today, I followed you in Green Park, and
they're long gone.' Tommy said.

'Okay, thanks. Pint?'

'Yeah, please. Bitter.' Lavery sat down in the corner, at Eddie's
table.

Maloney rose and ordered two drinks from the bar. The
barmaid gave him a look like he had shot her brother the week
before, and he stared at the pictures of old boxers above the bar to
avoid her gaze. People in London were amazingly unfriendly.
Maybe it was because he had sat there for ten minutes after meeting
the three ringleaders in the park, not buying a drink, looking at his
watch, waiting for Lavery to show up. The place was deserted apart
from the two of them. He returned with the pints. For once, that
lump Armstrong wasn't with him.

'No Jack?'

'He's busy.'

'Ah. Well, cheers, Tommy.'

'Cheers. How'd it go then?' Lavery asked.

'They're up for it. No surprise there.'

'I suppose not.' Lavery gulped down a large mouthful of beer. How the hell could he stand the taste? God alone knew what they made it out of. Maloney took a small sip of his own Guinness, the only thing remotely palatable.

'They were a bit cagey,' Eddie said.

'Well, you would be, wouldn't you? Stranger meets you in a park and says, "Can I interest you in a little bit of thievery?"' Eddie nodded. Lavery had a point. 'Except it's not a little bit, it's a fuckin' huge bit.'

Lavery thought he was so funny, and his sense of humour was already wearing thin on Maloney. Still, he was essential to the security aspect of the plan. Tommy claimed that he was well placed to keep a lid on things from the police end, something Pat Leahy, back home in Ireland, confirmed. He knew the right people in the right places. Eddie might have to put up with shit from him, but it would be worth it. There was no going back. He remembered the months digging out the contact on the trains, obtaining the leverage they needed to get their hands on the vital information. Then there was the surveillance of the track. He was going to let the gang go on the same journey of discovery he did. They had to feel the plan was their own, regardless of how they were going to be steered.

'Who were they, then?' Tommy asked.

'Goody again, then this Buster Edwards, and Bruce Reynolds.'

'I see.' Lavery looked to be thinking about the two new names. 'So?'

'What?'

'Do you know them?' Eddie asked.

'Only by reputation.'

'And...?'

'Edwards knows a lot of people,' Lavery began. He downed more of his drink, was two-thirds of his way through in a couple of gulps. Thirsty bastards, these northerners. 'He'll be the one they look to. He's got the contacts to get enough hands. They need more bodies. I need all the names of those on the job.'

'All of them?'

'Yeah, the bloody lot. I want to know who's doing our dirty work.'

Eddie thought about the reasoning. 'We're going to pay them to keep out of trouble?'

'That's the idea. I want to know who we're paying.'

'I'll mention it next time.'

Lavery finished off his drink. Eddie stared at the two small mouthfuls he had taken from his glass. Tommy sighed and set off for the bar, ignoring Maloney. He returned with another pint and two bags of peanuts, one of which he threw at Eddie.

'What did you make of Reynolds?' Lavery asked.

Tommy should have showed up at the meeting, rather than hiding in the bushes, if he wanted that much detail. Eddie thought about the steely face behind those glasses, the authority Bruce seemed to carry among the three men.

'I reckon he's the real boss.'

'Really?'

'He seems to be their leader. At least intellectually.'

'Well, that's not saying much.'

Maloney pondered the position of Gordon Goody. He was the man who brought the job to his friends, but wouldn't be leading on it. Buster Edwards looked like the muscle. Lavery interrupted his train of thought, slapping his new pint down on a beer mat.

'What did they say about my two men on the job?'

'They said they only work with people they know.'

Lavery appeared to think about this for a moment, then said, 'Well, we'd better get 'em to know Jack and Mickey then.' He was adamant about having his boys on the ground throughout. That was fine. Eddie had his lads poised to travel over at the crucial time to protect his own interests.

'I'll get them to agree,' Eddie announced confidently.

'They better fuckin' had,' Tommy exclaimed. 'No men on the job, no job. We'll pull the plug.'

Maloney felt Lavery was keen to lay down a marker, show those London criminals who was boss, that you couldn't mess with the hard lads from the North. All Maloney wanted to preserve was a successful robbery.

'D'you think we can trust 'em? They're not gonna just fuck off and do it under our noses?' Lavery asked, ripping open his bag of peanuts and crunching away.

'No, I don't think so. I don't know. Maybe. I think Reynolds is a bit more cautious than the other two. A planner. Don't forget, without our inside information, they have nothing.'

'No. Same goes for what the Flying Squad will do about it.'

'Also true.' Lavery was just reminding him of the leverage he held, all part of the game. He still wondered how deep he reached, and how far up in the Met he could control an investigation.

'Come on, then. What did they say about the million quid?' Tommy asked, spitting peanuts on the tabletop.

Eddie wiped his hands on his trousers before replying. His pint stared back at him. How could he put this subtly?

'They fucking hated the idea. Obviously.'

'Greedy bastards.'

The irony wasn't lost on Eddie. 'They said a million was too big a drink for someone who wasn't getting their hands dirty.'

'What about Jack and Mickey? I'm giving 'em two good men for free? Cheeky fuckers.'

Lavery didn't look angry. He smiled, must have known the objection would come. Eddie didn't blame the ringleaders, but the money wasn't negotiable.

'I told them again that without our information they would have nothing.'

'What did they say to that?'

'Just grumbled.' Eddie swallowed a mouthful of Guinness, buying time to think. Lavery filled the pause anyway.

'What else did you discuss?'

'I told them all about the train again, and the three new coaches that are more secure than the older ones. We're going to put the new ones out of action at the right time.'

'It's already in hand. I have two men in Crewe at the workshop.'

'Good.' Eddie wondered how close Lavery might have got to working out who his inside sources were. Without those, the Beast would have no need for him. He would be squeezed out, not only financially, but, probably rather painfully as well.

'What about the guns?'

'I don't think they'd thought that far ahead. They raised no objections.'

Eddie thought back to the faces of the three men when he had broached the subject of nobody being armed. Reynolds looked shocked. Edwards simply smiled and said he had a favourite cosh he was taking, and they wouldn't need shooters. Such naivety. Maloney knew his boys would need to be carrying when they picked up their share, fight fire with fire if Tommy's men were armed. He couldn't return back home empty handed if the robbery went ahead, knew he would be dead if that happened.

'So, what now?' Lavery asked.

'I keep up with them, on and off. Do you fancy meeting them?'

'I'm not sure yet. Let me know if there are any issues I need to address. Key thing is, I need to know the names on the job.'

'Sure.'

Eddie wondered again why Lavery needed that much detail. Maybe he was going to infiltrate the gang somehow, manipulate them. Eddie was fully aware he and his lads needed to be ready for anything when the share out came.

The woman who had looked so disdainfully at him from behind the bar walked over and whispered something in Lavery's ear. He nodded, and rose to his feet. 'Excuse me a minute.'

Lavery walked over to the end of the bar and picked up the receiver of a public telephone. He nodded a couple of times, and said something Eddie couldn't hear, despite the quiet in the pub. Eddie's partner hung up and walked back to the table, finishing off his second pint as he stood there, forcing Eddie to study his own meagre attempt. This was a military operation, not a drinking contest. He would have all the contingencies in place; ready for whatever Lavery threw at him after the robbery. Tommy looked to be in a hurry to get moving.

'See you, Eddie. I gotta go, someone to meet,' Lavery said, looking at the door. 'Go careful.'

'I will,' Eddie replied, knowing care would be central to his next three months.

6

'His bastard legs are stuck,' Mickey Griffin announced.

Not more bloody problems, thought Jack. This was supposed to be simple, a gentle reminder to one of Tommy's men up the police ladder. Jack Armstrong joined Mickey in lifting the man out of the car boot. Why he chose to nick a bloody Viva for this sort of task was beyond him. What was Mickey playing at? It meant that DI Barclay had been folded in half in there.

They sat Barclay down in the chair. The sunlight snuck its way in through a broken window, reflecting on the metal of an abandoned car door, propped up in the deserted service bay. They were in one of the latest garages they hired in West London, Marriott's, in Ealing. The smell of oil and the taste of stale grease hung in the air. Griffin untied Barclay, who groaned. When Mickey undid the gag in his mouth, expletives spewed out.

'Fuck you doin', you fuckin' arsehole?'

Jack folded his arms and stared at the man in front of him. He had no time for bent coppers, they were worse than straight ones as far as he was concerned. At least you knew where you were when they were on the level. Unfortunately, his boss had developed rather a taste for them, cultivated moles at a number of levels, from what he could see. There were probably many more out there, paying for past crimes with a revised sense of loyalty towards Tommy Lavery. Barclay gingerly stood up.

29

'Please sit down,' Jack insisted.

'I'll stand.'

'Have it your way,' Armstrong replied. He kicked Barclay hard in the balls. That was for Archie Hamilton, fitted up for the post office raid in Chorlton. He didn't care that Barclay had nothing personally to do with it. He was one of them. Barclay keeled over and knelt on the dirty floor, and stayed there until Lavery's face appeared at the door.

'What do we have here, then? Help him up will you? He's a friend of mine,' Tommy said.

Griffin and Armstrong lifted the policeman up on to the chair. Barclay's demeanour changed as soon as he saw Lavery. He sat upright with his hands on his knees.

'I done what you asked,' Barclay said.

'Have you?' Lavery replied, arching an eyebrow.

'Yeah. I'm in the fingerprints division now.'

'Good. That's good.'

'Why all this? What have I done wrong, Tommy?' Barclay pleaded.

Jack had been given no reason as to why they had to pick up the copper. Just that they needed to bring him somewhere secure, so that Lavery could have a quiet word with him. Normally this meant bundling people into the boot of a car, and that was what they did. Maybe they had misjudged this one. He would blame Mickey.

'I just wanted to have a chat, Cliff. You know, man to man.'

'Why you got these two beating me up? They shoved me in the boot.' Barclay scowled at Jack, who returned the glare.

'Did you beat the nice Detective Inspector up, boys?' Lavery asked, rolling his eyes.

'We didn't know,' Griffin replied. Jack was glad it was Mickey that spoke first. He knew perfectly well they were dealing with a bent copper, Mickey must have forgotten.

'Oh, well. Next time, just go easy on him, will you? He can travel in the back seat if he wants.'

Lavery seemed to be amused by the discomfort they had put the policeman through. Their boss feigned surprise at their rough tactics, and maybe that was the point of the exercise. Deep down, Tommy would have no objections to a copper receiving a decent kicking every now and again. It was good to keep them on their toes.

Lavery pulled a chair over, from a tattered old desk in the corner, and sat astride it. 'Cliff, I just wanted to make sure you had your eyes and ears open.'

'Of course.'

'Good. I want you to keep it that way.'

Barclay looked confused. Griffin shuffled about from one foot to the other, annoying Jack. God only knew what it was doing to Tommy's frame of mind.

'Cliff, I need to know you're still on the right side. You're still on my side.'

Barclay looked defiant, but Jack had seen that look before. Inside he would be bricking it. 'I'm on your side, Tommy.'

'Good. That's good. Please keep it that way. I'll be in touch soon.' Lavery turned on his heel and headed for the door. 'Jack, I need a lift,' he added.

'What about him?' Griffin asked.

'He's got a pair of legs, hasn't he? He can walk back to Scotland Yard. Jack, come on.'

Armstrong followed his boss out into the yard. Dozens of tyres were stacked along a brick wall and Lavery leant against the end of one pile, lighting a cigarette.

'Jack, did you hurt him much?'

'A bit.'

'Good. Nothing wrong with that. He is one of them, after all. Come on, I've got a doctor's appointment.'

Armstrong wondered if this was a euphemism. Tommy Lavery was indestructible. The thought of him needing medical help was a curious one. Nothing could bring down his boss; he was a force of nature. He led the way to the Viva, realising they were going to leave Mickey Griffin alone with DI Barclay, of the Met, and no transport. They could play together on the North Circular for all he cared.

7

23rd May 1963: Twickenham

Bruce arrived first for the meeting at Buster Edwards's flat on St Margaret's Road. He was still conscious of being tailed by the police, and parked his Lotus several streets away. The initial responsibilities were going to be shared out that day, and he was going to have to field a lot of questions. The next ten weeks would go by in a flash, and there was so much to cover.

Buster greeted him with a huge grin, looking excited. They shared a cup of tea while they waited for the others to arrive. They had been busy in the week since they had met the mysterious Ulsterman in Green Park. The more he thought about the job, which was just about every waking moment of every single day, the more he found new questions popping into his head. The hope was to iron most out before a mass meeting was called. This was going to be his stage, when he stood up in front of the assembled friends and told them how they were all going to become rich. It called for a military operation and he would be their commander.

Gordon arrived next, along with Charlie Wilson, a veteran of many jobs together. Charlie was a force to be reckoned with, only last week he and two of his friends had beaten a man close to death in an alley in Lee Green, because he thought he was being swindled over a few used cars. There would be a need for controlled muscle on this job, because they would have to persuade reluctant Post Office employees to allow them to walk off with millions of pounds. All you needed was one 'have-a-go hero' to stick a spanner in the proverbial.

The remainder of the local crew assembled soon after. Roy James was normally their getaway driver, good enough to race professionally; he had beaten Jackie Stewart on the domestic circuit. He shared Bruce's love of fast cars and they would often sit for hours contemplating which set of wheels to buy or steal next. John Daly and Harry Smith, two more close associates from the past, completed the usual group. They were a tight knit bunch, despite the fact that they occasionally worked with other firms as well. Jimmy White, an ex-paratrooper who they knew and trusted implicitly, sat calmly in a corner. It had been a few years since Bruce had worked with him, but Buster thought he would be invaluable. Bruce felt comfortable that this was a strong nucleus for the job.

When they were all supplied with drinks, Bruce stood up and addressed everyone.

'Lads. We have a tremendous opportunity in front of us. This is a chance to pull off a massive robbery. You have, no doubt, heard the number we are looking at? Four million quid.' There were nods of approval around the room. He had their interest, and carried on, staring at their faces. 'We are going to rob a train. All we need to do is stop it, relieve them of what we want, and disappear.'

'Sounds easy.' There wasn't a hint of sarcasm in Roy James's voice. He lived his life at high speed and had a positive outlook that mirrored this.

'Well, Roy, it won't be easy, but we have a few factors in our favour. Let me tell you more.'

Bruce went into a description of the train that ran from Glasgow to Euston every day, its schedule, and precious cargo. A few of the team appeared to glaze over as he related the detail of where the money was kept, and how many employees were stationed on the train, according to the Ulsterman. He needed the team to concentrate.

Buster stuck his hand in the air after Reynolds completed his summary. 'Please, Sir, please, Sir. How do we stop the train, Sir?' Bruce smiled as the men in the room laughed. Trust Buster to lighten the mood.

'We need to think about that. We know sleepers across the line don't work.' More nodding in the room, the underworld was full of apocryphal stories on that front. 'We also know there are no passengers on the train, only Post Office employees. So, no communication cord to pull.'

'Can't we get a job on the train?' Roy James asked.

'Not in time. Anyway, there's no way to be certain of being on the right train.'

'I've got a question, Bruce.' Charlie Wilson spoke calmly, and with authority. 'Why's nobody done this before?' It was a fair point.

'Nobody's had this inside information before,' Bruce replied swiftly, thinking it was a neat answer. 'We all know how important that is to any job. We've got a man on the inside who knows all about the train, may even be on it.'

'Who is this informant, then?' Charlie had taken over the questioning.

'Gordon?' Bruce pointed to Goody.

'We call him the Ulsterman.'

'The Ulsterman?' Several voices questioned at once.

'Yeah. He tried to hide his accent, but he's definitely lived in Belfast before. That doesn't matter I suppose, it's just a name we use for him. He calls himself Jock, actually.' A couple of the group chuckled. 'Thing is, this information looks solid.'

'Railway's full of fuckin' Paddies, ain't it?' Charlie grumbled.

Bruce tried to wrestle back control. 'Regardless of where he's from, he's got good information, that's all that matters.'

'Bruce. What does our informant want? I mean, this is four million quid, right, and he knows it. How much of a drink is he after?' Harry Smith had touched on a subject Bruce wanted to cover at the end, when they were fully on board. He swallowed, and prepared himself for the backlash.

'Quite a big drink, I'm afraid. A million quid.'

There was instant protest, particularly Charlie and Roy. Bruce had got used to the idea of giving up the first million on the job. If the load turned out to be as big as promised, it wouldn't matter.

'You're fuckin' jokin', right? A million. What, up front?' Charlie led the clamour.

'Yeah. A million. Those are his terms.'

'What if there's only a million on board? Or less?' Charlie's face was turning purple.

'Then we nick the fuckin' lot, don't we!' Gordon picked up the thread as planned. There was no way they were going to put all that effort in without a fair reward.

Roy had an alternative suggestion. 'Can't we just say "No" to him, and go and do it anyway? He can stick his million where the sun don't shine.'

'Yeah. Let's say we're not interested, and then just go and do it,' Charlie agreed.

Bruce eyed the rest of the room. Jimmy White had been quiet so far. He bet he was already thinking through logistics. Once a soldier, always a soldier. His brother-in-law, John Daly, was also mute, smoking impassively.

Bruce had an ace up his sleeve in this debate. 'Thing is, he came to us because he was impressed by us. He went to the Heathrow trial. Sat and watched us walk free.'

'Except Mickey Ball,' Harry interrupted.

'Yeah, except Mickey,' Bruce accepted. Poor Mickey was the one casualty from the robbery.

'He was watching us?' Charlie sounded more positive.

'Yeah, he was.'

'I just think a million's a bit steep, that's all.' Charlie had always driven a hard bargain. Normally they split every job down the middle. Nobody got a master share, that wasn't how they operated. They were all in things together; shared the risks and the spoils.

Jimmy White finally spoke up, and all ears in the room listened.

'I just reckon if there's four million, that's more than enough. We're nicking a train, for God's sake. There's plenty. I actually think we might need a bit more help.'

'I agree.' Gordon stepped in. 'Our man says there are only five or six people in the HVP coach we're after. But, we've got more to do. We might need to move the train. We might have to uncouple it to keep the sorters in the other carriages away from us. We might need a few more hands.'

Bruce picked up on Gordon's words before anyone could interject. 'I want to discuss who else we think might be useful on a job like this.'

'Freddie Foreman.' Harry threw the name into the air, and there were slight intakes of breath. Foreman was a high profile face, living off the glory of a quarter of a million bullion heist in Central London, six months before.

Buster Edwards knew him best of all. 'I'm not sure. He's lying low. He's made anyway, he's got plenty.'

'He's a fuckin' liability,' was Charlie Wilson's violent reaction. Bruce shared this point of view.

'Anybody else?'

'Jimmy Hussey, maybe?' This was Roy's suggestion. They had worked together in the past. Everyone knew Jim. He was a good old lad, handy with his fists in his youth, totally reliable.

'Yeah, that's a possibility. Anyone object?' Bruce asked. Shakes of the head followed. 'Anyone else?'

The silence that followed was long enough for Bruce to drop in another demand they had to discuss.

'Our friend on the inside has offered us a couple of his men to help on the job.'

'Who the hell does he think he is?' Charlie rounded at Bruce, staring him down. It wasn't my suggestion, Bruce wanted to shout.

Gordon rallied. 'He's the man who's come to us with a chance to make millions, you idiot.' Goody faced up to Wilson. 'Listen, he says these two won't eat into our share at all. He pays 'em out of his cut.'

'He bloody well ought to. A million, for God's sake.' Charlie sat with his arms folded, defensive again. He'll come round, Bruce thought, when he focuses properly on the rewards. He decided to target the others, isolate Wilson.

'Think of the amount of money we'll need to unload off the train. Have any of you seen how much four million quid looks like?' Bruce scanned the room. They looked eager for the job, probably waiting for him to tell them what to do. 'I trust we're okay with these two extra pairs of hands?' Bruce continued.

Everyone nodded, with the exception of Charlie, who carried on scowling.

'When do we meet these two?' Harry asked.

'When we gather everyone on the job, they'll be there,' Bruce confirmed. He focused on the financial lifeline they were being offered. 'He's going to pay for everything we need up front. That includes a wage for each and every one of us, from now up until the job. A hundred quid, cash, each week.'

This raised a few eyebrows, Harry Smith most vocally. 'Really? A hundred quid? Each?'

'Yeah. I've got an envelope for when you leave.' Gordon was the wages clerk.

'He's serious about this?' Roy James seemed impressed.

'Yeah, he is. Has anybody got any big jobs on at the moment?' There was silence around the room. If they had anything planned, they weren't telling. Charlie would probably still be at it the day before.

'Well, maybe it would be a good idea to lie low until August,' Bruce suggested. 'That's when we're looking at the job, the Bank Holiday. We don't want any of us getting picked up. You don't want to miss out on this money for the sake of a few nicked motors, do you?' He wasn't looking at anybody in particular, but they would all know this was directed at Charlie and John. The room concurred again.

'Anything else, lads?' Bruce asked. They had decided to keep a future meeting with an electronics expert, from the South Coast Raiders, quiet for now. Charlie would blow a gasket if he thought they were going to bring another crew on board.

'One question.' Bruce saw Harry Smith's steady hand in the air. 'What if this is a fit up?'

Bruce was ready for this one. 'Why set us up for a job later in the summer, in August? When they could just as easily fit us up now?'

'Yeah, Bruce is right. It makes no sense,' Jimmy White chipped in. 'They'd want us locked up now, not later.'

'You're all right, Whitey. They're not bloody after you, are they?' Wilson replied. Bruce looked at Gordon and Buster, two men also conscious of the fallout from Heathrow.

Most of the eyes seemed to be focused on Charlie Wilson. Maybe they thought he was over playing this idea of being picked on by the police. Bruce was going to have to watch him. Charlie was always the one that picked holes in plans, and that was one reason he was extremely useful. Another was his attitude to violence. Bruce hoped that wouldn't be needed on this job, but if the difference between being caught and getting away with it was Charlie Wilson whacking some over-enthusiastic GPO employee on the head, then that was a risk he was prepared to take.

Bruce was pleased by the looks on their faces, as Gordon handed everyone their envelope, just before they left. There was a lot of work to do yet in terms of planning, but with a little extra help they should be able to pull it off. This robbery was going to go down in history. It would be two fingers up to the police as well as the banks. Doubly satisfying.

'Stay out of trouble, boys, will you?' he said as a form of ultimate sign off to his team.

'Yes, Sir!' shouted Buster in return.

Where would they be without him? As a group they were more solid than they might appear, because despite the odd squabble, they always had the same end goal in sight. Thieving something that was worth their while, and watching each other's backs. A tight unit was more likely to succeed.

They filed out in ones and twos a few minutes apart, still conscious of possible interest from the Met. Bruce allowed himself a satisfied smile as he watched everyone depart, sharing a cigar with Buster. If they could bring these extra hands into the fold seamlessly, keep the togetherness; this was going to be a titanic success.

8

A ticket inspector entered the carriage, and the man opposite pulled three first class tickets out of his jacket pocket. They were studied carefully, before being punched and returned to the Ulsterman. This return journey to Rugby was on him. Gordon Goody watched their insider throughout the transaction, to see if he gave any indication of being a railway man. He appeared to give none.

'Where were we?' The Ulsterman smiled as they were left in peace. He looked enormously relaxed, despite being in a train compartment with two notorious thieves.

'Where to stop the mail train.' Bruce Reynolds spoke quietly, and Gordon struggled to hear him over the noise of the engine as it entered a tunnel, north of Watford. It wasn't far now until the proposed intercept point.

Bruce stabbed a long finger at a spot close to Cheddington on the Ordnance Survey map. The Ulsterman had pulled it out of his briefcase a few minutes before, and Gordon and Bruce went back to leaning over it. There were crosses marked all along the railway line between Tring and Long Buckby, just like there was on their own version. If he had been doing the same research they would represent possible places of attack.

All three men studied a familiar stretch of the track and surrounding countryside. The B488 ran partially parallel to the railway, and then veered away. A side road off it ran under the line, to a place they knew well. Bridego Bridge, known in railway circles simply as Bridge 127.

'This looks a good spot. Very isolated,' Bruce announced. They had gone through many other possibilities, but kept coming back to the same place. Gordon looked up at the squat figure opposite, who examined where Bruce's finger had been, and then smiled at the pair of them.

Gordon explained their reasoning behind the choice. 'There are no properties in the immediate vicinity, apart from a farm about three quarters of a mile away.'

'This is the best place to unload it all,' Bruce added.

'How many of you are on the job now?' the man asked. 'Remember, we need to know who is getting the hundred quid a week. I can't be giving you money for nothing, you know that.'

Gordon looked across at Bruce, who now seemed to be more interested in gazing out of the window. They were approaching the most interesting part of the track.

The Ulsterman pulled a notebook out of his pocket and continued. 'I mean, we can trust you, but you must understand our position.' He smiled and Gordon felt comfortable. There were worse ways to get by.

'Please don't write anything down.' Gordon put his hand out to stop the Ulsterman, before withdrawing it. 'We don't want any stray lists lying around, you understand?' Gordon reeled off the names; the man nodded, and tucked his book away. Hopefully he had made his point.

'Okay, that's what, nine men, yes?'

'Yeah.'

He addressed Goody, staring at a distracted Bruce Reynolds as he did so. 'I'll leave it to you to distribute. You can have your money in a minute. Someone is dropping it off for me.'

'On this train?'

'Yes. Nine, is that going to be enough?'

'Eleven, if you count your men as well.'

'You might need more.'

'We're looking to be selective. We know how tight this job needs to be.' Gordon enjoyed this negotiation back and forth.

'When do we get to meet your two extra men?' Bruce asked, still staring out of the window.

'You'll meet them very soon,' the man retorted.

They passed slowly through Cheddington station without stopping. A few seconds later, everyone watched the location that would become a focus of their lives, pass by.

When the crossing point disappeared in the distance, their companion jumped up. 'Would you excuse me for a minute, gents?' He turned left out of the compartment into the corridor. Gordon and Bruce exchanged a look. The Ulsterman had left his briefcase in the carriage, having folded the map back up again and placed it carefully away. He would be back.

Seconds later the door slid open and he returned, followed by two large men.

'Don't be alarmed.' The Ulsterman resumed his seat opposite Gordon and Bruce, but the two new occupants remained standing.

'We're not.' Gordon sat up to attention, knowing there would be nothing to be gained by an attack in broad daylight. The two eventually positioned themselves either side of the Ulsterman, on the long seat opposite.

'Meet Jack and Mickey. These are the two men I mentioned.' The recent visitors nodded, but didn't make any moves to shake hands.

'Hello, Jack, Mickey,' Bruce and Gordon echoed.

One of the two men sported a scar cutting across his forehead, probably carried as a warning. The other was slightly taller, no less broad, and was completely bald, as if it had been deliberately shaved. Gordon suddenly placed them. They were the two men he saw in the park when he first met the man opposite, his minders. They looked like they might prove useful if things cut up with the GPO staff.

43

'This is Bruce, and Gordon. I mentioned them before.'

'Afternoon,' they chorused. That was all they needed, Gordon thought, a pair of northerners on the job.

An uneasy silence descended in the compartment. These four men were going to have to work together.

'Mickey, could you fetch our guest?'

The one with the scar stood and stepped outside into the corridor. A tall man appeared and slid the door open, taking his place. He sat down between their original passenger, who shuffled up to make room, and the northerner called Jack, who was staring at Bruce and Gordon intently. The two sides were clearly drawn. The recently exited guest stood in the corridor, looking up and down the passageway. Gordon got the distinct feeling they were not going to be disturbed.

'Gentlemen. It's a pleasure to meet you.' The newcomer sat unnervingly still as he spoke. Another northern accent, they were bloody everywhere. 'Which one of you is Gordon?' Goody offered his hand and the man shook it firmly. 'Pleased to meet you, Gordon. Brian has said so much about you. All good, I might add.' He chuckled to himself. Bruce shot Gordon another look, which he couldn't work out. The atmosphere remained strained. 'So, you must be Bruce.' The man shifted his eyes towards Reynolds and another handshake was exchanged.

The Ulsterman resumed the conversation. 'This is my partner. We are the people you are working for. You wanted to meet both of us, well, here we are.' The pair opposite laughed, but the tension on Gordon and Bruce's side failed to lift.

'Who exactly are you?' Bruce asked.

'You can call me Mark.'

The penny dropped for Gordon Goody. This was the man who had escorted him from Brian Field's office to meet the Ulsterman for the first time. The cheeky bastard, he even asked who he was when he entered the compartment. The visitor must have worked out what he was thinking, and held his hands up in mock surrender.

'It's you. You had a beard,' Gordon said. The man nodded and smiled. What were these people playing at? It was like working with Kim Philby. 'I'll explain later,' Gordon whispered to Bruce, who seemed totally confused.

'Nothing changes. Our terms are the same. It's a million for the pair of us, and that includes our two men on the job.' As the Ulsterman spoke, his partner remained impassive. God only knew what their real names were. Maybe they would never find out. These men knew exactly who they were, and the names of everyone on the job, yet they had no clue what they were dealing with. That would be a job for Buster, to go digging for information.

'I just wanted to meet you two properly. I'm sorry if I didn't let on the first time we met, Gordon. I'm sure you understand we were sizing you up. There's a lot at stake here. We had to make sure we picked the right people.'

'And have you?' Gordon asked. The two men opposite exchanged a glance.

'I think so,' the new visitor replied.

'Which of you is it that has the inside information?' Bruce asked. A good question, no partnership was ever truly equal.

The northerner pointed at the Ulsterman. 'This man here has all the information. I'm providing other support. I have a different role to play. Security, that sort of thing. They know about the newer, more secure coaches, don't they?' he turned to his partner to ask.

'Yes.'

'Well, one thing I'm providing is a guarantee they will be out of action. My neck of the woods. In fact we're heading up there now to have a good look around. It'll make your job ten times easier. We'll do it one at a time, make it look like natural causes, to ensure nobody suspects anything. You can concentrate on getting the money off rather than breaking in. Oh, and I'm paying your weekly wages as well. That's my doing.'

The Ulsterman smiled faintly. Gordon wondered if they had only been dealing with the messenger so far. He might have the inside information, but here was the real brains and balls behind the job. He looked at the character opposite, and wondered just what they were getting themselves into.

'Well, I'll leave you to your journey. It was quite a coincidence to bump into you on this train.'

This Mark, or whomever the hell he really was, looked pleased with himself. The suit looked to be particularly expensive, out of even Bruce's league. He was the man in charge, checking out the two men who were going to lead the train robbery.

The man stood to shake hands again and stepped over to the door of the compartment, which Mickey had slid open.

'Good luck. I'm sure you won't need it.'

Jack followed Mark out of the door. He didn't say a word throughout the whole meeting, boring a hole through Gordon's head the entire time. The Ulsterman shuffled along in his seat, back to the middle.

As soon as the door closed, and the three visitors had disappeared from view, Gordon started the questioning.

'Who the hell is he?'

'Oh, you don't need to know that.'

'But Brian knows him, doesn't he?'

'Yeah, well I suppose he does, yeah. Just ask around. I'm sure you'll find out.'

'We will.'

Gordon understood. Brian Field would tell them, because the mystery man who had just left the compartment wanted them to know. This was a big player.

The man's very presence seemed to leave a large hole in the compartment now he had gone. Gordon knew there were more pressing things to think about. How and where would they stop the train? How far were they likely to have to move it to the ideal unloading point? Should they uncouple the HVP coach from the rest of the train? More importantly, how would they move the money, given there was going to be so much of it? Who precisely they were working for paled into insignificance compared to those issues.

The Ulsterman had one more question. 'Gordon. Bruce. Have you thought about what you're going to do once you've got the money off the train?'

'We're working on it,' was all Bruce came back with. Perhaps it was best to reveal as little as possible, given the surprise they had just been given.

'Good. You know it will make sense to take the money somewhere safe afterwards. That way we can ensure everyone gets their share.'

Gordon could see what he was driving at. The two men who had put them up for the job didn't trust them an inch. Everything would have to be played straight down the line. That would mean finding a base to hole up after the robbery, rather than a fast getaway. Roy James would be pissed off, had set his heart on leading a fleet of speedy Jags back to the capital. It didn't look like that was going to be an option.

The Ulsterman just smiled. Maybe they should put a tail on him, work out where he lived? Harry Smith was an expert in skulking around in the shadows, staying hidden. This would be a job for Smudger when they got back.

'Let's stay in touch,' the Ulsterman said.

'Sure, Jock,' Bruce replied. The name they were using out loud was becoming a bit of a joke.

'Say, in two weeks time?'

Bruce and Gordon nodded their agreement.

'Oh, I need to give you your envelopes.' The man handed a bundle to Gordon, tied up with string.

'Let's meet outside Buckingham Palace. I'd prefer to meet in a more public place.' Bruce was making a sound point. Next time it had to be on their terms. They could also ensure they had plenty of the boys in the area, just in case.

'That's fine. A fortnight? Two o'clock?'

'It's a date,' Bruce chuckled. All three smiled in unison for the first time in the past hour. They were going to be working together; they might as well have a civil relationship. The engine slowed as they pulled into Rugby station.

'Gentlemen, this is your stop. I'm travelling on to Manchester. I shall see you next week.'

They shook hands all round, and Bruce and Gordon collected their coats from the rack above. There would be another opportunity to view the attack point from the other side, during the return journey. Gordon thought about the previous three weeks, and how he had gone from being an everyday thief to a man sitting at the helm of a massive robbery. It was funny how life could just throw opportunity in your lap. His future was looking up.

9

'Wait here. I'll come and get you when the coast is clear.' Buster's face was creased with concentration as he asked Bruce to hang back by the ticket office.

Reynolds watched as his friend greeted a large man in his forties on the opposite side of the station concourse. They turned and walked towards the buffet room, paused outside to share what looked like a joke, and entered. Bruce did as he was instructed, and stood outside, watching from a safe distance. Buster had told him some stories about Tommy Wisbey in the past few days. How he was an old veteran who was totally trustworthy, the same way Buster was viewed across London. They had both been in Freddie Foreman's gang in the late fifties, and made quite a name for themselves. Buster stuck his large head out of the buffet room door and waved at Bruce to follow him in.

Inside he saw Wisbey sitting at a table, sipping tea, with a small wiry man beside him. This looked more like an electronics expert, the key to unlocking their major obstacle. Stopping a speeding express train.

'Tea?' If Buster was offering to buy, you took him up on it, whatever it was.

'Yeah, please mate.'

'Gents?' Buster gestured to the two men already sitting down.

'Nah. I'm good.' Tommy Wisbey responded. The other man just shook his head.

Bruce scanned the faces in the room while he waited for Buster to return, two mugs in one hand. They sat down opposite the men from the South Coast Raiders, a title they had been given in the pubs of London.

'Here you are, Bruce.' The mugs clinked and Buster spilt one of them over his hand. 'Fuck, sorry mate.' Buster gave Bruce the one with half its contents missing.

'Buster here tells us you might need help.' Wisbey wasted no time, and delivered his words through gritted teeth. It didn't scare Bruce, but he could imagine it frightening a guard or a train driver into doing as he was told. Involving both of these two might not be the worst thing they did.

Buster was the first to reply, as Bruce sipped at lukewarm tea. How could they serve it up so tepid? 'Yeah, we have something we'd like to ask you.'

'Go on, then.'

Buster continued. 'We hear you boys have been holding up mail trains on the Brighton line.'

'Where'd you hear that?' Wisbey looked angry. It was common knowledge.

'We just heard it. Word gets around, you know.'

'We don't want nobody talkin' about all that stuff. Nobody can do us for that. If that's what you've come to talk about, well you can piss off.'

Bruce eyed the little man sat next to Wisbey. He looked more like a bank clerk than a thief. Maybe that was to his advantage.

'No, that's not...' Buster hesitated. He told Bruce that when he phoned Tommy a couple of days before he was all sweetness and light. Keen to have a chat about a job he and this man might be able to help with. Now he was on the defensive. Bruce decided to join in the conversation to establish his credentials, just in case it was he that had got his hackles up.

'Tommy, isn't it?' he asked.

'Yeah. You know that.'

'Tommy, we're not bothered about anything you've done in the past. Not in terms of talking about it.'

'Good.'

'We heard you were stopping trains, messing with signals, is all we heard.'

The two men sitting opposite looked at each other. Wisbey jumped in again, anger rising in his voice. 'Told you, we're not havin' anybody fingerin' us for those. Leave it.'

Buster joined in, calmly. 'Look, you know me, Tommy. We're not gonna do anything like that. We're here to talk about a touch of possible work. You know you can trust me. We go a long way back.'

'I know.'

Bruce outlined the basics of the plan, without giving away the amount of money involved. Then he moved on to the area where they needed assistance.

'We're looking for somebody to help us stop a train.'

'What sort of train?' The small man blinked at Bruce. This was the first time he'd said anything, and his voice was annoyingly nasal. He knew Charlie would hate him instantly.

'A mail train.' The man's eyebrows arched as Bruce spoke. 'But not just any old mail train. This one's gonna have millions on board.'

'Millions?' Wisbey nearly spat out his mouthful of tea.

'Yeah, millions.'

'How d'you know this?' The little man asked Bruce. He decided to draw a brief pause to his description of the job. More information was needed first.

'I'm Bruce Reynolds. You are?'

'Roger Cordrey.' Bruce nodded, as if he knew the name by reputation. In truth he'd never heard of him, but there was no other reason for him to be sitting with such a lump as Tommy Wisbey in a station buffet room.

'Anyway, Roger, we're talking about a daily mail train that travels from Glasgow to Euston, and back again. It carries hundreds of thousands of used notes in a special coach, and that's what we're after. Only on certain days the load can be many times more than that. We're looking at up to four million quid in one night.'

'Fuck me!' Wisbey muttered under his breath.

Roger looked momentarily impressed. 'You didn't say, how d'you know all this?' he asked.

'We know a man on the inside. We've got some excellent information.'

'Such as?'

'We can talk more if you can help us.' Bruce had to play things cagily.

'Sometimes trains can be a bit of a gamble,' Roger said authoritatively. Bruce knew the South coast mob had struggled to make a good living off their exploits.

'Indeed. We can reduce the risk. We'll know when it's the right time to strike. We need someone like you to help us stop the thing.'

'You can't get on the train?' Wisbey asked.

'No, no passengers, just GPO employees.'

'Your insider isn't going to be on the train?' Cordrey enquired.

'I can't tell you that.' In fact, Bruce had no idea where the Ulsterman's informant fitted into the picture. He had been wondering for days whether it was even a man in the HVP coach itself, whether they might just let them in. It was more likely to be just an employee who knew what got moved around where and when.

'I think I can stop those trains, easy enough.' Cordrey announced, sounding smug.

'You do?'

'Yeah. I had a look at the Irish Mail train a few months back.'

'I remember that,' said Buster. 'Balls up, wasn't it?'

Roger blushed and turned to look at the wall to his left.

'Yeah, I heard Bobby Welch ended up running round with no coat and shoes,' Buster continued, chuckling to himself. Wisbey looked fiercely at him. Bruce worked hard to suppress a laugh.

'There were a few problems with it. But I've studied the line North of Tring, I know it pretty well,' Cordrey said, looking back at them. 'If you want someone to stop a train using signals, I'm definitely your man.'

'Good. We hoped you'd say that,' Bruce smiled.

'There could be four million on this thing, could there?' Wisbey was obviously interested.

'Yeah. We're only going to strike when the load is at its biggest.'

'A Bank Holiday, then.' Roger got right to the point.

Bruce tried not to give away the fact that this was a correct assessment. He was getting more comfortable with this little expert. 'You seem to know what you're talking about.'

'I like to think so. I can stop this train for you using the signals. I have a unique way of doing it.' Cordrey hesitated. 'But there are a couple of things I need if I'm going to help you.'

'Go on.' This was the bit Bruce was dreading. At least he had Buster with him, in case things cut up rough.

'My friends, including Tommy here, need to be on the job.'

'Who's that, then?' Bruce asked, confident that Buster would know them by reputation.

Roger looked at Wisbey and made his request. 'Tommy here, and Bobby Welch, and Danny Pembroke. These lads need to be in on the job, or I won't help you.'

Buster pulled a face, and Bruce tried to play it straight.

'I'll have to talk to the rest of our boys.'

'If my lads aren't in on it, then it's no deal.'

Bruce pondered the very idea that the crew in question were Roger's 'lads'. From what Buster had told him, Cordrey was very much a part time thief.

'I'm sure we can sort something out.' This was as much as Bruce could promise. He knew how Roy and Charlie would react, they would be furious with spreading the rewards. But as Jimmy White said, there was plenty to be had because they were stealing millions.

'Oh, and I need a fee up front.'

'I don't think that's going to happen.' Buster went instantly back at Cordrey. 'Don't get too greedy. I don't care what you can do with signals, don't take the piss.'

'I just think you need my help, and I should be rewarded for it.'

'Look, we're all gonna get even shares, there's no masters and servants on this one. Same whack for everyone.' Bruce looked at Buster as he said this. Don't you dare mention where the first million is going. Buster stared ahead blankly.

'Same whack? No fee for you? Or your informant?' Wisbey asked, sounding surprised.

Bruce chose his words carefully. 'It's an even split between everyone on the job. No matter what time anyone comes in on it.'

'That sounds fair, I suppose.' Roger sat there blinking, swilling the dregs from his cup of tea.

'And there is one thing that might soften the blow,' Bruce added. 'We're offering fifty quid a week to anyone on the job, as soon as they sign up, like a wage. As a reminder to keep out of trouble in the meantime.'

'Fifty? Jesus.' Wisbey seemed pleased.

'Yeah. For everyone on the job, every week.'

'How long for?' Roger asked.

'Nice try. Let's say well into the summer.'

'August Bank Holiday, then?'

'We'll talk more if you can help us.'

Roger offered his hand to Bruce. 'I think we've got a deal. When do we start?'

'Tomorrow, if you're free?' Bruce was anxious to finalise where the train was going to be stopped, as well as where it would be unloaded. The rest of the job needed planning, especially the getaway.

'Tommy, d'you wanna come?' Roger asked.

Wisbey laughed. 'What, lookin' at a load of trains and signals? No thanks, all the same.'

10

10th June 1963: Hyde Park, London

'No Mickey Mouse names, these have got to be genuine,' Eddie Maloney insisted.

Reynolds nodded. 'We won't take the piss, Jock.'

'I hope not. My partner, you met him, he'll know straight away if it's a load of old bollocks.'

Maloney pointed at the two men sitting on a bench about thirty yards away, by the entrance to Hyde Park, the pair they had met on the train. He knew they had already made enquiries about Tommy Lavery, via Brian Field, so they should know what they were dealing with. This was a one off, a never to be repeated opportunity. If they were sensible they would take their chance regardless of whom they were ultimately working for.

'You know the names,' Bruce said.

'Indulge me again,' Maloney asked politely.

Reynolds listed the thirteen men they had now drawn into the gang. Maloney wrote them down in a small notebook.

'Don't worry, I will destroy this,' he reassured them. 'You can't expect me to memorise that many.'

Maloney stared at his borrowed back up men, Jack Armstrong and Mickey Griffin. Lavery had given him the assurance that they could be trusted, but he was only going to feel safe when his own boys were over. Fitzgerald and Ryan were busy on a job in Belfast, and he was struggling to get the hierarchy to free anybody else up to provide personal security until August.

'Sounds like a big crew to manage?' Eddie asked.

'There's them two as well,' Gordon added, pointing at Jack and Mickey.

That would make fifteen in all, Eddie counted, but the numbers didn't matter. Lavery simply wanted to keep tabs on everybody involved, which made sense. They had to guard against this lot running around the countryside and losing touch with the money.

'We're still getting rumblings about you taking a million off the top,' Reynolds chipped in. He didn't look concerned, smiled as he made the challenge.

'It's not up for debate. You can take it or leave it.'

The two men shared a look, and Eddie decided to head off the issue.

'Gents, please don't think about turning us over. I'm not stupid and nor is my partner. I'd think about doing the same thing, I don't blame you for considering it. But that's why I'm working with those men over there, and their boss. We're a partnership. You steal from me, you steal from them, and I'm sure, if you've done your homework, you'll know by now he's not a man to piss off. Just do your job, and everyone's happy.'

Maloney reached into his pocket and pulled out an envelope. 'It's for you to distribute, you know that.' He handed it to Goody, and both Bruce and Gordon looked around nervously at three men in suits, walking towards them. They passed without incident. These two seemed to be a little out of their depth. Decent thieves, by all accounts, but nothing more.

'Listen,' Bruce began. 'We've got a full meeting on Saturday. We'd like you and your friend to come and meet the whole crew.'

'Are you sure that's wise? The less everyone knows, the better.'

'I know the boys will want to see who they're gonna be working for.'

Eddie relented. 'I'm happy to come along, but my partner is busy at the moment.'

Lavery had been adamant about staying out of the limelight. His reputation, along with Mickey and Jack, would suffice, and he knew Maloney was less concerned about being recognised. He would be on a boat to Ireland within twenty-four hours of the robbery. This lot would be busy running with their money and saving their own hides.

Bruce passed on the details of Buster Edwards's address in Twickenham.

'Three o'clock we start. This is the one and only big meet up. After Saturday, we split into small groups, once we're clear on responsibilities.'

Maloney studied him. He seemed to enjoy being in charge, organising everybody. A job of this size needed men like Bruce Reynolds.

'And you're all going to stay quiet, keep yourselves out of trouble?' Eddie asked.

'This will help,' Goody said, putting the wages envelope in his jacket pocket.

The three men walked further along a tree-lined parade. Reynolds kept looking around, and Goody stared straight ahead. Armstrong and Griffin followed about fifty yards behind the trio. Maloney felt relaxed, knowing there was plenty of support nearby. Not that he ever felt threatened by Bruce and Gordon. If they only knew what he had done in the fifties back home. All that invisible torture and death was history, he had a more important role for the organisation. He was a moneyman now, no longer an executioner.

'You know somebody on the inside, obviously,' Gordon started. 'Do you know a train driver we could borrow?'

'No,' Maloney chuckled. This was their problem, not his. 'No, sorry, I can't stretch that far. You looking to move the train, then?'

'Yeah.'

'My inside information isn't coming from a driver, if that's what you're asking.' Both men fell silent. 'Can't you use your skills to persuade them to move? Shouldn't be too difficult.'

'Just covering every possibility.' Bruce sounded insulted. 'What if the driver has a heart attack when he sees us jumping into his cab?' Reynolds seemed extremely thorough.

'I don't know what to advise. Maybe you could find a retired driver in the pubs?' That was their problem.

'We want to lie low, remember?' Reynolds replied.

Maloney turned left as they approached Hyde Park Corner, walking parallel to Park Lane. Who was watching them? More of Tommy's boys? Or members of this train gang? As long as it wasn't the police, it wouldn't matter. Nobody else could hear what was going on. He needed to pin these men down on a hideout, because lining it up would take time and legwork.

'Gents, I assume you're looking for somewhere to lie low for a few days?'

'We're coming round to it, yeah.' Bruce and Gordon must know now there was no other option, not with between two and four million pounds in tow.

'Here's a thought,' Maloney began, trying to make it look like he was coming up with this on the spot, when in reality he and Lavery had mulled over how to address this for a couple of weeks. 'A hideout. We can take care of the process, fund it, and even find it for you. That way it's all at arm's length. So long as you tell us where you'd like to be.'

'We have to choose it.' Bruce sounded firm.

'That's fine. But we can facilitate everything. Keep your faces a long way away from the purchase.'

'Sounds good. We pick it, though.'

'Fine.' As long as Maloney and Lavery knew where it was, everything else was possible. Brian Field's firm could front it, and use false identities to hire or buy the place.

'Do the police know who you are?' Bruce's question appeared to come from nowhere.

'Do you? I don't mean that in an insulting way, Bruce, Gordon.' Maloney kept on walking, not breaking stride as he talked. 'What I mean is, I'm in this country under an assumed name, you've probably worked that bit out. It wouldn't be too difficult to arrange the purchase of an appropriate location for you all to stay hidden for a while. The money will weigh a ton, you know. You'll need a place that's pretty large, and out of the way.'

Bruce looked across at Gordon and seemed to speak for both of them. 'Right. We'll start looking straight away.'

'Excellent. Talk to Brian Field, tell him first, it'll be quicker.' Maloney watched the two men exchange a look. 'You do trust Brian, don't you? He's integral to this whole project.'

'Yeah, we do,' Bruce said, but their faces told a different story. In truth Field was disposable to everybody, and Maloney knew it.

'Good. Well, I shall see you on Saturday,' Eddie announced, after coming to an abrupt halt. 'Bye.'

Maloney reversed his direction, and headed for Hyde Park Corner tube station. He was anxious to return to Kilburn, where he had been holed up for the previous three months. He was renting an anonymous bedsit above a row of shops on the High Road, and managed to blend into the background. He would be the saviour of the IRA, assuring their future for years to come, helping them to become an active force again. Eddie was already counting the days before his return home, and glory, feted by Whelan and Leahy. His name would be made. No more would Eddie Maloney be seen as an old timer.

11

'I have that list for you. Care to take a look?'

Tommy Lavery handed a slip of paper over to Detective Sergeant Joe Watson. Joe looked around the pub and slipped it under his beer mat. He scanned the few faces seated around tables and at the bar, and relaxed. It was clear that nobody was interested in them. *The Three Feathers* was not the type of place where coppers or villains hung about. It was a boozer where office workers and builders mingled throughout the day. It had become a regular meeting point for the Manchester criminal and junior officer in C Division at New Scotland Yard.

Lavery said he was extremely pleased with Watson thus far. Joe was keen to climb up the ranks, knew he had more sense than many of his colleagues, which helped him make progress. That, and the odd tip-off, courtesy of the 'Beast of the North'. Joe knew how the world of crime worked, was a disciple of a future head of the Flying Squad, DCI Frank Williams. There were two types of bent copper. Firstly, there were the ones who would bend the rules in their favour, work the rackets and take the backhanders. Then, there were men who prioritised the real scum on the streets, and used every resource at their disposal, to nail them. Joe was falling into line with his new boss in the second camp, working to cull the nastier villains who washed around on the streets of London.

Lavery and Joe had been in touch for a couple of years. Watson cut his teeth in COC10, the Yard's stolen car unit, cracking a major ring the year before, largely thanks to information received directly from Tommy. Watson had just made the switch on to the robbery team, which seemed to please his benefactor.

'I'm going to work on the Squad now, COC8. Hatherill okayed it for me and I'm working under Frank Williams as of last month.' George Hatherill, Commander of C Division, was too straight to be of any value to men like Lavery, an untouchable.

'Great news. Well done, young man. I'm pleased for you.'

'I was getting a bit bored of chasing nicked cars around the place to be honest.' Watson tried to lighten the conversation.

Tommy just stared straight back at him. 'Well, you would do.'

'Same again?' Joe asked. Lavery nodded, so he rose to fetch two more pints with chasers. It was the middle of the day and both men were working. When he returned, Joe studied the names on the list. There were thirteen in all.

'Anyone familiar?' Lavery asked, casually.

'A few.'

'Might I enquire which ones?'

'About half of them I know pretty well already.'

'Which ones?' Lavery asked more insistently. Joe swallowed hard.

'The ones at the top. Reynolds, definitely Wilson, a few others.'

'Wilson? Indulge me.'

'Car thief. Bloody idiot, gone a bit quiet in the last month.'

'Well, I need to know what you boys know about all of them.'

'Sure.'

'I want you to do some digging for me, a little bit of background. Their records, their personal lives. Wives, girlfriends, bits on the side, dodgy activities their mates aren't aware of, that sort of thing.'

'Really?'

'Yeah. Really.'

'Why d'you want this?'

'Come, come now, Joe. You know you shouldn't ask me questions like that. We have an understanding, you and me.'

Watson sighed, tipped his whisky into his pint and sipped. The burn ripped into him. 'Yeah, I guess we do.'

'You know we do. Please don't forget it.'

How could he? Lavery had appeared out of nowhere a couple of years before, with some blinding information. It helped him crack a ring of dodgy number plate providers, and bought him a ton of brownie points with Williams and the section head, Hatherill. Like a bloody fool he lapped it all up, and acted alone and off the cuff. The arrest of a gang of four men scattered from Birmingham to Watford made quite an impact. Two of them were still serving. The official line he took with Frank Williams was that he had to protect his informant. Williams was used to this type of approach, positively encouraged it. His boss was well known for fraternising with villains, it was the way he got things done, and here was bright young Joe Watson, a man after his own heart. Lavery had given him a nice 3.8 Jag in return, far more than a copper on his salary could afford. He stuck to taking the bus to work, kept it a secret, parked out in Bromley where his mother lived. The arrests had apparently reduced some of Tommy's competition in the lucrative and murky 'cut-and-shut' area of the motor trade.

From that day on, Lavery continued to drop him titbits of information, almost all of it helping with convictions, or shutting down operations. At first it was mostly cars, but now he was receiving tip-offs on robberies too. It might have been considerably after the fact, but the arrest of George Brain and Manny Eastman in January came from Joe establishing that they were behind a series of jewellery heists on Bond Street. The case was about to come to court, and he was fast becoming Frank Williams's golden boy. His new boss seemed to approve of his methods, asked no questions as to his sources, just allowed him to carry on picking up the collars.

Most of the credit went to Williams, because that was how it worked. Joe knew he was trapped; Lavery had him where he wanted him, caught in a web of lies that meant he had no alternative but to do his bidding. He wondered about being fed a list of names. There were mutterings about a big heist in the offing somewhere, but there always was. In one pub you would hear about train hijacks, in another it would be bullion robberies in the City, elsewhere it could be a boat full of diamonds about to get hit. If the grapevine went quiet, he and his colleagues would be more suspicious.

'You want information on them. Do I need to do anything else? Should we be sweeping them up?' Joe knew these were never social calls. If Lavery wanted to meet him in person, then there was a task to perform, probably in exchange for another tip-off. He stared at the piece of paper in front of him.

'Absolutely not. Quite the opposite in fact.' Tommy looked stern-faced. 'I want them left well alone.'

'You know there's nothing I can do to control what the Squad does.'

'I know that.' Lavery would be well aware that Joe was still a junior officer, a humble DS. The man opposite lowered his voice considerably. 'I'd like you to tell me what you know about these men.'

'These? They're all crooks.' Joe started to laugh, but quickly reined it in when he saw Lavery's expression, those eyes boring in at him.

'Are they? You tell me, Joe, you tell me. If they're on a list of mine it's pretty likely they're not vicars, don't you think?' Lavery stared at Watson, making him realise the seriousness of the situation. Tommy eventually cracked into a smile, but said nothing more.

'Can I keep this?' Joe asked.

Lavery chuckled. 'No. Write them down. On your crossword or something. I want that back in a minute when you're done.' Joe had no idea if this was in Lavery's handwriting, but there would be prints on it. COC3, the newly formed forensics division, were doing amazing things, some of it even legitimate. It was the future for solving crime. Every criminal made mistakes, and often it was dabs that tripped them up.

'No problem, Tommy.'

Watson thought about the list in his hands. Just what was Tommy Lavery up to? It never crossed his mind to turn him in, not for a second. He knew by reputation the consequences of messing with Lavery. It was rumoured that a couple of the Manchester force had been disabled out of their crime squad last year for simply daring to bring him in for questioning. He knew which side his bread was buttered. There was also the occasional sweetener as well.

'Am I getting anything for this task?'

'I'll think of something,' Tommy grinned, showing his irregular teeth. 'Once you've done this for me. I want you to memorise those names, all right?'

'Memorise them?'

'Yeah, remember them well. I might ask you to refer to them in the future.' Lavery looked calm, but Joe knew there was a killer lurking underneath. No longer by his direct hand, Tommy was too smart and well protected for that.

'When do you want this by?'

'You've got a couple of weeks. I need to start planning, once I get your information.' Joe must have betrayed his puzzlement, because Lavery stared forcefully, deep into his soul. 'All will be revealed in time.'

'Sure.'

'Have I ever let you down before?' Lavery asked. Joe had to agree, he hadn't. He wondered just how well his career might have gone if it hadn't been for the help of this big, bad gangster from the North. He considered how many of his colleagues were also on his payroll. Maybe there was no such thing as an honest collar any more. Or an honest copper.

'No, Tommy. You've never let me down.'

'Good. You come through with this little job for me; I'll see you right. Okay?'

'Okay.'

'Is Tommy Butler still kicking around?' Lavery asked.

'Of course.'

Tommy was always asking how his superiors were getting along, like a nervous tic. The Grey Fox would never retire. He worked eighteen hours a day, seven days a week. Ernie Millen, Hatherill's number two, was currently leading the Flying Squad, and received all the credit, but it was Butler and Williams who got the results.

'And Frank's still rattling a few cages, is he?'

'Frank's always rattling cages.'

Joe tried to smile. He wondered if his colleagues had similar conversations on a regular basis. There was no way he could raise the subject. If any of them were legit, he was screwed if he talked about what was going on. If he was honest, he looked up to Lavery. Tommy was a businessman, making his way in a complicated world. He cut a few corners it was true, but then again, who didn't? Were all accountants or solicitors on the level? He doubted it, from what he had seen. Why should he be any different? And the same rules could apply to coppers. The Big Picture, as Tommy described it to him once before, think of the Big Picture. He was trying to.

Lavery finished off his pint in rapid style. 'I'd best be going, got a train to catch.'

'Going anywhere nice?'

'No.' Lavery retorted coldly. 'Fuckin' Leeds. I hate Tykes.'

Joe simply nodded. These northerners, they were a race apart. He raised his glass in salute as the criminal, who had him well and truly by the balls, left. He eyed the list of names written on the back page of his newspaper, scattered around the crossword. They weren't major criminals. Maybe Lavery was looking to trade them in? His reputation would be shot if he worked with any of this lot. As a crew they were questionable, made up of rival firms. The list was littered with small time bandits, dodgy bookmakers, and failed car thieves. He thought a few of them were in retirement, not up to the job. Lavery would know what he was doing.

As he sat on the top deck of the bus, on his way back to New Scotland Yard, Joe watched the shoppers scamper by. Their lives looked simple, and he was struck with jealousy. As he fished his ticket out to show the bus conductor, he found Lavery's piece of paper with the names on it. Joe had picked it up, careful to ensure nothing was left behind. This might well be a test; he had been put under the microscope by Lavery before. That time he ended up with a pair of busted ribs, a black eye and regrets over the reporting of a security breach in Edgware. He screwed up the sheet, and set light to it with his cigarette, watching the writing evaporate as it glowed. He knew it never paid to be walking round with evidence in your pocket. This task had to be his focus when he returned to work. Tommy Lavery was going to be pleased with his detective work. It paid to know exactly who your real friends were in this game.

12

Jack Armstrong studied the faces around the room. They certainly looked like thieves, some more intelligent than others, some perfectly capable of looking after themselves. Eddie Maloney was stood in front of them all, proudly talking about the inside information he had. They were lapping it up, greedy little dogs salivating at the thought of all that money heading their way. They were going to be in for a nasty surprise later.

Jack was stood with Mickey Griffin at the back, watching the crew intently. Occasionally one of them would stare at he and Mickey with what they must have thought were threatening eyes, but none of it carried any weight. Maloney seemed comfortable because of their presence. The Mick droned on and on about how all the money was untraceable and how lucky they all were to be sat in Buster Edwards's living room. If this place was representative of the kind of rewards they had been picking up thieving, they weren't very good at it.

Smoke hung heavy and close to the ceiling. Men coughed and spluttered and drank beer. One of them, Bob Welch he thought his name was, kept passing wind and made a couple of the others laugh. Many looked plain bored when Maloney revealed the massive amount of money on offer. What a rabble. The only ones who seemed to know how to conduct themselves professionally were the two they had met on the train, Reynolds and Goody. There was one quiet guy, near the back, called Jimmy White who did intrigue him. He seemed to be taking it all in, not diving in with questions and accusations. His steely eyes were fixed on Eddie Maloney as the Irishman spoke.

'I just wanted you all to know there is a face behind this job. I'm here to guarantee you will be attacking on a night when it's worth your while.' Maloney smiled at them. Only a small number seemed to return the favour. After he finished his little speech, Eddie sat down next to the drawn curtains.

Bruce Reynolds then took centre stage. 'The night of August the sixth, boys, that's the plan. It's a Bank Holiday just before that in Scotland, and there'll be plenty of money on board.'

'That's correct,' Maloney added. 'It's the perfect time to strike.' Again he forced a smile, but they seemed to be a tough crowd to please. They would have to watch themselves on this job.

'What if it don't run? Or if it's runnin' late? Fucked if I wanna stand around in the cold and the dark for fuck all,' one of the larger men said, staring at Maloney.

'Tommy, our friend here can tell us if anything is amiss,' Bruce intervened.

'Yes. I can warn you off if anything doesn't add up to the maximum haul for you. We attack when the coach is full of money.' Maloney smiled again.

'I hope so. Given you're nickin' the first bloody million.' Another of the group laughed as he said this, a tall man with fierce eyes. Around the room there were murmurs.

It was Gordon Goody who stood up to counter. 'All we're doing is paying off our inside source. You always do that on jobs, right?'

'Not a fuckin' million quid's worth.'

Maloney made to leave, call their bluff. Jack and Mickey stood still. Bruce told them they had to hang around when Maloney left the meeting, which he was scheduled to do. They were a part of the team now, would be treated as such.

'No, wait, Jock. There's plenty to go round, isn't there?' Gordon pleaded to the men in the room.

Jack smiled to himself at the ludicrous name they called Maloney. He'd also heard them refer to him as 'the Ulsterman', which was more accurate.

Jimmy White spoke up for the first time. 'Jesus, we're nickin' a whole fuckin' train. There's plenty for the rest of us. Jesus.'

'One thing I will say, and then I'll be on my way.' This time there was silence and concentration as Maloney spoke. 'If you get nothing, we get nothing. If you take less than two million, we'll split everything in half. I can't say fairer than that.'

There were nods of approval around the room. He was a cheeky bastard, Lavery hadn't agreed to anything of the sort. Half a million was coming his way regardless of what the Irishman said. Maloney avoided eye contact with Jack, searching the sea of faces in front of him.

'That seems fair.' A small man in the corner contributed. Most faces swivelled around to watch him, then turned away as he carried on talking. 'I mean, there is plenty to go round.' Some of the others muttered agreement.

Bruce cleared his throat. 'Look, lads. We've done a deal and that's that. Our friend here just wanted you to be reassured the inside information is going to work in our favour.'

Maloney gave a final farewell. 'I want to wish you good luck. Obviously, I'm pulling for you all on this one. I shall see you again when the job is done.'

As Bruce escorted Maloney away, everybody started to talk at once. Jack threw a look at Mickey Griffin, who seemed to be more interested in the dirt under his fingernails. It had taken them a good half an hour to bury Billy Arnold up to his neck that morning, eventually persuading him to reveal the whereabouts of a consignment of shotguns that had gone missing. Mickey obviously didn't bother to wash his hands afterwards.

When Reynolds returned, Buster Edwards switched off the

lights and started fiddling with a projector. They were then subjected to a tedious ten minutes of photographs of the place where they were going to stop the train, as well as pictures of mailbags. They ought to be able to recognise a few million quid if they saw it without all this slide show nonsense.

Reynolds proceeded to drone on about uncoupling the coaches and what the driver and the fireman would do when they stopped the train. Jack tried to focus on the details. Lavery wanted a blow-by-blow account of the meeting that evening. Nobody was taking notes, and he was trying to commit the more interesting pieces to memory. Mickey was still engrossed with the dirt on his hands.

The conversation threatened to boil over when they started discussing how to move the train a thousand yards down the track, to where the money would be offloaded. One of the men, Roy James, he thought it was, kept banging on about wanting to drive the train. Bruce and Gordon resisted.

'I still reckon I can drive it. I've got two months to master it.'

Goody countered. 'Roy, I know you're good on a track, but this is different. We need to know if you can definitely move it.'

'I reckon I can.'

'Yeah, but can you stop it?' Jack thought this was Danny Pembroke, pointing his finger in James's direction. 'You nearly killed me at Stonebridge Park. Crashed the bloody thing. We had to leg it.'

The little man who talked about the signals backed him up. 'It's much harder than it looks. I reckon we need somebody who knows what they're doing.' Roy shot him a fierce look. 'What I mean is, somebody trained in it. Years of experience.'

Charlie Wilson, a face he had been warned about, had a preferred method. 'We just bloody well make sure the driver moves it for us. We just have to persuade him, don't we?' He smiled at Buster Edwards. It was clear what their preferred method would be, and Jack found it hard to argue against their logic.

The signals man interjected. 'We need a contingency. Train

drivers are notoriously stubborn. If whoever we've got decides he won't move it, he won't bloody move it.'

'Why wouldn't he?' Charlie Wilson raised his hand as if holding a cosh. A few of the men laughed.

'I'm just saying we might come across one who's a bit bloody minded, that's all.' Maybe this bloke was right, Jack thought. Imagine a driver saying, 'Go on then, hit me.' They'd still be buggered, and the train would be going nowhere.

Reynolds tried to placate Roy James. 'We need to cover all the angles, everything from every direction. Roy, you can be a back up, but we need more security. Basically if we can't move this train, we're knackered. Do you fancy taking the risk of lugging dozens of heavy mailbags a thousand yards down the track? I'm not sure I do.'

Jack was buggered if he would. There were murmurs around the group until Reynolds cleared his throat and made an announcement.

'I've found us a retired train driver.' Bruce smiled, but it didn't catch on at first.

'That's brilliant. Where?' Jimmy White looked surprised, and wasn't alone in the room.

'Doesn't matter where. He can move the train for us. Thing is, there's one thing that comes with him. Or one person.'

'How'd you mean?' Roy James must have been keen to retain his status as the only recognised driver of any vehicle in the gang. It was comical to watch. Even Griffin had stopped his manicure to take in proceedings.

'I found our driver through an old lag I know. He's a hefty lad, my mate, straight as they come, we can trust him.'

'Who is it, then?' Charlie Wilson asked.

'He's one of us. I've done time with him.' There were audible sighs of relief around the room. Anyone who had served was automatically more trustworthy than a regular member of the public. 'It's Ronnie Biggs.'

Jack didn't recognise the name, but then again, why would he? These southern monkeys were well outside of his normal sphere.

'Biggsy?' Charlie Wilson asked.

'Yeah.'

One of the larger gang members, he thought it was either Tommy Wisbey or Jim Hussey, wanted to know more. 'Who is he, this Biggs?'

'An old time thief. Like it or lump it, he knows about the job now.' Reynolds faced up to the whole room. It looked like he had taken a decision without consulting the rest of the gang.

'You told him?' Wilson asked threateningly. Jack knew he was one to watch.

'I had to, in order to get at this driver. We need one.'

Jack watched the discussion escalate about this Biggs. What a pain in the arse. They thought they had a definitive list of all the men on the job, just like Lavery asked, and now here was another one. He would be well hacked off.

Bruce tried to round off the debate. 'I can vouch for him. A hundred percent. He's solid.'

Gordon backed him up. 'Look, if Bruce says he's good, then he's good. Another pair of hands won't do us any harm, will it?'

The consensus in the room seemed to be with allowing this Biggs character in on the job. Jack pitied every single one of them. They had no idea what they were letting themselves in for. If Lavery got his way, none would survive with both their share of the money and their liberty.

The meeting dragged on. Reynolds raised something that did interest Jack and his boss. The share out. Bruce stood in front of them to tackle the thorny issue. Armstrong was ready to rebut any more challenges that came their way about the first million.

'Lads. We're splitting everything evenly between us. That's after our insider gets his share.'

'Fuckin' hell!' Charlie Wilson spat.

'We've had that debate, Charlie, let's move on.'

Jack watched Wilson scowling in the front row. Your time will come, he thought.

Reynolds continued to talk like he was a military commander. A few of the gang smirked when he adopted this manner; others sat up to attention. He could bet it was the rival group from the South coast that were less appreciative of Bruce's approach.

'We've given up on the fast getaway, roadblocks,' Reynolds began.

Jack was expecting a prolonged discussion on the subject, but they must have talked about it before they arrived.

'Brian Field, who some of you know, is going to front up the purchase of a hideout,' Bruce Reynolds continued. 'We'll lie low there for a few days until it's safe to leave.' Jack looked at Roy James, the racing driver. He looked totally pissed off. 'We've got a place lined up, and its perfect. Nobody will find us.'

'Where is it?' Jack was shocked to hear Mickey Griffin asking a question. What was he playing at? Both he and Lavery repeatedly had to tell him to stop thinking for himself.

'All will be revealed soon enough,' Bruce blinked back, obviously taken aback by the source of the question. 'Our friend Jock is working with Brian to secure it.'

Griffin looked bemused by the response. Jack would have to have a word outside. They were supposed to observe, and look mean. Nothing else required. The extra name on the job made the trip worthwhile. It was also vital for the gang to feel comfortable with the pair of them.

Reynolds then carried out a two-way conversation in front of everyone with Jimmy White about supplies, which had most of the gang yawning and reaching for their beers. This Bruce might think he had the air of a military leader, but clearly had no idea how to retain the interest of his troops.

Gordon Goody picked up a final thread. 'Remember, boys, let's stay out of trouble and keep our heads down, just for a few more weeks. Don't change your routines too much; we don't want to disappear off the radar entirely. We want to be seen about, but inactive. Are we all clear?'

There were a few mumbles of 'yeah' around the room, and more nodding. It felt to Jack that sheer boredom was bringing them all into line.

'Don't forget gloves, everyone,' Bruce threw in. 'Bring your own, and spares, we can't be leaving any clues lying about.'

There were many sighs around the room. Things had gone on too long and Reynolds was testing their patience. They were all experienced thieves; they should know the preparations you had to take for a job like this, for any job. Especially gloves.

13

The wig itched like mad, but, for Eddie Maloney, the disguise was a necessity. He had no plans to be in the country twenty-four hours after the robbery, but he knew his features, especially his lack of hair, made him memorable. Brian Field was going to do all the talking, and even though he could adopt a passable English accent, he planned to fade into the background during the visit to the farm. The clerk made all the viewing arrangements with the estate agents, and received the property details in the post. On paper it looked ideal, and he was posing as an advisor to a prospective purchaser. He even dressed down for the part, buying an old suit from a second hand shop in Colindale.

The message from Bruce Reynolds was that this was the property they wanted to use for their base after the robbery. The cost was £5,550, and the plan was to lay down a deposit simply to ensure they gained access to the farm in August. Field said he had a stooge set up to front the purchase.

Maloney went over his conversation with Bruce Reynolds two days before, as they bumped along the track that connected the farmhouse with a quiet country road. He sounded excited to have found the right spot to lie low. It was shocking that Reynolds and Daly both visited the farm the week before in person. Why were they being so reckless? He said he had used the name of Richards, and insisted it would be a dead end lead; nobody would remember the people who came to visit, but didn't buy. Eddie wished he shared Bruce's optimism, and wondered how long this bunch would stay safe after the robbery if this was how they operated. Not his problem, if he was sitting in the safe haven of Dublin.

A farmhouse appeared behind a cluster of trees in front of them. It looked abandoned, which might be an advantage. Who would come nosing about in a place like this? They would probably be able to strike a quick bargain for it. A woman emerged from the front door, as Brian parked up his Ford Consul. She looked well over sixty and Maloney hoped they were desperate to sell. A secluded base was central to both his and Lavery's objectives, and this place didn't even feature on Ordnance Survey maps. Who wouldn't want an invisible hideout?

After an exchange of pleasantries, the woman showed them both around the farmhouse. Maloney wouldn't have touched it with a barge pole if it were his own money. The place was a mess. There was running water, and a generator provided electricity, but it had a distinct pre-war feel. It felt rather like stepping into a rural farm in western Ireland. The nostalgia for home was hard to ignore. In a few weeks he would be back, prominence in the organisation confirmed, finances in place for the future of the struggle. This little farmhouse was going to be an integral part of all that.

They took a tour of outbuildings that were spread around the property. Lavery asked for details about the layout, so he paced a few of the distances out, an old reconnaissance trick. He was buoyed by the news that Fitzgerald, Beard and Ryan were due over the week before the heist, and it would be good to catch up with old comrades. Maloney concentrated on his accent, shortening the vowels and saying as little as possible. Field wouldn't see him again after that day; didn't seem to think he was the mysterious 'Ulsterman' the gang were talking about. Eddie was a phantom, whatever title they gave him, and he would disappear into the Irish mist once he had his money. He was using the name of 'Dawson' for the day, an advisor to Tommy Lavery as far as Brian Field was concerned.

Brian continued to engage Mrs Rixon in conversation, and she asked what 'the client' was going to do with the farm if he bought it. Eddie ignored the question, leaving Field to whittle on about re-development. The place was big enough to house the whole gang comfortably, could keep the transport Bruce wanted to use under cover, and was well hidden. Little else mattered, as long as they could set the purchase in motion rapidly.

As Field went up the stairs with the owner, Eddie's thoughts turned once more to Tommy Lavery. At least he was going into this thing with his eyes wide open, knew what he was up against. He pitied the gang, a bunch of would-be big time criminals who didn't know what they were dealing with. He had to be prepared for a double cross even though the hierarchy were preaching trust. Word from Whelan, on the mainland, was that there were too many deals in the pipeline for Lavery to turn on his Irish business colleagues. No matter how big he thought he was in England, there was an army waiting across the Irish Sea that would break him if he tried anything. But Maloney still had to make contingencies. Two boats would now be heading from the Welsh coast to Cork, the money split up. They were coming armed, taking no chances.

When they returned to the kitchen, where Eddie had been contemplating the future, Field and Mrs Rixon wrapped up a discussion about the surrounding countryside.

'That just about does it for me, what about you?' Brian Field avoided using any names. Eddie didn't even know who the front man was going to be.

'Fine,' Maloney replied in his best English accent, 'I've seen enough. I need to talk to my client next.'

'Oh, good.' Mrs Rixon appeared delighted. Maybe they really were struggling to offload the place. Well, they were still going to be stuck with it, he thought, the sale wasn't going to go through. Six hundred quid was the ceiling Lavery had placed on any deposit, and he would be leaving all those arrangements to the firm of James & Wheater. All operations were being kept securely at arm's length.

He studied Brian Field as he drove back up the track to the Thame Road. Lavery was confident that he would hold up under pressure if anything went wrong. Gordon Goody seemed to trust him as well, but there was something behind the eyes that worried Eddie. Nobody got to be that successful as a solicitor's clerk unless he was crooked. His aim was to keep his distance and remain invisible. His sources needed that level of protection, because if this went off as planned, there would be a massive investigation into where the inside information came from, within the GPO. He had men to look after in this country, even if they were the ultimate enemy.

14

'I really appreciate your work, Joe.'

'Thanks, Tommy.'

'No, I really do. And my associate here appreciates it too, don't you?' The tubby, balding man simply nodded, without looking at Joe Watson. In fact he had made no eye contact at all since Joe had arrived at the water's edge.

'It was no big deal, really. They're mostly very well known to us.' DS Joe Watson knew there were a couple of exceptions, but everyone on the list had a record.

'I suspected as much.'

The three of them strode down the Thames embankment, opposite Mansion House. The watery sunshine cheekily offered its help in warming the day, peeking out from behind scattered clouds. All three men wore suits, and Lavery's companion also carried a coat over his right arm. Joe felt the heat of the day as he fingered his collar, struggling to remain composed. Just what was he doing here with men like this? His life was in a tailspin. He was paying for poor decision-making.

'Where's the information then?' Lavery asked gently. Joe felt more nervous when Tommy spoke quietly, the threat just below the surface. The stories you heard.

'Oh, yeah, they're in my bag here. Do you want them now?' Watson held up the shopping bag he was carrying, with a blue cardboard file sticking out of the top.

'When we're done. It's everything I asked for?'

'A one page summary for each one. Well, for a few there's not as much as the others, to be honest with you.'

With some, Joe had needed to pad it out a bit to at least make it look like he had done a bit of work. For the likes of Wisbey and Wilson, it was a matter of what you left out. It was an oddity that four of the thirteen surnames began with a 'W'. They appeared to be a strange gang of men, if that was what they were. Some of the names could almost be characterised as enemies. He didn't have the confidence to ask Lavery why the hell he wanted to know about them, he valued his limbs too much.

Joe looked across at their companion, who stared out over the Thames, ignoring him. He decided to elaborate.

'A few can handle themselves. Tommy Wisbey, Jimmy Hussey, both big lads. Charlie Wilson, definitely can be a hothead and Buster Edwards is not averse to giving someone a backhander. And Bob Welch may be a bit past it, but he's solidly built, always been a rough house.'

'But not a gang of thugs?'

'Not all of them, no.' Joe thought about the more lightweight names. Roger Cordrey, what was he doing there? Jimmy White, a safebreaker, but known to be a loner. Were they men Lavery wanted to hire for a future job, like an elite, handpicked crew? If that was what he was playing at, it was a strange collection of names, an odd bunch. Certainly not what he would classify as a crack team of criminals.

'Well, maybe they're just a bunch of idiots whose time is nearly up. Do you catch my drift?'

Lavery let the comment hang in the air and Joe Watson's heart raced. Was this a hot list? A group of men who had pulled off a job that they didn't even know about? People who had crossed Lavery over the years, and now he wanted them behind bars? Surely he had enough resources to settle scores?

'Just keep your list of names, Joe. Don't throw that crossword away yet. It might prove useful in a few weeks time.'

Maybe they were a crew for a job coming up, and Tommy was handing him a list of those taking part. This had to be a bad dream.

'What d'you want me to do with the names?'

'Right now, nothing at all. Wait 'til I give you the nod. Then you can use 'em however you see fit. By then it might be obvious.' Lavery wheeled and put his hands on Joe's shoulders. 'But don't fuckin' use 'em before I say so, all right? You know what'll happen if you do that, don't you? Just don't get any clever ideas, all right?'

'I understand,' was all Joe could reply. What did he mean, that it would be obvious? His thoughts were interrupted by another request from his generous benefactor.

'Oh, yeah, I've got one more name I need a quick check on. Another to add to my list.'

'Who's that?'

'Ronald Biggs.'

'Never heard of him.'

'No, I didn't think you would have,' Lavery replied dismissively. 'But I still want him checked out. Same details as all the others, addresses, acquaintances, affairs, the lot. Understand?'

'I won't let you down.' Joe prayed that he never would.

'Good.'

Lavery stopped to lean over the embankment wall, staring out over the Thames, and both his companions joined him to watch as a boat slowly inched its way to the opposite shore. It reminded Joe of the progress his career was making lately, stalling in the low waters. He needed something to get his teeth into soon, or he would go mad. The Flying Squad wasn't as glamorous as people made out. There was only so much sitting in cars, eating sausage rolls, nursing cold coffee and watching empty houses a man could take. Maybe these names would change all that.

'Joe, I think our meeting has concluded.'

'Oh, right. Sure.' Watson made to shake hands and Lavery

ignored him. 'Here you go,' Joe said, dropping the shopping bag to the floor.

'Not in public, you idiot,' Tommy muttered towards the sulking current.

'When do you want this information on this Biggs character?'

'Tomorrow.' Lavery turned to face Joe.

'Tomorrow? You're asking a lot, Tommy.'

'Yeah, I am. And you're gonna get a lot in return, if you do as I say.'

Joe Watson shrugged. Something was brewing. The jungle drums were beating a steady rhythm; rumours of a massive job were on the cards, although nobody could quite work out what. A few of the names on his list had gone quiet. Perhaps he was going to get a tip-off in advance of an operation. It was best to sit back and be ready for whatever was coming.

'You want to meet tomorrow, then?'

'Yeah. Right here, midday. Don't be late, I've got an appointment with the Commander.'

Just what the hell did he mean? Surely not George Hatherill? Maybe it was code. 'No problem. I'll be here.'

'Good, see you, hotshot.' Lavery turned his back and flicked the remains of a cigarette into the river.

Suitably dismissed, Joe trudged up the hill towards The Strand, and then turned left, to begin the long walk towards New Scotland Yard. He preferred to make the journey away from the river, among the throng of shoppers. Maybe this Biggs was clean, and that was why he was a late runner. Certainly nobody Joe had come across before. What was Lavery up to, dealing with amateurs? He supposed he would find out the truth soon.

★ ★ ★

When Eddie Maloney turned back from staring across the Thames, the police officer had disappeared.

'Can you trust him?' Eddie asked Lavery. English coppers were never going to be his cup of tea, as they said. This one clearly worked for Tommy, which made him doubly untrustworthy. Still, it would be interesting to know how deep into the force Lavery reached.

'I think that's my problem, isn't it?'

'It could be mine, too.'

'You've got nothing to worry about. Just make sure there's enough money on this mail train, and you're on your way with your share. No more questions asked.'

'He doesn't know who I am? You've not told him, have you?'

'He hasn't got a fuckin' clue. He doesn't know anything unless I fuckin' tell him.'

'Good.' Maloney wished he could feel more assured. It had surprised him when a member of the Flying Squad joined them for their meeting along the river. Lavery seemed to know what he was doing.

'You're going to turn them all in?'

'I don't know yet. But it's always good to have a fallback position, don't you think? For our security.' Maloney considered this point of view. Asking for a million off the top could always invite jealousy and anger from a group of thieves. It would be second nature to want to keep it all.

'They might get away with it,' Eddie declared, watching the current. 'The robbery, I mean.'

'I doubt it, actually. Not in the long run.'

'You sound confident.'

'You've seen their hideout, yeah?'

'Yes.'

'Think they can stay there for several days and not leave any clues behind? Not a single one?'

'You never know.'

'Course they fuckin' won't. Too many of 'em, no way they'll keep it clean.'

'Will that be an issue?'

'Could be.'

Eddie thought about the latest news. Bruce had confided in him that Billy Still had just been arrested. They had planned to pay him to burn down the farm afterwards, destroy the evidence after the men and the vehicles had gone.

'They might need a bit of help.' He explained the Still situation, and Lavery laughed.

'My boys might do it. If they paid 'em.'

Maloney thought about Lavery's two men. 'Are your boys thorough in their work?'

'Been known to cut a few corners from time to time, be forgetful, know what I mean?'

'I do.' Eddie turned to something he had been meaning to ask. 'What are we putting Brian Field's way for this?'

Lavery looked insulted. 'Nothing.'

'Nothing at all?'

'No, he gets his share out of their lot. Have they not worked that bit out yet?'

'No, I don't think they have.' This would go down well, he thought.

'We need to insist that he gets a full share.'

'Are we in a position to do that?'

'I think we are, yeah.' Lavery held up his bag, and Eddie saw his point of view.

'What you got in there? I didn't quite get the gist.'

'Information. On all our thirteen friends. Soon to be fourteen.'

'What for?'

'Information's always useful, you know that Eddie. It's why we're both standing here now.'

If only Lavery knew how simple it had been to obtain, Eddie thought. Two different contacts, employees of the GPO, separately their knowledge was of limited use. But, when you stuck the two pieces together, it was infinitely more powerful. One was a member of his organisation, the other a relative of a contact, from Warrington. Still, it wasn't how easy something was to obtain that determined the value of a piece of information; it was what you could gain from it.

Maloney watched a passenger boat gently ease its way down river. Lavery was trading information on the gang with a bent copper. Whatever Tommy was up to, he would be long gone when that lot were shopped to the police.

'You sure you don't want to get involved?' Lavery asked.

'In what?'

'I don't think our friends will get far with their money.'

'Really? That's a shame.'

Maloney pondered the consequences of Lavery turning on the gang, or simply handing them over to the police. Surely they would make plans for the future? They couldn't be that foolish? It proved he was right to bring over more security for his share.

'We haven't talked about how we split up our money,' Eddie added. 'We need to agree that now.'

'We get this lot to count it out for us,' Tommy held his bag up in the air again. 'Then we take it away.'

'And how should we share it out?'

'You decide where you want to do that. My boys will bring it to you. You can follow them if you like, of course.'

Eddie had thought about turning up at the farm to collect his half a million, but dismissed it when he saw the limited escape route, one dirt track. If the police gave chase or worked out where they were hiding quickly, he didn't want to be sat at the farm with his trousers round his ankles.

'Jack and Mickey can bring it along. Somewhere a long way from the farm and the scene of the robbery,' Tommy suggested. 'You choose where we meet.'

'Excellent. I trust them.'

Lavery was offering to pick up the initial risk, transporting the million away from the hideout. He would go searching for a place on the way to the Welsh coast to complete the transaction, to ease their escape with the half a million. He wasn't going to let the organisation down; Eddie Maloney was going to be a national hero.

15

'That'll do, boys, half time.' Gordon called everyone in, to gather round. 'Sit down, boys. Here, Jim, have you got those beers?'

Jim Hussey opened up a box containing twenty-four bottles of beer he had stolen from an off licence the week before. Gordon knew most of them didn't care what Bruce said about keeping out of trouble, they couldn't help themselves. There were two weeks to go, and mass meetings like they had at Buster's flat were out of the question. He had hit upon a good way for a large number of the gang to gather together out in the open. A seemingly impromptu game of football on Wimbledon Common fitted the bill. What they were doing looked perfectly normal on a summer's day. Gordon picked up the idea watching a couple of matches there the week before. His team were leading 3-1 and he could see the likes of Buster and Tommy Wisbey blowing hard. It was good to get those South coast boys running around, because apart from Roger, they had done precious little for their share so far.

Most of the preparation work had been done in small teams. Jimmy White and Danny were busy gathering together the materials for the job and the supplies for the farm. Roger had been training John Daly and Harry Smith in tampering with signals. Himself, Bruce and Buster were monitoring the Up Special trains every night, logging the times that they passed by the stopping point, known as Sears Crossing. With one exception, when it ran over half an hour late, their train passed through no more than five minutes off schedule. This regularity provided great comfort. They knew much more than the authorities. That kind of knowledge had you fit to burst with excitement.

The beers were passed around liberally to all fifteen men. It was eight against seven, but putting both Bob Welch and Tommy Wisbey on the larger side ensured that things were even. The only man missing was Ronnie Biggs, who was checking on his driver friend, because he had promised to undertake a few refresher trips with old workmates. Gordon was still worried about how secure the little man was going to be, and he wasn't alone. Buster, for one, had questioned his reliability about the job. He had no experience, and would be vulnerable. Gordon's solution was to keep him out of everything, ensure he spent very little time with the rest of the gang. It was also nice to see Jack and Mickey there. They were starting to feel part of the team.

It was Bruce who wrestled control of the updates, as they sat on the grass, soaking up the sun and drinking.

'Gents, we have a dress rehearsal coming up this Tuesday night, Nine Elms depot. Gather there at midnight, we want to ensure there are no mistakes.' Bruce adopted his military style of command again. His method had become tired, and Gordon knew a few of them were getting pissed off with him. If it weren't for the considerable prize, they might have given up on the job by now. Most simply wanted to get on with it. The next two weeks would feel like forever.

'From the top, then. Let's start with an update on the travel arrangements. Roy?'

Roy James went through the routes a couple of times, but this was of no interest, apart from the three men who would be driving on the night. It was going to take about thirty-five minutes to drive from Bridego Bridge to the farm, maybe more if they split up. The detail was getting everybody down.

Jimmy White updated them on vehicles. There was an Army

lorry and two Land Rovers, along with a back-up vehicle hidden ten miles from the farm, in case of emergency.

'Remember, it's vital we lay low when we're at the farm,' Bruce Reynolds picked up. 'Nobody go buggering off, please? It is isolated but there are a few other farms scattered about, and some houses out on the road. We don't want anybody getting clocked, do we? We don't want to balls it up before we've started.'

The men continued to drink their beers, and Charlie Wilson opened up a second. It was a warm day after all, and he put more effort into the match than most. 'I can't wait, to be honest,' he pronounced, necking half his second bottle in one go. 'I can't wait to get stuck into it.'

Bruce sounded determined to keep everybody calm. 'Nor can I. But the date is set, and that's it.'

'I know, but fuckin' hell, Bruce.' Charlie grinned at everyone, and it caught on.

Gordon knew that Charlie hadn't touched a motor for weeks, and it must have been killing him. He had even joked that he was getting rusty. Maybe this job would mean he could retire from the game altogether.

They went through the rest of the plan in detail, a fifteen-minute stoppage in the action. Charlie was finishing his second beer when Bruce called everyone together for one last pep talk.

'Don't forget your gloves, boys, really important. And those of you attacking the HVP, bring your coshes.'

'Oh, we will,' laughed Buster. He made as if to crack a head open with an empty bottle. The boys joined in the mirth.

'I don't reckon we'll need to. The driver will see sense when he sees the size of us,' Charlie chuckled. More laughter. Gordon watched them all. They looked a happy bunch; this really was going to work.

'Bruce. How long we gonna be holed up there?' Charlie asked.

'I reckon we have to plan for up to a week.'

'A week? Fuck me.' They were all hoping to get back home

sooner than that. A week with that amount of money would be torture, as well as dangerous.

Gordon tried to reassure them. 'We need to play it by ear. If the coast is clear, we're off. But there might be a bit of a fuss, so we may have to sit tight for a bit, be patient.'

Charlie would go mad, cooped up in a farmhouse. They would have to bring a bit of entertainment, playing cards and board games, that sort of thing. Gordon made a note to pick some up on the way, perhaps a game of Monopoly. Nobody was going to catch Gordon Goody out; he was the most careful of all. They would have loads of money to keep them company while they waited for the right time to leave.

Jimmy White turned to Gordon and smiled. 'Don't bother eating beforehand, mate. We got tons of food. Danny found a load of stuff that fell off the back of a lorry last week, didn't you, Dan?'

'Yeah,' Pembroke chimed, chewing a piece of grass. He rarely said a word. 'Funny how that happens.'

Gordon was conscious that they had been sitting down for too long. 'Come on, lads. Let's get back to the game. Jack, you can have Roy on your team, swap him with Bruce.' They had made the two northerners captains, even though they were reluctant leaders.

'Oh, fuckin' cheers,' Bruce said, pretending to be insulted.

Everyone laughed. Bruce would never make a footballer. But as a disguise for a gathering this was ideal. Gordon felt they were set, ready to go to work. Weeks of planning meant that everything was falling nicely into place. All they needed was a coach load of money to fall off the train and they would be sorted. In a couple of weeks, they would be rich.

Gordon gave everyone the final reminder before they resumed the match. 'Don't forget, rehearsal at Nine Elms, Tuesday night. Midnight. Don't be late. That train won't be.'

16

Jimmy White concentrated fiercely on the road ahead, even though he was extremely familiar with the route. He told Bruce he had approached the farm from three different directions at least a dozen times, could find it with the lights off. That was the last practice drill Roy James had insisted on. Today was Tuesday, the sixth of August, and their night of destiny lay in front of them. By the same time tomorrow they would all be very rich men. Bruce slept fleetingly the night before, images of hundreds of mailbags drifting through his dreams. There were stuffed full of money, but every time he reached out to take one, it moved away, dodging and weaving from his grasp, before flattening him like Brian London. Now it was all very real.

Three other men sat in the back of the van, along with a collection of airbeds and sleeping bags, plus boxes piled high with supplies. You could literally feed an army on what they had, probably for a week. Bruce hoped it wouldn't come to that.

'This is home for the next few days,' he announced as the farmhouse came into view.

'Looks a fuckin' dump,' was Buster's first impression, straining to see over Bruce and Jimmy's heads. Biggs and the old train driver were pressed against the rear of the vehicle.

'It is a bit.' Bruce had returned the day before to have another look around, and check everything was as he remembered it. He left his car in a lay-by half a mile away and walked the rest. The most important thing was the size of the outbuildings, somewhere to hide the big vehicles after the robbery. Both the Land Rovers and the Austin lorry had been painted khaki by Gordon and Harry to keep up the military theme. His uniform carried the insignia of the Paratroopers. He was poised to lead his men into battle.

'Get your bloody gloves on, mate,' he shouted to Buster, as they jumped down. His old friend looked at him sheepishly, like a schoolboy who had been caught scrumping, and then smiled, pulling a pair out of his back pocket.

Bruce opened the main door to the farmhouse wide and propped it open with a stone from the garden. It was the first time he had even considered the grass at the back of the property. His mind flitted through the many tasks that needed to be completed before the rest arrived. He wondered if the others had made plans. Gordon, undoubtedly. Buster, maybe. His friends were used to being drilled by him, but the South coast lot could sort themselves out. In twenty-four hours they would be on their own.

It took the best part of ten minutes to carry all the provisions from the Land Rover into the house, and then Jimmy and Buster busied themselves storing the food in the cupboards and the expansive pantry. Everything else was lined up in the empty living room, apart from the airbeds, which they carried upstairs.

Roy James arrived earlier than expected in another Land Rover containing Jim Hussey, Charlie and Harry. They carried bottles of ale with them, along with all the uniforms they were going to wear, dark clothing to make the gang look like railway workers or military personnel. Spare black balaclavas were unloaded in case anyone forgot his own. Jimmy White returned to London in the early afternoon, to collect Roger's team with their electrical equipment and the walkie-talkies.

Whilst Jimmy was away, Jack Armstrong and Mickey Griffin loomed up in the garden. They must have trekked their way across the field to get there, carrying their own sleeping bags and rucksacks. After a quick 'Hello' from Armstrong, the pair went upstairs to grab a corner in one of the bedrooms. Bruce gained more confidence after seeing them in action at the trial run the week before. They were strong boys, and picked up on the tasks quickly. Jack in particular looked like he would be a useful asset on the job.

Bruce walked around the house for the next few hours, checking every detail he could think of. The tension rose as the sun set across the fields at the back of the farm. Charlie started pacing about anxiously, walking from room to room. Buster was also on edge. On the outside, Bruce felt that he was looking calm, but his insides betrayed him. He knew he was close to the big one; the chance to retire and live the high life with Franny was within touching distance. One more night, a perfectly executed plan, and the future would be rosy.

As the clock ticked closer to nine o'clock and darkness descended, a flashlight shone in the direction of the house from down the track. As it neared, it became clear that Gordon Goody was approaching. He walked into the kitchen, switched off his torch, and pulled a bottle of whisky out of his coat pocket. Bruce had never seen him drink on a job before. Something was up.

'Job's off for the night. Postponed twenty-four hours,' Gordon blurted out.

'What?' Bruce replied.

'Yeah. Got the call half an hour ago. Brian Field dropped me off at the end of the lane. The Ulsterman confirmed there's a very light load on tonight, much less than a normal night. Reckons the train will be heaving tomorrow, though.'

'He'd better be right. You fancy telling 'em?' Bruce said.

A few faces had joined them in the kitchen, including Roger and Charlie.

'What's up, Gordy?' Charlie asked. Goody offered his whisky bottle around. It was pretty full, so it was obvious he had only just started drinking.

'Postponed. Just for twenty-four hours.'

'How come?' Charlie was the inquisitor.

'Extra day's Bank Holiday in Scotland. They were light by the time they left Glasgow, and the stations on the route are nearly empty.' Gordon looked at his watch. 'Best get some sleep, lads, we're gonna be busy tomorrow night.' He looked incredibly tired, and the whole atmosphere in the kitchen deflated.

'Fuck it.' Charlie smashed his fist into a kitchen cupboard.

Bruce opted for the positive. 'But that's good news. It means there should be loads more money from the banks waiting for us tomorrow, right?' He looked at Charlie and Roger as he announced this. The four million they had talked about could well be on the cards, if they had the patience to wait another day.

Gordon pulled his head up and addressed them all. 'It is good news, yeah. That money's still sitting in the banks, waiting to come to London. There'll be bloody tons of it tomorrow night.'

'There'd better be,' Charlie shouted. 'Or there's gonna be a fuckin' Ulsterman, or wherever you say he's fuckin' from, gettin' a fuckin' visit from me and my friends.'

Charlie stormed off up the stairs to tell the others. Bruce heard the reaction from one of the bedrooms. There were groans and shouts. But Gordon was right. This did mean there would be a bumper load of mailbags and money packets running on the GPO train the next night.

'What if it's a trick? You know, it's full tonight and they've got someone else to rob it further up the line?' Cordrey asked.

Trust Roger to say something stupid, thought Bruce. 'You mad? That makes no sense,' he replied.

'No,' said Gordon. 'Remember, there's no million in it for Jock if there's nothing on the train.' Roger shrugged his shoulders and sloped off, out of the kitchen.

Bruce looked at Gordon. 'Did it sound kosher to you, Gordy?'

'Yeah. And Brian was definitely surprised.'

Bruce doubted if the solicitor's clerk would be in on any conspiracy, even if there were one. Field was a bit player in the whole thing, even if he was taking a share for himself, after arranging the ghost purchase of the farm. Gordon took the call at Brian's house; the clerk had dropped him off at the end of the track. Bruce thought Charlie was going to have a heart attack when he heard that Field was on a full whack.

'Well, we just sit tight until tomorrow then, don't we?' Bruce asked.

'I guess we do, yeah.' Goody agreed.

Bruce walked around each room of the house, making sure everyone had heard the news, pushing the positive aspect. The complaints were widespread, but there was nothing they could do. Their positions as the richest thieves in the land had simply been postponed by twenty-four hours.

17

7th August 1963: Leatherslade Farm, Oxfordshire

Jack Armstrong parked up before opening the back of the Humber, and Tommy Lavery unfurled himself into the yard at the side of the farmhouse. His boss was in a hurry. Gordon and Bruce stepped forward to greet them, and Lavery seized the initiative.

'Gordon, good to meet you again. And you Bruce.' Lavery was all smiles.

'Hello, Tommy.' Bruce let out a low laugh. They knew who he was, then. Lavery carried a briefcase in his left hand, and indicated they should go inside.

'I've been rather busy. As, indeed, have you.' He indicated the farm. Jack looked around at their temporary home. It was a dump. They paid over five hundred quid as a deposit for it. They were robbed.

'Come inside.' Gordon ushered them in nervously.

'I'm not stopping long. Could you do me a favour? I'd like to talk to everyone, if I may?'

Armstrong thought about the polite manner his boss was employing. If only they knew how difficult he found it to act that way. Goody ran off, and within a few seconds the entire crew were gathered in the living room. Lavery walked in with Jack at his side. Griffin had stayed behind to keep an eye on everyone while Jack went to pick up the boss, and stood within the throng.

'Gentlemen. I'm the partner you may have heard your Irish

96

friend talking about. I'm the man who's been putting up the money for this job. I just wanted to meet you all.'

Buster jumped in. 'If you're here for your money, we haven't even done it yet.' A couple of the gang laughed.

'I know. Brian Field told me about the postponement. No matter. I'm sure everything will go off without a hitch. I just wanted to talk to everybody. I know many of you wanted to meet me, well, here I am. I have something to share with you. It will hopefully bring you more confidence about tonight.'

Murmurs washed around the room. Jack knew that this was an important territorial moment.

'Gentlemen. I want to thank you all for being here, for being on this job, first of all. You're probably wondering who the hell I am. Bruce here can tell you, he knows my name. It's unlikely you'll know my face, unless you've served time in Strangeways, or worked in the North. That is my domain.'

Armstrong looked around the room. The faces ranged from defiance, like Charlie Wilson and Tommy Wisbey, to what simply looked like confusion; Roger Cordrey for example.

Lavery pressed on. 'A few of you might know me by reputation. Now, I know you've discussed the man you call the Ulsterman a few times in your meetings. He is a business partner of mine, and this robbery was our joint idea. That is why we insisted on our share of the proceeds. I know many of you think a million is too high a price to pay for providing you with the opportunity. I understand this feeling, but believe me gentlemen; tonight you are going to become very rich men. Your take will far exceed ours.' Lavery looked around the room trying to make eye contact with everybody. Jack watched as many simply stared at the floor, disinterested. If they knew what the future held, they would pay more attention.

'Now, I want to make one thing very clear. I don't exist. I'm not here. This man you call the Ulsterman, that's a very good guess by the way,' Lavery passed off a smile and continued. 'He doesn't exist either. You understand? If anybody asks, it might be tomorrow, it might be in twenty years time, but if anybody asks, we don't exist. It was all your idea, all your inside information, from a source inside the GPO. I hope you get what I'm saying?' There were nods around the room, and a few mutters that Jack struggled to make out.

'I trust you're not armed, any of you?'

'Only with these little beauties.' Buster held up his cosh, a length of lead piping wrapped in cloth. 'We might need these.' There was laughter around the group.

'No problem with those, you might find the odd employee who doesn't want to play along, fair enough. But no guns, lads. You don't want to be looking at the rope if something goes wrong, do you?' Jack and Mickey were going to pay everyone a discrete visit before they set off, to check if anybody was carrying.

'We're the ones taking the risk holding up a train, loading tons of money.' Charlie Wilson interjected. 'You're just gonna sit there and take your share, are you?'

Lavery held his hands up in mock surrender. Jack knew this sort of challenge would come from Wilson. Seeing Charlie, close at hand a few times, had backed up what the bent copper told them. He fronted up to everything.

'Look, I've been sat where you all are in the past, and I've worked my way up to where I am. Have any of you heard of me? Apart from Bruce?'

Everybody turned and looked at Bruce Reynolds. 'His name's Tommy Lavery,' he announced.

'I have, then,' Harry Smith volunteered, his hand wavering nervously in the air.

Lavery paused, Jack presumed to allow his name to sink in, before carrying on. 'Good, well let me say what I came to say, and then I shall leave you to it. Bruce here has heard of me, and this gentleman here too, so I shall allow you to discuss me behind my back, when I've gone. How's that?'

There were more murmurs around the room, but nobody spoke up. Lavery pushed on. He looked at his watch. Jack knew his boss needed to be in London that evening. Apparently he had an appointment with a senior policeman, as solid an alibi as you could get. Armstrong had taken possession of the briefcase when they entered the room. He opened it up as planned, and pulled out a handful of loose sheets of paper.

'One last thing,' Lavery began. 'My friend here is passing something around, there's one for each of you.'

Jack walked slowly about the room, shuffling the papers as he went, handing one to each member of the gang. The men studied their individual sheets. A few laughed. Others looked deadly serious. They were neatly typed, contained only basic information, but enough to keep the gang in line.

'Don't be alarmed, gentlemen. I'm showing you these to give you confidence. If I can get my hands on this type of information, you must know that I have a considerable degree of reach in certain quarters, shall we say? I just want you to be aware of your obligation to each other, and to secrecy. Nobody must reveal the identity of any other man on this job. That is paramount. What goes on inside this job stays inside this job. I hope you all get my meaning.'

'Where the fuck did you get this?' Roy James was staring at a sheet detailing his racing career, and the names of three women he had been seeing in the past two years. It also contained a list of his previous offences.

'I'm sure you can guess. You can be reassured that we're on the same side. You have a job to do, I'd better leave you to it.'

Lavery turned to leave, but Buster Edwards stood in his way. Jack stepped in between Buster and his boss and Edwards retreated half a step, his sheet held behind his back.

'Please. Let's not squabble. I merely want you all to know we're in this together,' Lavery addressed the room again. Most were still studying their own typed sheet. Jack watched as his boss cleared his throat to make a final announcement.

'Listen. Did you think I would enter into such a serious enterprise as this without knowing who it is I am employing?

Gentlemen, you're all thieves, that's why you're in this room. I know you will have discussed at some point taking the entire load for yourselves.' A few glances were exchanged. 'I'm not worried about that. I would have considered the same thing if I was in your position. I'd think more than once about turning over the inside man, you'd be idiots not to at least have thought about it. But you must drop that idea. You have to understand, all I'm trying to tell you is, that I know who you are, where you live, and what you do. I'm simply protecting my investment. It's all any of you would do in my position. Think about it. You would do the same.'

Tommy Wisbey ripped up his sheet theatrically, staring at Jack's boss. 'We need to talk about this. Properly. When he's gone.' He jabbed a finger at Jack and Mickey in turn. 'And without you two.'

Armstrong looked at Griffin and understood. They would have to leave this lot for a few minutes. If they were sensible, nothing would change. The fact that Lavery knew everything about them should be irrelevant. They still had a massive opportunity. Jack signalled to Griffin, and they followed Lavery through the kitchen, and into the garden.

Outside, Tommy addressed his two men. 'Take it easy, boys. I don't want them to get jumpy. Let them concentrate on the job, okay?'

'Sure, Tommy,' Jack replied. 'We know what to do.'

'Good. You're part of this gang now. For a few hours that's how you have to behave.'

★ ★ ★

Bruce went outside and checked that Jack and Mickey had followed their boss out of the farmhouse. They were standing in the garden smoking, as if nothing had happened. Lavery had already disappeared down the farm track in the Humber.

When he returned to the living room, uproar reigned. Everyone was speaking at once, some to all assembled, others talking to the man next to them, comparing notes. It seemed they all had a personal sheet, complete with names of wives, girlfriends, addresses, car registration numbers, and criminal records. This man held a lot of information about the team. Bruce felt he needed to regain control, and called the gang to order.

'Everyone. Everyone!' Bruce had to yell the second time. They needed to get themselves together; they were due to rob a mail train in a matter of hours.

'Who the fuck does he think he is?' Charlie Wilson yelled. 'Fuckin' tellin' me this. Where we live, names of my three kids. What the fuck is this bloke?'

'He's our boss. Let's face it, he's the one who's given us this job,' Bruce said.

'What you got us into, Gordy?' Charlie yelled at Goody. Gordon seemed too absorbed in his own piece of paper to reply.

Buster was sceptical. 'How do we know he's not settin' us up like a right bunch of tits? The track could be covered with police tonight.'

Roy James interjected. 'All they would have to do is raid this place. If they wanted us, they'd just swoop now. They'd be here already.'

'I think he's right,' said Jimmy White. 'He's on our side, and maybe we should be grateful for that.'

'I think it fuckin' stinks. Did you know all this?' Charlie stuck his nose in Gordon's face.

'Course I bloody didn't. Jesus. What the fuck d'you think I am?'

'I'm not sure any more.'

Bruce stepped forward and raised his arms for quiet. 'Look, boys. We need to stay calm. Nothing has changed. He and his mate are getting a million; we might be getting three million. Remember that, boys, three million quid between us. That's a lot of money.' He hoped that bringing them back to reality would help to restore order.

'I'm still worried about that bloke,' said Charlie.

'Tell us what you know about him then, Bruce. What you heard?' Roger Cordrey asked.

Reynolds looked at Smith. 'Harry, you said you knew him as well, right?'

'Yeah, I do.'

'What you heard?'

'You go first, Bruce.'

He had found out more about this Tommy Lavery character from his old friend, Jimmy Darwin. The advice was unforgettable. It served as a warning, but by that point there was no turning back on the job, not one that big. Steer clear, was Jimmy's first direction. Keep away; he's a nasty bastard. Run for the hills. Imagine the Kray twins, but without the moral compass and the doting mother.

The room stared at him. He needed to convey as little of the truth as possible, in order to keep everybody motivated. Too much time and effort had been invested. He took them through the details that Darwin had passed on about Lavery's hold over the police in the North, as well as the rumours that he reached into the Met. He left out the colourful comparison to the Krays. The important thing that he stressed was that Lavery seemed to be a powerful ally, not an enemy.

'If he's on our side, then that's good, isn't it?' Gordon argued.

'Look,' Bruce summarised, 'I just think we're miles better off working with him than against him.'

'What you heard then, Harry?' Charlie asked, calmer now.

Harry Smith leant against a wall by the edge of the drawn curtain. The lone bulb shone in the enforced dark, and when he spoke everybody hung on his words.

'He's big, yeah he is. He's a bookie an' all.' Smith looked at Tommy Wisbey, who was in the same line of business.

'Is he?' Wisbey uttered quietly.

'Yeah.'

'And?' Charlie led the desire for more.

'Well, that's about it. He don't take no credit. Run a few rackets.

I also heard what Bruce said, about having the Old Bill in his pocket.'

'Can we trust him?' Charlie asked.

'Dunno. He's bent, ain't he? But so are we.' Harry chuckled. 'What I mean is, he's done a few things in his time. Word is, now he's untouchable.'

'Well, surely that's a good thing. He won't be turning us in, will he? He's on our side,' Jimmy White concluded.

Bruce watched as most of the assembled gang seemed to come to the same conclusion. Better to be with him than against. He decided to wrap up the discussion, because they had a job to focus on. There were final preparations to check and double check. It bored some, but they needed it. Planning was everything, and this was proving to be a distraction.

'Listen, boys. He might not be everybody's cup of tea.' Bruce stared at Charlie and Buster, who were stood bolt upright in the middle of the room, with their arms crossed, anger on their faces. 'But he's put us on to this, and nothing's changed. He's not demanding more money, that's the same. If anything, we've gained a little from this. We know who he is, we know what we're working with.'

'Not some poxy Irishman, then?' Roy chimed in.

'Both of them. But I think we know which one of our business partners wears the bloody trousers,' Bruce replied, addressing the whole room.

'I don't see what difference it makes,' said Roger. 'We still go ahead as planned, so long as we get the okay, Gordon? We give them a million, and we take the rest, we have the biggest payday we could ever imagine, and then off we go.' Bruce admired the more positive view.

'I agree,' said Gordon falling in line. 'We have to stick together, maybe even more now. He was right about one thing, though. We say nothing to nobody. Even if it goes wrong, we say nothing. Agreed?'

There was a chorus of 'aye's, and 'yeah's, around the room.

Gordon pulled a box of matches out of his pocket, and set light to his own piece of paper. 'What's written on these won't matter. We're gonna be fuckin' rich,' he announced.

He dropped his sheet to the floor, and a few of the others joined in, either adding their sheet to the pile or burning their own. There was laughter in the house once more, something it had been distinctly lacking for a while. A happy crew would be more focused.

Bruce knew they had to remain vigilant. He cast his mind back to one uncomfortable moment in the afternoon that he was forced to deal with. A local farmer had wandered down the track and engaged him in a conversation about renting a field from the new owner. Fortunately, everybody was out of sight upstairs. He made up a cock and bull story about them being a small team of decorators preparing the place for a Mister Fielding, the first name that popped into his head. Imagine if the raid had gone ahead as planned the night before, he might have walked in on millions.

His attention turned to an old friend. Bruce spotted Biggs looking sheepish in the corner. 'What's up, Ronnie?'

'Oh, nothing, nothing Bruce. All's fine.'

'How's Stan? He ready?' Bruce was fully aware that the driver's presence on the job was unsettling. Whenever he entered a room, everybody either left immediately or covered their faces. Nobody wanted to be picked out of a lineout by a civilian whose only contribution was that he could move a train a few yards. Roy James was still pushing for dumping the old guy and driving the train himself. Bruce was merely covering all the angles. Until the visit from Lavery, this Stan had been the main source of tension in the camp. If it wasn't one thing, it would be something else.

'He's fine.'

'What's up?' Bruce looked at Biggs, and then realised that Ronnie wasn't holding a sheet of paper. Lavery hadn't written out his life story for him.

'He doesn't know you, then?' Bruce laughed.

'I bet he does,' Biggs replied.

'Maybe you're in the clear,' Bruce reassured his old friend. Ronnie laughed, but it wasn't the deep, throaty sound Bruce had grown accustomed to hearing. This was an expression of nerves. 'Don't worry, mate. It'll all turn out fine. We're gonna be loaded soon. Could be for the best that nobody knows who you are, Ronnie. Being unknown might be handy.' Biggs nodded. As an afterthought, Bruce added, 'You keeping your gloves on?'

'Course. Yeah.'

'Good. Make sure you do, mate.'

18

When Jack Mills saw the red signal it was no surprise, because he had been warned of a problem by an amber one, a mile earlier. This kept happening on the night specials. He would just be getting his cup of tea at Euston a little later than usual. Mills looked at the clock to the rear of the engine cab, which read just after three. A glove covered both green lights, and Roger Cordrey had fixed the second signal to show red after hooking it up to six Eveready batteries on the gantry above.

Down on the trackside, fourteen men waited to pounce in anxious anticipation. This was it. At long last, after weeks of planning, the big job was on. Pulses raced, minds sped, and dreams of what they would do with their fortunes focused attention. Bruce Reynolds was already on his way back to the main group in the second Land Rover, John Daly at the wheel. Bruce was the one who gave the first all clear to tamper with the signals from way up the line, just south of Leighton Buzzard station. John had brought about the warning amber light at the dwarf signal; his technique mirrored that of Roger Cordrey up on the main gantry. It was standard procedure to call through to the nearest signal box to check for a fault if the light stayed red for too long. All the team by the trackside knew this, as they did the fact that the coach just behind the engine contained millions of pounds in unmarked notes.

Fireman Dave Whitby was riding along with the driver and

jumped down to check what the problem was. He had to telephone the Cheddington box, convinced it was another signal error. They had become more commonplace throughout the summer on this line, especially at night. When he reached the trackside phone, he found there was no connection. Just what were they buggering about at? He was walking back towards the front of the train when he saw two men ahead. He thought they were engineers, sorting out the communication fault.

'What's the problem?' he called out, as he approached. The men didn't answer at first. Then one muttered something he couldn't quite catch, heading towards an embankment. He followed them, and caught up alongside the rear of the two men by the track, and repeated his question.

'What's the problem?' The words were barely out of his mouth when one of the men turned and shoved him to the ground. The other sat on top of him and covered his mouth with a glove.

'Don't say a word, or we'll kill you.' The menace came from a figure wearing a dark uniform, but this was no railway engineer. A mask covered his face, and he was holding an object above his head, threatening to strike. Whitby nodded, indicating he wouldn't make a sound. Both men lifted him to his feet, and marched him back towards the engine and Jack Mills.

'Come with us,' one instructed as they walked, 'but don't say a word.'

Up ahead, the driver peered out into the darkness. He could see two figures walking his way, and if they were track engineers they would give him the all clear. He turned and saw a man climbing on to the footplate from the other side. Mills tried to push the intruder back down on to the track. As he did so, something hard thumped into the back of his head, and he slumped to the floor. Within seconds, his cab contained three masked men.

'Hell you do that for?' an angry voice shouted.

'Had to.' The other voice sounded different, but Mills could also hear a ringing in his ears.

'Let's get on with it, shall we?' A third voice spoke in the cab, trying to wrestle back control. 'No more whacking unless we have to, all right? Come on.' Mills was dragged down to the trackside, where he saw Whitby lying face down on the ground. Blood oozed from his own head, and he tried to stem the flow with his hands.

'Lie face down. Now. Or you'll get some more.' Mills lined up alongside the fireman and saw the look of fear in Whitby's eyes. Jesus, someone was robbing the mail train.

Back on the engine footplate it was getting crowded. Charlie Wilson was frustrated with the stupid old man they'd brought along on the job. It was another one of Bruce's little gestures, one that might end up with them getting caught.

'Why the fuck can't you move it? You're only bloody here to move this bloody thing. Now move it.'

'I can't. I don't know why, it won't…'

Charlie looked into Ronnie Biggs's eyes and struggled to control his hatred. Biggs was only there because he knew the bloke who could move the train down the track. And now he seemed to have no bloody clue how to do it.

'It's not like the trains I've shunted before,' the man shuddered.

'Oh, for God's sake.' Charlie raised his cosh to batter the stupid old man. What a liability. Bruce's soft spot for his old cellmate might cost them. He should have backed up Roy James, insisted the racing driver was at the controls.

Buster Edwards seized the initiative. 'Right. Bring the driver back in here. We'll get him to move it.'

'Have you seen the state of him?' Jim Hussey had jumped up from the trackside.

'We need him. Go.'

Moments later Jack Mills was sitting back in his driver's seat.

Buster Edwards took over. 'Now, we don't mean you any harm, okay? All we want you to do is to move the train down the line until you see a white sheet across the tracks, okay?'

Mills sat still, afraid to move.

Another voice, one he recognised from the first incident in the cab butted in. Not a London accent, muffled by a mask, it was the man who hit him earlier. 'Just do as we say. Or you'll get another whack.' Mills knew the game was up. He looked down the track and thought he could make out something ahead of him. He summoned up the courage to ask a question.

'How far are we going?'

'Only about half a mile. You'll see where to stop. Just do it.' He was unaware that this was the voice of an increasingly annoyed Charlie Wilson, but realised he had no choice but to do as he was told.

★ ★ ★

'This is Three. We are in position.' Bruce Reynolds had insisted on everybody using numbers rather than real names. 'Three' was Gordon Goody, and this meant that the train had been shunted along and was ready for unloading at Bridego Bridge. He and John were closing and he could just about make out the hulking shape of the Royal Mail train, the subject of his dreams, in front of them on the bridge. John parked the Land Rover in a space by the fishing lake. Another Land Rover with identical plates and a large Austin lorry were already in place under the bridge. They would move this into position when the other Landy was full. Bruce walked over to the vehicle under the bridge and spotted Ronnie Biggs in the cab with the old driver. Biggs looked over and shook his head, mouthing 'sorry' at Bruce. Nothing appeared to have gone wrong. The train was up there, where it was supposed to be. It was time for everyone to get to work, and Bruce jumped at him first.

'Ron, I don't care what's happened. We need your help unloading. You up for it?'

'Course I am, yeah.' Biggs spoke soothingly to the shaking figure beside him. 'Just stay here, right?' The boys must have persuaded the original driver to shunt it along to the attack point, either that or Roy had finally mastered stopping a train. However it was done, they had the HVP coach, and as long as the promised millions were on board, nobody would mind. They were all going to be rich in a few minutes.

Back up on the track, the fireman and driver were handcuffed together, and lay face down on the ground. Charlie Wilson offered both men a cigarette, which was rather impractical.

'If you lie still and say nothing, there might be a bit of money in it for you.' Both men seemed to nod. Wilson simply wanted to ensure they saw as little as possible. Harry Smith arrived at Charlie's side.

'You look after these two. This one's had a bit of a bump,' Wilson instructed. Smith looked at the back of the older man's head. There was blood flowing freely, despite the man holding a handkerchief against the wound.

'Just lie still lads, and all will be good,' Smith soothed. Charlie set off for the HVP coach where the attack was about to begin.

Inside the carriage, Frank Dewhurst, the Head Postmaster on the mail train, strained to hear what was going on outside. He peered out of the high window, standing on a bank of mailbags. They heard steam coming from the rear of the coach, so they knew they had been uncoupled from the rest of the train. They were being held up. Dewhurst had already pulled the communication cord, but this made no difference. He could see the odd figure outside, and heard voices. There were only six of them in the coach, all GPO employees. His assistant, Thomas Kett, started stacking mailbags against the entrance to the coach, and everyone joined in. Frank knew it would ultimately be futile. If someone had taken the time and effort to stop the train, uncouple and shunt them away from the rest of the coaches, they weren't going to give up if they encountered a few mailbags in the way. And his men were likely to be significantly outnumbered. He heard a shout from outside.

'They're barricading the doors. Get the guns.' The words sent a shiver through him. Dewhurst looked at the rest of his men, who stopped stacking bags. He might be a dutiful employee, but nothing was worth getting killed over, not even this amount of money. He looked at the bags around the coach. Most sat in their wire cages; or in the pile by the door, and a few were lying on the floor, the recent subjects of an argument about West Ham's midfield formation for the coming season. The world was going to be far more interested in the men about to attack, rather than what they had been up to with the red mailbags.

Two windows smashed above their heads one immediately after the other. The end doors sprung open, and three hooded figures jumped into the coach, finding six GPO men standing against the cages. Dewhurst put his hands up as if to ask the men to stop, but this was futile. Both he and the man standing next to him, Leslie Penn, were battered around the shoulders with coshes. All the employees hit the floor.

'Lie down. Don't move, or you'll get some more,' shouted an angry voice. Dewhurst looked about for any guns, but couldn't see any. That didn't mean they weren't carrying any.

'Move down that end. And hit the floor.'

The GPO employees shuffled along to the front end of the coach, and lay down. Two men stood over them with heavy instruments in their hands, their eyes staring fiercely through black ski masks. Frank could feel his bowels losing control. These men meant business. God, they had got lucky, what a night to rob the mail train. For years he had been making this run down from Scotland to London and back the next day. Tonight was one of the biggest loads in memory. The transport police at Tamworth station joked that it would be standing room only for the rest of the journey, although there was plenty of space to manoeuvre when the bags were in the cages. He thought about the newer, more secure coaches. They had metal grilles that made entry through anything other than the end windows impossible. They were all out of service, and had been for at least a couple of weeks. These masked men had got very lucky indeed.

★ ★ ★

Out by the track, a human chain of ten men had been formed. The GPO mailbags were lifted out of the coach, and passed down from the bridge via an embankment into the Land Rovers. The large lorry was already full. Bruce looked at his watch and noted that they were close to the time limit.

'Position two. Any sign up your end?'

'Nothing. They all seem to still be inside the train. Can't see anybody,' Cordrey replied.

'You on your way down?'

'Nearly there.'

Roger pedalled his fold up bicycle as fast as he could. Earlier he had jumped from the signal gantry and walked down the track towards the stranded HVP coach, then back up to the main bulk of the train. His job was to watch for activity in the main carriages. It only took one nosey mail sorter to get involved and they would have to divert manpower from unloading the packages to giving him a clobbering, and that would reduce their takings. All the telephone lines along the railway line, as well as those to and from nearby properties, had been cut beforehand. No lights were on at Rowden Farm half a mile past the bridge, where he could see the outline of their target getting closer. He struggled to talk and pedal at the same time. 'I'll be there in a couple of minutes.'

'Good. We're nearly done this end. Get a move on.'

Bruce Reynolds joined the human chain at the bottom of the embankment, moving the mailbags about to make more space in the last of the vehicles. He looked at his watch, and knew it was time to stop. There was no need to get too greedy. He scrambled up the embankment, past the heaving bodies to the stranded engine and coach.

'Right, boys. That's it. Time's up,' he announced.

'There's not many to go. Just a few.' Despite the darkness and the ski mask, he knew the words belonged to Buster Edwards.

'No, he's right. Let's cut it there. Come on.' Jimmy White was the voice of reason. There was no need to add unnecessary risk.

'How much is left?' Bruce wanted to check how accurate their information had been.

'About ten bags, something like that.'

'Make this the last one. Come on lads, time to go.' The Colonel barked out his orders. Well over a hundred bags, he reckoned, stuffed full of money. The inside information had proved to be excellent.

The exit strategy from the HVP coach had also been mapped out. Everyone inside was tied up or handcuffed, lying face down in a corner of the carriage, as well as the driver and his fireman. Gordon Goody and Jack Armstrong were the last to leave.

'Right. Now we're going, most of us. Two of us are staying behind, just to look after you lot. I'm going to be sitting outside with my friend here.' Armstrong held up his cosh for them to see.

'Yeah. I'd stay put for a bit if I were you.' All the faces strained to look up at Goody, who then jumped out of the coach.

Armstrong re-emphasised how important it was to remain inside. 'I'm warning you. You've seen what we're capable of. Now sit tight. Nobody move for thirty minutes. I'll be watching, and I won't be alone.' With that, Jack jumped through the battered door, closed it, and ran down the embankment.

'All done?' Reynolds was waiting for Armstrong at the bottom.

'Yeah. I've told 'em not to move.'

Bruce's face expressed the demeanour of a leader, and the pips on his shoulder were a constant hint towards the status he craved. He was living the dream, heading up his forces.

'Shame about the remaining bags,' Gordon added.

'Don't worry. We've got plenty. Let's go.' Bruce pointed down the road. He walked up to the main lorry, where Jimmy White was sitting at the wheel.

'Remember, split up, don't drive too fast. We don't want to draw attention to ourselves. Just drive smooth, remember what Roy said.'

'I will. See you.'

Jimmy White jerked the lorry forwards and Bruce watched as the main bulk of their takings slipped away into the night.

He put his head inside Roy James's window in the first Land Rover.

'Go easy, Roy. This isn't bloody Brands Hatch, remember?'

'I know.'

'Stay away from Jimmy, we don't want to look like a convoy.'

'I know,' Roy James answered, barely disguising his annoyance.

Bruce tried to ignore the dissent. 'Good. See you later.'

'Bruce?' Roy studied their leader. He would have to admit that the planning had paid off, everything was properly organised.

'What?'

'I could've driven it, you know. I could've been the driver.'

'Get lost. Go.'

Bruce banged the side of the car. He walked back to his Land Rover, which would set off in the opposite direction and double back, before heading for the farm. The idea of using a hideout was the right decision. There was no way Roy and Jimmy would have been able to control themselves in the rush to get back to London. Every man in the three vehicles was turning over an important question in their head. How much had they taken? The line of mailbags seemed to go on endlessly, bulging with money. The Ulsterman's information was spot on.

★ ★ ★

Ron Baxter had been a train guard for ten years, and was used to signal faults and engineering works at night. Delays were commonplace. Because he heard the brakes go on, he knew there was a stop signal up ahead. Looking out, he could see the red light above the gantry in the distance, so he went back to his game of patience in the cab of the last compartment. After another five minutes and another failed hand, he checked again. This time he stepped off the train in search of a phone line, following procedure. He spotted a GPO inspector he knew to be Eric Little heading towards him, swinging a torch.

'What's up?' Little was breathing heavily, as if he had been running down the track.

'How'd you mean?'

'Well, why we stopped? You heard anything?'

'No, nothing. I'll make a call.'

They headed over to the box stationed at the side of the track. The line was dead.

'Funny. Maybe they're testing?' Baxter suggested.

'What, up ahead?'

'Maybe.'

'Let's go take a look.'

Both men walked up the track towards the front of the train. They struggled to pick their way at times, as the stones slipped underfoot. Baxter was astonished when they reached the position where the HVP coach and the engine were supposed to be. They had vanished.

'What?' Little scratched his head. The signal was still on red. Where were the coach and the engine? Baxter tried to peer ahead in the murk.

'Wait here,' Baxter instructed Little. There was something in the manual for this type of situation. The GPO knew nothing about what to do in times of crisis; they were simply travelling postmen.

'Where you going?' Little asked.

'A job I've got to do.'

'Shall I come with you?'

'If you like. It's up to you.'

Baxter walked briskly back to the end of the train, into the final compartment, and applied the hand brakes. He picked up two packets from a cupboard and jumped back down beside the track. Little had followed him all the way.

'What are they?'

'Detonators. They're a warning for the next train behind. Luckily it's still on amber back there, so nobody should come up behind us. It's procedure, so I must obey it.' You covered yourself and did as you were told, if you wanted to keep your job.

It took Baxter nearly fifteen minutes to place his charges on the track behind the train, measuring them as precisely as he could at the correct distances apart. He then walked with Little further north up the track towards Leighton Buzzard, looking for another telephone housing. He planned to ring the nearest station in Cheddington, as well as the signal box again. That line was also dead. The two men then set off back towards the front, in search of the missing part of the train, the section with all the money in it.

After about five minutes they saw a train coming in the opposite direction, and Baxter tried to flag it down. It slowed, but continued on about a quarter of a mile past. The lights allowed both men to pick out the lost part of their train, stationary on a bridge up ahead. As they approached, it became clear that the windows in the HVP coach had been smashed. Baxter shouted out, asking if anybody was there. Two faces comically appeared at one of the windows, emerging with great caution.

'Are you alright?' Baxter called into the coach. The two men clambered out through the broken window and jumped down to the trackside.

'Thank God you're here. They stole the whole bloody lot, you know,' Frank Dewhurst said, blinking into Little's flashlight, still surprised about what had happened.

'Stole what?'

'The whole bloody lot from the coach. The High Value Packets, the bloody lot. We've got a man badly hurt. The driver, they hit him.'

'Hit him? What, Jack?'

'Yes, Jack Mills.'

Baxter knew Mills, had worked with him on many a run over the years.

'The bastards. Come on; let's get over to the train on the other line. They'll take us back to Cheddington station. We can phone from there.'

19

The short wave radio crackled into life. The police were waking up to what had happened.

'Get this. Someone has stolen a train. A whole train.'

Everyone in the Land Rover laughed. This was a moment to savour. They were at least one step ahead, as the Ulsterman and Lavery assured them they would be. Bruce smiled, thinking about the line of bodies passing bags down the embankment. The HVP coach was almost emptied out, it had bloody well worked. Lights were on in the kitchen of the farmhouse up ahead at the end of the track. There was little sound, but from what they could see there was much frantic activity. The vehicle rocked its way up the lane, and John Daly at the wheel began to quietly sing 'The Good Life.' Four men joined in, not caring who heard the sound in the dead of night.

As they pulled up, Bruce could make out more singing and shrieks of joy from inside the farmhouse. The job wasn't over yet, but the hardest part was done. Reynolds ran into the kitchen, and heard 'I like it,' ringing out from Ronnie Biggs and Jim Hussey. A line of mailbags snaked its way from the kitchen to the living room, where four more men were shifting them about into piles. There was also a growing stack of bank notes, stretching towards the ceiling. Gordon Goody was opening each sack in turn, inspecting for tracking devices. They had thought of everything.

Goody stood in the middle of the room with his hands deep inside one of the red bags. The contents were being transferred to an area where James, Edwards and Pembroke stood, piling up the notes. Bruce's eyes were drawn to a heady mixture of fivers and tenners. The money kept on emerging like endless kittens from a sack.

'Found anything, Goody?' Bruce asked.

'Nothing yet,' Goody barked, ferreting away. 'I'll keep looking, nothing but lovely cash so far.'

His teeth glowed with a smile illuminated by a solitary bulb from the ceiling. Pembroke was carrying discarded money packets back into the kitchen, where Jimmy White was collecting them up in a black plastic bag. A procession of full mailbags kept making its way into the room. This was going to take a while to count.

Despite the euphoria, tiredness struck Bruce Reynolds like a Sonny Liston right hand. Weeks of planning and plotting suddenly weighed him down, and the urge to close his eyes and sleep hit hard. He could leave the counting to others. Bruce climbed the stairs and crashed out on one of the mattresses, and slept like a baby, dreaming of Franny and the South of France.

★ ★ ★

'Two and a half bloody million, Bruce. It's over two and a half bloody million.' Buster woke Reynolds from his fantasies, but reality was pretty damn exciting as well. 'It's all there, like they said. Fuckin' millions, Bruce.' Edwards let go of Reynolds's arm and shook his hand frantically. 'Mate, it worked. It worked.'

Buster handed him a piece of paper.

'We've worked it all out. Once we take off the first million, it's a hundred and ten thousand each. Give or take. Yeah, Bruce, we done it!' He hadn't seen even Buster this animated before. As he walked down the stairs the excitement could be felt all over the farmhouse. He spotted Ronnie, suddenly remembered the date, and shook his hand.

'Happy birthday, Biggsy.'

'Yeah, Bruce, it's fuckin' magic.'

'Everyone, it's Biggsy's birthday,' Bruce announced. A small cheer went round.

Charlie Wilson handed Biggs a five-pound note. 'Happy Birthday, Ronnie. Here you go. Don't spend it all at once.'

This set off a cascade of well-wishers handing fivers to Biggs. Spirits were high. Bruce sought out Gordon, who was drinking a beer in the kitchen, still wearing gloves. He was a consummate professional.

'Well, Gordy. We pulled it off, didn't we?'

'We bloody well did, mate. We bloody did.'

'You checked every bag did you?'

'All of 'em, yeah. Nothing.'

'I reckon what your little Irish friend said about it not being traceable might be right.'

'Possibly, yeah.'

'Fuckin' great.'

'Cheers, Bruce. You fancy one?' Goody held up a beer.

Reynolds decided he had to remain sober, it was only half seven in the morning. 'No, better not. No offence.'

'None taken, mate. Cheers.' Gordon finished off his bottle, and carefully placed it in a black bag sitting by the sink.

Bruce needed to clear something up that was supposed to be Jimmy White's responsibility. Small tasks were tumbling into his head, and all of them needed to be completed before they left the farm.

'Where have all the bags and the packets gone?' he asked Gordon.

'Big pile of 'em, outside by the back door.'

'We still gonna bury 'em?'

'Reckon so. Jimmy's already digging an hole.'

'All the vehicles out the way?'

'Yeah. Nobody will know we're here.'

'Good. You need to get some sleep yourself, Gordy.'

'Later. I'll sleep when I'm out of here. We've still got lots to do.'

'I know.'

Bruce was painfully aware that virtually all their planning effort had gone in to getting hold of the money. Very little time was spent in thinking about what they were to do now; it was every man for himself. The vehicles were a concern. He was worried that the farm visitor had clocked them the day before. He also remembered passing a hitchhiker on the way to the job. All it needed was for either man to turn up in a police station and their escape vehicles would be compromised. They had to re-think how they would leave the farm. New plans needed to be drawn up, involving getting their hands on different transport. They were all relying on the lorry and the Land Rovers, and had no back up plan, apart from the extra vehicle, which they couldn't reach. He cursed himself for missing out on such an important detail. Bruce went back into the living room to talk to Buster Edwards.

'We all set?'

Edwards pointed at a series of piles in a corner. 'We got all the big notes spread out among the shares.'

'Was there a lot of pound notes and ten bobs?'

'Bloody masses of 'em.'

Money was money, no matter what denomination. In fact, he knew that the larger notes would be harder to spend, more noticeable.

Jack Armstrong appeared in the doorway. His menacing frame blocked out the faint sunlight that crept into the room through the kitchen. Mickey Griffin loomed up at his shoulder. Bruce knew what they would be asking for, and wasn't disappointed.

'Good morning,' smiled Armstrong. 'Do you have our money?'

'Of course we do,' grinned Buster. 'It's over there.'

He pointed at several piles of bundled notes. The million looked substantial, sitting there in front of them. Despite the temptation to keep it, and tell these two to fuck off, they all knew it would be wise to hand it over. Armstrong and Griffin walked over to inspect it. They pulled some money off the top of one pile and started counting it. Armstrong then picked a few notes out from different parts of other stacks, holding them up to the light.

'It's all there, your whole share,' Buster announced.

'Oh, we don't doubt you. Only a fool would double cross our boss. Remember, he knows too much about you all.' Armstrong gave a friendly chuckle.

They were all bound together by an act that was going to define each and every man involved. Bruce hoped Ronnie and Buster's counting had been accurate. The two men continued to leaf through the notes.

'How are you transporting it away, then? This million pounds?' Buster asked.

'All will be revealed,' Armstrong replied cryptically, smiling.

Bruce was keen to see the last of the men, so that they could get on with planning their own departures. Both schedules and vehicles needed changing.

Abruptly, the counting stopped, as the two men picked an assortment of bank notes out and arranged them in two piles on the floor. Armstrong pulled a canvas bag from out of his rucksack, emptying the money into it. Were they stealing from their boss? Not a wise move, thought Bruce.

'Oh, don't worry,' Armstrong responded, as if he could read his mind. 'This is our share. Remember, it comes out of the first million.' Bruce nodded. They certainly weren't going to eat into the gang's money, and he couldn't stomach asking Ronnie and Buster to re-count everything. Armstrong dropped his bag in the corner of the room.

'We're going for a little walk,' Jack announced, grinning again.

'Where you going?'

'Oh, not far. Don't be surprised if you see something coming back down the track. It's only us, coming for all this. Keep your eye on our bag will you?'

Bruce nodded. The two men swept out of the room, through the kitchen and out into the yard. Reynolds followed Jack and Mickey to the external door and watched as they turned right and walked across the field in the direction of Oxford, the second time they had done this in the past couple of days. He pondered what was different about the likes of him and Gordon, compared to those two northerners. Class, and a touch of style, he thought. They knew how to live their lives, the right way to spend this amount of money. All he had to do now was get it out of there, to somewhere safe. He had to get a message to Mary Manson.

★ ★ ★

The horsebox bumped its way down the track towards the farmhouse. From an upstairs window, Jimmy White shouted down to the main living room.

'There's someone coming. With a horse thing.'

Bruce walked up to the top of the stairs. 'Who's in it?'

'It's those two northern blokes. I think it's just them.'

They were returning as promised, this time with a substantial vehicle to remove a million pounds. The gang needed to know more about what was going on in the outside world, before venturing out. Bruce had decided that at least two advance scouts would be required. He had spoken to Roger and Roy already, and was surprised to hear that Cordrey had a reservation at a guesthouse in Oxford for a week. At least somebody had been thinking ahead.

He returned to the living room to find Gordon peering through the corner of a pulled-back curtain. These two happily trundling along the track served as a reminder that they needed to vacate as soon as possible. Buster had moved the money up to the top floor, to ensure that it was out of sight from outside, just in case anybody happened by, like the neighbour the day before. The first million, which belonged to Lavery and the Ulsterman, was the only money still sitting on the living room floor.

The vehicle drew up and Armstrong and Griffin stepped out, each carrying a pair of large suitcases. Gordon and Bruce reached the front door in order to meet them, and several eyes were trained on the outsiders from upstairs.

'Hello again,' said Armstrong, his accent stronger than Bruce remembered it before. 'It's okay, we'll just help ourselves.' The two men breezed into the living room and inspected their piles of money. To Bruce, who followed them in, they appeared amazingly detached, given the massive sums lying in front of them.

Buster went in to help. 'They're in piles of fifty grand each, you've got twenty piles, okay?'

'We need to split this money in half,' Armstrong instructed, and he and Griffin began counting and separating the stacks.

Bruce watched as Buster gave a hand in dividing up the money. Why was he aiding this pair? It seemed strange. Maybe he was angling for more work with this lot in the future? Separating the load into two halves took a couple of minutes. Armstrong and Griffin filled up their four large suitcases, brimming with notes. There was still a huge amount of the first half left over, and Griffin made a return journey to the horsebox for three more suitcases, which they also filled. Half a million quid, thought Bruce, his own share was just over a hundred grand, and these two men were just about to walk away with nearly ten times that. He assumed it was an even cut between the Ulsterman and Lavery. But still Bruce couldn't help thinking about the injustice. He had led all the planning, applied the brainwork, took the risks. He was glad Charlie was upstairs rather than down at that moment. The very sight of this would have driven him nuts.

Buster helped the two men with their full suitcases outside, and Bruce stayed in the living room. They soon returned carrying a large trunk, which they dropped to the floor and opened. With Buster's help they three-quarters filled it with the other five hundred thousand, before closing the lid with a thump. Bruce looked around the room, which now gave off an eerily empty feeling. The rest of the money was safely upstairs, but it felt strange for the space to contain nothing but the odd stray note lying around.

'Please give us a hand,' Jack asked politely.

All four men carried the trunk out to the horsebox, and shoved it inside. The back was full of money.

'Where's our bag?' demanded Armstrong.

'It's safe. In the stove.' Bruce had ensured this was out of reach for now. They needed these two men to return for one final part of the job later.

'I'll go,' Griffin announced, sweating. He looked like the one that did the donkey work among the pair, Armstrong the relative brains of the outfit. Bruce, Buster and Jack followed him into the kitchen. Mickey fished the canvas bag out of the stove and took it out to the vehicle. When he returned, Bruce remembered there was something he had to check.

'You're coming back aren't you?' Bruce asked as matter-of-factly as he could.

'Yeah, we are. In three or four days, *he* said.'

'He?'

'Brian Field.'

'Yeah, that's right.'

Bruce remembered the panic when he heard the news that Billy Still had been arrested. The idiot. He was going to get forty grand to clean everything, take away all signs of their occupation at the farm. He had promised to remove any fingerprints and equipment that was left behind, possibly even burn it down. Still was as sound as they came, but the fool got himself nicked two weeks before the job. Brian Field had found an alternative, and it seemed that meant the two northerners. They ought to be able to trust them; they were on the job together. He was sure they had been wearing gloves all the time, just like him. Would they even bother to come back? They would if their payoff was still waiting there.

'We'll leave your payment in the same place, in the stove,' Bruce said.

'Good. Thirty grand, yeah?' Armstrong asked. Brian Field must have knocked them down.

'Yeah. It'll be there.'

'Good. Just don't piss us about.' Armstrong looked threateningly at both Bruce and Buster in turn. They simply nodded in reply.

Bruce absent-mindedly picked up a small pile of pound notes off the kitchen floor, probably twenty quid in all. Buster seized them out of his hand, and passed the money to Armstrong.

'Here, a tip.' Buster laughed.

Jack Armstrong stared him in the face, and pulled out a gun. Bruce and Buster froze. There was nobody else in the kitchen to back them up; they were alone with the Beast of the North's henchmen.

'Woah, woah, I didn't mean anything,' Buster pleaded, hands in the air.

'You fuckin' better not have. Take the piss like that. You cockneys are all the same, fuckin' amateurs.' He pointed the gun at Buster's face. 'Now, back off.' He switched his attention to Bruce. 'And you.'

Bruce and Buster walked backwards into the pantry. The place was stuffed full of tins of soup and baked beans, as well as mountains of fruit and potatoes. Bruce thought Armstrong was going to lock them in. Then Armstrong's mood seemed to change, and he put his gun away. Jack took a deep breath and put a hand to his head, as if he regretted pulling a shooter on them.

'Look, sorry. I didn't mean anything by it. We just want to leave peacefully,' he responded. 'There's no need to take the piss, that's all,' Armstrong said. He looked like a different man to the one who had threatened them moments earlier.

'You had 'em all the time?' Bruce asked, holding back the anger, but failing to hide the surprise.

'Course we did.'

'Both of you?' Buster asked this time.

'Yeah. Think we're, stupid? There was two of us and fourteen of you. We've got someone's investment to protect. Now, just remember what we talked about yesterday. And of course, none of this happened, right? If they find out anybody was carrying on the job, and they catch you, you know what they'll do to you, don't you?'

Bruce was unable to answer. All that talk about not taking guns because of the risks, and they were armed all along. They had been nicely set up. It was bloody infuriating, but then again, there was the money to soften the blow. He focused on the situation Lavery's two men were in.

'You're not keeping it for yourselves, are you?' Bruce asked, pointing out to the yard where the horsebox was parked. There had been precious little opportunity to get to know Jack and Mickey in the run up to the job, or the immediate aftermath. They kept themselves to themselves, rarely said anything, and only got involved when it was necessary. He wondered what it was like to work for their boss.

'Course we're not. You think we're stupid? You do, don't you?' Jack laughed, but suddenly dropped the happy face. 'No, we know who we work for, we wouldn't do anything as daft as that.' His northern accent grew stronger. 'We want to live. Make sure you're not here when we get back to clean up, we don't want to piss about waiting for you lot.'

'Don't worry, we'll be long gone,' Bruce replied, knowing their plans were coming forward. The longer they hung around, the more likely they would be caught, it was that simple.

'We've just got a drop off to do. It's been a pleasure.' Armstrong's tone gave no indication that this was true, and he tapped the side of his nose as the northerner headed outside.

Bruce and Buster followed him into the yard, where Griffin was already starting up the engine. Reynolds looked up at the window and saw the faces of Tommy Wisbey and Charlie Wilson staring down. Would Armstrong have been as brave if those two

126

were in the kitchen as well? But he could see their point. They might have felt outnumbered, conscious that a gang that large could turn them over with ease.

Jack leant out of the passenger side window. 'We'd better be going. Don't worry, we'll be back to tidy up.'

'Will you?' Buster asked.

'Yeah. We keep our word. Look, sorry about pulling a gun on you like that.' Jack Armstrong looked like he meant it.

Buster smiled back. He seemed to have forgiven it already. There were several thousand reasons to do so upstairs.

'Good luck with your money, lads. I hope life treats you well,' Bruce said, as they pulled away.

The horsebox trundled its way back down the track and away from the farm. The dust caught in Bruce's throat, and when he turned around, Charlie Wilson had emerged at his shoulder.

'Buster tells me they were carrying.'

'Yeah, they were.'

'Fuckers. Bloody fuckers. After all that bollocks.' Charlie was unsurprisingly furious.

'I know. But what does it matter?' Bruce thought about it logically. So long as they had their money, who cared?

'Don't worry about it, Charlie. Water off a duck's back,' Buster said to Wilson.

Bruce had to focus on the tasks in hand. 'We should get the place tidy, you know, clean it up, we don't want to leave any dabs about, do we?'

'They're coming to do that for us, aren't they?' Roger Cordrey asked. His voice was irritating and high pitched, still grated on Bruce's nerves.

'Yeah, they are, Brian organised it. But we might as well do it ourselves, just in case. We still got to be careful.'

Buster went inside, and along with Jimmy White, retrieved the cleaning equipment from under the kitchen sink. Everyone gathered and was issued with duties by White, the typical

Quartermaster. Bruce Reynolds took Biggs to one side, for a particular task.

'Ronnie, do us a favour; start a fire, not too big. We need to burn the wrappers. If they won't catch, then bury 'em.'

'I've already dug an hole.'

'You might need to dig another.'

'Jesus, Bruce. Can't I just stuff 'em in the cellar?'

'Whatever you like, Ronnie. Just get rid of it all.'

20

Eddie Maloney watched through his binoculars as the horsebox pulled into the farmyard. Greatbatch Farm was situated a couple of miles from a village called Hawbridge, halfway between the towns of Pershore and Worcester. They chose it because it was heading in the opposite direction to London from the original hideout, and everyone was going to assume train robbers would head towards London, not Wales.

Lavery told him that only Armstrong and Griffin were going to be bringing the money, but Eddie wanted to make sure. They planned to let the vehicle draw up and park, before making their way across the field. Mick Fitzgerald and Brian Beard were to the West, also out of sight, and Ciaran was at his right hand. The thought had crossed his mind a few times that they could hold those boys up, and take the full million back to Ireland. Each time this flickered in his head he could hear Whelan's voice, warning him not to make any waves with the Beast of the North. There were too many successful business ventures in motion, so it was too big a risk even for an extra half a million pounds. Whelan was very specific about his instructions. Take only our money, and defend it with your lives. They were armed, because they knew Lavery's men would be.

They paused for five minutes, but nothing else appeared along the farm track. The four of them had been waiting for over two hours, had checked the area thoroughly. This place was even more secure and remote than the one Brian Field managed to obtain with Lavery's dodgy deposit. No neighbours for two miles in either direction. Maloney flashed his torch towards the woods, which replied twice. It was time to claim their prize.

Armstrong was sitting on the rear edge of the opened horsebox, smoking a cigarette, when Maloney and his men approached. Eddie failed to make the man jump as he loomed up from behind; so reasoned that Griffin was inside the cottage and Armstrong was not alone.

'Do you have the saddles?' Maloney asked.

'Where the fuck you been?'

Armstrong didn't seem to be bothered with the pre-arranged code for the handover, and threw his butt down at his feet. Griffin appeared at his side, as if part of a conjuring trick.

'We got held up,' Maloney smiled.

'Ha ha, very funny. You better not be pissing us about. I've had enough of that for one day.'

'Don't worry, we're not. You got the money?' Eddie asked.

'You been followed?' Armstrong replied.

'Course not. What do you think we are?' Jack didn't respond, ignoring the question. 'And it's all there?' Maloney continued. 'The full million?'

'Your half million is, yeah. Ours is long gone.'

That put paid to any consideration of taking it all. The northerners were being extremely careful, and suspicion was mutual. Maybe that feeling would help them both to simply head off in different directions. His life would be worth shit if he pissed Whelan off. He would drop from conquering hero to corpse in an instant.

'Can we see it?' Maloney enquired, as calmly as he could manage. He was about to take half a million pounds over the Irish Sea, the biggest financial boost to the cause in history. It would make the American negotiations look like chicken feed. Armstrong looked about him at the four faces, only one of which he had seen before. Despite this, both he and Griffin appeared unperturbed, confident that they wouldn't be attacked.

'Sure. Help yourselves.'

'Ciaran?' Maloney gestured to Ryan to take a look inside. 'So, how much did they take altogether?'

'They didn't say exactly, but they was happy to hand over the whole million to us.'

Maloney struggled to hide his surprise. The early editions of the evening newspapers had reported that just over a million was stolen. They must have either been mistaken, or winding up the gang. Goody's men wouldn't have simply handed over everything, not after what they would have gone through.

'Actually, I reckon they must have had more than us, judging by the piles.' Griffin simply nodded, as always letting Armstrong do all the talking.

'Ah, it's stuffed, look.' Ciaran pointed inside, and all the Irishmen took a peek. The massive trunk was three quarters full of bank notes, wrapped up in a series of bundles. The sight gave Eddie Maloney a warm glow.

'Fetch the van, will you?' Eddie ordered, aimed at Fitzgerald. Within a minute they heard the engine drone its way around the corner of the farmhouse. They had parked their vehicle in a shed around the back. This was their initial means of escape, and the other was parked over thirty miles away, in an abandoned warehouse on the outskirts of Ludlow.

The plan to split up the cash was a defence mechanism, born out of Maloney's suspicion of their business partner. They were going to head off in two different directions, just in case they were followed. Both would ultimately end up on the southern coast of Ireland, at one of their secret entrance points, close to Cork. Maloney's three men loaded the trunk into their van, and they took another look inside. There certainly looked to be half a million in there, he guessed. The four men exchanged smiles, interrupted by Armstrong, who walked up close behind.

'They gave you the Irish notes, and the Scottish ones as well, hope you don't mind?' Armstrong laughed, lighting up again.

'Ah, they'll do.' Maloney grinned in return. It would all be broken up and sorted when they reached Ludlow.

'You not gonna count it?' Armstrong asked. He seemed totally bored by the whole meeting.

'We trust you,' Maloney countered.

'Good.' Armstrong sat back down on the tailgate of the horsebox.

'Is that everything?' Maloney checked.

'Why, are you expecting something else?' Eddie thought that Armstrong always seemed to talk with a sarcastic air.

'No, just checking.'

'Nah, that's your lot.'

'Nice doing business with you,' Maloney offered his hand to Armstrong.

Nothing came in return other than a murmured, 'Aye, mind how you go, lads.'

'Come on, let's go.' Maloney called to his men and they bundled into their van. Fitzgerald took the wheel, with Maloney in the passenger seat, and Beard and Ciaran Ryan in the back, along with the trunk.

Armstrong and Griffin waived nonchalantly as they pulled away.

'That was bloody easy,' Fitzgerald said, as they powered along the main road in the direction of Wales.

'Too easy,' Maloney mused.

'Ah, they're just doing their jobs, just like us,' Ryan added from the back.

'Maybe,' Maloney answered, thinking of their reception on the mainland. Four conquering heroes were set to return.

21

The words of Tommy Lavery echoed in DS Joe Watson's head, as he pulled on his coat.

'Hold back for the moment. It's got to look like it's coming from an informant on the street, and we don't want it to look too prepared. Do it in two stages, starting with what will look like the ringleaders. You will just be verifying another source with your list.'

How did someone like Lavery know so much about everything, including his phone number at New Scotland Yard? His boss Frank Williams had called his team to a meeting just as they were planning to leave that evening. Now they were heading for the pubs to find out what the word on the ground was about this train robbery, to shake and rattle a few faces, and see what fell out.

His list of names was memorised. Lavery had identified the first ones to be leaked, which meant that the heat would be on Reynolds, Goody, Wilson, Edwards and James before the rest. His boss had told him that he would be working alongside Frank and DS Slipper on the robbery investigation to begin with. Joe had wondered about the names for a few weeks, thinking about the odd assortment of characters. Some were very surprising, like Roy James, a man who was supposed to be a budding racing driver. Still, his father used to say that crime made for strange bedfellows. According to Williams, who had attended a senior briefing earlier in the day, there were few clues to be had. The gang warned the GPO employees not to move for thirty minutes, which told them all they needed to know about how far away they might be hiding. According to reports, they were using lorries and Land Rovers, so wouldn't be able to move too fast. Roadblocks had been set up by the local force, but turned up nothing overnight. COC10, the stolen car unit, were already on the case with the vehicles.

Lavery had made it abundantly clear, at the risk of both his mind and his body, that the names could not be released until the weekend, which was a couple of days away. Joe knew he was unlikely to be out of his grasp for a while. All evening he hung around the usual haunts, and bumped into Frank Williams on a couple of occasions. Both of them were probably targeting the same men. None of the pubs he visited harboured the men on his list. It seemed that Tommy Lavery had given him the names of the thieves in advance of the biggest robbery the country had ever seen.

Watson felt himself weaken as he listened to the whispers around *The Lamb and Flag* in Elephant and Castle, *The Crown* in Camberwell, and *The Meat Packer* in Lee Green. Hearsay abounded, mutterings, but nobody was naming names. It was as if those involved were protected. He knew tongues were normally a hell of a lot looser than this after a major robbery. Everybody would have a theory, how it was done, who might have been involved. The fact that this looked like the biggest of them all hadn't got anybody sinking ships. Leaving Frank Williams in a corner talking to two women, he trudged off to catch his bus to Penge. Maybe they were all safely back home with their share of the loot, having been on his doorstep all this time. Speculation in the pubs was that the take was bigger than the million in the newspapers. He pondered what it would be like to have that amount of money, and not be stuck in a job with your balls in a sling to a character like Lavery. He yearned for freedom, but for now he knew it had to be earned.

Soon he would turn up with some extraordinary revelations. He thought about what it felt like to have that much dangerous knowledge, and the consequences if he ever let slip where his intelligence came from. Lavery wanted the names to be leaked gradually, to make it look genuine. Despite the talk of a corroborative source, Joe could still take the credit. He hoped Tommy wasn't setting him up to look like a fool.

'Take courage, Joe,' Lavery said as he rang off. He would need plenty of it in the coming days.

22

Both men lay dead at the side of the road.

'Fuckin' 'ell, the Irish really do stink, don't they?' Griffin laughed.

Armstrong stared at his partner. He would be happy when this caper was over, and he wouldn't have to drive around the country with the miserable git. Never said a word, and then when he did open his mouth he had nothing useful to contribute. Still, Tommy Lavery trusted him, and that was all that mattered. Jack tossed a cigarette end on to one of the corpses, as if offering a valedictory goodbye. They looked pretty well set men, but they were very careless, in the past tense. If he were transporting that amount of money about the country he would have kept his hand on his gun, even when he was taking a piss.

'Come on, get the money in the van.' They transferred the suitcases from the back of the Irishmen's Land Rover into their Bedford, and hid them under packing cases and a tarpaulin.

'You think he's gonna be pissed off?' Griffin asked.

'Why?' said Armstrong, indicating the suitcases they had just retrieved.

'Well, this don't look like all of it, does it?'

'No. They split up didn't they? Fuckers.'

Armstrong contemplated how difficult the choice had been. They placed the homing devices in two of the money bundles, and another in the lining of the large trunk. That stayed motionless outside a one-horse town in the middle of nowhere, so they picked up the trail of the other two. They anticipated the Micks were going to head for the coast, and they were right. The signal was easy to follow, and they caught them up in Shropshire at first, despite giving the Irishmen a twenty-minute head start.

However, the crafty bastards then split up their money and headed off in different directions, using separate vehicles. Dropping back, they managed to pick up the signal from both devices hidden in the bundles of notes, but it appeared they had ended up in the same car. Armstrong guessed they recovered about half the cash, perhaps slightly less. They tracked the two dead men down to a remote spot, close to a place ludicrously called Fishguard, where they had foolishly stopped to relieve themselves. That was the point at which he and Mickey intervened. They had no idea where the rest of the money was; it could even still be back in that warehouse on the edge of a town called Ludlow. At least they had something for their efforts.

Jack had studied the map in the front of their van when they followed the trackers. There was a dotted line from Fishguard to Ireland, across the sea. Maybe they were heading for a ferry, but there was no way they would be allowed to leave the country with money Lavery viewed as his own. They intercepted the urinating Micks only five miles from the coast, in a place they couldn't begin to spell, let alone pronounce. Two silencer bullets deposited into the heads of the men beside the deserted roadside, and the job was done. Once the money was loaded up, all they had to do was bundle the bodies down a bank, out of harm's way.

Jack and Mickey had switched to their van a mile from the initial meeting point in Worcester, and it was a bugger to drive, judging by Griffin's performance at the wheel. They now headed along the southern Welsh coast with their reclaimed suitcases for a while, then pulled up in a picnic spot after dark, and retrieved them from the back of the van. Griffin pulled out a jemmy, and after a few assaults, the locks were opened. They were all stuffed full of notes. He was sure Lavery would be pleased that they had recovered a decent amount of money. Armstrong was surprised they hadn't met any greater resistance.

They found guns on both dead bodies, before tossing them aside. What use are they stuck in your back pocket, when someone is standing over you with their own weapon pointed at your head, asking you to kneel down right now or I'll blow your fucking head off? Jack grimaced at the memory of Griffin's sick sense of humour. 'Your money or your life?' he bleated at the two men, before shooting both. They had no option; Lavery had already made that decision. There were at least two more Micks out there, including that Maloney. Probably on their way to Ireland, no idea that their pals had been hijacked.

Griffin smashed their electronic tracker from the front of the van with one swing of a hammer. Armstrong rifled through the contents of the suitcases, checking that they hadn't been duped. There was only money inside, no bundles of newspapers.

'Should we go back to that warehouse? Maybe they left part of it there, were planning on going back for the rest?' Mickey asked.

'Don't think so. Would you?'

'Nah, suppose not. But they are bloody Irish, you never know.'

'Nah, I really doubt it. We'd best work out how much we got first of all.'

Armstrong continued checking the nearest suitcase. He reckoned, as a first guess, there might be sixty grand in it. Multiply that by four, and that was well over two hundred grand. Not bad for a night's work, but it was still just under half of the Irishman's share. Would Lavery be happy with that much?

'What if the boss asks what we did about the other half?' Griffin asked.

'Well, what the fuck could we do? They were smart enough to split it up, weren't they?'

'Yeah, suppose they were. And they got a bit lucky. We should have had more devices,' Griffin mused.

Oh, he was all fucking theories now after the fact, wasn't he? Stupid bastard. Maybe they should have had more trackers, but to be honest he only had three available, and it made sense to stick one in the trunk. Besides, there was no way they could have followed two vehicles at the same time.

'Suppose they weren't quite smart enough, though,' Griffin chuckled. Jack thought about the two dead bodies lying anonymously at the bottom of a bank. Would that be him one day?

They needed to keep moving now that there was a manhunt on for train robbers. Mickey had been following the news like a radio ham, continually switching from one station to another as they drove along. Griffin slipped their van into reverse and they pulled on to the main road, in the direction of Swansea. It would take them a few hours before they reached Manchester. Lavery should be pleased. Not only did they have their own half a million safely hidden in a lock up in Redditch, which they would collect on the way back, they had a nice tidy bonus as well. It wasn't every day you persuaded someone to hand over more than two hundred thousand quid, just like that. Even if you asked after they were dead.

23

Bruce Reynolds was picked up within a couple of minutes of leaving the farm. Two men in a Ford Anglia stopped at the roadside, and offered him a lift.

'Where are you heading?' the driver asked.

'Thame, if you would,' he replied, mirroring the well-bred accent.

Reynolds was dressed in a Burberry sports jacket and carried a backpack, trying to look like a country rambler rather than a train robber. He was happy to escape from Leatherslade Farm. The mood was still upbeat, buoyed by the fact the police hadn't got their act together yet. The huge piles of banknotes raised the spirits every time he laid eyes on them. However, every moment spent there increased the chances of being caught. The key thing was not to be found in possession of the money. Almost anything else could be explained away, as their Heathrow experiences had demonstrated.

Bruce engaged in light conversation with the two men, and the subject of the robbery eventually cropped up, it was apparently all over the news.

'Yes, I do hope they catch them, don't you?' Bruce threw in, with as posh a voice as he could muster, playing his Colonel role again. He had mixed with that level of society before, and it was only an outstretched arm away now. Bruce thanked the men when they dropped him off in Thame, and soon met Mary Manson at the bus station. They hugged, and Bruce felt that mild frisson return. He loved Franny, but Mary was more than a family friend. She held the key to escape.

They bought an Austin Healey from a car dealer in the same town for £900, a kind of down payment on his glamorous future. Mary paid the salesman, as Bruce tried to stay out of sight. There was no way to avoid paying in fivers, but that was how people purchased cars like that. He was determined to escape in style. Manson had showed up in a small Bedford van, parking it in a quiet side street. She followed Bruce back to the farm, where they loaded both his and John Daly's shares into the back of her vehicle, inside a set of packing crates. Bruce reckoned they would be the first of the gang to leave with their money intact.

The rest of the team were going to need vehicles, and a logistical operation that they had mapped out that morning had begun, involving moving men and cars back and forth. Harry Smith gave Daly and Reynolds a lift back into Thame in the Healey, promising to return it later, and they waved Mary off in the Bedford as they left. Nobody would suspect a thirty-year-old woman driving a van to be carrying two significant shares from this monumental robbery. Bruce and John Daly hoped that two men travelling together with no luggage would pass unnoticed, and they caught a bus from Thame to Victoria coach station. One nervy cab ride later, they met up with Mary again, at her flat in Streatham.

The brothers-in-law took their money to a lock up in Mortlake, that Bruce had already rented, and hid their loot inside a couple of wardrobes at the back of the garage. They went their separate ways, Bruce to visit Franny in Putney, where she was already packed in readiness to move on, and Daly in his own car to Cowes, looking to buy a boat. He told Bruce he thought this was the best sort of hiding place, floating on the sea. They agreed to avoid any contact until the end of the month.

Bruce greeted Franny with delight when they eventually met up, and hugged their son for what he feared might be the last time for a while. He didn't think the police would have any evidence against him, they had been extremely careful both at the scene of the crime and the farm. But they had a close shave with the Heathrow robbery, and the Flying Squad were going to be looking for him on this one. He had mapped out contingencies for Franny and little Nicholas. If the others didn't plan ahead, that was their lookout. He was confident nobody would grass. The only potential weak link was Biggs's train driver, Stan, or whatever his name was. Despite Ronnie's protestations to the contrary, he was the only unknown quantity. You could never really trust civilians.

There was one more matter that nagged at him. He had twice been sighted in connection with the farm. Bruce had visited the place, as well as the estate agents, when they were searching for an appropriate base. His face might also be remembered if the police put enough pressure on the visitor that they had the day before the robbery, although he suspected they would need more concrete evidence. With memories of Heathrow hanging over him, he knew caution would have to be his watchword for a few days. There was little he could do other than to tread carefully. He hoped, for their sakes, that the rest of his group were doing the same.

They took Nicholas over to Mary, who agreed to look after him for as long as necessary, and he and Franny moved into a friend's empty flat in Clapham. Nobody could link him to James and Betty Madison. They would be safe there, as would the money in the lock up. It would be just a matter of sitting tight and letting it all blow over. Then he and Franny could poke their heads out and enjoy the spoils. If they were patient, they would be in the South of France living the high life by Christmas.

24

'The Maid Of The Sea' pitched and rolled, making Eddie Maloney sick to his stomach. It was always this way with sea crossings, he preferred flying back to the mainland. As the small boat bobbed on the Irish Sea he thought of home, and the reception they would get. Not when they landed at Cobh, but when they returned to Dublin with all the money. Five months spent in lousy England, listening to their stupid accents and all their complaining about football or weather or modern music. As a nation they were contemptible. Ciaran Ryan was down below, guarding the suitcases, sleeping on them in fact. They were the only passengers on the fishing boat, especially 'chartered' from the Cork area over to Holyhead and back, no questions asked. Geraghty would be waiting at the dock, as arranged, with a van, to transport everything over to headquarters, most of the cash going straight from there to the bank, the rest heading for various hideouts along the West coast.

They drove steadily from Ludlow up to Holyhead, winding their way through mountains and then deserted lanes in the middle of nowhere, a deliberate ploy to check if they were being followed. It was still difficult to trust that Lavery, and splitting up the money was designed to keep them one step ahead, even if it meant spreading the numbers able to guard it. Ryan stopped their vehicle several times, pulling into lay-bys. On one occasion they waited for twenty minutes, but either their pursuers were exceptionally gifted, or didn't exist. At the quay they easily found the fishing boat, along with their escort who was referred to only as 'Bertie'. Whilst Ryan loaded the suitcases on board, he abandoned the van in a pub car park. His walk back through Holyhead town reminded him of home, and the streets of Limerick. Maybe Wales would one day look to break free of the shackles as well. They were pioneers.

His thoughts turned to Beard and Fitzgerald, and the other load being transported across from Fishguard to the same destination. His journey was longer both across land and sea. He had to trade the greater time on a boat for accompanying most of the money. His instructions were not to hang around in Cobh when they arrived, as Leahy and Whelan wanted to meet him as soon as possible in Dublin. The moment he set foot on home shores he and the money would part company for good. The others should make it across first. Those two boys could certainly look after themselves; he pitied any of Lavery's men if they tried to take them on. He wouldn't dare try an ambush, there was too much at stake in the relationship with the organisation. They were apparently providing cheap labour and willing hands for a massive black market operation in the North West of England.

Ryan's head popped up from the tiny cabin, down below.

'Ah, Ed, how ya faring?'

'I'll be fine. Just, ya know.'

'Ah, I know. Here, take these.' Ryan offered a packet that contained oval-shaped tablets. 'Antripol', according to the label.

'What's this?'

'It's for the stomach.'

'What is it?'

'It's for your stomach, Ed, do ya the world o' good.'

'Get down there with the cargo.'

'Sure.'

Maybe Eddie was being over cautious, ensuring one of them was with the money at all times, out there in the middle of nowhere, but he had felt on edge ever since Armstrong and Griffin handed their money over so readily. It wasn't every day you gave half a million English pounds to near strangers on a farm. He knew that if the Coastguard stopped the boat, they would have to shoot their way out.

The nausea still clung to him like a Galway mist as he swallowed the tablets, and Ryan disappeared below deck, confident in his own sea legs. There was no way he would be able to survive down there, if he could at least watch the horizon he might make it across in one piece. Just another couple of hours and he would be home, the conquering hero.

25

Gordon Goody watched the last of the visitors leave 'Kabri' from the upstairs window. The place had been christened thanks to a combination of Brian and Karin Field's names, resulting in an ugly title. Jimmy White, who spent most of the day before selflessly driving back and forth, was at the wheel, with Ronnie Biggs and the failed driver in the back. Ten of the gang had stayed there the night before, and Karin and Brian had hosted an impromptu party. Only a handful missed the celebration. Cordrey never returned after a trip to Oxford, taking all his money with him. Bruce and John were already in London.

There had been a series of exoduses throughout the day. Three of the South coast group and Jimmy Hussey had disappeared earlier that morning, heading for Reading they said. Roy James returned, as promised, for an increasingly nervous looking Charlie Wilson and Harry Smith, before they left in yet another van. Gordon suddenly felt rather lonely after three days cooped up with the gang. He had his hiding places sorted. His money was going to be buried in Bob Corden's garden in Barnes, a man he could totally trust. He had a room ready above *The Windmill* pub in Blackfriars, a place he had stayed before. Gordon never removed his gloves on the farm, even to take a piss. They would have nothing on him, even though he knew the Met would come calling. He even had an alibi placing him in Belfast at the time of the robbery.

He came down the stairs with the last of his suitcases, and saw Brian Field slumped in his armchair, drinking.

'I can give you a lift to the station, Gordon,' Brian offered.

'No need. I've got the Rover outside.' One of the motors used to ferry people and suitcases back and forth was still there.

Field fell silent. He looked incredibly sad for a man who was over a hundred grand richer than three days before. Brian might be used to the criminal fraternity in his line of work, but Gordon supposed he wasn't as comfortable having a gang of wanted men staying under his roof, along with over a million pounds of stolen money. Had he got in too deep? Gordon began to wonder for the first time how reliable this man, who had wheeled and dealt on his behalf in the past, would remain. This robbery was special; they were front-page news everywhere. It was time to move on, and more importantly, put some distance between himself and his stolen money.

'What are you gonna do now?' Gordon asked.

'Oh, we got visitors coming. Just my parents. But, best not to have loads of money lying around, you know.' Brian made a valiant attempt at a smile, but Gordon could see he was struggling.

'Apart from yours, Brian.' It was worth reminding the clerk that he was up to his neck in this thing.

Field threw a question at him from nowhere. 'D'you reckon those boys will show up to clean the place?'

'I don't see why not. They're getting paid for it.'

Thirty grand was a lot of money for a bit of tidying up and dumping three vehicles, but they had few other options. Gordon was the last one to leave the farm as well as Kabri. He felt like the parent of the family, always tidying up after them. They had scrubbed the place so clean that Jimmy Hussey joked they should have started up a business. Nobody had seen or heard anything of Jack and Mickey since they disappeared with their cash, and he hoped for their sakes they didn't double-cross their boss. Gordon had heard tales of the exploits of Tommy Lavery, and none of it made for happy bedtime reading. He chose to say nothing when he showed up at the farm. With men like him, it was best to stay as invisible as possible.

'I hope they come back,' Field said nervously.

'Why d'you care? You weren't there?'

'Was their money there when you left?'

Gordon struggled to recall the green holdall that Buster said he had put aside. 'I didn't see it, but that doesn't mean it's not there.' He might have mentioned something about it being in the kitchen, or the stove. Maybe they took it with them when they shot off with the horsebox. They looked to be in a big hurry at the time.

Gordon's lack of reply made Brian's eyes widen. 'Oh, God.' He slumped even further into his armchair and reached for the bottle of scotch. He shakily poured a measure into a glass, knocked it back, and repeated the dose. Gordon looked at him sorrowfully.

'Look. It probably won't matter.' Gordon tried to smile, couldn't understand why Brian was so concerned. 'Maybe they came back and cleaned the whole place after we left yesterday. Maybe it's already burned down.' Gordon didn't think that was likely, and Field didn't look convinced either. Why was he bothered? Brian hadn't spent any time there over the past few days.

'You reckon?' Field asked hopefully.

'Look at it this way. There's nothing you can do now, is there?' Gordon looked down on Brian, trying to sound concerned, which in many ways he wasn't. 'You could go down there and do it yourself, if you liked.'

'No.' Brian was right. If the police stumbled across the place, nobody wanted to be caught cleaning it up or in the process of torching it. There were appeals out for deserted farms and warehouses in Buckinghamshire and all surrounding counties. It would be found soon.

'You can't do anything about it now. You need to think ahead, what you're going to do next. You have to carry on as normal, Brian, not arouse any suspicion. The rest of the boys will be doing that.

You've got to as well.' Gordon finished his pep talk and headed for the door, suitcases full of money in his hands.

Field finished his drink and made to reach for the bottle once more, but his hand fell limp in his lap. He looked like a lost schoolboy who had wandered off the path and desperately needed guidance, which Gordon didn't have the time or inclination to provide. He had to press on, couldn't become embroiled in Brian's personal mess.

'Look, Brian. I'm sure it will be all right. You need to carry on, like I say.'

'Okay. And thanks, Gordon.'

'What for?'

'Oh, I don't know. You just seem to understand my position more than the rest of them.'

Goody smiled. It might look that way, but inside he felt no sympathy for this greedy little man. He was just a clerk, and now that he had infringed too closely on the realities of crime, it was too much for him. Gordon hoped that Field would stand up to questioning if the police came calling, and felt the need to provide a degree of reinforcement.

'We stick together, Brian, remember.'

'Of course.' Field seemed to perk up a little, stood and came to the front door to shake Gordon's hand, and see off the last of the robbers to leave his home. Gordon eyed the Rover parked outside, the final vehicle to pull out. It was his passage to Bob Corden's back garden, and hiding his money.

'Good luck, Brian.'

'And you Gordon. And you.'

Gordon had a feeling that Brian Field was going to need it, especially if somebody discovered the farm before it was burnt down.

26

Bob Welch leant against a tree and took a breather, drawing on yet another cigarette. He had smoked almost constantly at the farmhouse. The claustrophobia clawed at him all the while he was there, drove his desperation to escape. Now they were free, he could relax again. He watched as Danny Pembroke carried on digging. His friend still hadn't taken his gloves off, even slept in them.

'Help, for fuck's sake,' Pembroke pleaded.

'Just a minute.'

Welch inhaled, tasting the nicotine. They were burying over two hundred grand in the undergrowth, by a clump of trees at the back of their new cottage. Unlike the rest of the gang, Danny and Bob had made plans. They anticipated a major stink brewing up over a robbery of this size, and had rented a place in The New Forest. While the rest of them were busy fretting over what exact times a particular train passed a certain point, all they were focused on was where and how to hide their money while the fuss died down. They were sure they would be at least one step ahead of the police, as well as the rest of the gang. They didn't really trust that Reynolds and his mob, reckoned they were a right bunch of fancies, swanking around Soho and the West End like they owned the place. If it hadn't been for Roger coming in on the job, as well as their muscle, the robbery wouldn't have happened.

Pembroke leant against his spade, stuck in the ground. They were three feet down by now, and the earth was getting increasingly tough to move.

'You're not fuckin' helpin' me, are you?' He paused and blew out hard. 'You reckon that's deep enough?'

'Yeah, think so.'

Welch leant on his own shovel. What they were doing made perfect sense. They had no idea who the police might have in the frame for this one, but were determined to stay out of it. Their alibis were secured with men they could trust. Heaving those mailbags had blistered their hands and given them sore arms, but all the pain was worth it. All you had to do was look at the piles of money and you were cured. Welch and Pembroke decided that they would stick together, to mutually assure that their money would stay safe.

They walked over to the metal chest they had hidden beneath a pile of woodcuttings two weeks before. They researched a few places before hitting on this one, an isolated cottage with a large garden and trees at the back. There were no neighbours, and no reason for anyone to come near, sniffing for stolen money. Rented under a false name, they had taken all the necessary precautions. Pembroke and Welch lowered the chest into the newly dug hole, and then dropped their eight heaving suitcases inside. Two hundred grand sure weighed a lot, satisfyingly enough.

'Fancy a beer?'

Bob Welch pulled two bottles of Pipkin ale out of his shoulder bag. Danny laughed. Why not? They had worked bloody hard for this load of money; nobody sweated more than they did. It was their problem if the rest of them had made no plans.

'Cheers, Dan,' Welch said.

'Cheers. To the GPO,' Pembroke added.

'The GPO, yeah.' Both laughed.

When they had downed their drinks, they set about re-filling the hole with earth, placing their two bottles inside the chest full of money before closing the lid. They even re-planted some bushes to disguise the recent activity.

Both men trudged back to the cottage, and checked the surfaces again. The last few days had taught them to be exceptionally careful. After a final clean up of their equipment, which they put away neatly in the small shed that adjoined the property, the two men jumped back in their small van and drove off for Lyndhurst station. The vehicle was then abandoned in the car park. Bob and Danny took the train back to London, arriving well after dark, and went their separate ways. They trusted each other, which was a hell of a lot more than the rest of the gang could say for themselves.

27

Roy James pulled up outside the lock up in Chiswick, and Harry Smith and Charlie Wilson looked at each other, sharing a smile. Every time you got in a car with Roy it was a showcase for his driving talents. He could have been a professional racing driver, as he kept repeating, if he hadn't been so busy having fun being a thief. This job was only fun in the respect that they had each got away with over a hundred grand. They knew there was going to be a nationwide manhunt, so places to hide their money and ways of staying hidden were needed.

Charlie and Roy both planned to keep the majority of their money hidden in garages. Judging by the conversations in the car on the way down, Harry's plans were more sophisticated. He had multiple places to stash his money, as well as a means of laundering his cash quickly. Danny Regan was lined up, and ready to go. Harry Smith was going to move into the property business.

Wilson did most of the talking on the journey, telling them of his intention to spend his share on cars and his family. Roy was going to plough his money into his racing career. Harry kept quiet; confident he had a better long-term plan. The police would be looking for large quantities of cash, and his aim was to liquefy his quickly. Buying property and renovating it was the perfect route, a simple way to make it disappear.

Wilson's talk about his family jarred with Harry Smith. He was unlikely to see Shirley and their two daughters again. If the police came looking, that was the first place they would try. A different woman was going to shelter him, all arranged in advance. Margaret Wade lived on the other side of London, in Shepherd's Bush. They would struggle to make any connections to her, as even his wife didn't know she was his bit on the side. Maybe in the future he would ensure his girls got part of the money, but if he wanted to stay free, Plaistow was the last place he could be seen.

They sat and waited until darkness descended, another thirty minutes passing as the windows steamed up. They were parked outside a row of deserted garages, the lights dim and distant, ideal for stashing bags of stolen bank notes. Charlie Wilson eventually got out of the van and cautiously opened up one of the doors, as if expecting someone to leap out from the shadows. Charlie flitted his eyes around nervously, which made Harry jumpy. Roy got out and joined Wilson in unloading their shares, which were now contained in black sacks, into a large chest towards the back of the garage. Harry left them to it, keeping a look out in the street.

His own money was packed tightly into four large green holdalls, still sitting in the back of the van. Roy James startled him when he poked his head back inside the vehicle.

'Where to, mate?' Roy laughed, trying to sound like a cabbie. Harry stared him down. It was his money that would get turned over if they did anything suspicious now. Wilson padlocked the garage door and climbed back into the van.

'Where to?' Roy prompted again.

Harry was going to stick to the plan, even if a hurried phone call from a telephone box down the lane from the farm had brought it forward by two days.

'Heston.'

'Where?'

'Heston. Just off the Bath Road. I'll direct you, it's not far.'

Roy looked suitably annoyed, given that they had driven along it about an hour before, idling away the time before it got dark.

'Fuck's sake,' was all he offered.

'I'm meeting a mate. Don't worry, it's someone I trust.'

Charlie looked at his watch repeatedly as they drove slowly back out to pick up the A4. Wilson was desperate to get into his local pub and start celebrating. Harry wasn't planning to do anything that stupid. They should all be looking to stay out of sight, there was no point drawing attention to yourself.

Harry directed Roy into a deserted trading estate close to Heston Aerodrome. They drew up outside a warehouse that had most of its windows smashed in. Doors hung off their hinges and the wind whistled through like a ghost town. Nobody would be happening down there purely by accident at that time of night. Danny Regan was waiting in a battered Ford Cortina, smoking a cigarette, and dangling it casually out of the window. This was a pre-arranged signal that all was clear. After Roy James pulled up, Harry grabbed his holdalls from out of the van and laid them out on the tarmac, before poking his head in through the passenger door.

'All the best, lads. Don't get caught out, now.' Both men inside smiled.

'Mind how you go, Harry. Be lucky,' said Charlie.

'Bye,' was all Roy muttered.

Harry tapped on the side of the van, an old habit, and Roy James performed an expert three-point turn before speeding off back in the direction they came. Harry picked up two of his heavy bags and walked over to Danny, who was still sitting in his car, finishing his smoke.

'All right, Dan, you good?'

'All good, mate, all good.'

'Give us a bloody hand, then,' Smith barked.

Regan flicked his cigarette past Harry's shoulder, and got out of the car. 'It went well, then?'

Danny must have read the reports of the robbery, but Harry was looking forward to giving him the inside track on the past three days.

'You could say that, you could say that. Blinding in fact. No heat on you at all?' Smith asked.

'Me? Nah, nothing mate, nothing at all.'

28

'It must be here somewhere. I'm sure of it. Try left here.'

'We've already gone down here. Fuck's sake, Bill, thought you said you knew where it was.'

'I did. I do. Just can't seem to remember.'

Bill Boal was sweating in the passenger seat, and Roger Cordrey inwardly cursed himself for not bringing a map. It seemed that Bill didn't even check the location of the deserted house they were trying to find, before they set off. Big Clive Hanson was apparently on the run and living in Benidorm. Boal said he remembered visiting the house about three years before, and was certain it had been boarded up. It had a garage that would be ideal to hide Roger's money in.

'I'm sure it was round here. In Westbourne. I know it was.'

'Oh, for God's sake.' Roger pulled up. There was no point having a go really, they were in this together now. 'Look, let's park and think about this.'

'It's here, I know it.'

'You've been saying that for an hour. Come on, Bill. I've got an idea. We need somewhere to stick this car.'

Bill Boal was the first person Cordrey had turned to when he left the farm for good. He owed Bill over six hundred pounds, which he had borrowed to cover a gambling debt. He promised Boal five grand if they could meet up in Oxford, and his old friend seemed happy to help. Bill Boal knew Cordrey was a thief, but this was something else. It would be tremendously exciting to help one of the infamous train robbers secrete their money. When Roger asked him about potential hiding places, Hanson's house, in one of the better areas of Bournemouth, seemed an ideal spot. However, there was a problem associated with Bill becoming involved. His wife Rene.

After leaving Oxford the day after the robbery, they headed straight for London, and Bill was forced to confess to his wife what they were up to. Rene was far from pleased. Roger also took the opportunity to give a few hundred to his sister, Maisie, to look after, just in case anything happened to the main part of his share. She and her husband were going to vouch for him if an alibi was needed for the robbery.

Excuses were given, and stories set, and the pair then headed for Bournemouth in separate cars, Bill bringing his family with him. They hoped to blend in with other holidaymakers whilst they took the opportunity to hide Roger's money. Rene and Bill's three kids were left to play on Bournemouth beach while the two men set off on their expedition around the town. The plan would have worked if they could only find the bloody place. Now they were forced to re-think, and Roger decided on a change of approach.

Cordrey drove back into the centre of Westbourne, an area they had passed through a couple of times during their fruitless search. They visited a local newsagent, looking for adverts of garages for rent. Eventually they found two that fitted the bill in Bournemouth, close to Victoria Park. A quick scouring of the local newspaper helped them to buy an additional car, a second hand Anglia from a car dealer in Poole. With the search for Hanson's house abandoned and the focus switched to new hiding places, their afternoon started to bear fruit.

In a shop window, Roger spotted an advert for a rental flat above a florist, in Winton. They secured this first and placed three of the suitcases in the wardrobe. Both men sat on the bed as Roger made cups of coffee. Boal looked anxious.

'Look, Rog. Rene's giving me real gip about this, you know. Are you gonna give me the rest of what you owe me? You're hardly strapped.'

'Just be patient, mate. You know I'll pay you back.'

'I know, but we left 'em on the beach hours ago. I'm sorry I couldn't find the house.'

'It doesn't matter. We've got a Plan B now, haven't we?'

'Yeah.'

Roger studied his share in its various receptacles. A sudden wave of panic hit him as he counted the items. It had been hard to keep track of everything, what with moving money about within the farmhouse, then to and from a guesthouse in Oxford, down to his sister's house in London, then finally to Bournemouth. There was an awful lot of it, and the six small suitcases made sense. The number of holdalls did not. It looked like he had more than his share, he wasn't quite sure. Everybody had carefully guarded their money down on the farm. He was no different, keeping part of it in the pantry under tins of baked beans, and the rest in his pile of suitcases. This was why he was keen to get away from the place as soon as possible. They were a bunch of thieves after all.

He tried to re-gather his thoughts as he sipped his coffee. He had to focus on getting it hidden as quickly as possible. It couldn't stay in one place.

'Bill, mate, we need to get this lot out of sight. Those garages we saw in the paper, let's get to work.'

'But what about Rene and the kids?'

'Can't you pack 'em off back home?'

'What, already?'

Roger fell silent. He didn't know what to say. Bill insisted on bringing them along, for a trip out if nothing else. Maybe he'd told his family that they were going to Bournemouth for a proper holiday. All paid for by his money, his electronics expertise.

Boal was insistent, looked extremely worried. 'Rog, she'll be suspicious.'

'Isn't she suspicious already? That money we left at yours? The money I took to my sister's? Is she blind?'

'Come off it, Rog. Don't start on Rene.'

'Look, we've got work to do. We can't sit on this, have it lying around in here all day.'

Both men agreed. The newspapers were full of the robbery and there was an enormous reward out there. He picked Bill Boal because he was a loyal friend from his days in Kingston. They went back too far.

'All right, Rog. Give me an hour. I'll go down the beach, say goodbye. Maybe take 'em to the station.'

'While you do that, I'll start working on the garages in the paper.'

Boal departed and Roger sat looking at the suitcases and bags of money. It was mind-boggling, there was so much cash just sitting there. Cordrey knew that once it was clear the signals had been tampered with, the police would come looking for someone with a track record like his. The reason he got involved in the first place was because of his expertise, so it wouldn't take a genius to put him in the frame. His alibi would hold up though, especially with Boal's help. Without the money there would be nothing to pin this one on him. He began the process of transporting three suitcases back into the boot of the Anglia, ready to be stashed in the first garage he could rent. All he had to do was lie low for a few days, and he could begin his life again.

29

Jack Armstrong and Tommy Lavery took their places at the table opposite the prisoner. Jack looked at his boss, who had dressed in a donkey jacket for the visit, playing down his status. There was no need to advertise who was there to see little Alf Walker. They knew he had had two important visitors the day before, both senior policemen, all behind closed doors. It wouldn't do Alf's chances of survival much good if he started getting noticed. Not that he was likely to remain inside for much longer after the previous day. The police loved an informant, especially one with the names of the men who stole over two and a half million quid.

Jack studied the scruffy sight that presented itself opposite, biting nervously at its fingernails. He ought to be showing his boss more respect than that, given the opportunity that had been thrust upon him. Lavery sighed, and Walker looked up at them both, before settling on the man that really mattered.

'Good morning, Alf. Did you sleep well?' Lavery asked.

'So, so.' Walker had massive bags under his eyes. No doubt up all night tossing and turning over what he had spilt to the police the day before.

'Did you have any visitors yesterday, Alf?'

'Yeah.' Walker closed his eyes, appeared to be trying to will Lavery to disappear. He was going nowhere for now.

'Was it Hatherill?'

'Yeah.'

'Just Hatherill?'

'Nah. Someone else as well. Forget his name.'

'Do you? You'd forget something that important, would you?' The menace was evident, despite a soft tone in Lavery's voice. With Tommy you watched, listened and learned.

Walker struggled to make eye contact with Lavery, and Jack willed him to face his boss. Tommy had more respect for those who at least fronted up. It might not mean they lived any longer, or avoided injury, but they were respected nonetheless.

'Miller or something like that.'

'Millen?'

'Yeah, that was it.'

Lavery nodded to himself. The two big boys were there then, that was handy. Tommy knew a lot of senior people, and boasted he had dropped a nugget of information in Hatherill's Club. The vain fool had taken the bait. Attacking the suspect list from two ends was a sensible plan.

'Their names don't matter, Alf.' Lavery cleared his throat. The visitor sitting to their right looked round, stared into Lavery's eyes, then turned away again. Tommy lowered his voice another notch. 'What matters, Alf, what matters very much to me, is what you told them.' Lavery lit a cigarette and offered one to the prisoner, who refused. Jack smoked his own rollies and Lavery never bothered with him any more. Armstrong decided to busy himself with his tobacco. His boss had asked him to come along, but keep quiet. Simply playing the role of chauffeur to Tommy was perfectly acceptable, especially after the recent hectic days.

'I did what you asked,' Walker said, nervously.

'Did you? Tell me what you told 'em.'

'I told 'em what you wanted me to say.'

'I'm sure you did that.'

'I did. Truthfully.' Walker still struggled to make eye contact, stared at Jack instead. He indicated with his eyes that Alf should look back at Tommy immediately.

'Good.'

Lavery flicked ash into a small pot fixed to the table, and studied the little man. Jack was the one who had given him the relatively simple task the week before, with the knowledge that what he was providing the police would be looked upon extremely favourably, particularly in light of the sentence stretching out in front of him. Ten years for robbery, a bungled wages snatch in Reading. Walker was known in London criminal circles, and was familiar to the Flying Squad. Lavery also revealed that he was desperate to get out, because his wife was expecting their fourth child. Only sent down five weeks before, he was searching for a way to reduce the stretch he would serve, but at the same time would not wish to be seen as a grass. Here was a man who would name names, but only to the most senior of officers. Millen and Hatherill showing up in secret yesterday to interrogate the informant was the ideal result.

'Now, tell me what they asked you. And what you told them. Precisely.' Lavery accentuated the last word ruthlessly. Walker was bound to understand what was needed of him.

'Nobody knows I told 'em.'

'Good. Tell me what they asked you,' Lavery asked patiently.

'I did what you asked. Gave 'em nicknames, names of girlfriends, like he told me,' Walker stabbed a shaky finger in Jack's direction. 'Then in the end, I said their names.'

'Which ones did you name? Tell me exactly what you said.'

'The ones you said.' Walker pointed again at Jack, who wanted to snap the bloody thing off. The prisoner leant forward slightly, and Lavery moved in to meet him, so that their faces were inches apart. Armstrong could smell the fear from where he sat. 'Goody. Edwards. Reynolds. James.'

'Any more?' Tommy asked, curling his fists into a ball. Jack knew this was never a good sign.

Walker appeared to be thinking, trying to dredge up more

names from his memory. 'Nah. Yeah. Yeah, Charlie Wilson. That was all I gave 'em.'

Jack studied what looked like shame in the face of Alf Walker. See how easy it was to grass? Anyone could do it, if you were persuasive enough. Breaking his brother's arm, and bringing a photograph of it with him the last time he visited, also helped to provide focus.

'Those were all the names you gave, yeah?'

'Yeah.'

'You didn't mention Jimmy White, then? Or Bob Welch?' The man hesitated, a look of horror across his face.

'Ah,' he offered, his face reddening. 'Sorry, I...' Walker looked like he was going to cry.

Lavery rocked back in his chair. Walker had been instructed to deliver seven names, and managed five. Jack supposed that a week was a long time inside, stewing on the betrayal he was supposed to carry out. Maybe fear had made him forget the other two.

'You bastard,' Lavery spat with conviction, staring at the little man. 'You fuckin' bastard.'

Walker covered his face with his hands, crying. Not in here please, thought Jack, don't draw attention to us. Imagine if they found out who this visitor really was.

'Sorry,' was all Walker offered, and his eyes turned now to the floor, afraid to look up. Would Lavery launch an attack on Walker for failing to do as he was told? Not in there. When he got out, he would be fair game. There was a reputation to keep up.

'Did they seem happy when you told 'em those names?' Lavery asked, still looking annoyed. Walker nodded. 'And you were evasive, weren't you? You didn't offer 'em up straight away, like he said?' Jack felt his boss's eyes piercing his skull, as his faced turned towards him.

'That's what I told him to do, Tommy,' Armstrong pleaded. Lavery had to believe him. The senior policemen had to believe it was a genuine tip-off, and that it wasn't being given too easily. Walker came to Jack's aid.

'I took ages to tell 'em. They was getting really pissed off with me, were just about to leave. It was almost lock up time and we was in the chief warden's office, just me and them. The warden was having kittens.' Walker forced a smile. Lavery lost his.

'Did the warden hear any of this?'

'Nah, it was just me and them, in his office. He was outside.'

'Well, we'll see how this goes. I'm sure your brother will be fine now, he's receiving good medical attention.'

'Thank you.'

Jack thought about the man on the other side of the table. He should be thankful. Lavery was offering this insignificant failure of a thief a chance to get time off of his sentence, just for spilling names to the police. He should be on his hands and knees in gratitude. His side knew there were other sources for names, but Walker wasn't to know it.

'We won't be seeing you again. Obviously, this meeting never happened, you've never met us before. You're a sensible lad, aren't you, Alf?' Walker made no reply, save for a nod of the head. 'You know what to do now. Keep your head down, and say nothing more. Don't give 'em anything else if they come back, you understand?'

'I understand.'

'Forget everything you told 'em.'

'What if they ask me again? Ask me more questions?'

'I just told you. Jesus wept,' Lavery swore. 'Look, they won't.'

Walker looked confused, and Tommy didn't seem to have the energy to bother explaining how insignificant a piece of the jigsaw he was. Lavery smiled and rose from his chair. The meeting was over.

'Come on, Jack. We've got work to do.'

Armstrong stood up as Lavery indicated to the guard that he needed to leave. Tommy had been furious when he heard about part of the Irishman's money escaping over the water. It was a good job he was on the end of a telephone line at the time. He ranted on about cheating and swindling Paddies, not really seeing the irony of what he was saying. Jack simply kept quiet and took the anger. By the time he met up with the boss that morning, it seemed to have been forgotten about.

When they reached the car, Lavery had calmed down, and focused on practical matters.

'We've got to start on them. We know where they are, where they'll hide things.'

'Most of 'em, yeah.' Jack thought back to the conversations he and Mickey had with the gang members about their plans after the robbery, whilst they were idling time away, waiting. Some played their cards close to their chest, but what information they managed to glean suggested similar strategies. Bury it, and go into hiding.

'Well, you two better get your skates on. Oh, and George needs your help.'

'Parlane?' Jack tried to hide the dread in his voice.

'Yeah. Says he's had some luck already.' Lavery handed Jack a telephone number. 'Give him a call, will ya?'

'Sure. You know Mickey and me's got a little job to do?'

'What's that?'

'Burning down the farm.'

'I wouldn't bother, Jack. They paying you?'

'Yeah.'

Lavery sighed and paused for a moment. 'Well don't get caught. I need you. You got more important things to do for me. You do that in your own time, okay?'

'Sure, Tommy.'

It was fifteen grand each, they would find the time. Mickey was very insistent that they have a play with a box of matches.

'Right. Come on. I want you to take me to Barnes.'

'Where?'

'It's in West London. I've got someone to look up. You can drop me off, and go and see George after that.'

Jack pondered Lavery's motivation once again. He was already rich, could draw upon financial resource and muscle for pretty much anything he wanted. Now he was after the robbers' money as well as his own cut. When would he stop? When would he have enough? He would pursue each and every one of the gang and their money, he was sure of it. The poor bastards, it was hard not to feel a degree of sympathy for the robbers. He and Mickey did share a massive job with them after all. They were scattering, and the police were already poised to pounce, names in their sweaty, bent palms. It would be an interesting game to watch from the safety of the touchline.

30

Joe Watson was feeling lucky. He was one of the first fifteen officers drafted into the Robbery Squad, all gathered for an initial briefing. He wondered if Lavery's tentacles even reached into New Scotland Yard, to ensure he was on the team. Frank Williams was going to be his lead officer, directing them under Detective Superintendent Tommy Butler, largely because he knew a number of faces in London. Both Williams and Butler would be very familiar with the names on the list that was indelibly imprinted in his head.

Ten minutes after the team meeting dispersed, Watson sat down with Williams in his superior's cramped office, on the premise that he had prime information about suspects. Joe had had enough of waiting around. As soon as he leaked the names and got the job done, he would be out of Lavery's clutches.

Only those of a certain rank got their own office spaces, and even these were small. In truth, Williams spent very little of his time cooped up in the room, choosing to be out and about in the pubs and clubs, closer to the action and the criminals. Joe felt it was time to drop the names.

'I've got a few good suspects for the robbery.'

'Oh, have you?' Williams leant forward at his desk, pushing papers about, searching for something, but not looking up.

'Yeah, I have. A few names.'

Williams deigned to raise his gaze up this time. 'Go on then, we can compare notes.'

Watson swallowed. Given his own contacts, Frank was bound to have drawn up a list already. He wondered how closely they would match and how many of his own were genuinely involved. It wasn't unknown for grasses to land people in it that they simply had a grudge against. Maybe that was all Lavery was up to, lining up men guilty of past crimes against the Beast. He tried to appear nonchalant at the start of his roll call.

'Okay. I assume you're thinking of the same names, right? Goody, Edwards, James, Reynolds, Wilson?'

'Of course.' Williams returned to rooting about under piles of paper on his desk.

'I picked up a few more.'

Joe needed to be central to such a huge case as this, Lavery had made that abundantly clear. Everything else was being dropped for the time being, but when the dust settled he needed to still be in on the investigation, rather than merely gathering intelligence. According to Williams, although Butler didn't mention it in their briefing, there was a lot of pressure coming down from Government as well as the GPO, whose money it was that got stolen.

'Go on. Aha!' Williams pulled a newspaper out from under the paperwork, much of which had now fallen to the floor, and placed it on the desk. He looked at the front page. 'Robbed!' screamed the headline. You could always rely on *The Daily Mail* to sum things up concisely. Watson tried to re-focus.

'Well, I have some information there was another crew involved, along with that London mob. Bob Welch, Roger Cordrey and Tommy Wisbey.' He was throwing more names out there, ignoring the instruction to filter them gradually.

Williams stared at Watson, unnerving him. Had he laid out too many, too soon? He swallowed, then realised he should be looking like he had been really clever. He tried to smile, and realised that his boss was beaming.

'Now then, they've been busy on the trains before, haven't they? I was wondering about Welch and Wisbey,' Williams nodded to himself. 'How good is this information you've got, Watson?'

'Oh, very strong.'

'And where's it coming from?' Williams asked. Did he know about Lavery too? Surely someone as long in the tooth as Frank Williams wouldn't be as weak as me, thought Joe.

'Just a good source, Guv.'

Williams nodded, and didn't pursue it for the time being. Joe needed to be on his guard, his boss would probably set a trap for him, to reveal why he knew so much, so soon. Frank returned to his pipe, a continual source of inspiration, as if he was a modern day Sherlock Holmes. If Joe's boss considered these names to be legit, that would help add weight.

'Come on, who is it?'

'Sir, you know I can't tell you, not just yet. Maybe later.' Never, more like.

'Really? Is it anyone I know?'

Maybe he was just trying to steal a source. The more Joe thought about it, it didn't feel like he was doing anything wrong. Just as with any other crime, they tapped people for information on the perpetrators. The only difference here was that he had the names of the thieves before it took place, without even knowing what the job was. They were looking at the same end result though, if they caught the robbers, so why worry?

'I don't think it is, no. I've known him a little while, Guv.' Watson was sticking to the truth as much as he could, had no choice but to keep his informant's identity quiet if he wanted to carry on breathing. He decided to widen the focus. 'I heard a few contradictory things, but this was pretty solid information. Came from a bloke who claims to have been offered the job, but turned it down.'

'Every criminal in London claims to have been offered this job,' Williams muttered. Genuine enquiries were showing this to be the case, they had come across a few faces saying the same thing, but if you believed everyone, half of London was in on this robbery from the start.

'How does he know all these other names? The South Coast Raiders?' This was a common term for Wisbey, Welch et al.

'I dunno. But he seems certain. Said he asked who else was in on it, just to check if it was a real job, not a fit up, you know.'

'As if we'd do that,' Williams chuckled, puffing away. He nodded some more, then played an imaginary tennis shot over his desk, making Watson jump back. 'Maybe your source wants to land somebody in it?'

'I suppose that's always possible,' Watson replied. Stay calm, and don't give anything away, he told himself. His boss seemed to think that this was genuine. 'And there's a couple more.' The cascading of names was turning into a random process.

'Oh, go on?' He really had Williams's attention now. Time to lob a few hand grenades in while he had the chance.

'How about Jimmy White and John Daly?'

'Jimmy White?' His boss did look surprised by that one. 'Thought he'd retired.'

'Maybe he has now,' Watson replied.

'Daly makes sense, if Reynolds is in on it. Their wives are sisters.' Watson nodded dumbly, and then remembered unearthing the connection when he was doing research for Lavery. He was bluffing, reading off a series of words that were hand-written into *The Daily Telegraph* crossword weeks before.

'Jimmy White was definitely a part of it, so he says.'

Williams shook his head, then smiled. 'I'm not sure, petty thieves, some of these names, Watson. Let's leave White out of this for now, shall we? He's got no connection to the others. We can keep that one to ourselves, can't we?'

'Of course, Guv.' Joe wondered how much Frank might already know, and why he objected to White being in the frame. 'I suppose it is a large gang, they're not all going to be master criminals, are they?'

'I guess not, no.' Williams pulled at his pipe and spent the next two minutes carefully re-filling and lighting it. Watson stood impassively, not knowing what to do next. Smoke billowed around the musky office, rising in circles over Joe's head, raising the tension in his mind. Was his boss going to buy all this?

'That is pretty good information you've got there, Watson. Most of it adds up. Can you draw up a list for me, a proper one, and we can shove it under the noses of COC11, see what they think? They can at least give us a load of addresses.' Williams continued to puff away. 'But let's keep this between us for now, okay?'

'Of course, Guv.'

'Good. By all accounts it was a large gang.' Williams stared at Joe. 'I want to ensure we don't go charging around until we're ready. I'm sure Uncle George will be happy if we've made early progress.' Even a relative newcomer to the team, such as Watson, knew he was referring to the big man, the Commander of C Division, George Hatherill.

Frank Williams rose from his desk and poked his head outside of his door. 'Tommy?' he shouted. Seconds later, Butler entered the room, dressed in a creased suit. He looked like he had slept in it, even though he arrived at the office less than two hours before. What he lacked in elegance, he more than made up for with his wits and determination as a copper. His presence made Watson doubly nervous. Would the Grey Fox see through his list, and guess the original source? Butler was a legend in the force, a workaholic, and a forceful example to everyone. His list of solved cases was long and heralded, ranging back to just after the war. As of that morning it had become official. Butler was going to head up the Robbery Squad, who were taking over the investigation from those stiffs out in Buckinghamshire. This made sense, because all the villains in the frame were from London. Joe almost felt sorry for the provincial boys, with no resources at their disposal.

'Chief. Watson here has been working hard on our sources. Between us, we've got a good list of suspects.' Williams winked at Joe.

'That was quick.' Butler's eyes flashed with interest.

'We've been working the streets since Friday,' Williams saved Joe by talking to Butler. 'There's a lot of interest out there in this robbery.' Joe felt that if he spoke his voice would fail him, and he would sound like a pimply schoolboy.

'I wasn't expecting a list of suspects until tonight, that's very good.' Butler's eyes twinkled mischievously. 'Who you got?'

Williams continued the conversation with Butler, Watson happy to melt into the background.

'The usual ones you might guess. Edwards, Reynolds, James, Goody.' Butler nodded. Doubtless with his knowledge of London criminals he might have worked them out. Williams pressed on. 'We don't think there's anyone from the big firms in on it, least word is they're not.'

'But who'd grass them up?' Butler said, smiling. Joe hadn't considered this, but the Grey Fox clearly had. Nobody would put a Richardson or a Kray, or any of their important lieutenants, in the frame for anything.

'True. Maybe they're behind it, but weren't there.'

'We got tails on them all the time. If they'd been brewing this one up, we'd have known, wouldn't we?' Butler asked.

'I'd like to think so, yeah. Certainly there's no real link from this list of names to the Krays.'

'What about Foreman?' Butler threw in another name that fitted the bill for this type of job. Freddie was big, brash, and loved money. Tommy Lavery hadn't mentioned his name.

'He's a maybe,' said Williams. 'Edwards knows him from way back. Wisbey does as well.'

'Tommy Wisbey?' Butler asked.

'Yeah. We got him in the frame for this.'

'Hmm. Well, it would be good to pull Freddie in,' Butler smiled.

'There's a few we'd like to bring in,' Williams said. Watson wondered exactly which criminals they meant, because he had no idea. 'Apparently Foreman's already sitting on a fortune, the word goes,' Frank said.

'Anyone else I should know about?' Butler asked.

Williams turned to Joe. 'Watson. Anyone else of major class?'

'Not really. Lots of small timers, we think, from what we've heard,' he added, still trying to make the source look as genuine as possible. He could feel the sweat building. Strange how, when a figure like Butler got up close, the pressure built. 'Bob Welch, Wisbey, Charlie Wilson.'

'Not that bastard? Jesus, what a mixed bunch.' Butler shook his head. 'Wonder who pulled this crew together?' he thought out loud. It was a good question to ask, and if he hadn't been privy to his own particular brand of inside information, it would have been one Watson should have considered. The answer must have been Tommy Lavery.

'We're going to look into all of them,' announced Williams.

'Good. Millen and Hatherill want to see us at twelve. Got something they want us to hear, apparently...' Butler paused to look at the heavens. 'So, I'd like you to be there too. Don't be late, Frank.'

'I won't.'

A knock on the door broke the tension, and one of the new team, DS Slipper, pulled Butler from the meeting.

'See you later,' Butler said as he exited. Williams closed the door after him.

'He seems pleased,' Frank said, and Joe wondered if he was being sarcastic, but couldn't see any signs of mirth in his face. Joe was providing the key pieces of intelligence so far, and felt uneasy about it.

'What about the scene of the crime?' Watson asked. Every criminal left evidence behind, however small, and if he could shift attention on to something else, he might be able to relax.

'Ah, yes, well, I'll tell you this, Watson, seeing as you're here now. There was a bit of a balls up.' Joe raised his eyebrows. 'Seems the engine and the carriages were shunted about a bit. They've brought the carriages back to Buckinghamshire now, but they've been all over the place. COC3 will be having a look at them this week, but I don't think we'll get much. Nothing we could use as evidence anyway.'

Williams looked forlorn. Joe pondered what kept this man going. When he got to fifty, he hoped to be sitting on a beach somewhere, rather than in the dungeons of New Scotland Yard.

All they really had so far was his list of suspects. Pinning the names might be tough if there were no prints and none of them got caught red-handed with the money. In the meeting he had sat through earlier they were told that only a very small number of the bills were traceable. Much of it was going to be destroyed, and that wasn't going to help in tracking down the gang. Maybe Lavery would feed him more in the days ahead, perhaps even the whereabouts of the thieves.

'Right, come on, Watson, let's get digging. Write out the names for me, and I'll take them over to Parish in COC11, see what they've got to tell us. We'll keep this under our hats, until Parish comes back to us. Well done, lad, well done.'

Watson beamed what he hoped was a smile of pride. Inside, he knew he owed everything to a criminal who still had his bollocks in his fat, greedy fist. He was going to give up figuring out Lavery's motives, would focus his mind on tracking down the men on his deadly list. That way he might emerge on the other side of the investigation with his credibility intact, his first step to becoming a legitimate police officer again.

31

12th August 1963: Leatherslade Farm, Oxfordshire

'I've fuckin' had enough waiting about.'

Mickey Griffin didn't have many virtues, and patience was certainly never going to be one of them. Jack Armstrong scratched his head and continued to wonder. They were supposed to be gone by now, but you would never know judging by the state of the farm. Nothing appeared to have changed since they had left a few days earlier; it certainly looked like the vehicles were still parked up. If the police had found the place by now it would have been cordoned off, so it was probably all clear. In this game, experience and a nose for trouble had taught him a few nasty lessons. They had to pick their moment to come out into the open. They were sitting in the bushes, a couple of hundred yards away from the farmhouse, and he was the one observing through the binoculars. Griffin was just moaning and shuffling about in the undergrowth. Unless he had a cosh or a gun in his hand, his contribution was usually minimal.

Jack was tempted to tell his accomplice to 'just wait another five minutes,' but he was also getting fed up with hanging around. Lavery was on his back about other tasks that needed to be carried out, including meeting up with George Parlane.

'Come on. Let's go take a look.'

'About fuckin' time,' was all Griffin had to offer, and he followed in Armstrong's tracks as they strode across a field up to the walled garden. The farmhouse was down in a small dip, and as they approached it, there were no signs of life.

'They've fucked off, ain't they?' Griffin retorted. Armstrong had to agree with his powers of analysis for once.

'Let's check the vehicles first,' Jack instructed.

They walked over to the largest outbuilding, where the Army truck was still parked up. Both men wore gloves, as befitted professionals. Armstrong smiled, thinking about the number of times he saw members of this so-called expert gang of thieves walking around without them on. The most laughable was the getaway driver who thought he could drive the train, Roy James. He didn't seem to be bothered about taking precautions, even fed a stray cat a saucer of milk with his gloves off. It was their necks they were risking, not his.

'Go and look at the Land Rovers, will you?' Armstrong ordered Griffin as he headed for the farmhouse. Because he was the brains, he got to be the 'boss' most of the time. Griffin didn't seem to mind, just got on with the job, and went over to the nearest shed to take a look. The lorry was padlocked up, and they needed to locate their payment before they went any further.

They had returned as a result of a special request from Brian Field. Thirty grand was waiting for them in either the kitchen stove or the pantry, according to the clerk. Field panicked a little when Armstrong suggested burning the place down. That would be quicker, would mean there was nothing to clean. They were also supposed to take the vehicles away, and dump them. Griffin was all for driving the Land Rovers into a river, but this felt a little clumsy.

Jack had moved to the farmhouse when his partner wandered into the kitchen, with a bemused look on his face. Not that this was a particularly unusual sight.

'Jack, we got a problem.' You wait until I tell you there's no money in the stove, Armstrong thought.

'What's that?' There might be good money for them personally in this job, if they could find it, but complications were something he could do without.

'They're fuckin' locked!'

'What?'

'Locked up. The Landies, the sheds they're in, they're padlocked.'

'What?'

'Are you deaf or something? They're both padlocked, and fuck knows where the keys are.'

'Jesus wept,' cursed Armstrong. This gang would be the death of him. Why would they ask he and Mickey to return to take the vehicles away, and then lock them up?

Ten minutes of fruitless searching in the farmhouse followed; sleeping bags and other rubbish left behind being tossed about. What a bunch of idiots. Armstrong considered whether they were being set up. If they were, he'd hunt down every single one of the gang, even if it were in his old age, and kill them.

Then Jack threw his bombshell at Griffin, who hadn't even picked up on the lack of money yet. 'And guess what else?' Armstrong asked, grimacing because Griffin already had a face like thunder.

'What now?'

'The stove. There's nothing in it. Or the pantry.'

'You what?'

'It's empty. Nothing.'

'But that's our cut for cleaning this place up.'

'I know.'

'You checked the kitchen?'

'What the hell d'you think I was doing while you was pissing about outside?' Armstrong shouted, staring Griffin down. It wouldn't help to argue; not now there was no reason to hang about at the farm any more. 'Let's look in the cellar. Maybe they put it down there.'

A quick visit down the stone steps revealed nothing but potatoes and hundreds of empty mailbags. No thirty grand. Armstrong felt a wave of disgust pour over him. Those bastards had fucked off with their money, still hoping they would come back and clean up afterwards. What did they take them for?

'No money, no clean up,' he announced.

'Too right. I wonder who did it? I bet it was that fucker Wilson, bet it was him,' Griffin speculated.

'It don't matter who it was, there's nothing here for us. The bastards. You wait 'til I tell Tommy,' Armstrong seethed.

'Maybe they locked it up in one of the Land Rovers?'

'Well, why the fuck would they do that? What, just to piss us off, or something?' Armstrong wondered at the sheer stupidity of Griffin.

'Well, I don't know. You tell me where it is.'

'Let's check the garden, and the garage where the truck is, one more time.'

'The garden?' Mickey looked like he had forgotten there was one.

'Yeah, you remember, one of 'em was digging an hole, wasn't he?'

'I'm not digging up any holes.'

'You want your money?'

'Fuck's sake, yeah, but Jesus, I'm fed up with this.'

Armstrong held his hand up, thinking he could hear a noise. It sounded like it was coming from the track that led down to the main road. They walked out of the kitchen, and peered around the corner of the house, up the lane. A small tractor was lurching its way towards them.

'Who the fuck is that?' Griffin whispered, as they ducked back behind the side of the house.

'Jesus, I don't bloody know,' Armstrong rebutted, taking another peek. 'It looks like a nosey bastard on a tractor.'

'What do we do?'

'Hide. And lock the back door, take the key with us.' It was ridiculous. The gang had padlocked the Land Rovers in the two garages out back, and left the door to the house unlocked, with a key on the inside. It was like a guidebook on how to screw up a hideout. Armstrong was determined to avoid getting caught, just because of their stupidity.

179

Griffin turned the key, locking the farmhouse, and placed it in his pocket. They both scrambled across the field to the trees where they had been hiding earlier. There was plenty of time; they could still hear the tractor plodding its way up the track as they ducked into the undergrowth. After what seemed like an age, a man dressed like a scarecrow emerged outside the kitchen entrance. He looked like a country local. If it was the police in disguise, it was clever. The man walked around and tried the back door, shouting, 'hello' a few times. He then took a quick look at the large outbuilding where the truck was parked, and disappeared out of their view. He must have gone to look at the sheds.

Whoever this person was, undercover police or just a nosey bastard, there was no way they were returning to the farm to finish off any cleaning up. Or burning it down. No money meant no work, as far as Jack was concerned. Loyalties counted for nothing. If the rest of the gang didn't wear gloves and tidy up after themselves, that was their problem. The visitor was bound to report the place to the police, and they could be visiting the farm very soon. Screw them, thought Armstrong. One of the gang took off with their pay for the clean up, or simply lost it, and they were going to get what they deserved. He knew nobody could put him together with a gang of London thieves. Lavery had plenty of work for him in the next couple of weeks, maybe longer. 'Retrieval services' he called it. Maybe the opportunity would come to discover who took off with their thirty grand at the same time. They could pay a few personal visits and undertake specialised interviewing of their own. Whoever took it had it coming, sooner or later.

32

'I've got a few names for you,' Commander Hatherill announced. Ernie Millen was sitting alongside him in Hatherill's office, looking particularly smug. Frank Williams and Tommy Butler, the two most senior officers appointed to the Robbery Squad, faced them. Hatherill looked excited, and hinted that he was going to provide some significant help in the investigation. Unless they had just been interviewing the Krays, Frank doubted they could be ahead of his team already.

'That's good news,' Butler said, sharing a glance with Williams. 'Who you got, Sir?' Frank looked across the table at the most senior figures in New Scotland Yard. They were now seen as suits, their aversion to roughing it among the criminal class was well known.

'We met up with an informant two days ago.'

'Oh, that's good,' said Butler. 'Who? Where?' This was exactly what Frank wanted to ask. How on earth could those two get access to sources that might provide information on this job? Millen sat smiling while Hatherill continued.

'I came across a piece of information at my Club, in St James's Square.' Frank resisted the temptation to look at Butler. Those two lived in a different world.

'I see,' said Butler. Williams admired his subtlety, his ability to avoid diving in.

'This information led us to believe that an informant was

181

willing to talk. But only to men of the highest rank,' Hatherill added. The pair across the table looked like they were engaged in a manic grinning contest. Frank wondered where this connection, with an alleged informant, really came from. He would bet his life someone had been lifting their legs.

'This source is reliable, and we can't tell you this informant's name.'

Frank knew Hatherill had travelled up North on the Saturday, because his driver told him he wasn't required for the day, annoyed that they had used a regular taxi firm. He wondered who the informant might be. Jack Squires was in Durham prison, as was Eddie Blackburn. But he struggled to see how they would know anything. They had been inside for well over a year each. Mickey Ball knew some of the names that Watson had provided, but he went down too long ago. Hatherill carried on, as Frank racked his brain for someone who might fit the bill.

'It took a while to get the information out of our man, but we think we have a few names for you.' Butler and Williams shared a look. They had to humour their senior officers. Go on then, give us a load of old nonsense you've just made up, just to look like you've still got your fingers on the pulse, Frank thought. Hatherill reeled off a short list, consulting a piece of paper in front of him.

'We've got Ronald Edwards. We've got Bruce Reynolds. Charles Wilson.' He stopped to look up and check the faces of the two men sitting opposite. Williams tried to remain impassive. Joe Watson's list threw up the same names, and he had heard whispers in the underworld about Edwards and Reynolds. Hatherill continued. 'Roy James and Gordon Goody.'

Frank Williams knew every criminal in London, and wasn't going to bring up their list yet, not in this company. The overlaps were interesting, but this was nothing new. Millen and Hatherill had simply been wasting police time and money travelling north.

'That's very interesting,' Tommy Butler began. Trust his immediate boss to handle the situation better than him.

'Yes, I suppose it is,' Millen added guardedly. 'Have you been digging as well?'

'Yes, we have,' Butler replied. 'Those names sound like good ones, they mirror the ones we're picking up.'

'Well, that's good, isn't it?' Millen asked, looking at Hatherill, who smiled in reply. The pair looked very pleased with themselves, playing at being proper detectives again.

'Oh yes, of course it is,' Butler said. 'We're looking at a gang of at least a dozen men, judging by the statements taken from the witnesses at the scene.'

Millen and Hatherill didn't look deflated at the thought they had only fingered less than half of the gang.

Millen switched to another subject. 'The thing is, we are receiving considerable pressure already to make arrests.' Frank wondered why they were in a meeting if that was the case.

'I understand,' Butler said diplomatically. Williams studied his boss, who was doing all the talking with the senior brass. He looked calm, and sitting back suited him fine. These types of meetings normally made him uncomfortable. They were wasting time sitting about in New Scotland Yard when they should have been out there looking for suspects, hitting the pubs and clubs and asking questions.

'So, how far have you got?' Millen's question sounded like an accusation. The Robbery Squad had only been in existence for three hours, what the hell did they expect?

'We have a good list of suspects, and a few of them are on your list, Sir.' Butler ignored Millen's implication of inactivity. The two men opposite nodded. 'Thing is, it looks like a combination of groups who've come together. We have a lot of linked names.' He hesitated.

'Go on,' said Millen.

'Well, there's not much evidence from the crime scene to date,' Butler confessed. Frank knew the Chief wouldn't reveal why.

'Not much?'

'No. Buckinghamshire CID said there was nothing at the scene. We have a team of three officers out there now, working with them. But we need more men,' Butler added.

'We need to throw every man we can, every resource we need into this,' said Hatherill. 'It's high profile.' Millen nodded in agreement at the Commander. 'And there's that thirty minute clue, isn't there?' Hatherill added.

'Yes, there is. Bucks CID are co-ordinating searches at the moment, looking for a hideout.'

'And have they found anything yet?'

'Not yet, Sir, no.'

'Tommy, you will keep us posted on daily progress?' Hatherill asked.

'Of course we will, Sir.' Frank tried to suppress a smile as Butler responded. He was notorious for just ploughing ahead with cases, even working alone into the night. This often led to those under him, and more often his superiors, not knowing the full picture.

'Good, well, we're done here. Good luck, Tommy,' the Commander said as he wrapped things up.

Frank and the Grey Fox left quickly, and it was over a minute before they felt they were out of range of their superior officers. Standing in a corridor of New Scotland Yard, Butler released the pressure that had been building in Hatherill's office.

'What a pair of idiots. If they think we're going to tell them everything, they're going to be waiting a long time,' he laughed. 'Let's get out there hassling those names, see if any have surfaced. If they're missing at the moment, that gives me a good feeling. They might still be lying low.'

Frank agreed. He had no idea how long the robbers planned to stay hidden. He thought about what he would do in their position. Getting into the mind of a criminal was central to catching them. If he had a big share of two and a half million pounds, he would already be out of the country, but he doubted that many of their suspects had the wherewithal to arrange something like that. Many hated setting foot outside of London; must have struggled to leave the smoke even to carry out the job. There was one notable exception. Reynolds. He'd be gone, probably lying on a beach in the South of France already.

33

'You took your fuckin' time. Where the fuck you been?'

George Parlane's greetings were seldom erudite.

'What's the hurry?' Jack replied.

It had been a busy week for Armstrong. Taking part in the biggest robbery the country had ever seen. Chasing a load of Irishmen around Wales after their money. Visiting the nick. Abandoning an attempt to burn down a farm. Ferrying Lavery all over the place. And here he was in the bloody countryside again. At least they were sat outside a pub, even if it was one in the morning.

'Tommy wanted me to bring you in. He says it needs two of us.'

'How come?'

'One to keep watch, one to strip the place.'

'What place?'

'His caravan.'

'Whose caravan?' This was getting him nowhere. 'Look, take me through what you've seen,' Jack pleaded, sighing.

He had worked with Parlane several times before. He could certainly look after himself, was smarter than Mickey Griffin, although that wasn't saying much. Lavery seemed to use him for sneaky tasks like this one. Parlane revealed the job Lavery had given him as they walked from their meeting point, up Box Hill. It was bloody steep and both men struggled with the gradient.

Parlane had been instructed to follow Jimmy White after the

186

robbery. He was of particular interest, apparently, because all the information the bent copper turned up revealed him to be a loner. He hadn't been inside for over five years, and apart from his wife, there was nobody obvious to help him hide his money. That was why Parlane was called in. He took Jack through a potted history of the previous three days, as they climbed the hill in the dark, his torch leading the way. Jack was used to setting the pace with people like Griffin, but Parlane cut out a high tempo. His colleague had broken into White's flat in Clapham, stolen his passport, but found no money. When White eventually showed up, he tailed him to Reigate, where Jimmy and his wife went on a shopping spree. Parlane chuckled as he described the couple being interviewed in the street by a pair of uniformed coppers. Mr and Mrs White apparently drove off without attracting suspicion. The poor saps had no idea they were talking to one of the most wanted men in the country. Jack resisted the temptation to remind Parlane that he was one too.

As they turned a corner, at the top of the steep climb, Parlane drew to a halt. Jack saw a set of locked gates, and shone his own torch at a sign, which read, 'Clovelly Caravan Site'.

'This it?'

'Of course.'

They climbed the gates and leapt down the other side. Jack half expected to hear the sound of a barking dog as they landed, but thankfully nothing approached. Parlane returned to his story, whispering this time. He had been on his own for the past three days. Maybe he was simply desperate to talk to someone.

'I followed them, and they came here. They bought a caravan.'

'Why?'

'I dunno why. Maybe they wanted a holiday home?'

'What, rob millions and plough it all into one of these?' Jack eyed the static caravans around him. It seemed an odd way to take a break from modern life.

'I dunno. Well, thing is, they bought it and then took a load of suitcases and plastic bags inside. Then they drove off, but I'm pretty sure some of the bags and suitcases are still there.'

'You mean he's hidden his money in a bloody caravan?'

'Yeah.'

'What an idiot,' Armstrong laughed softly.

'Yeah.'

'They've not been back?'

'No. I've been hanging around for a few days waiting for help. I reckon it's safe to go in there.'

The caravan wasn't bloody booby trapped, Jack thought. 'Why didn't you just go in and take the money back to Tommy?'

'Ah, I didn't want to get caught. He must have hidden it in there and it might take some finding.'

'In a caravan?' Jack couldn't help but sound incredulous. Where did Lavery get his people?

'In a caravan, yeah,' Parlane repeated.

'Look, which one was it?'

'This one here. Number twenty-three,' Parlane said.

They had stopped outside a white home on metal legs. Jack had never been inside a caravan before. He supposed he was broadening his horizons.

'How do we get in?' he asked, half expecting a stupid answer. He wasn't disappointed.

'Through the door.'

Armstrong tried the handle. It didn't budge. 'Let's try a window.'

The caravan backed on to a group of trees, so they broke in out of sight, through the rear window. Armstrong smashed the glass, then propped it open as they waited for someone to come running. After five minutes he reasoned it was safe to go inside, and pushed the window up far enough so that he could climb in. Parlane sat on the doorstep of the caravan and kept watch.

Jack swung his torch around the interior of the van. It looked incredibly cramped. Who would volunteer to spend time in somewhere like that? There were cupboards all over the place, and he opened everything in a hurry. He was starting to lose patience with both the stupid little holiday home, and Parlane, when he opened up the stove. Something about his recent experience at the farm made him look there. The inside had been removed to leave a hollow storage space, which was filled with a large black bag, and when he shone his light inside he saw bundles of bank notes. Poor Jimmy White. He was going to lose the lot.

Buoyed by his discovery, Jack went back over all the cupboards again. He found a couple of small suitcases laden with money, hidden under a pile of blankets. There was a fair amount, but he thought over a hundred grand would look bigger than that. There had to be more. He shone his torch around the walls. There were tools sat on a shelf by one of the windows. Had White been building a secret compartment to hide the rest?

'Jack. Someone's coming,' Parlane hissed from the other side of the door.

Armstrong abandoned all thought of continuing his search, and threw the bag out of the back window, followed by the two suitcases. He had no idea if Parlane had already legged it or not. Lavery wouldn't forgive him if he left any of this lot behind in the caravan. The fallout from losing part of the Irish money had still not really settled. Tommy was putting up with his presence at the moment, but underneath there was still an undercurrent of anger. He couldn't leave empty handed.

Jack threw himself out of the window; face first, and landed with a thump on the concrete. His head throbbed, and he felt blood as he touched the side of his face. His knees were killing him, the impact ripping his trousers. Pain was irrelevant, he had to get moving, and so he raised himself to a crouch and listened. He thought he could hear a faint rustling in the distance, like something moving. He prayed it wasn't a dog. It sounded like it was going away from him. He looked around on the ground. The plastic bag was missing, but the two suitcases lay in an unruly pile where the trees met the concrete. Parlane had fucked off with the bag and given up on the heaviest items. The bastard.

Armstrong grabbed a suitcase in each hand, and headed into the trees. He stumbled several times in the dark, his legs stinging and reminding him of the fall. All he wanted to do was get away from Jimmy White's caravan as fast as possible. He stopped at a large tree to catch his breath, and listened for the sound of barking, frozen to the spot. Armstrong had a reputation for violence, but vicious dogs were his greatest fear. He realised there was no crazed animal out there after him, and relaxed. Human beings were easier to handle. Jack wondered what had really startled Parlane. If it was a wind up, he would kill him.

He slowly picked his way down the hill after waiting in the trees for a good twenty minutes. It was slow progress, because he had lost his torch during the escape. Jack found Parlane sitting in his car outside the pub, at the bottom of Box Hill, where they met earlier. Armstrong dropped his suitcases into Parlane's boot, where they joined the black bag. At least he hadn't left that behind. As he opened the door, he saw Parlane casually lighting up.

'Where the fuck you been?' Parlane laughed.

'Don't start that again,' Jack replied, and sank into the passenger seat.

34

'HIDEOUT DISCOVERED.'

Buster Edwards breathlessly dropped the newspaper on to the table as he swung into his seat in the café. All four men stared at the headline that was screaming at them.

'We're nicked,' Roy James whispered.

'Fuck,' Charlie Wilson echoed.

Bruce looked around the empty café. Reynolds, James, Wilson and Edwards were sat in the 'Copper Spoon,' just off Hanger Lane. Bruce had gathered the group to discuss a crucial subject. A series of coded messages had led to this summit of the leaders. The only man missing was Gordon Goody, who they couldn't trace. The clean up of the farm was worrying Bruce, particularly the removal of the mailbags. They had put a lot of effort in to wiping the place down, working deep into that Thursday night. The loose ends still worried him. The vehicles they had already given up as lost; nothing they could do about them.

Bruce wouldn't put it as strongly as Roy, but he had a sinking feeling in the pit of his stomach. Something had gone wrong, and it was out of their hands. He understood the personal concern. He remembered several occasions when Roy took off his gloves. For a few of the group the farm was never going to be discovered, so there were no issues with fingerprints. That was the only explanation he could think of for their lack of caution. The likes of Bruce, Gordon and Jimmy White were painstaking in their care. He felt certain there was going to be no evidence to convict him, should he be questioned, which he had no intention of letting happen.

'I thought Brian Field was sorting it out?' Charlie asked. He looked to be concerned; although he also said there would be none of his dabs lying around.

'He was, but only after our first plan went up in smoke. He was using those two northerners,' Bruce explained.

'Gordon said it was all fixed, money was put aside for them in the kitchen,' Buster added.

'How much?' James asked, sounding desperate.

'I think it was twenty grand, I dunno, Gordy knows for certain.' Bruce had to admit that he couldn't remember exactly what Gordon had said. It was all being sorted out when they decamped to the Fields' house, and he was already well out of the picture by then. He couldn't oversee everything.

'Oh, fuck,' Roy exclaimed.

'I don't think it's necessarily a problem,' said Bruce. 'They were on the job too, remember?' He tried to stay positive. 'They'll have cleaned it up. Besides, we did a pretty good job of it ourselves, didn't we?'

'You reckon we can trust 'em?' Buster asked. Bruce's mind went back to the incident with the guns.

'Yeah,' he replied. Jack Armstrong and Mickey Griffin. He had been thinking about the northerners since the raid. To be fair to them, they definitely pulled their weight on the night. Nobody shifted more mailbags, and their muscle proved to be extremely handy. All they were doing was protecting Tommy Lavery's investment.

'Jesus, I'd go back for twenty grand, even now,' said Roy. Bruce knew he also wanted to wipe the place thoroughly clean one more time.

'The question is,' began Bruce, 'should we go back and check?'

'But, like you said, we cleaned the place top to bottom, didn't we?' said Buster. The image of Edwards wearing an apron and cleaning kitchen cupboards jumped into Bruce's mind, making him smile for the first time in a few days.

'Yeah, we did. But there are the mailbags. They're still there.' Bruce surveyed the faces around the table. Roy looked distraught.

'Unless those boys took 'em away?' Buster said.

'But we got no prints on the bags, we made sure of that, didn't we?' Charlie asked.

Bruce was still thinking about the Land Rovers, because he bought one before the operation. It was under a false name, but he knew the police would come looking for him anyway, after Heathrow.

Buster picked up the newspaper and folded it in half, hiding the headline. 'None of it matters now, does it?' There was no going back to the farm; all they could do was cross their fingers and hope. Or run.

'I wanna do something,' Roy said.

'There's nothing we can do,' Buster interjected. 'The place will be crawling with police. We won't get near it.'

'We're nicked, I told you,' Roy re-iterated, dropping his head into his hands. He looked close to tears. Here was a brilliant driver, a man who might have become World Champion if he only had the financial backing. Now he was reduced to a wreck, just because a local plod had stumbled upon a farm.

'Look, boys. The place is clean, right?' Bruce thought he should try to keep spirits up, but there was little response. 'The farm's clean. The train was clean, or they would have said something by now, right?' If there had been anything left at the scene their names would be out there already.

'Bruce is right. We can't go back there, however tempting it is,' Buster said. 'We've got to lie low. Just look at the shit storm we've created.'

'Brilliant, isn't it?' Charlie chuckled, the first sign of levity in the entire meeting.

Bruce had to admit, they had kicked up a right stink. Everyone was talking about the robbery, the world wanted to know who did it. And here were four of the gang, sitting in broad daylight, the staff in the café none the wiser. He just had a feeling that things wouldn't stay that way for long.

'Look, let's keep the same signals as we have now, but we need to be extra careful.' Everyone agreed with Bruce.

'Shall we arrange a meeting now?' asked Charlie.

'Let's say, if we can wriggle free, we meet up at that garage in Sheen we all know, yeah?' Everyone nodded at Bruce. 'I'll arrange a date.' Gerry Madden, an old acquaintance of Charlie's from way back, owned the place, and they would be guaranteed privacy.

'If we're not in total bloody lock down, yeah,' Charlie commented, pitifully.

Bruce tried to summon up some strength in his troops, maybe for the last time. 'Until then, boys, let's go our own ways. Be careful everyone, yeah?'

35

'Well, that was a right waste of bloody time, wasn't it?' DCI Peter Vibart announced loudly to everyone in the room. There were a few murmurings of agreement, until Tommy Butler begged to differ.

'I don't know. It shows they're on the run. It shows we've got the right names.'

Vibart looked embarrassed, and Frank Williams agreed with Butler. 'Yeah. I think our suspect list is spot on.'

They had called at five addresses that morning, from Shoreditch down to Putney, and the whole team bloody well missed breakfast to take part. Butler and Williams selected the five names they thought were certainties to be hanging around their usual haunts, and be at home. Edwards, Reynolds, Welch, Wisbey and Daly. Not a sight of any of them.

'Can we go through all the other names we have again?' Vibart asked. There were a few on the list that they failed to visit that morning. Joe Watson shuffled uneasily in his seat. The fact that these men weren't at home might mean the names were right and he wasn't being used to lead the Robbery Squad down a series of dead ends. He needed the identities to be right if he was going to emerge from this investigation with any credit. Vibart for one already viewed him with suspicion.

There were eight men gathered in the room, including their

commanding officer, Tommy Butler, as well as his boss Frank Williams. Thirty in all were working the case, Williams said, but this was the group chosen to work on the ground and look for the arrests. A large team from forensics were already down at Leatherslade Farm. Watson wondered just what Lavery had arranged to be found there, because it felt like he was pulling all the strings.

'Before we revisit the names, let's analyse what we found this morning. Or didn't find,' said Williams, eyeing Butler. The Grey Fox had left no doubts over his disappointment at the lack of arrests so far. They had no warrants, or any direct evidence at all when they knocked on the doors at seven in the morning. It had been a fishing expedition, as Butler termed it. Everything stemmed from Joe's suspect list, and they had nothing.

'Yes, let's do that,' Butler agreed.

Vibart spoke up first. 'Wisbey. His wife was at home, but no sign of our friend Tommy for a few days. She was saying nothing. She lets us have a nice look around, too. But nothing.' Vibart stared anxiously at Butler. Everyone knew what would happen to any evidence obtained without a warrant. They were just testing the waters out there.

'They're hardly likely to have piles of stolen money lying around,' Williams responded. Again, this was a fact that everybody in the room knew. 'Okay, what else did we find?'

Watson nearly spoke up, but Slipper beat him to it.

'Reynolds, nothing at all. Even his wife has gone away, according to his neighbours. Daly, the same, that's Reynolds's brother-in-law. Him and his wife weren't home.'

'Sounds like he's right in the frame, then,' Butler remarked. The Grey Fox suspected everybody, no exceptions. They all knew how tenacious he was, and that he would not rest until these men were found. Joe also knew this meant he would be working extremely long hours.

'What about Edwards?' Williams asked.

DS Moore replied. 'The same thing. His missus was also away.'

'It's like they knew we were coming,' Butler shouted. 'Did they know we were coming?'

Silence descended on the packed room. Smoke billowed upwards, escaping from nervous, tired mouths and nostrils. What Butler was suggesting was unthinkable. That one of their own had tipped off the robbers that they were about to be questioned, and their homes searched. Watson surveyed the other faces in the room, hoping that he didn't stand out. Everybody, apart from Frank Williams, appeared worried, but nobody looked as guilty as he felt. His boss moved things on.

'The last one was Bob Welch. That was very interesting, wasn't it, Watson?' Frank said.

Joe jerked into life. 'Yeah, Guv, it was.'

He decided to say no more, allow Williams to tell the extraordinary story. There was no doubt that their attempted questioning was the weirdest.

'Well, come on,' Butler coaxed. Joe stared at Frank Williams, who relented.

'Well, we were at Welch's house, his wife let us in, said he was already out for the day.'

'What time was this?'

'Seven this morning. Anyway she made us a cup of tea, didn't she?' Williams again looked at Joe for confirmation, and he nodded as confidently as he could. 'So, she makes us this cup of tea, and the phone rings.' Six faces focused intently on Williams, as Watson tried to look away. This was going to be embarrassing. Frank was building up to something, however nobody could find out everything that Joe heard.

'She answers it, and says, what did she say? I think it was, "Sorry, we're not planning to have our windows cleaned this week," and Joe here grabs the phone off her before she can say another word, and then hears, what did you hear?'

'I heard a man at the end of the phone say, "Got the message", then the line went dead,' Watson told the rest of the room. At least that part was true.

Butler was quick to interject. 'A code, then?'

'Probably,' Williams said, 'meaning don't come home. Welch has been warned off.'

'They'll all know we've come after them by now,' Butler replied. 'So, was that it?'

'See, that was the interesting thing. We know this sort of code goes on. No, what happened was that ten minutes later, we've had a good look round, and we're all about to leave, when the phone rings again. Joe?'

Watson swallowed. Williams wanted him to carry on with the story. They would get the majority of it. He tried to look as relaxed as possible, betraying the feeling deep in his guts.

'Yeah, he almost seemed to be expecting one of us to answer. He said "hello", and then asked what we were doing at his house. I told him we were looking to ask him a few questions. He asked what about, I said the robbery in Buckinghamshire, the train robbery.' Watson broke off and looked around the room at his fellow Squad officers. He was the only one to have any contact with a suspect so far, let alone anybody he was reliably informed had carried out the raid. It didn't fill him with any pride, or self-belief.

'Go on, Watson, please,' Butler asked. You couldn't deny the Grey Fox.

'Well, he said he would drop in to talk to us, in about an hour.' There were looks of incredulity around the room.

'Really, he said that?' asked Vibart.

'Yeah. Said he would come home and answer us a few questions, so long as we promised to go after that and leave his wife alone.'

'Bless him,' Vibart retorted. A few chuckled.

'I assume he never showed, then?' Butler asked.

Watson fell silent.

'No, of course he never showed,' Williams added. 'I can only think he was hoping to check if we were still there, if it was safe to go home. Maybe he was watching the house.'

The rest of the meeting moved on to discuss the other potential names they had, and known associates of the prime suspects. Williams concluded with an update on the next actions in the investigation. Superintendent Ray and his forensics team were already camped out at the farm, poring over it for evidence. The stolen car squad were at work on the vehicles, trying to track down their history. Maybe that would give them a solid lead for suspects, or simply confirm the ones they already had. The Fraud Squad was also looking into the purchase of the farm. The Yard was all over the case, it seemed like every angle was being covered. Joe Watson sat there with a complete list of suspects in his head, all but a small handful now transcribed on to paper, being carried around in Frank Williams's pocket. Lavery had asked for about half to be held back, but he had thrown some out there in panic. He and his colleagues were after the same result; it was just that he was going about it from a different angle.

There was uproar when Butler finally revealed plans to release names of suspects in the next few days. Apparently this decision had come down from Millen and Hatherill. Everybody on the Squad knew that as soon as they published photographs of known criminals, hoping for the public to spot them, they would go to ground for good. This would be easy for a gang of extremely rich thieves, given the resources they would have available. There was also the issue of whether any resulting trial could be argued to be prejudicial, if the jurors knew who the robbers were supposed to be in advance. There was a reward of over a quarter of a million pounds out there. Somebody would be tempted to grass, whatever the risk. Watson was confident that if the names Lavery supplied were the right ones, and many had been verified through other sources, according to Frank Williams, these men would be found.

What unnerved Joe the most, as the meeting broke up, was the memory of the words of Bob Welch on the telephone. Just before he rang off that morning, he had a goodbye message; one Joe failed to pass on to the team. He was standing at the kitchen table in the house; Williams and Mrs Welch were by the front door. It was a phrase that sent a shiver through him when he heard it. There was no way its use could have been accidental. 'Take courage', Welch said, just before hanging up. The same words that Tommy Lavery, the orchestrator, used less than a month ago, when he was passing on a list of names.

36

15th August 1963: Bournemouth

Roger Cordrey looked blankly back at DCI Fewtrell. Frank Williams studied the scruffy little man who looked to be an unlikely thief. His name had emerged in Watson's list, mostly unnoticed, and certainly attracted few comments from other members of the Squad. He found it remarkable that such a lightweight would be involved on a massive job. He did have previous in stopping trains, a similar modus operandi, but Cordrey was strictly a small-time crook. Fewtrell read aloud from a typed piece of paper in front of him.

'Roger John Cordrey, you are charged that on the eighth of August 1963, at Mentmore, in the County of Buckinghamshire, being concerned together with other persons at present unknown and armed, you did rob Frank Dewhurst of £2,631,784 in money, the property of Her Majesty's Post Master General. Do you have anything to say?'

Cordrey said nothing, just stared at the ceiling. Bill Boal had given a similar response when he was formally charged earlier. Apparently he had plenty to say the previous evening when the local force brought him in, shouting his innocence around the room and banging on tables. He claimed that Cordrey had set him up. Williams and Fewtrell had rushed to Bournemouth as soon as they got word that two men had been apprehended with over a hundred and forty thousand pounds of robbery money. Detective Sergeant

Davies briefed them on the fun and games of the night before. He and his colleagues had discovered their cash in a series of cars and garages dotted about the town, and Cordrey admitted the money was from the train robbery. He had also hidden suitcases in a flat he had just started to rent. Frank had to laugh when he heard the story of where he hid the key. It took a desperate man to hide a Yale up his backside.

Now that he and Fewtrell had showed up, both of the men refused to say a word. No official statements had been taken, but Williams knew they had their first thieves in custody. Boal didn't appear on their list of suspects, but that was hardly a problem. The pair had been caught red-handed, and this meant they had started knocking down the wall, a significant boost to the investigation. Hatherill and Millen would be delighted, because it would keep the politicians off their backs for a while. The arrests gave him the confidence that their intelligence was going to be more fruitful than that which came from the Commander.

Boal particularly fascinated him. He proclaimed his innocence long and hard, according to Davies, but there he was, holding the keys to over a hundred and forty grand. Despite this, he continued to deny knowledge of the money. He was either panicking, or an idiot. Boal was bang to rights. He was an unknown quantity, had no criminal record. Maybe the gang were clever, and had used a mixture of established faces and unknowns. It also made Frank think there could have been as many as twenty men on the job.

Both men were going to be transferred to Aylesbury for the time being. It had been decided by a combination of Butler and Hatherill that the local station would be used to house the thieves as they were apprehended, and act as a holding ground for all the relevant evidence. This arrest gave him more confidence that Maurice Ray and his fingerprint team would turn something up at the hideout. If the gang were as clumsy as this pair, they probably left dabs all over the place. Such a total lack of professionalism would help, all criminals made mistakes. The embarrassment of the hijacked train getting shunted all the way out to Crewe, before it was inspected, could now be swept under the carpet.

Frank was eager to return to London. This would give the team renewed optimism. The capital was his hunting ground, and would be where this gang were from. Tomorrow they would be raiding the Cordrey and Boal homes, as well as the principal faces on the list, and this time they would have warrants. Now Hatherill had given the go-ahead for more manpower from the Met, they could even start staking out the homes of suspects. None of them could stay on the run and invisible forever, all criminals returned to the nest sooner or later. If those two heading for Aylesbury jail were anything to go by, they would have the whole gang banged up inside a week.

37

16th August 1963: Leith Hill, near Dorking

Jack Armstrong's attention was drawn to voices to his right, deeper in the woods. He motioned to Reggie Field to be quiet, and crouched down low, taking up a vantage point behind a cluster of thick bushes. He peered out and saw a man and a woman walking hand in hand, laughing. You cheeky bastard, I know what you're up to, he thought. He saw the couple stop and kiss against a tree. They appeared to be dressed in work clothes, he in a suit, and her in a summer dress. Were they having an affair, about to have it off right there in front of him? He would watch. Why not? It would break up the boredom of the search, already over an hour long at eight o'clock in the morning.

He was on a mission to save the lives of two men. Reggie Field was Brian Field's father, and the solicitor's clerk had panicked. Jack and Tommy Lavery had showed up the evening before at Brian's place in Oxfordshire, to remove him of the burden of his share from the robbery. Because the farm had been discovered, and he could be linked to its purchase, Brian said he had hidden his money in his father's garage. Tommy was inclined to believe him, because Jack had his hands around Brian's throat at the time, and was pushing his face in the direction of an open fire. In something straight out of an Ealing comedy script, it emerged that Field Senior had found it in his garage, and dumped it in the woods, south of Dorking, a place he used to go walking when he was younger.

Jack was getting sick of running around. He, Tommy and Brian Field had travelled directly to Reggie's house in Middlesex, and had to wait for the old man to return home from his attempt to rid his family of the robbery money. Reggie was greeted by the sight of three men sitting in his living room, and one of them (Jack) pointing a gun at his son. Tommy Lavery insisted on Reggie returning to the spot where he left the money. Only the old man struggled to remember exactly where it was in the dark. An hour searching in emerging daylight had also been fruitless, Reggie becoming increasingly panic-stricken, until they spotted the amorous couple.

Jack had made one discovery during their time in the woods, although he struggled to rationalise it at first. He found a small, plastic wallet in the undergrowth, which contained a thick wedge of fivers, wrapped in familiar bands from the robbery. Reggie Field denied all knowledge of it, said they were looking for three suitcases and a green holdall. The thirty grand those backstabbers had cheated out of him and Mickey drifted into Jack's mind. The news that the hideout had been found still made him smile, it would serve them right if they had left any evidence behind. It didn't look like there was more than about five hundred quid in the bundle. Maybe it had fallen out of the holdall somehow. The look on the old man's face at the sight of the wallet seemed to be genuine. He had just dumped the luggage somewhere he thought it would be found as soon as possible, not examined all the contents.

The couple stopped kissing, and they bent down towards the floor. You dirty little devils, Jack thought. Then he froze, as he watched the man hold up a grubby holdall, inspecting it. They were having a conversation, probably about what to do with their find. He couldn't quite make out what they were saying, and watched as they looked briefly about them, before running off in the direction they had come, towards what he thought was the main road. Frankly, he was rather disoriented by this point. The couple must have parked up back there, and slunk into the bushes to screw each other.

He thought about what to do next. It looked like they might have stumbled across Brian Field's share of the takings, cash that Lavery viewed as being his own. He cursed his bad luck. They had wandered around for over an hour since dawn, and that couple had turned up and walked straight into what they were looking for. He watched carefully as the couple disappeared from view, and decided to go over and take a look, telling Reggie again to stay put and out of sight.

Partially hidden underneath a hedge were three suitcases and a large black plastic bag, which, upon inspection, contained the hefty dark green holdall, as well as a briefcase. How the hell did he miss all this? There was no justice. Jack quickly decided there wouldn't be enough time to remove everything; he would have to be selective, especially with the old man in tow. If those two were off to raise the alarm, and God knew the whole country had heard about this bloody train robbery money by now, he wouldn't be able to carry much. He was worried about Reggie doing something stupid and getting them caught.

Tommy would be delighted if he returned with some of the cash; any amount would cheer him up after the past twenty-four hours. He had swung from being happy that everybody was under wraps, and all the pieces were in place, to near hysteria when he found out that the fool Cordrey had been caught red-handed. Then Brian Field panicked and hid his money in his father's garage. Surely this would soften the blow, even if it wasn't the full amount.

He thought he heard more noises back in the direction of the road, and forced himself to stay calm. Jack made his decision. Removing the suitcases would make it obvious he was in the area, and slow them down. That couple might even be on their way back already. The cases would be heavy and impede their escape. He remembered the holdall being held up in the man's hand, so snatched up the briefcase, and ran back to where he had been hiding. Fortunately, Reggie Field was still cowering in a hedge. He pulled the man up forcibly by the arm, and dragged him back in the direction where he thought his car was hidden. The last thing he needed was to be picked up close to money from the train robbery. Lavery knew he would never talk, would swallow any sentence that came his way, but Armstrong was also fully aware he couldn't help his boss's cause sitting in a prison cell.

As he drove off in the direction of Dorking, dark memories of that night in the caravan park nearby flashed through his mind. He passed a police car with sirens blazing, coming the other way. They were going to be salivating again about their newest find. Jack had pocketed the five hundred; he would definitely keep that to himself. He mulled over what to do with the briefcase and its contents. Reggie Field would be too scared to say anything, was hiding flat out on the back seat as he drove. He didn't stop to check how much was in there, would examine it when he was safely out of range, and then decide what to do. Keeping secrets from Tommy Lavery wasn't necessarily wise. However, a member of the gang had cheated he and Griffin, and they deserved more for the work they had put in. It would be a fair reward for all this buggering about.

When they returned to Reggie Field's house, Lavery and Brian Field had disappeared. Tommy would have taken him somewhere safe, waiting for his telephone call. He was glad his boss would be on the other end of the line again. The Beast did not take well to bad news, even if there was nothing Jack personally could have done about it. He did not envy Brian Field. Not only were the law going to be on his case soon, but Tommy would probably have asked Mickey Griffin to take care of him as well.

38

'I've never been to Aylesbury.'

'You sure, Bob?'

Joe Watson watched intently as DCI Vibart continued to press Bob Welch. He had to admit the suspect was stonewalling the questioning with ease. Joe was happy to let his colleague carry on, he was outranked after all, and it was well known that Vibart hated to be interrupted while he was interviewing.

'Very sure, yeah. I've never been to Aylesbury, or no towns near there, neither.'

'Let's go back over this again, one more time.' This was an old trick, and everybody, including Welch, knew it. You kept asking the same question over and over again, looking to trip them up. 'Where were you on the seventh and eighth of August, just over a week ago?' Welch was having none of it, repeating his alibi once more.

'I told you already,' he said, but stayed remarkably calm. 'I met a couple of me mates, Jimmy Kensit, Charlie Lilley. I was with them. Just ask 'em.'

'Oh, we will,' Vibart replied, a little too sarcastically. Watson cringed. Sometimes you had to be more flexible in your approach. How he yearned to get Welch alone, off the record, and ask him if he knew Tommy Lavery. But that was never going to happen.

'Well then, ask 'em.' Welch sat back in his chair, looking

satisfied. The suspect looked at Joe, who stared back. What was he thinking? Would he know it was he who was on the end of the line when he rang his house?

'Tell us again what you did over those two days.'

'We met up at a café in the Elephant. I forget what it was called, but Jimmy goes there a lot, he'll know the name.'

'Go on.'

Welch sighed. 'And then we went to a betting shop in Aldgate. Lenny Rose runs it. He'll tell you I was there all afternoon.'

'And the evening of the seventh?'

'I told you. We went to the dogs, Wimbledon dogs, me and Charlie. Somebody must have seen us there, bound to.' Watson knew there would be faces out there that would vouch for Welch, even if he said he was on the Moon. He was a genial criminal, who could look after himself. His main problem right now was that he was a known associate of Roger Cordrey, who had coughed for involvement in the robbery already. Bob's name was written on the wall of the incident room.

'And then after that?'

'I went home, about nine, ten, something like that.'

'Where to?'

'Home.' Despite the incessant badgering from Vibart, Welch looked relaxed. Watson felt like smacking his colleague one, even if Welch didn't. 'To my wife,' he added, laughing.

Vibart failed to see the funny side, but Welch caught Joe smiling. Was that a shared moment? Was he working for Lavery as well? Watson wondered how deep the connections ran; those words uttered to him over the phone about courage still had him thinking. How on earth would he know who was on the line, or if he was also working for Tommy?

Vibart's next question brought Joe back to the present. 'All night, at home, then?'

'Yeah.'

'And in the morning, what then?'

'I met up with Jimmy and Charlie for breakfast again, same café in Elephant.'

'And you can't remember it, the name of it, even though you went there two days in a row?'

'That's right. Ask Jimmy.'

Vibart fell silent for once. Watson wondered what on earth he was hoping to achieve. Welch was on their suspect list, but apart from that there was no evidence against him. He knew Williams and Butler were placing an awful lot of their hopes on the forensics team. But, for now, there was nothing to nail anybody with, apart from the two clowns Cordrey and Boal who got caught with the money. He beckoned Vibart over to a corner of the room.

'I don't know what else we can do. We got his statement. We know where he lives.'

'It just pisses me off, that's all,' Vibart responded.

'But, what can we do?' Watson looked over at Welch, who was expressionless.

'I suppose so. Fuck it. Look, you write this one up for me, will you?' Vibart whispered. Then, louder, to Welch, 'Okay, if you sign this statement, we'll let you go. But don't think we aren't going to want to talk to you again.'

'That's fine,' Welch replied calmly. He seemed utterly confident there would be nothing on him. Bob's name was on the list, therefore in Joe's mind he must have been in on the robbery. They just had to bide their time.

'You're free to leave,' Vibart announced, after ten minutes of paperwork had been sorted out.

'Mind how you go,' Welch offered, as he left. Joe watched him exit, smiling. He had the air of a man under protection. Joe had resisted the temptation to throw the word 'courage' into the conversation to check for a reaction, even during the small talk at the end of the interview. He was too scared to reveal anything in front of Vibart. He had no idea how high and wide Lavery reached.

★ ★ ★

In the incident room, Frank Williams gathered a few of his team together. Tommy Butler had given a briefing for the next stage; they were going to step up the observation of the suspects on the list. The stolen car unit were due to report the next day, and that would provide them with more concrete evidence to work on.

'I want to keep watch on the main suspects, discretely from a distance, but round the clock.'

Everybody nodded, but Joe knew they were dreading the extra hours this would mean. The team were on Tommy Butler time now. Cigarette smoke rose towards the ceiling, gathering in clouds of renewed hope.

'We didn't come across anybody else today, other than Welch?' Shaking of heads followed Williams's question. There had been another series of raids, and Bob Welch was the only one at home that morning. 'Not even Goody?'

'No,' Watson replied. He had accompanied Vibart to the flat above Goody's salon. 'His mum let us in, she's a nice old dear.'

'I wouldn't trust anything she says,' Williams remarked. 'She knows exactly what her little boy gets up to, mark my words.' She seemed such a sweet thing, made them both a nice cup of tea as well. Vibart had pulled a fast one, said they had a warrant, which they didn't, and she just let them in without checking any paperwork. Whilst Joe kept the old woman busy chatting, Vibart went around the whole flat searching for evidence.

'Well, we found nothing there. Not a sausage,' Watson reported.

'That don't surprise me,' Williams replied. 'Goody is very particular, very careful.'

'We can always hope,' Vibart piped up.

'No, not Goody. We're going to have to do something special to nail him.'

'True,' Watson added. Everyone looked at him, one of the newer boys on the Squad. 'Word is he was still involved.'

Williams stuck two photographs on the massive board in front of the team. 'Roger Cordrey and Bill Boal,' he announced to his men. Everyone stared at the two faces. They didn't look like big time thieves. 'We picked up Cordrey's sister, his brother-in-law and Boal's wife this morning for receiving. They all had stashes of bank notes, all of it from the robbery, we're sure. They're up in Aylesbury now.'

Bill Boal was the one that puzzled Joe. Unless he was dragged into the robbery at the last minute, he seemed odd. He had no record, and was missing from Lavery's list. Frank Williams grabbed his attention, announcing their focus for the rest of the week.

'Right, lads. Priority is keeping our eyes on our suspects, and then following up anything we get from Maurice Ray and his team, all right?' The room nodded together, creating more smoke patterns in the air. 'We're going to accumulate evidence, watch them, and then pounce. The Chief doesn't want us bringing them in one at a time, like today. We swoop for the lot in one go. Until then, we watch them like hawks.' Joe could see the shoulders slump, and the faces drop. There would be more watching and waiting.

Joe was due to meet his major informant in a couple of days, and he hoped that things would become clearer after that. He was desperate to free himself of the burden of knowing every name involved from the start; they pulled him down like a deadly weight. His fear of Lavery was almost matched by the dread of being found in possession of too much information. The sooner they were all caught, the lighter he would become.

39

Frank Williams met DCI Malcolm Fewtrell on the drive leading up to Brian Field's house, as arranged. The Buckinghamshire CID man insisted on Frank joining him for an interview with the solicitor's clerk. It appeared that he was up to his neck in it. As they stood outside in the light rain, Fewtrell explained more about why the visit would be of interest.

'His firm worked on the purchase of the farm. He knows a few of the names you mentioned. Goody and Edwards.' Any link to the suspects was worth pursuing. 'But we've discovered something else. You heard we turned up a load of money in Surrey? In a place called Leith Hill?'

'Yes, I did.' Frank recalled the news of the suitcases coming into the incident room at New Scotland Yard, over a hundred grand was recovered. This was a huge step forward for the investigation, although they had no idea how it got to be there.

'Well, there was a holdall, too. In it was a receipt for a German hotel. See if you can guess whose name was on it?' Fewtrell showed Frank a copy of a bill, contained in a transparent bag.

'Not?' was as far as Frank Williams got, pointing to the house, then staring at the piece of paper in Fewtrell's hand.

'Yeah. Mr and Mrs Field. Bit of a coincidence, don't you think?'

'Just a bit.'

Frank contemplated what made people in the legal profession

get so heavily involved with criminals. He would have thought they were not only bound to behave properly, but would also see the downside of crime. This didn't stop there being plenty of bent briefs around, as his daily life reminded him. The two men crunched their way down the considerable drive.

'Nice house for a solicitor's clerk, don't you think?' Frank said. Both men knew there was more to Brian Field than a mere office worker. Perhaps he was the mastermind behind the whole robbery?

'Let's try and keep him relaxed. We don't want him doing a runner, do we?' Fewtrell asked.

'He won't be able to. We're going to watch him like a hawk from now on. I've got two men on their way up this afternoon.' Williams was still trying to establish the level of manpower both the Yard and the Met could provide over and above this country outfit.

As they approached the house, the front door opened, revealing a short man wearing a casual shirt and slacks. He looked like someone who was about to take a trip to the local golf club, rather than a man who had pulled off a recent train robbery. Frank did notice there was a scar running down the left side of his face.

'Can I help you?'

'Yes, I hope you can,' Fewtrell opened up. I'm DCI Malcolm Fewtrell, from Buckinghamshire CID.' Frank's new colleague showed Field his identification, which the man studied for a moment, then nodded. 'And this is DCI Frank Williams, from New Scotland Yard.'

'Come in, please.'

Fewtrell waited for Williams to produce his own identification before stepping inside. They had no warrant but apart from that he was doing this by the book. Field led the policemen into his living room, and offered them both a drink, which they declined.

'May we sit?' Fewtrell asked. This was all extremely formal, Frank thought. Maybe that was how they did things out in the sticks. He was going to listen and watch, rather than lead the questioning. This Field didn't look like a man who had orchestrated a dramatic and high profile train robbery. Outwardly he appeared very calm, hands steady as he poured himself a glass of whisky. Frank had seen many a white-collar criminal go to pieces at even the slightest questioning before, but this Field was astonishingly relaxed.

When they sat down, Fewtrell wasted no time in asking Field about his links to the dramatic discovery near Brill.

'As you might have guessed, we're investigating the purchase of Leatherslade Farm.' Field simply nodded, and took a sip. 'Could you tell us what you know about the purchase of the farm?'

'I think I can.' Field appeared to be racking his brain to recall information. He would know everything, Williams was certain.

'Please, Mister Field, any details would be useful,' Fewtrell continued.

'Of course. I do remember, because the farm isn't that far away, I think. North of here, isn't it?' Fewtrell nodded. How handy, thought Frank. 'Our firm arranged the purchase for a client of ours. Mister Wheater arranged everything, as far as I can recall.'

'That's John Wheater, your boss?' Fewtrell asked.

'Yes, that's right. Mister Wheater did all the paperwork, all the conveyancing for the purchase, as I recall.'

'And did you have any involvement in the purchase?'

'Not really.' Field looked evasive this time.

'Is that so?' Fewtrell asked. Field didn't reply, took another drink. The local DCI pressed on. 'The thing is, Mister Field, that we have reason to believe you may have visited the farm before it was purchased, is that right?' Field appeared to be thinking over his reply.

'Do you know I think I might have, yes. I think I might have gone to look at it with the client. The purchaser.'

'A Mister Leonard Field, is that correct?'

'Yes, that's right.'

'This Leonard Field a relation of yours?' Fewtrell asked, and Field laughed.

'No, no, that's just a coincidence.'

'And you just went to the farm the once, is that right?'

'Yes, just the once. Lennie, Mister Field, wanted me to take a look with him. As I live not far away.' They were probably no more than twenty-five miles from Brill.

'And that is the only time you went to the farm?'

'Yes, the only time. And that was weeks before this, this robbery thing.'

'We understand,' Fewtrell reassured him.

As discussed beforehand, they didn't want to put Field on red alert. Frank had been studying their suspect all this time. He rarely made eye contact with Fewtrell throughout all this questioning, was probably hiding something. The thing Frank wanted to know was how deep his involvement went. Fewtrell asked more questions about the process and paperwork for this type of purchase, and Field's role in it. At all times he said that it was John Wheater who knew the detailed information, they should talk to him if they needed to know more. Fewtrell promised that they would.

Williams led the distraction towards a new line of subtle questioning, pointing to a photograph of Mr and Mrs Field on the mantelpiece.

'Your wife not home today?'

'Oh, she's out shopping in Oxford. I expect she'll be back this afternoon, doubtless after she's bought half the town.' Field forced a laugh.

'She spend a lot of money shopping?' Williams asked.

Field was reserved at first in his response. 'Not really. Sometimes, you know, like any woman.'

Frank looked at the photograph again. She appeared to be good-looking, and much younger than Brian. His suspicious mind began to tick over. He wondered how an ordinary solicitor's clerk, who was no Anthony Newley in the looks stakes, could ensnare a young and attractive female like her. After more idle chat about wives, Williams changed the subject of conversation.

216

'Do you go on holiday much together?'

'Yes, when we can. When work permits.'

'Do you go abroad for business?'

'Occasionally, yes. But it's more pleasurable when Karin and I go together.'

'Yes, I can understand that,' Williams agreed. He and his wife never went overseas, strictly Margate for them. 'Have you been anywhere really good? You know, that you might recommend?' Fewtrell watched intently.

'A few places. France we like. And earlier this year we went to Germany.'

Williams's face lit up. 'Germany? Oh my wife would love to go to Germany. She's always on about it.' If you couldn't eat whelks, Margaret had no interest.

'Really? It was lovely there.'

'Where did you go? Would you recommend it?'

'Yes, I think I would. We went to a little place in Southern Germany, in Bavaria.'

'What was it like? Maybe my wife would like it?' Williams asked, reeling him in.

'If she likes the fresh air, she will.' Frank nodded keenly. Field continued. 'Lovely places to sightsee.'

'What are the hotels like?' Frank asked. 'My wife is very particular about hotels, you know,' he smiled. Field was relaxing, unsuspecting.

'We stayed in a lovely one. Not far from Munich.'

'Sounds great,' Frank replied.

'Oh, Karin really loved it.' Field jumped up and went to a cabinet drawer in the corner of the room, ever anxious to please the policemen who were setting him up. He pulled out what looked like a brochure, and copied down the name and address of a hotel, the Pension Sonnenbichl, and handed it to Frank. 'Here, you could try this one.'

'Would you recommend it?'

'Oh, yes, definitely.'

'Thank you,' said Williams. 'You've been most helpful.'

Frank stared at the jagged writing in front of him. The same hotel that appeared on the receipt made out to a Mr and Mrs Field, found in the bottom of the holdall, that was discovered in Leith Hill three days earlier, full of stolen money. Not only did they now have a clear link between Field and the purchase of the farm, they could establish that he must have handled the stolen money as well. All they needed to do now was work out his precise role in the robbery, how high up the command chain he sat. Fewtrell wrapped up the interview casually, indicating they might need to talk to Field in the future. The policemen made their excuses and left, hopefully leaving him none the wiser.

Once they reached the end of the drive, Frank carefully placed the piece of paper with the address written on it in a bag. Another one for the fingerprint boys, he thought. Field had no criminal record, and there was no need to alert him to their suspicions by asking him to submit to printing. They would keep Brian Field under observation for the time being, see who made contact with him.

'I think we should let DCI Mesher in the fraud squad take over from here, don't you?' Frank said, insisting, rather than seeking opinion. Fewtrell nodded in agreement.

'We're stretched,' he admitted reluctantly. 'There's so much evidence now.'

Frank Williams thought about the resources that the Yard had at its disposal, and how Hatherill was throwing everything at the case. His reputation was on the line. He knew that he wasn't one of Uncle George's favourites, and that while he was in command he would struggle to climb the ranks any further. Personal gain had to be put to one side. He had to focus on sniffing out this gang, driving them out of the shadows, and unearthing the suspects and their money.

40

'Some of you already know Detective Inspector Barclay, Cliff Barclay.' The man standing in front of the Robbery Squad nodded to a few of the others in the room, as Tommy Butler addressed them. Watson thought he might have seen him before, but he couldn't place where. 'DI Barclay is here to update us on the latest from the forensic and fingerprinting team, from COC3. As you may know, he's been working alongside them for the past week, and now he's coming back to our team. Apparently there's loads of news for us to get our teeth into.' Butler stepped back to allow Barclay to speak. The incident room was packed with fumes and the rank odour of unwashed men. Joe Watson struggled to concentrate, drawn to the sweat marks on Barclay's armpits as he addressed everyone.

'Gents, we have a few developments I think will be very useful to the investigation.' Barclay seemed comfortable centre stage, a place Joe still had difficulty holding. 'We have managed to develop some prints from the farm, and many match up with your suspect list.'

'Who have we got, then?' DCI Vibart asked enthusiastically.

Barclay walked around to the chart on the wall, which had the list of names written in thick pen on it. He pointed as he verbally ticked them off.

'All these men, we can place at the farm, through fingerprints.

Roy James. Charles Wilson. John Daly. Bruce Reynolds. Robert Welch. Thomas Wisbey. Ronald Edwards.' He stood back, as if admiring his work, and looked around the room. There were smiles everywhere.

'That's a good haul,' Butler said, stating the obvious. Seven men, along with Cordrey and Boal. They had evidence to convict well over half the gang, based on their latest information. This was going to send a rocket through the underworld, Joe thought. Lavery seemed keen to keep tabs on how they were progressing with the investigation. He would be delighted with this news.

'Nothing on Goody, then?' asked Peter Vibart, one of the officers he had run rings around on the Heathrow robbery.

Barclay sighed. 'Not yet. We've got plenty more dabs to sort through, and some we haven't identified positively yet. If you've got the names of known associates of the suspects, we can check through those next, use it as a short cut.'

'We'll get that done for you,' Butler said.

The Chief looked at Vibart, who nodded in reply. Joe Watson felt exposed. Frank Williams was the source he was planning to filter the last of the names through, and he shared a look with his boss, who shrugged his shoulders. After all, the Grey Fox was the man in charge. Joe felt uneasy dealing with Vibart, having worked closely with him recently. His rabid fanaticism was almost scary, and unlike Frank Williams, few criminals seemed to respect him. His immediate boss was frequently found drinking in pubs and clubs with villains, and Joe supposed he too was adopting this style of policing.

'Watson, can you share any more information with us? Perhaps you can give DI Barclay and the forensics boys a bit more help?' Butler addressed the room, and Joe was unsure what to say next. Now Butler was asking for more, and he felt the Chief's eyes burn into him. Joe had already moved away from Lavery's script for cascading names to the investigation, had become confused about who was supposed to be known about, and when. He had confided the rest of the definitive list to Frank Williams the day before, who decided to keep that information under wraps until they found more evidence. His boss gave him a subtle nod. With all the fingerprints at the farm, there was no reason to be cautious any more. Even though Lavery had asked for the last few to be held back, he was going to reveal the rest.

'We have more intelligence; principally on associates of the men we already have on the list. This is fresh information.' Watson hesitated, realising all eyes in the room were looking at him. What the hell, he thought. The sooner he got the other names out there, the quicker his ordeal would be over. Lavery would be happy, what difference would it make when the whole squad knew? Besides, they might have come from other sources, so how would Lavery ever find out?

'Go on, Watson. Frank dropped me the hint last night that you might have more for us,' Butler encouraged. Joe cleared his throat.

'Some of the newer names we have talked about already. Others are associates of the men on our list here.' Watson pointed to the names on the wall. Eyes moved back and forth around the room, settling on him again. 'Right, Danny Pembroke, we think, is definitely in the frame. He's a good friend of Bob Welch.'

'I know him well,' Vibart remarked with disdain. 'Nearly nicked him last year.'

'Two more names. Jimmy Hussey, he knows Edwards.' Watson paused to allow interjections, rebuttals, but none came. 'Then we have Ronald Biggs.'

'Who?' Butler asked. There were other looks of surprise around the room.

'Who's he?' Vibart demanded.

'He's an old acquaintance of Reynolds; they served time together. The word out there is that Ronnie has gone back into crime in a big way.'

'This is way too big for him,' DS Slipper chipped in. 'He's a small time car thief, nothing more. Or he was.'

'Maybe he helped with pulling the vehicles together?' Butler asked.

'It's possible,' Vibart added. 'The stolen car squad say they think they have a few leads for us, don't they?'

'I was coming to that,' Butler replied. 'Yeah, they think they can link the purchase of one of the Land Rovers that we found at the farm, to Bruce Reynolds. They tried to play clever games with reg numbers with the Landies. Both were the same.' The whole team had received a briefing on the vehicles involved an hour earlier, and Reynolds was the only one with a definite link to the cars. Joe looked at Frank Williams, who was surprisingly holding his counsel.

'Please carry on with our wider suspect list, Watson,' Butler demanded. All eyes shifted back to Joe, who swallowed something sharp. He checked Frank Williams again, who offered a thin smile. It was time to go all out.

'The other one we want to start considering is James White.'

'Ah, yes, Jimmy,' Butler said. Again there were a few nods in the room. 'Jimmy is a safe cracker though, what's he doing on this job?'

'I don't know,' replied Watson. 'All the word out there is telling us, and we have this from an extremely reliable source indeed, is that Jimmy White was central to the whole operation, one of the ringleaders. And nobody knows where the hell he's gone. He's been missing for nearly three weeks.'

'Maybe he's just fucked off to avoid the heat. Knew the job was coming?' Slipper asked. Watson paused, waiting for the others to contribute. He knew White was no longer one of Lavery's biggest concerns. It sounded like Welch and Pembroke had drifted up the order of priority, according to his last phone call with the Beast.

'Word is, that White is in hiding for some reason. Most people think he's involved.' Watson decided to leave it at that.

'Right, we go looking for White,' Butler announced. 'And these other two as well. Is there anybody else we should be looking for, according to your information, Watson?'

'Those are the new ones that have appeared on the radar in the past couple of days. Of course we're still looking for Smith, Goody and Wisbey as well.'

'We think we're getting close to identifying the whole gang,' Frank Williams added at last. Maybe he was helping Joe to take the credit for all his inside knowledge?

'Good. We'll get those added to our official suspect list. Commander Hatherill needs an update tomorrow.' Butler wrote the names on the board as he addressed the team. 'Then, we're going to be making a decision about our strategy with the newspapers and radio.'

'I assume we're going to keep following our suspects, waiting for even more forensic evidence?' Vibart suggested.

'That's what we want to do. But as you know, Hatherill likes big publicity. We're trying to resist, but he's very keen to appear busy. The politicians are probably putting a lot of pressure on for arrests,' Butler replied with a heavy sigh.

'We've got five already, including two of the robbers,' Slipper said. Nodding heads around the room indicated agreement that this was good progress.

'I know. We think we can limit Hatherill to only going public on two or three, while we keep tabs on the rest,' Williams said. Butler confirmed with a nod of the head.

'I assume, Chief, the plan is to go after those where we have the evidence? The ones with the fingerprints,' Vibart said. Joe could tell he was keen to get stuck in.

'Yes, we will. Let's draw up plans for the middle of the week, make our visits to this wider list. I want to co-ordinate everything neatly. Peter,' Butler turned to Vibart, 'I want you to get this all ready, prepare us for a move on everyone, by Wednesday or Thursday.'

'Why are we going to wait that long, Sir?' Slipper asked. Few on the team trusted Slipper, he would sell his own mother to jump ahead and steal an arrest.

'We need to make sure it's all aligned to the public appeal that goes out. Hatherill will be pissed off if we go charging in too soon. We watch the high profile ones, go after them as the appeals and the photos hit the press.' Butler sounded resigned to waiting.

'We're not going after them immediately?' Vibart asked, sounding frustrated.

'Not just yet, in a few days, it has to be properly co-ordinated.' Butler wrapped up the meeting. 'We need to keep up the observation, link together the evidence we have so far with all this forensics and fingerprinting. Spend our time getting the cases ready for when we lift anybody. We need to be prepared, not just bring them all in and then scratch our balls wondering what to ask them about, okay?' The nods in the room showed they knew what he was talking about. Even Watson was aware these suspects would be able to acquire decent briefs, and they needed anything they brought to trial to be watertight. They would only get one chance to bring in this many men. Butler would kick their arses around the Yard if any of the team cocked this up.

The room dispersed quietly, and Joe Watson thought through his situation. The introduction of the rest of the names seemed to have gone pretty well, even that of Biggs. He was very much the surprise late package, but Lavery was adamant he was to be linked to the robbery. The Beast of the North wouldn't make such a selection lightly. All Joe did was undertake sound police work, following up on an extremely solid tip-off from a reliable informant. He was simply doing his job.

41

Buster Edwards peered nervously out from behind the curtain. He and his wife, June, had been in a perpetual state of fear for about a week, ever since the farm was discovered. They had moved out of their flat in St Margaret's Road, because the police would come looking there first. Now they were holed up in a friend's spare bedroom, not daring to go out. If this was to be the life of a train robber, Buster didn't want it.

The man knocking at the door looked familiar. It was one of Lavery's men from the robbery, Jack Armstrong. He remembered him as being very quiet, but determined to ensure everything went smoothly on the job, one of the first to storm the carriage, showing no fear whatsoever. Then he noticed another smartly dressed man standing about five feet behind him, looking up and down the street. He couldn't appear more suspicious if he tried, and Buster felt like he had little choice but to let them in. They didn't need those two characters drawing attention to the flat in their quiet street. If he was with Armstrong, he was unlikely to be the police. Buster eased the door open a few inches.

'Can we come in, Buster?' Armstrong asked, pushing against the entrance and walking straight through into the hallway of the flat. The other man followed a couple of steps behind, and Buster closed the door. June and Nicky were out grocery shopping, and would be back any minute.

'How are things, Buster?' Armstrong enquired.

He wondered about telling the truth, and decided against it. 'Things are fine, Jack. How's everybody else?'

'I can't speak for everybody else. I've got a message for you from my boss.'

'Tommy Lavery?'

'The very same. Look, can we sit down for a minute?'

At least he wasn't about to be wrestled through the door, packs of coppers waiting for him outside. He had read the news about Cordrey, but they didn't seem to have any more of the gang. He felt sure that Roger wouldn't say anything, but you never knew who else had been picked up, and was currently being interrogated. Bruce and Roy looked on edge the last time they met, and he wondered what Reynolds was up to. It would be a safe bet Bruce had a support network ready to help him out. All Buster had was this old friend who was putting them up, and he was getting really twitchy now that the robbery was all over the news.

They moved into the living room, and Buster switched on the lights, keeping the curtains drawn. Ralph Simpson was at work until five o'clock, and they were already getting used to having the place to themselves until teatime. Both visitors sat down on the sofa, and Buster dropped himself wearily into a worn armchair. He was hardly living the high life.

'Buster, we've got a bit of news that should interest you,' Armstrong began.

'Oh, pardon me, would you like a drink? Either of you?' Edwards asked. He was so on edge that he had forgotten his manners.

'No, thanks,' Armstrong answered for both men. 'You need to be moving on soon.'

'How d'you mean?' Buster asked, sensing the inevitable. He felt he could trust Armstrong. The man sat alongside Jack was totally expressionless.

'I'll come to that. Now, my boss has some information for you. Your name is on a list of suspects that is being bandied about New

Scotland Yard. The Robbery Squad are on to you. You're not the only name in the frame. We know they're already going through known associates of everybody on a list, to see who is harbouring people they think were on the job.' Buster shrugged his shoulders. With Tommy Butler leading the investigation, and Frank Williams out on the streets asking the questions, it wouldn't take long before they were tracked down. Ralph wasn't in his immediate circle of friends, but eventually they would come knocking on his door, just like Armstrong did today.

'How did you know I was here?' Buster asked.

'It didn't take us too long to work it out. And the point is, the police won't be too far behind us.' The seriousness of the situation was obvious. Buster suddenly wanted June back by his side, and looked at the clock on the wall. What was keeping her? Had they picked her up already?

'Tomorrow is going to be a big day for the investigation. Tomorrow they're going to swoop all over London. They're also going to name names, and publish pictures of people they want the public to turn in. For a big reward.'

'Including me?' Buster struggled to stay calm.

'As far as we know, you won't be one they go for tomorrow, not in an appeal to the public. But they are raiding your house again and your friends. It's a huge operation.'

'Who are they after?' Buster asked, wondering how they decided who was a priority.

'Tomorrow, we understand it will be Bruce, Bob, Charlie, and maybe Jimmy White.'

'Jimmy White? Why Jimmy?' Buster thought this one over. There were no obvious links between White and the men involved in the robbery. He would only be in the frame if someone had grassed him up, or maybe if they'd tracked down the Land Rovers. There was no way Jimmy would have left any dabs at the farm. There had to be an informant helping, and when that happened, all the rules went out of the window.

'I don't know why. But apparently those are the four that will get their mugs splashed across the papers. Everyone knows you've worked with them all in the past, Buster. They'll be on to you soon.' Armstrong was right. Edwards was sure there would be no evidence to link him to the hideout, and unless anybody else talked, he would be fine. But it wasn't worth taking chances, not with Butler on the case.

'Here's the thing, Buster. I'd like you to meet Geordie Adams. Geordie, this is Buster.' The man reached across and shook Buster's hand. His grip was firm and decisive. Armstrong continued. 'My boss would like to help you out. Geordie here is available to assist you, keep you hidden. He can be your link to the outside world. He can place you in hiding for as long as you need. You, your wife and your daughter, if you want to go together.'

Buster studied the other man again. He looked to be about fifty, had his hair slicked back and was heavy set. He wore a smart suit, the type Bruce might go for, and had an air of respectability about him. Geordie looked like a solicitor, and God knew he might need one of those soon. At last, the man spoke.

'Buster, I can help you. Mister Lavery has authorised me to assist you in any way I can. I have a place you can move into tonight, if you wish.'

'Where?' Buster knew June wouldn't want to move outside of London.

'In Shepperton. It's a quiet street, very pleasant, trees, gardens, and no nosey neighbours. We've also got a new name for you both if you want to use it.' Buster knew where it was, out West of London, suburban.

'Go on, what name?' he asked, expecting it to be something ridiculous.

'Green. We have a rental agreement for six months in the name of Mr and Mrs Green already arranged for you, to live in a quiet street called Old Forge Crescent. The rent will be twelve guineas a week, payable to myself.'

'To you? Twelve guineas is a lot.'

'It's a very nice house, in a very nice area,' Jack interrupted. 'Of course, if you don't want to take up Tommy's kind and generous offer, that's up to you.'

'Can I talk to June about this?' Buster asked. Everything appeared to have been taken care of.

'Of course you can. But you need to decide by this evening. Tomorrow may be too late,' Geordie said.

'As I said, the police are planning raids,' Armstrong added. 'We don't know exactly where, but they may come looking for you here. We managed to find you, Buster.' He was right. Edwards had already made the decision; there was no need to discuss it with his wife. They were going to move out to Shepperton, and become Mr and Mrs Green.

'We'll go,' Buster heard himself say.

'You'll need to pack right away. The sooner we go, the safer everything will be,' Geordie said.

Buster knew he had no choice. Then something he should have thought of earlier popped into his head. There would be a price for all this.

'How much is Lavery asking for hiding us?'

Armstrong came back immediately. 'Ah, well, Tommy isn't after any money from you, Buster. The important thing is that you, and your share of the money, wherever that is, are safe.'

He couldn't help but be sceptical. 'Really? He doesn't need payment for this?'

'Not now, Buster. The priority is to get you, June and your daughter to somewhere safe,' Geordie interjected.

At least my money is safe with me, he thought. He had a feeling he was going to have to start tapping into it soon. Ralph had refused to take anything for harbouring them the past few days, but he was getting increasingly nervous. It would only be fair on his old friend to spare him the stress, especially if he was likely to receive an early wake up call from the police the next day.

'So, Lavery doesn't want anything?' It didn't seem likely.

'As we say,' Armstrong insisted, 'he's interested purely in you, June and Nicky's safety for now. There may be other things he can help you with later, but we want to hand you over to the care of Mister Adams here. I do believe the services of a minder like Geordie will need to be paid for. To him and him only.' That was the catch, thought Buster. He was going to be paying Lavery, but by a different route, a layer of protection for the big criminal from the North. No wonder these people never got caught.

'My fee is a hundred pounds a week, on top of the rent. Payable in cash.'

'And how long for?' Buster asked.

'As long as you need it,' Geordie replied calmly. 'If you feel you want to move on, out of our protection, that's up to you.'

'I sense you are wavering a little,' Armstrong said, standing up. 'I'll tell you what.' Buster's fellow robber headed for the door, Geordie following him. 'We'll give you until seven o'clock tonight to make your decision, if you want to move or not. Talk it over with your wife. The heat is gonna come down, mark my words. Remember, if we move you, and Geordie here is looking after you, then you are a step ahead of the game.'

'You have people inside the robbery investigation?' Buster asked. It wouldn't surprise him if Lavery did, judging by what Bruce Reynolds had told him.

'Let's just say that we know what's going on, day to day, and leave it at that.' Armstrong held out his hand to shake with Buster. 'Good luck. I hope you make the right choice. Geordie here is excellent at his job, and you'll be in very good hands. And I hear Shepperton is a very respectable area.'

Geordie shook with Buster as well, and the two men headed for the front door. The key in the latch made everyone freeze momentarily, until the face of June Edwards appeared at the entrance to the living room.

'Hello darling.' She stopped still, and stared at her husband. 'Don't worry, love, just friends come to help us pack our bags. We're moving on.'

42

Joe Watson and DS Slipper brought Charlie Wilson into the charge room.

'It must be strong if you've brought me in?' Wilson muttered.

Joe said nothing, remembering the instructions from Williams and Butler the night before. Give nothing away until the Grey Fox got to interview them. They had picked Wilson up in an early morning raid, and Joe was getting hungry, nothing to eat since a bacon roll at half past six. The clock on the wall ticked its way up to ten o'clock. They had to lift Wilson before his face appeared in the early editions of the evening newspapers, along with Reynolds and White, all part of Hatherill's latest public appeal. If they had him in custody, he wouldn't be able to warn the others. Pat Wilson, his wife, had told Charlie she was going to 'ring the plumber' as they took him away. The message would be out there already that one of the key suspects was in the nick.

'I said, it must be strong, then?' Wilson repeated.

'Just wait, will you?' Slipper replied.

'Fine.'

Wilson sat with his arms folded, staring at the wall. They had found nothing at his house in Fulham when they swooped, but only a fool, unless his name was Cordrey or Boal, would have robbery money hanging about at home.

The door opened, and Tommy Butler swept in, smiling. Joe

relaxed, and watched as the Chief whispered something in Slipper's ear, before his fellow DS left the room. He was going to watch the Grey Fox in action.

'Ah, Charlie Wilson. So pleased to see you,' Butler began. Wilson said nothing in reply. 'I'd like you to take notes, Watson, if you would,' Butler said. This felt slightly unusual; normally an officer from the station would do this, but Joe was getting used to Butler's very particular ways. Wilson didn't seem too fussed by the arrangement.

'Charlie, do you know Cheddington in Buckinghamshire?' Butler asked, sitting down opposite the suspect.

'No, never been there.'

'Do you know Leatherslade Farm?'

'No, never been there.'

These were the agreed standard questions for every interview from now on. The aim was to determine, or get the suspects to deny, whether they had been at the scene. Then they would use witness testimony to counter this if they were seen on the train or at the hideout, and failing that, forensic evidence.

'Where were you on Thursday the eighth of August last, Charlie?' Wilson hesitated before answering. An instant response would have given away too much preparation.

'Like normal, I would have left home about five in the morning.'

'Where were you going?' Butler continued.

'Spitalfields Market. I'm there nearly every day, just like I was this morning, Mister Butler.' Joe remembered from his earlier research that Wilson was ostensibly a greengrocer by trade.

'And, can anyone vouch for that?'

'I'm sure there'll be plenty of people to back me up,' Wilson replied confidently. They knew well that he had a solid band of acquaintances that would say he was in China that day, if Charlie asked them to. It was the fingerprints that were his weak spot, and Wilson didn't know it yet. Frank had told him they weren't going to show their hand on the forensic evidence until later, they would see how much rope each suspect would need to hang himself first.

'Give me their names. We'll check into every one.' Wilson listed about seven men, some of whom Joe recognised as crooked. His group was very tight, would be hard to break up. Butler persisted with repeating his questions about what Wilson had done throughout the day of the robbery, and he batted everything straight back. After about half an hour, Butler decided to call it a day.

'I've heard enough for now. We'll get you, Charlie, you know we will.'

'You seem to know a lot. Maybe I made a mistake somewhere.'

'I'm sure you have along the line, Charlie,' Butler replied nonchalantly.

The Chief formally charged Wilson, and informed him of the items that were removed from his house by Slipper and Watson; two pairs of shoes and trousers, and a set of keys that they couldn't place a lock for. Slipper returned to take Wilson down to the cells, and when they had left, Butler turned to Joe.

'I want to spice it up a bit. You've got a good imagination, haven't you, Watson?'

'What do you mean, Sir?' He could guess where this was going.

'It was a bit bland, wasn't it? My memory is playing tricks on me already, Watson. I'm sure I remembered him say something about the money, didn't you?' Joe wondered how to respond. Butler went on. 'I'm sure he said we couldn't make it stick without the money, am I right?'

Joe Watson looked down at his scrawled notes. He struggled to focus on the words on his pad. 'I think maybe he did.' Joe knew redrafting of statements went on all the time. He had witnessed Frank Williams do it more than once.

'Hmm. I'll leave it to you to write up the report, present his statement for the rest of the team.'

Butler rose from his chair and departed with a flourish, leaving Watson alone in the room with his conscience. The implication was clear. He went back to a desk and typed up the statement and his report of the interview. The end of the conversation included Wilson's words, 'I don't see how you can make it stick without the poppy, and you won't find that.' This was a well-known word among London criminals for stolen money, and it would do. Wilson was stuffed anyway; Barclay had told the team that the fingerprint evidence was conclusive. He was simply bolstering the case, making things easier in the long run.

43

Bruce Reynolds was idly looking through an estate agent's window, when he caught the reflection of the headline on a news stand. He turned around to read it from across the street.

'TRAIN SUSPECTS NAMED BY YARD,' it screamed.

Bruce froze, and then switched his brain into gear. He inched towards the newsagents and saw his face on the front pages, along with Jimmy White and Charlie Wilson. The bastards. This was a surprise, publishing photographs. What evidence did they have then? Nobody would have grassed, surely? Maybe it was that little weasel, Roger Cordrey, who had already been arrested. He had to move quickly.

He sought out a phone box, and called the flat where he and Franny were hiding out. An old friend, who was looking after them in Bayswater, owned it. This was his first sortie outside for five days. He was searching for somewhere new to live in Hertfordshire, well away from London. Franny was getting her hair done in Bond Street, she said. There was no reply. He had to think. She would surely see the newspapers if she were out and about, would begin to worry about him. He dialled a number in Chiswick. Terry Hogan could be completely trusted.

'Tel, it's the postman,' he said, as soon as Hogan answered the phone.

'Ah, yeah, hello.' They had a system in place, just in case the heat was suddenly on, and phone lines started being tapped. The police knew Hogan was an old friend.

'Can you tell me where the postmistress is?'

'I can go and find her if you like?'

'That would be great if you could.'

'I shall put her somewhere safe. Call me back when you are.'

'I will. Tell the postmistress everything's gonna be okay.'

'Sure. Bye.'

Hogan hung up. The police would probably be looking for Franny too, hoping she would lead them to Bruce. But there was another concern, far weightier. The money. Not just his, but also John's. Both shares were safely squirrelled away in a lock up in South London. The problem was that he had rented the place well in advance of the robbery, anticipating the need to hide his share while the pressure died down, but used his real name. Bruce had to get that money out of there before the police made enquiries, and beat him to it. There was no way he was going to let Tommy Butler and his squad get their filthy hands on both their shares, not after everything they had gone through. His brother-in-law was hiding in Kent, in the safety of a quiet bed and breakfast. He would have to move the money for them both.

One more phone call was made before he sped to the garage in Mortlake. He needed someone trustworthy, who would have a van available, to help him move the money. He breathed a massive sigh of relief when Tony Barrow answered the phone. There would be no need for code words with Tony, he was totally off the police radar, had no criminal record to speak of. Barrow was straight down the line, an old school friend.

They met outside Parson's Green tube station an hour and a half later, and sped to the lock up. Tony looked petrified, must have seen the newspapers as well. But, to his credit, he turned up to help, and Bruce was grateful. They circled the lock up three times, just in case it was being staked out. In the end, Bruce thought they had to go for it, the manhunt was on, and the clock was ticking. It took just a couple of minutes to retrieve the suitcases from the furniture in the garage, and they were on their way.

'Where to, mate?' Tony asked.

'South Circular. North Circular. Then the A1,' Bruce replied. 'And drive steady, we don't want to attract attention.' Reynolds had one person in mind, a man far away from London and the Met. When they eventually pulled off the A1 and swung through the quiet streets of Lincoln, Bruce finally felt he could relax.

'All I need you to do is pull in at someone's house, and then you can go.'

'Thank fuck for that,' Tony uttered. He had been shaking throughout the entire journey.

'I want you to have something for your trouble,' Bruce suggested. Making a small hole in the money would be worthwhile. Tony had gone out of his way to help, a favour he would never forget.

'Look, Bruce, mate, I don't want anything. Honest, nothing.'

'Not even a little bit, just to say thank you.'

'Nah, mate. I want well out of it.'

With that, Tony left Bruce standing in the front garden of a house he had visited a couple of years earlier, along with over two hundred grand. He was confident that Jimmy Darwin wouldn't let him down in his hour of need.

44

23rd August 1963: Welford Road Police Station, Leicester

Gordon Goody sat back in his chair and sighed. What a bloody mess. The most ridiculous thing of all was the fact that he was picked up because a stupid woman thought he looked like Bruce Reynolds.

They woke him at two o'clock that morning, rousing him from slumber at the Cross Keys Hotel in the centre of Leicester. If everything had gone completely to plan he would have been lying next to Jean Perkins, one of his girlfriends. They had arranged to meet the night before in the hotel bar, and his intentions were not exactly honourable. For some reason she went lukewarm on him, and decided to go home early. After a couple more quiet drinks alone, he went to bed.

The day had hardly gone to plan before that. He had borrowed Charlie Alexander's Sunbeam, which broke down on the way up. The big end had gone, which would mean a hefty repair bill, a reconditioned engine probably. Charlie wasn't going to be pleased about that. The Alexanders had been very good to him since the robbery, because he knew there was no way he could return home to Putney and his mother. Word had already reached him that the police had visited their flat and searched the place. He knew there would be nothing incriminating lying about, either there or at *The Windmill* pub in Blackfriars, where the Alexanders were renting him a room upstairs. His money was buried, his clothes from the raid burnt.

He was forced to look at the face of DCI Vibart across the table into the bargain. What a bloody weasel he was. A few of the officers in the Met were trustworthy, but not that one. It was pure bad luck, that woman thinking he resembled the subject of a widely broadcast manhunt. He could ride it all out; they wouldn't have anything concrete on him.

Only his alibi had gone wrong so far. He had flown to Belfast two days before the original robbery date, and set up a friend to fly back under his name two days after the heist, to show that he was out of the country. For some reason the friend decided to return a day earlier than planned, and with the twenty-four hour delay, his alibi was sunk.

He made one small mistake earlier in Leicester. When the two policemen woke him and asked him his name at two in the morning, he gave it as Alexander, because that was what he checked into the hotel under. It seemed they then contacted the pub and found Charlie at home. Still, this was a lie that could be explained. He then gave them his real name, and the truth behind why he was in Leicester. That must have led to Vibart being sat opposite him.

'Gordon Goody. We're surprised to see you here,' Vibart began, sounding delighted to have found him. A copper called Moore accompanied him, and it appeared that the local force had left the pair to it.

'Are you?'

'Of course we are. You live in Putney.'

'Not any more.'

'Oh, why is that, Gordon?'

'Because you lot are after me. I know what you think about that Heathrow thing. I'm skint after that, cost me every penny just to clear my name.'

'Yeah, we know how that one ended up,' Vibart hit back. He still looked furious, several months later. 'We don't know how you did it, but you wormed your way out of it.'

Goody just shrugged his shoulders and tried to give nothing away. They would have to work that out for themselves.

'What are you doing, living in Blackfriars?' Vibart asked.

'Just staying with friends.'

'Why?'

'Why not? You lot want me for this robbery, no doubt. I was just staying out of harm's way until you catch the people that done it.'

'Oh, we're doing that all right,' Vibart said angrily. Goody felt comfortable. They had nothing, were just testing him out.

The questions rained in on Gordon, and he batted them all away easily.

'Have you ever been to Cheddington, in Buckinghamshire?'

'Have you ever been to a place called Leatherslade Farm?'

'How well do you know Bruce Reynolds? And Jimmy White? And Charlie Wilson?'

'What were you doing on the eighth of August this year?'

Goody just played it tight, said as little as possible.

'What about this money in your wallet? You said you was skint?' Vibart asked. They found fifteen pounds in his possession, including two five-pound notes. Gordon knew the police were focusing on fivers, a rare sight.

'Miss Perkins gave them to me. You can ask her.' This was true; she offered to pay for his hotel room as well that night. Jean was a lovely girl, even if she wasn't interested in anything more than a drink.

'We will, Gordon, we will.'

'Fine. I've got nothing more to say.'

'We're going to take you down to New Scotland Yard, if that's all right with you?'

'No problem for me. You've got nothing on me.'

It took another twenty-four hours before Gordon was released from the Yard, without charge.

'We've got our eye on you,' were Vibart's parting words, as he left the building. Gordon knew they were after him, but was still confident they had nothing that would stick.

45

Charles Alexander appeared to be happy to let the police officers search the tiny room above his pub. Gordon Goody must have reassured him that there was nothing to worry about. DI Barclay and a forensic officer called Stannard had joined Joe Watson and DS Slipper at the property.

They had already searched the room thoroughly, and found Goody's passport on top of the wardrobe. There was minimal clothing to be found, suggesting he was only intending to stay for a short while.

After a brief and hushed discussion, Barclay and Stannard ushered both Watson and Slipper out of the room, whilst they continued their own search. Slipper interviewed Alexander and his wife again at the bar, to go over their statements about the car and check the insurance and registration documents. Watson sat alone downstairs on a stool, smoking and contemplating the investigation in general. Things appeared to be progressing well, and one thing that reassured him was that all the names on the list that Lavery gave him seemed to be genuine. Nobody was being fitted up for this one, although he knew this sort of thing had happened in the past. Everybody was aware that occasionally pieces of evidence turned up out of the blue and people changed their statements, or suddenly remembered things they had previously forgotten. This case seemed to be different. Whatever his motivation, Lavery was actively helping the police with their enquiries.

Tommy had failed to turn up for their last meeting, replacing this with a hurried telephone call the night before. They were due to meet at midday in a pub in Stoke Newington, a new venue. Lavery was obviously extremely careful about where he was seen, and with whom. Every location had been discreet, places nobody would suspect a policeman and an informant to meet. Aside from the development of Goody being picked up in Leicester on an apparent tryst, and Charlie Wilson coming quietly but confidently, the only other thing of note was the disappearance of Roy James. Slipper was going mental, having chased him down to the South coast the day before. He was officially on the run, and his car had been abandoned in Chiswick. Williams and Butler were delighted with the intelligence that he kept providing. The Grey Fox even announced that Joe was going places, after he read the revised statement he prepared for Charlie Wilson. An officer with an eye for detail and a sensible head on his shoulders, the Chief said.

Watson was starting to have mixed emotions about the whole investigation. The full set of names was in the hands of Butler and Williams now, but there was a problem. Lavery said he wanted Smith and Pembroke to be removed from the list. Unfortunately, the entire team had already heard them, so they couldn't be deleted. He decided it was best not to ask Lavery what he was up to, just keep his head down. The past few days had gone by in a whirl, as they checked address after address where informants alleged the men still on the run were hiding, all to no avail. Goody, the subject of this raid, had been apprehended somewhere in the Midlands, but that was about it.

Barclay and Stannard emerged from upstairs with their hands full. Stannard carried a sack in two hands, with clothes peeking out of the top, and a pair of suede shoes bulged from Barclay's transparent bag.

'We've got what we think we need,' Barclay proclaimed. 'You

can go now,' he said, annoying Joe. Who did he think he was? Butler seemed to place an awful lot of faith in this Barclay. Maybe he was just thinking about things too much, seeing devils in every corner. Slipper came over, looking pleased with his work.

'I think we're done here, Joe, shall we head back?'

'Yeah, there must be loads of paperwork to catch up on,' Barclay snorted. 'We'll be off, too. A good morning's work,' he announced, holding up the bag with the shoes. 'Who's for a drink?' he laughed. Stannard chuckled, and Watson looked at Slipper for guidance.

'Come on,' he directed. 'We've got real police work to do.' Barclay raised his eyebrows at the other two officers.

All four men left the pub, and Watson excused himself to catch a bus towards Camden. He never arrived in a car to meet Lavery, preferring to use public transport. Joe still felt the need to blend into the shadows when preparing to go head to head with Tommy. You could never be too careful, dealing with a man who appeared to be in total control of the game.

46

26th August 1963: Margate

Frank Williams knocked on the door of the guesthouse. DS Joe Watson was with him, and stood watching, checking the upstairs windows. This was the third address they had visited that morning with a positive sighting of John Daly, but there was no way he could have been staying at all of them. Frank suspected that Daly was long gone already. Watson had insisted on coming along with him for this one, which Williams was happy with. The young officer was getting increasingly involved, and he felt a strong common sense of purpose. Joe seemed to have an excellent work ethic and was developing solid underworld contacts. Both were useful attributes for a modern police officer.

They knew that Daly was a fringe criminal at best; his only real link to the robbery was that he and Bruce Reynolds had married a pair of sisters. However, Barclay and his team had given a reassurance that there were fingerprints placing him at the scene, from a Monopoly set. In fact it appeared that one harmless board game was going to bring conclusive evidence against four men. Frank pictured them with the brass neck to play it with real money.

When Frank showed her the photograph, the lady who faced him was positive. Yes, a man who looked like that did stay at her bed and breakfast the night before, but he had left early that morning. Williams cursed under his breath, and the woman looked appalled. Somebody must have tipped John Daly off that they were coming. There were massive internal objections to publication of his pictures in the newspapers, and Butler was furious with Hatherill. Their information had led them to the Kent coast just as Daly's face hit the news stands. If they could have waited just one more day, Williams kept repeating in the car on the way down. Many of the team were still in observation mode, and it seemed that this reported sighting in Kent was spot-on. Watson said he thought that they might even be a matter of streets away, if he was moving about, but Frank doubted it. He asked the lady at the door if she knew where the man had gone next, but she shook her head. Then she provided a small clue.

'I dunno where they went.'

Williams was quick to latch on to her. 'You said, "they", was this man not alone?'

'Nah, he was with a woman and another man when they left.'

'Did they stay here as well?'

'Nah, only him, that one,' she said, pointing at Frank's picture of Daly.

'Could you describe these two other people?'

'Oh, I dunno. She was younger than him, I think. He wore glasses, tall and thin, looked older. I only saw 'em for about a minute.'

'Where did you see them?'

'They was outside, here in the street, in a car waiting for him.'

'Can you remember what sort of car it was?' Williams asked.

'A red one. I dunno what make,' she smiled weakly. A woman. What the hell would she know about cars?

'Did they have an accent?' Frank continued the questioning. She shuffled from foot to foot, dragging heavily on a cigarette.

'Not really. Local, I suppose.' That could mean anywhere in the South East, which wasn't particularly helpful.

'Is there anything else you can tell us about the other couple?' Williams probed.

'Did they look like they were a couple? You know, like husband

and wife?' Watson threw in over his boss's shoulder. A perfectly reasonable question, Frank thought.

'They looked like they might have been together, I suppose.' Bruce Reynolds and his wife, Frank thought. He thanked her for her time, and they stepped back into the street.

'They've bloody scarpered, haven't they?' Frank stated, not really asking Watson his opinion. They rescued Daly when the pictures hit the press, and they might be back in London already.

'I reckon so. We could keep looking along the front. And the first street in,' Watson said.

'No,' Williams replied. 'They've bloody well gone. Those bloody photos,' he muttered. He was like Butler, devoted to his task. Pounding the streets, knocking on doors, asking questions in murky pubs, that was the Frank Williams way. That was how they were going to bring the gang in. 'Come on, young Watson, we'd better get back to town. I've got an idea. I know how we can ruffle a few feathers.'

47

26th August 1963: Eaton Square, London

'You'll be safe here,' Billy Goodwin said.

Michael Black seemed to agree, echoing what John Daly was hoping to hear. 'Yeah, Paddy, this is the place for you.'

Bruce Reynolds wanted to voice his objections to his brother-in-law, but he was his own man. They had argued long and hard over what to do about the money that was moved up North. John wanted his back immediately, and it took all of Bruce's calm to explain the reasons why not. Jimmy Darwin was taking a small fee, only ten grand for keeping over two hundred safe in a place the police would never think of looking. Bruce had been forced to act, to save both their shares, but John had forgotten all this. He wanted his money and these two old acquaintances of his were more than happy to help him.

'Bruce, what d'you think?' Daly asked. His face was thinner already, and he had told Bruce he was on a crash diet designed to change his appearance. He just looked unwell. If this was what big money was doing to John, he might be better off simply throwing his cash in the Thames.

'John, it's your decision where you stay. If you think you're safe, that's good.'

Goodwin and Black looked relieved, and Black seized the moment. 'Paddy, we can look after you.'

John looked desperate. Bruce knew all the parasites were

crawling around now, trying to take what they could from the most wanted men in the country. Thankfully he had planned ahead, which meant the friends he was using were solid. He and Franny were in their third safe house already, in Thornton Heath, and were establishing a place in Kensington to hide for good. John seemed to think he could blend in at this flat in Belgravia, with the help of these two men.

'They're gonna help me hide my share,' he told Bruce on the way up. He and John had been sitting in the back of the car while the debate raged, as Mary Manson drove them back up to London. She had looked impassive in the front, smoking continuously. They had to move fast when John's face was splashed everywhere, and she knew where he was staying in Kent, having visited him the week before.

'You sure you can trust 'em?' Bruce asked, constantly looking out of the window at what was following up the A2.

'Hundred percent, Bruce, hundred percent. Totally.'

What Bruce knew of Mickey Black could never be described as 'hundred percent.' Word was he was flaky and had turned somebody in before. Goodwin he hadn't heard of, and he wondered how and where John got to know those two characters. Maybe they approached him when they found out about the robbery. He was probably about to make a massive mistake, but there was no point in telling him in front of that pair.

Reynolds took Daly to one side as he left, in the foyer of the apartment building.

'Look, John, it's your decision. If you feel safe here, that's fine. But I need a bit of time to get the money for you.'

'Thanks, Bruce, I appreciate it. I'm gonna need a bit to pay these two, you know, for helping me out.'

'Just be careful what you pay 'em. And for God's sake, don't tell 'em where it's been, all right?'

'No problem. Where is it now?'

Bruce still hadn't divulged where he had moved their money to, the day his own photograph hit the front pages of the newspapers.

'I'll tell you later. In fact, it doesn't matter, does it? I'll bring it to you as soon as I can, maybe next month, is that all right? It's totally safe where it is.'

'You can't bring it any sooner?' Daly looked scared.

'Don't let 'em bully you, John.' This sounded ludicrous, looking at the size of Daly compared to the pair of weasels sitting inside. 'You hold the upper hand. They only want your money, and until you have it, they can't steal it from you.'

'I just want my share, Bruce.'

'I'll sort something out for you. It may take a few weeks, but I won't let you down.'

'Cheers, Bruce. And thanks again.'

Daly went back into the flat, and Reynolds contemplated what he might have dragged his brother-in-law into. It wasn't that he was averse to criminality, far from it. John could handle himself and loved the buzz of stealing. He had a long record of petty crime. It was the people on the fringes, the ones who were looking to relieve them of their rightful takings that they needed to be wary of. Bruce's helpers were a million times more trustworthy than John's, and he was glad of it. Daly would be penniless by the end of the year if he wasn't careful.

48

'So, you want us to run this straight away?' Jerry Crystal asked, sipping his beer.

You could say what you liked about him sailing close to the wind when it came to the boundaries of the law, or even fitting people up, but Frank Williams was a generous man, happy to buy the drinks on this occasion. Especially when he wanted a story planted in the national press.

'Yes, I do. You should tell your editor. I think we can drop the odd piece of information your way in the next few days,' he offered.

'What sort of information?' Crystal looked keen, which was how Frank wanted him.

'You'll find out, as it comes up. I know you're gonna be interested in who's a suspect.'

'You'll give me the rest of the suspects?'

'If you like.'

'But everyone's got a bloody list, Frank. Every bloody paper has their own list of train robbers. You saw those in *The Daily Mail* today?'

'Yes, load of rubbish.'

'Really? Can I quote you on that?' Crystal asked, with a smile.

'No, you bloody can't, and you know it,' Frank countered. 'We're not in here, I'm not sat here, you're not sat there, this isn't happening.'

Crystal carried on smiling. They both knew this was all a game, and Frank was certain he had the upper hand. He knew the press were talking to members of the team all the time, squeezing the officers for stories. He had no doubts that Slipper, and maybe even Nevill, were dropping information to the press. The investigation was like a sieve. Almost everything discussed in the incident room was turning up in the national newspapers. Some of it was then exaggerated, but most looked well informed. Now he wanted to use a reporter to his advantage.

'All I need the story to be, is that a significant proportion of the stolen notes have been discovered to be either marked, or the banks know the serial numbers.'

'Is that true?' Crystal asked.

'Does it matter?' Frank replied. 'It's a good story, either way. Just take it, and print it, will you?'

'I can quote a senior source inside the investigation?'

'Not senior, just a source will do.'

'I'm not sure they'll buy it. Earlier, you lot said hardly any of it was traceable.'

'Well, we've changed our minds, haven't we?' Williams studied Crystal's face. Of course he was going to print this, it was a significant twist in the story.

'My editor's gonna ask what the hell's going on.'

'You can think of something. Say anything, say whatever you like.' Frank considered the lowlife existence that was journalism. It was down there with the crooks as far as he was concerned, perhaps lower. At least you usually knew where you were with criminals.

'The police and the banks have worked more closely, and discovered that over half of the money is in known sequences.' As Crystal spoke, Frank could see the story developing in his head. He would take the bait.

'That sounds excellent to me.'

'Cheers, Frank. You gonna catch these men?'

'Of course we are. And you can help us.'

Apart from this little ruse to try and instil some panic in the robbers, Frank doubted the press were really going to be of much use to the investigation. The Squad would stick to their tried and tested approach – shaking the trees of the London underworld. Then prey on the insecurities and vagaries of villains, wait for the train robbers to fall to earth. And he, Tommy Butler, and the team would be waiting for them when they landed.

49

4th September 1963: Redhill

'That'll be him now,' Charmian Biggs announced, as a man entered the kitchen. Frank Williams looked at the thin face and recognised him from the file. Ronnie Biggs was a petty criminal, and a surprise when Watson added his name to the suspect list. He was an old cellmate of Bruce Reynolds, but that was the only possible connection to the robbery that he was aware of. A month earlier the local station had checked out Biggs as a possible candidate for receiving, because his wife had been spending money openly. All the evidence confirmed that he won it gambling, but now they had something far more concrete. Barclay's briefing was unequivocal. Biggs's fingerprints appeared in several places in the farmhouse, including a dish, a ketchup bottle, and on the Monopoly set. So what if he was a minor player, he was certainly one of the most careless.

Frank stood to greet Biggs, who looked forlorn as he entered the room, and kissed his wife.

'Hello, Mister Biggs. Your wife let us in.' A formal introduction, the way he liked to open up interviews with suspects he didn't know that well.

Biggs said nothing at first, apart from a brief accusing glance at the woman by his side. Williams continued as planned. 'We are police officers. We are here in connection with the train robbery in Buckinghamshire, and we are in the process of searching your house.' It was standard procedure to explain what they were doing. Everything had to be done by the book if they were going to bring this gang to trial.

'What, again?' Biggs replied, looking at Williams and DS Slipper, who also sat in the kitchen, sipping tea. 'The local law turned me over some time ago about that.'

'Maybe,' Williams replied, and watched the interaction between the husband and wife. He didn't look too impressed with her letting them in, even though they had a warrant.

'You haven't found anything, have you?' Biggs asked.

'No, nothing has been found yet.'

'That's all right then.' Biggs sat down at the table, opposite Slipper, and his wife mopped his brow.

'Please excuse me, we're just finishing up,' Williams said, beckoning his colleague towards him as he rose to leave the couple in the kitchen.

'Listen to anything they say, will you?' he whispered, before going back upstairs to join DS Nevill. Ten minutes later, they abandoned the search and came back to the kitchen.

'Anything said?' Williams asked Slipper.

'Nothing, Sir.'

Mr and Mrs Biggs were sitting together, holding hands. Biggs would have to go with them, because the evidence was too strong. Not finding anything there made no difference.

'Okay, Ronnie, we're going to take you to New Scotland Yard, where more enquiries will be made.'

'That don't sound too good,' replied Biggs, staring intently at his wife. Williams wondered what silent messages he might be sending her. Ronnie turned and looked at Frank. 'What are my chances of creeping out of this?'

'Not good,' Frank replied.

He wouldn't find out about the fingerprints until later; they would allow him the room to incriminate himself first. Biggs looked like a defeated man already. 'We may return to search later,

Mrs Biggs,' Williams addressed his wife, smiling. The woman nodded meekly. She didn't look much like a gangster's moll, too suburban and respectable. 'Come on, Ronnie, come with us.'

On the way out to the car, Biggs opened up his own questioning.

'I dunno how you tied me into that lot in the papers.'

'Do you know any of them?' Williams asked.

'I read about it, but I dunno any of 'em.'

'Are you sure?' Frank wondered why he was lying so openly.

'Oh, I know what you're getting at. Yeah, I know Reynolds. He'll want some catching.'

Nevill and Slipper bundled Biggs into the back of Frank's car and they set off for London. Biggs said nothing all the way, and Frank Williams wondered once more how such a low-level criminal got caught up in so massive a robbery. Sometimes it wasn't what you knew, but whom you knew, that got you into trouble. Well, Biggs's past association with Reynolds, along with his own stupidity, had landed him right in it. Ronnie was going to be one of the easiest to nail down and convict, destined to be an unremarkable criminal.

50

The sign inviting the general public to look around the hideout of the great train robbery swung in the wind. Jack Armstrong eyed the dilapidated farmhouse, and a strange uneasiness came over him as they stood outside the door. He was more familiar with the place than any policeman. DI Barclay, who stood alongside him, knocked, and a tall, burly man answered.

'Can I help you? You come to look at the farm? We're closed 'til the morning.'

He looked to be half asleep, his red cheeks betraying the fact that he had clearly been drinking. Barclay did the talking, as planned.

'Mister Rixon, is it?'

'Yeah. Can I help you? I said, we're closed. We're open to the public at nine in the morning.'

Word was that the previous owner of the farm had reclaimed the property now that the forensic teams had departed, and was setting it up as a tourist attraction. Ten shillings to walk around the robbers' hideout, and have a gander at all the bits left behind that the police didn't take away. It was greedy, and calculating, a joy to Jack, truly enterprising.

Barclay showed his identification to the farm owner.

'I'm DI Barclay from the Robbery Squad. This is DC Jones. Can we have a little look round please?'

Jack smiled at the name Barclay plucked from thin air. Not very

257

imaginative. He didn't bother to show any form of identification. There was a gun in his jacket pocket, if all else failed.

'Your lot have already been and done your business. I thought you'd finished,' the owner complained, scratching his head. He looked to Jack like he could rival Mickey Griffin in the intelligence stakes.

'We just need to have a final look round, if that's possible?'

'Go on, then. Where d'you want to go?'

'Can I try outside? The outbuildings maybe?'

'Go on.'

The light was fading, and Barclay seemed to have a decent grasp of the layout. They wandered into the garden where the partially dug pit was still obvious. There was a row of shovels and forks in a line, like a ceremonial parade. The remains of the bonfire represented a sad reminder of a failed attempt to destroy evidence. Otherwise, the outside of the property looked to have been tidied up, compared to the state the rest of the gang left it in. Jack thought about the men with whom he shared the place for a couple of days. They were scattered, and here he was coming back for another look.

Barclay headed for the largest building, where they knew the lorry was housed before. The space was empty, and they both looked around at the walls, and checked the contents of the floor.

Rixon appeared at Jack's shoulder. 'Everything's as you lot left it. Pretty much.'

'Good, thank you Mister Rixon. I can search for myself,' Barclay said.

'If you tell me what you're looking for, I might know where it is.'

'That's very good of you, but we'll be fine.'

'Are you sure?'

Would he ever leave them alone? Barclay stopped momentarily, and then turned to Rixon. 'Tell you what, I wouldn't mind a cup of tea.'

'D'you want something stronger?' Rixon asked, cheeks glowing. Barclay paused, and shot Jack a look. Bloody hell, he was going to have to keep the bloke occupied.

'Just a cup of tea would be lovely, thank you.'

'Tell me about the inside,' Jack insisted. 'Tell me what they left behind.' He led the man away from the shed, glancing back over his shoulder to see Barclay crouching down, pulling on a pair of gloves.

'Oh, well, they left a few bits in the cellar.'

'Come on, show me,' Jack smiled, as they returned to the farmhouse.

Inside, the kitchen was a mess, plates and glasses cluttering up the work surfaces. The man appeared to have no shame at the state of the place. He led Jack to the trap door leading to the cellar, and shone a torch down into the dark. He struggled to see what he was trying to show him.

'There was a few hundred quid left behind, down there,' he said.

'Really?' Jack replied absent-mindedly. 'Did you keep it?' he smiled.

'No. Of course not.'

'Good.'

Jack remembered whom he was supposed to be, and resisted the temptation to ask Rixon whether he had found thirty grand in a holdall.

He steered the old man back into the kitchen, and decided not to have another peek inside the stove, in case he had gone mad before. The place had apparently been examined several times since they left. Barclay assured Jack that there was no evidence of him or Griffin being there, despite there being dozens of dabs. Such was their sophistication; the fingerprinting squad had apparently identified a few of the gang from partial palm prints on the lorries. Jack suffered another five minutes of painful conversation with Rixon, before he spotted Barclay through the kitchen window, carefully carrying a can of squashed paint across to their car. The paint was dry, but its contents would be crucial. A missing part of the jigsaw puzzle to catch Gordon Goody had been found.

51

Joe Watson was dog-tired. He tried to focus on the names on the wall in the incident room. The forensics ended up being the big breakthrough the investigation was hoping for; they knew some of the gang were incredibly careless. The core team were discussing progress; eight men, plus Tommy Butler.

'Nothing on Pembroke, then?' Butler asked the room.

DS Nevill spoke up. 'Nothing. We even took his pubes,' he laughed.

'His pubes?'

'Yeah, forensics found a few in one of the sleeping bags. God knows how they match 'em though.' For once, there was light relief in the incident room. This investigation was exhausting; Butler demanded they work ridiculously long hours, leading from the front. Joe was out on his feet after ten non-stop days. How the hell did Butler manage it at his age?

'But we've got nothing else on him? Nothing at his flat in Camberwell?' Williams followed up.

'No, nothing,' Nevill responded sheepishly.

'He knows Wisbey well, doesn't he?'

Joe Watson didn't notice that Williams was directing the question directly at him this time. He must have looked a right Charlie, half asleep. Which he was.

'Er, yeah, he knows him, and Bob Welch, another on our list,'

Joe replied. 'Pembroke and Wisbey live on the same estate.'

'They worked together before?' Butler asked.

Joe was at full stretch on this investigation. None of his ex-colleagues in COC11, the Intelligence team, wanted to get too involved, so most of the work came down to him. Maybe Lavery had even arranged that as well.

'Not Pembroke and Wisbey, odd as it may seem. But Pembroke and Welch, yeah, a few times.' Joe recalled the printed records he pulled a few months back.

'So, we had to let Pembroke go. But we want to keep tabs on him, all right?' Williams directed. 'Get the Met to keep up their good work.' Resources were massively stretched, following up all the wild goose chases that were coming in after the public appeal, as well as genuine leads from sources on the street. The Met were lending a considerable number of additional officers to the investigation.

'And what about this character, our friend, Jimmy Hussey?' Vibart chipped in, tapping at his name on the wall.

'He's on his way to Aylesbury as we speak,' Butler replied. 'We got him in this morning. Denied everything, the bloody lot, then Maurice Ray and his boys checked his prints, against ones they found on the lorry, and bloody bingo. He's done for.'

'Any ideas where his money is?' Vibart asked.

Nobody seemed to want to reply, because this was one of the major problems with the investigation. They were making excellent progress with tracking down and keeping tabs on the gang, and in some cases securing firm evidence, enough to prosecute. The pressure from above was now about retrieving the money. Butler had replaced Millen, who was promoted sideways, as leader of the Flying Squad, and was flexing his muscles on the team.

'We don't know where most of it is,' Butler announced. 'Frank, can you set up a small group to help track the money down, just work on that aspect?'

Williams looked a little put out. Joe Watson knew his boss pretty well by now, he wanted to be out there on the streets and in the pubs, sniffing out the gang, not looking for piles of paper.

'I'll get a team together, but we're short of resources, as you know,' he told the room. Everyone knew this was addressed at Butler.

'Can you get Barclay or one of his team to help out?' The Grey Fox asked.

'I'll look into it. I still think if we find the gang, we find the money.'

Joe wondered how much his boss really believed this. After the initial haul from Cordrey and Boal down in Bournemouth, there had been the money in the woods near Dorking, followed by thirty grand hidden in the lining of Jimmy White's caravan. But apart from that, they had drawn an enormous blank.

'Back to Hussey, he's already in Aylesbury and will appear before the magistrates tomorrow.' Butler seemed to think that one was sorted. 'He's going to go down for this one.'

'Did he implicate anyone else?' Vibart asked.

'Not a chance,' Butler replied. Joe knew everyone they had pulled in so far was incredibly tight-lipped. Around South London there were too many theories and people in the frame to make sense of it all. The only reliable source in the whole investigation had been a sheet of paper handed to him by Tommy Lavery in a smoky pub months before.

'And Wisbey, Pembroke's neighbour, what about him?'

'He wasn't in,' Williams replied. 'DS Nevill and myself, we went down there this morning. We found nothing in his flat either.'

'No sign of him?' Butler asked. Everyone in the room knew that Williams had pulled Wisbey in the year before for breaking and entering, a case that didn't get to court. Joe heard that a deal had been done with Wisbey in exchange for information on a diamond heist.

'No, Rene made us both a nice cup of tea, seemed quite relaxed, but she would, she knows the score.'

'She told us he'd left her for another woman,' Nevill laughed. A couple of colleagues joined in.

'Oh, that old one,' Vibart added, not amused, as usual.

'It's possible,' Williams replied. Suddenly becoming a rich man could turn your head and make you more attractive to women.

Vibart snorted. 'Not Wisbey, Jesus.'

Williams dismissed Vibart's comment. 'Well, anyway, she says he's buggered off to Spain with a woman.'

'You know him, don't you, Frank?' Butler asked.

'Yeah, I do.'

'Bring him in, find a way,' Butler demanded.

'I'll think of something,' Williams replied, smiling.

Joe wondered what his boss was up to. He was capable of anything. Had Lavery reached higher up the investigation, as far as Frank? He always seemed to trust the names that he conjured up from his magical informant. Maybe he was in on the whole thing as well? Perhaps half the room were working for Lavery, and he was just a minor player? He wasn't sure whether believing the team was in on it reassured him or not. He had to focus on his own instructions. Now all the names on the list had been circulated, he was sending information on the investigation back to Lavery every other day. If there were others in the Robbery Squad doing the same, he would know everything. In a dream he had two nights before, Lavery was sitting there, smoking a cigar and orchestrating from a massive armchair. It might be closer to the truth than he imagined. The quicker this case was wrapped up, the sooner he would be free. If half of them were pulling in the same direction and working for one man, it wouldn't take long to round up the entire list.

52

9th September 1963: Bedford Prison

Gordon Goody edged his way into the visiting area. He was out on bail, but that didn't mean he was in the clear. It had been a close shave up in Leicester when he was mistaken for Bruce Reynolds. The important thing was that his money was still safe, as far as he knew, and that he had his liberty, up to a point. His bail conditions meant that he had to report to his local police station every three days. With this in mind, he checked in under the name of 'Joey Gray' to meet Charlie Wilson. He looked around the visiting room at the other prisoners. None of the faces rang a bell, but his natural caution still dominated. This trip was a necessity.

Some of the gang were already banged up in Aylesbury, so he felt safer visiting Charlie in Bedford. They had questioned Gordon for two days, and then released him, which could appear suspicious, given that practically everybody else they picked up had then been arrested. Someone might think he had passed information to the police. He always kept a safe distance from the people he worked with, and maybe that would come back to haunt him.

Charlie looked pleased to see him, offering Gordon a firm handshake. It didn't feel like there was any menace. After a couple of pleasantries, Goody leapt in.

'Charlie, I want to reassure you, mate. I've got nothing to do with you being pulled in.'

'I know,' Wilson replied, looking into Gordon's eyes, checking him out. He felt reassured by the reaction. Charlie was known to have a big temper, and he mixed with some seriously nasty people, almost in Lavery's league. He certainly wouldn't want to see the outcome of a scrap between any of his supporters in Clapham, and the Beast's men, if push came to shove.

'Honest, mate, 'cos if I was sat there, I might be thinking about it,' Gordon explained.

'Nah, mate. It's not you I'm worried about. Our whole crew are tight.'

'True.' Gordon agreed. The police would be receiving tips from people all over the place. Even if some snouts were guessing, eventually they would get it right.

'Don't be ridiculous. I ain't worried about any of our firm.' Charlie's eyes sparkled. He looked positively happy for a man looking at fifteen years.

'What about the South coast lot?' Gordon asked.

'Nah, I ain't worried about them either. Buster knows 'em, they won't land him in it. There's enough of both groups still out there.'

'What's it like in here?' Gordon asked.

'Fuckin' awful,' Wilson laughed. 'Nah, it's all right. I reckon I'm fucked though. Fingerprints, so the word is.'

'But you wore your gloves?'

'Yeah, thought I did. But apparently they got loads of dabs, including palm prints, even though we cleaned the place up.'

'Palm prints?'

'Yeah,' Wilson chuckled. 'Dunno how we left those, but apparently we did.'

'Didn't those northerners tidy up after us?' Gordon asked, hoping they had done the job for Brian Field.

'Nah, Gordy, that's not the problem. We made mistakes.'

'But they were supposed to tidy the whole lot up.'

'Yeah, well,' Wilson whispered, leaning in towards Goody. 'I heard someone fucked off with their payment.'

'What?'

'Yeah. They had money put aside to tidy up for us. And someone nicked it.'

'Fuck,' Gordon replied. He would be unaffected, he'd kept his gloves on for every second of the stay, including when he slept at Brian's house.

'Yeah. It was fuckin' Cordrey, and his mate, Boal.'

'How'd you know this?' Gordon asked.

'I just know, that's all. I hear a lot in here. People get moved back and forth to Aylesbury all the time.' Wilson smiled.

'Bloody Roger,' Gordon fumed. 'But who's this Boal?'

'God knows. Some mug he got to help him hide his money, I think. They got caught with more than his share.'

'Bastard.' Gordon stared at Charlie. All his old friend's anger seemed to be focused on Roger Cordrey. The little electronics guy got all their sympathy to start with, the first one of the gang to be arrested. 'Has he been talking?' Gordon couldn't help thinking there was more to his own arrest. They had nothing on him, yet they still swooped.

'Word is no, but you never know, do you?'

'But he's still going to trial, isn't he?'

'Oh yeah, they ain't letting him off. Makes me think he's not said anything.' Charlie looked at Gordon, and growled. 'Still, if I ever catch the fucker.'

'He's pleaded guilty.'

'Fuckin' good. He is guilty,' Charlie laughed.

'You don't think he'll land us in it? To save his own skin?' Gordon thought Cordrey might.

'He's dead if he does; he knows that. Besides, there's too many of his own firm still out there. If he rats on any of us, they're going down too. Tit for tat.'

Gordon hoped it wouldn't come to that. Everyone grassing was a recipe for disaster; prison beckoned, as well as over a hundred grand down the river. 'We don't want it to end badly.'

'Nah. And hopefully Roger gets that as well.'

'Shall I go and visit him? Remind him of his obligations?' Gordon was a cautious man, but this might call for action.

'Nah, mate. You're taking a big enough risk being here,' Wilson said, looking around him. Gordon carefully eyed the rest of the room again, nothing suspicious as far as he could see.

'All right. Anything else I can do, Charlie?' Gordon thought about his bail situation, and the police crawling all over him. They had searched his flat in Putney twice to his knowledge, upsetting his mother the second time. They took clothing from *The Windmill*, but he knew everything he wore, shoes and all, was gone. There was nothing they could pin on him.

'Yeah, there is one loose end, one man I'm worried about.'

'Who?'

'Biggsy's mate, that Stan, or whatever the fuck he was called. Anyone know where he is?'

Gordon thought for a moment. Nobody even knew where he lived, apart from Biggs. 'No idea.' Then Gordon thought there was a possible solution close at hand. 'Isn't Ronnie in here?'

'Nah. Aylesbury at the moment.'

'Shall I go see him? Ask him where the bloke is.'

'He'll guess. Might tip him off.' Gordon had to agree. Biggs might be a little reticent to come across with that information, if he got an inkling of what Charlie might want done to him. 'He's got to be silenced, one way or another,' Wilson said with a sinister tone.

'Fuck. Charlie, are you sure?'

'Look, Gordy. There might be plenty to get me, but some of you were more careful. That bloke saw all of us, didn't he? Imagine if old Butler gets his hands on him first. We're all sunk if he does.'

Charlie had a point. The retired driver got ten grand for doing nothing, and wouldn't be on the police radar. But one thing nagged at Gordon's brain. When they were discussing alibis, Biggs was going to say he was away on a tree-felling job with this Stan bloke. He didn't know where. If they checked out this story, they would find the old driver. Biggs had only just been brought in, so it might be just a matter of time before the police hunted the fellow down. He would crack under pressure from Butler, and they would all be sunk.

'We'd better do something about it,' Gordon stated obviously.

'You better had, yeah, Gordy.' Charlie pointed at him. '*You* gotta do something.' His tone made it clear what he meant.

'I'll sort it,' Gordon said, hoping to reassure Charlie. If he saw to this, then there would be no suspicion laid at his door by any of the others.

'Actually, I think Buster knows where he lives,' Charlie added.

'Buster's hiding.'

'You no idea where he is?'

'None. I dunno where anybody is now, they've all scattered, Charlie.'

'I don't blame 'em. I wish I had.'

Wilson looked resigned to his fate. This lifted Gordon's spirits in a strange way. He didn't want to be sitting around, twiddling his thumbs, while they came up with all the evidence and the witnesses they needed to finally nail him. There was nothing on him at that moment, and this Stan bloke was the only loose end. Gordon knew a man who might be able to sort this out for them, someone they could all trust. Jack Armstrong would know why it was important to eliminate him, for the same reasons. Stan could also identify the northerners. Gordon felt a little for the old train driver, but all of their liberties were at stake, and it was too late to back down now.

'I know how to fix it. Leave it to me, mate.'

53

Bob Welch dialled the number from a phone box on Wandsworth High Street. He knew the name to ask for, and waited for an answer to come.

'New Scotland Yard, can I help you?'

'Er, yeah, I'd like to speak to DI Barclay, please?'

'Just a minute, I'll get him. Who shall I say is calling?' an officious voice replied.

'Oh, just tell him it's a good friend.' The line went silent for nearly a minute.

'Barclay here.'

Even from just two words, the voice sounded familiar, his information was correct. Cliff Barclay from the old days. More importantly, he knew he could trust this man, regardless of where he was sitting that very moment.

'Don't say anything. It's Bobby.'

'Who?'

'Bobby Welch.'

There was a slight pause, and Welch imagined Barclay looking around his office to check he wasn't being overheard. Bob pricked the silence.

'Can you talk now?'

'Yeah.'

'Right. I was told to ring you.'

'Yeah. Look, Mister Harris, thank you for calling.'

Welch smiled to himself, and looked up and down the street. Everything seemed totally normal, he was certain that nobody was tailing him. He had been told there were men on the inside of the investigation who would help him to hide his money somewhere safer. Tommy Lavery's recommendation was a personal one. Bob knew more than all of the others in the gang, when his name was mentioned on the night of the robbery. A few were confused, others looked nervous, but Bob Welch was reassured. If Lavery was behind the blag, everything would be taken care of, including the police. There as even a hand-written note on the sheet of paper that Jack Armstrong handed him that night, saying everything would be taken care of. The day before this phone call to Barclay, Tommy Lavery had 'bumped' into him in a betting shop in Shoreditch, although there was no surprise in his face. Their meeting lasted no more than a minute, but he felt much better for it. All he had to do was make contact with Cliff, a copper he knew from years back.

'I'm told you can help me make my next move,' Welch said.

'Yeah, that's right. You and your friend.'

'Oh, yeah?' He must have meant Danny Pembroke. Did they know where they had buried the money?

'Yeah. Look, wait just a minute.' The line went quiet again, and Welch waited patiently. He felt confident in his protection. 'It's okay now. I'm on my own,' Barclay whispered.

'Tell me, then. He said you could help me.'

'First thing is, stay the hell away from home. Your name's on a list that's been all round the houses, Bobby.' People talked, Welch knew that, but apparently everyone was trying to get a piece of the action. Tongues were loose because the reward was tempting. Welch looked up and down the street again. All seemed quiet, Bob felt relaxed even though Wandsworth was far away from his home turf.

'You need to stay out of London, at least for now. There's raids planned in the next couple of days.'

'I get the picture.'

'You need a new safe house. You are gonna be watched very closely, as soon as they pick up your tail. Your old safe house is about to be blown.'

'What safe house?'

'Come on, Bobby. There are so many people talking out there, we know what everybody's eating for breakfast. The investigation knows you've got a place somewhere near the south coast, we start turning over farmhouses down there from the day after tomorrow.'

'Fuck.'

'Exactly. So, you need to move things, if you catch my drift.'

How could they know? They didn't have Danny, and if they did pick him up, he wouldn't say a word. The rest of South London was leaking, however. Bob thought about asking Barclay where he fitted into everything, but decided it would make no difference. His focus was going to have to be on moving the money.

'Can you help?' Welch asked, meaning Tommy Lavery.

'There is a new safe house, off the radar. A long way away.'

Bob wanted it to be in the South of France. 'Where?'

'You just need to catch up with Danny; he's meeting a bloke this morning who knows the place. I'm sure you know where Danny is.' Pembroke had been constantly on the move since the robbery, had moved out of Camberwell, and was staying with a friend in Clapham.

'And this is gonna be safe?'

'Absolutely. Nobody knows about it. I think you should stay there as long as you can. The heat will die down, eventually. We're coming looking for you Bobby, London is not the place to be hanging around.'

Bob loved the city. Even going out as far as Buckinghamshire, to carry out the job, was a pain in the arse. They just didn't know how to live out there; the pubs were useless, never any decent beer. And the way they talked, Jesus, he had no idea what they were saying half the time.

'Danny knows about it?'

271

'Yeah. Catch up with him, as soon as you can. Someone's back, I gotta go.'

'Thanks for your help.'

The man at the other end cleared his throat. 'That's right. We'll be straight on to it, Sir.'

Barclay hung up, obviously no longer alone. Things were starting to leak, and he and Danny needed to act fast. It was a good job he had all the angles covered, had inside information. So long as Barclay was working with him and Lavery, all would be good. Just like in that football match on Wimbledon Common the month before, it was who was on your side that really mattered.

54

13th September 1963: Shepperton, Middlesex

Mr and Mrs Green stared at the suitcases in the wardrobe. They were the focus of both their excitement for the future, and exasperation at their current incarceration. Buster reckoned that June would trade it all in for the freedom to move around as they wished, or simply to go back home. Both the Twickenham flat and Ralph Simpson's place had been abandoned in favour of this lovely close in Shepperton. Nice and suburban as it was, he wasn't far away from agreeing with her.

The door knocked and Buster froze. He went back to the automatic response, and hid in a cupboard while June answered the door. He heard murmurings downstairs, and then she shouted up for him to come down. Their 'minder', Geordie, was standing there, breathing heavily.

'We've got to move. Right now.'

'What, right away?'

'Right now, yeah. Both of you are gonna be in the newspapers, on the front page, in a couple of hours. Pack your bags and get ready, quickly. I'll take you somewhere safe.' Geordie was a large man, and they had become extremely reliant on his services. His broad presence made you listen when he spoke, and right now he had their total attention. 'I'll be back in twenty minutes, I've just got to make a phone call.'

'You could use our phone,' June offered.

'Nah, that's good of you, I know what I'm doing.' Geordie walked out of their front door and up to his Vauxhall Viva. An ordinary car, parked in an ordinary street. Except that shortly the residents of this quiet cul-de-sac were going to find out that their neighbours, that nice Mr and Mrs Green, who lived at 6 Old Forge Crescent, were in fact a train robber and his wife.

Buster raced around gathering together clothes, whilst his wife got their young daughter ready to move. Where would they be heading next? They had been there less than four weeks, and Buster had got used to the quiet area. He knew June would be sick of their life if they kept moving about. She already wanted to settle down and enjoy the fruits of his labour. Their goal was to head abroad, but it might take some time for that to be a safe option, according to Geordie. It would use up part of the money of course, because false passports and new identities didn't come cheap. Their minder had already dropped the hint that he could fix this up. He seemed to be a nice bloke, always ready when they needed him, providing updates every three or four days on the investigation as well. He must have had inside information. Buster wanted more than anything to talk to Bruce, who he knew from the newspapers, was also the subject of a manhunt. Reynolds was probably already out of the country, sunning it on the beaches of St Tropez. Bruce always had a plan, thought ahead.

Before they knew it, Geordie was back at the front door, and June simply opened it with none of the usual precautions. It could easily have been Tommy Butler standing there, but they were in a panic. So many things were being left behind, but Geordie pressed for urgency when he returned.

'We need to get moving, fast,' he announced, standing just inside the doorstep. 'Look, I can help with the luggage you want to take. I assume you want to keep the money in your car?' Geordie eyed the suitcases at the bottom of the stairs. Out of the five assembled; only two contained their clothes and possessions, the three largest their financial future.

'Let's just get everything out to the cars.' Geordie appeared to be calm, despite the urgency. 'You take the eleven hundred,' he instructed. They were getting used to doing as they were told.

Buster eyed the second hand Morris they had bought with cash four days after the robbery. Maybe that was going to be traceable as well. At least the green and black patterned suitcases containing the money were staying with them.

'Just follow me, and don't panic on the roads. If we speed, we'll draw attention to ourselves. You're gonna be perfectly safe.' Geordie exuded an air of calm that seemed to relax June a little. Their daughter, Nicky, thought this was another great adventure. The poor girl was going to have to change schools once again.

The Greens left many of their possessions behind, but they had little choice. Buster locked the front door as they left. It would probably make no difference to the police when they showed up. He wanted to hang around, and watch the frustration on their faces when they broke in and found nobody home.

Geordie led them into the late morning traffic, across the river and on to the North Circular. They eventually pulled up outside a warehouse in Ealing; this far North West of town was unfamiliar territory. Geordie got out, and beckoned the Green family to do likewise. Buster should have been wary of being set up, of police jumping out of the shadows and pouncing. But all he saw were a pair of tall men, who emerged from a parked van, which was poking out of one of the warehouse doors. They walked up and shook Geordie's hand, and then their minder wandered over to talk to the three of them.

'Right. We're all set, Mr and Mrs Green. And Miss Green.' Geordie smiled as he said their acquired names out loud. Buster knew that June appreciated everything he had done for their daughter, as well. 'We have somewhere for you to go for two days. Then we're going to a place in the country I know you want to visit.'

'Where?' June asked, holding Nicky's hand tightly.

'Wraybsury.'

'Wraysbury? How did you know?' June failed to hide her surprise.

'It's my job to know, Mrs Green. We can't go there straight away, but I know you'll like it there.'

'It's the same place?'

'I understand it is, yeah,' Geordie replied.

Buster was amazed. How the hell did he know? The previous year they had viewed a fabulous house in the southern edge of Buckinghamshire, in the village that Geordie was talking about. It had a large garden that backed on to the Thames. When they first visited, Buster imagined himself, dangling his fishing rod in the river, wiling away the hours. It sounded like an ideal place to go. Maybe June had told Geordie about it before.

'You mean Sunnymede, don't you?' June said.

'I think that's the name of the place. It's now up for rent. June, I can take you there in a couple of days, but we need to keep Mister Green under wraps for a little longer. You'll need one of your wigs.' He smiled, and then pointed at her husband. 'He's all over the newspapers.' He checked his watch, and paused. 'About now, I'd say.'

Buster looked at his wife, hoping she would be happy if they moved to the house she had fallen in love with. If they could stay hidden there, she might smile again. Geordie certainly seemed to know plenty about them, but perhaps that was all part of his job. They were paying this man a hundred pounds a week, but if they stayed free it would be worth it. He certainly saved them that day.

'Come on, these two lads will get rid of your car. Get your suitcases out now, we still need to keep moving.'

'What are you gonna to do with our car?' Buster asked.

'Lose it somewhere, doesn't matter where. It's traceable to you, so we need to get rid of it. We'll find you another one tomorrow. Meanwhile, get in the van if you will, all of you. We're going to a safe place, then we'll take June and Nicky up to this house.'

'I don't know how to thank you,' June said. Was this strange and generous man growing on her? Buster tried to push it from his mind.

'You don't have to, Mrs Green,' Geordie replied. Buster was impressed by the fact he always used their false names, regardless of where they were. He knew his job. 'Remember, my fee covers everything.'

What choice did they have? Buster remembered the three suitcases filled with the rest of his share from the robbery. They still had that for comfort. When things blew over, maybe next year even, they would go abroad. America, or perhaps Canada. It was their favourite game, dreaming of where they would live with Nicky and their fortune. A few hours in the back of a van was a small price to pay to reach their goal.

55

Mickey Griffin threw the keys to Danny Pembroke, as Jack Armstrong watched on, amused by the little game. 'You open it,' Griffin demanded.

Pembroke looked him up and down, and then put the large key in the front door. It turned easily, and nobody jumped out to arrest them. Did these two really think they were going to be led all the way out to Devon to be turned over to the police? If that was the goal they could have done this anywhere in London. Or just killed them and dumped them in the Thames, if they felt like it. But none of that could be done yet, because they didn't have the money.

'You might have to trust them for a bit,' Lavery had told him, 'and get them to trust you.' Jack wouldn't trust this pair as far as he could throw them. They didn't even bring the bloody money, as he had hoped. The plan was to meet them at Stonehenge, those two morons from the robbery, with their shares in tow. Then lead them to this isolated cottage, and take the cash one way or another. Maybe they were smarter than they looked, and left it behind. Perhaps it was still buried somewhere. He couldn't be arsed to follow Welch and Pembroke around for days, and figured that once they proved that the location was safe, they would return with the money and hide it there. Then they could pounce. Lavery was preaching what he referred to as a 'long game,' but Jack struggled to see the point. Still, if all the decisions were left up to Mickey Griffin, Bob and

278

Danny would both be bound and gagged, ready to be tortured. Sometimes you needed a little bit of subtlety.

'Bob, Danny, this is a safe house,' Jack took over the conversation. 'It's being made available to you, and any friends and family you have, for whatever you want. Nobody knows you're here, nobody knows where it is, you can hide out here for a bit.'

'Not another fuckin' farm,' Welch muttered. Jack picked up during the robbery how much Bob hated being in the countryside. Well, if he wanted to stay safe, there was no choice. The reality was that Armstrong and Griffin were in charge.

'You don't have to use it, you know,' he replied. 'It's a cottage, anyway, not a farm. Tommy is offering you a safe place to hole up in for a while, because things are about to crash in London. You know yourselves that the police are everywhere. They're not bloody well down here, are they?'

Pembroke and Welch looked at each other, and then stepped into the cottage. They slowly explored the place, finding a large stone floor kitchen and a living room on the ground floor. Upstairs there were two bedrooms, and Jack and Mickey left the two men to see their own way around. 'Get them comfortable, relaxed,' were Lavery's instructions. The beauty of the cottage was that you could see anybody coming down the lane for a good half a mile, and dense woods surrounded the rear of the property. If Jack was looking for somewhere to hideout, this would be a good choice, but he was far too busy. Word was that Cordrey and Boal, whoever the hell he was, had more than an average share in their possession. He was hoping they would be released, so he could find out the answer to where the extra came from. Armstrong knew he would stand a better chance of finding the money than Griffin. Mickey would hit first and inflict too much damage before asking, that was his style.

'This'll do,' Pembroke said, as they all stood in the kitchen after the two men had finished exploring the place.

'Yeah, it'll do, I suppose,' Welch added grumpily. Jesus, you don't know you're born, thought Jack. If you had the money with you, you'd probably be dead by now. Griffin broke the silence, but added more tension to the chilly room.

'Where's your shares, then?'

Pembroke and Welch looked daggers at Mickey, who just brazed them out.

'The fuck's it got to do with you?' Welch replied, almost spitting with rage.

'Look, we don't care,' Armstrong interjected. The last thing they needed was a scrap out there in the middle of nowhere. They were both armed, but dead men don't tell you where they've buried over a hundred grand each. He dreaded to think what the boss would do if this ended up in some stupid shoot out, and they came back empty handed. 'We don't care where your money is, do we, Mickey?'

'Nah, I was just asking.'

'He was just asking,' Armstrong continued. 'Do what you like with it.'

'We fuckin' will,' Pembroke replied.

'Good, good.' Jack tried to re-focus the pair on the benefits of staying out of harm's way in Devon. 'This place is under a false name; nobody can link you to this cottage. Rent's paid for a year, if you need it.'

'That's very generous of you,' Welch said sarcastically.

'It's very generous of Tommy,' Armstrong rebutted, 'and you know all about him.'

Welch nodded, Pembroke just stared at him, and then shared what looked like a nervous glance with his friend. The seed was planted. Somebody else was going to be watching those two for a while. He and Mickey would be coming back when the money arrived.

56

Brian Field looked forlorn as he sat in one of the cold interview rooms, deep inside New Scotland Yard. Frank Williams offered him a cigarette, but he declined. Butler was due to walk in later, after Frank had warmed him up.

'Brian, I want to talk to you about the mail train robbery,' he began.

'I wasn't involved. I didn't rob anybody.'

'Didn't you?'

'No.' Field looked scared.

'You've never been to Leatherslade Farm before?'

'No.'

'And you can vouch for your whereabouts between the eighth and ninth of August last?'

'I'm sure I was at home.'

'All that time?'

'I think so, yes.'

Definitely trying to appear unruffled, but betraying how implicated he was in this plot. He sounded a different man to the one he and Fewtrell had asked about German holidays a few weeks before.

'And have you ever been to Dorking, Mister Field?'

'Dorking?'

'Yeah, Dorking.'

'Er, no I don't think so.' Field seemed to relax a little.

'You don't think so, or no, you definitely haven't?'

'I definitely haven't.'

'Have you ever been on holiday to Germany, Mister Field?'

'I already told you. My wife and I went there on holiday in February.'

'Was it nice?'

'Very pleasant, thank you.'

'Stay anywhere nice?'

'Yes, a nice little hotel.' Field stopped to think. 'You asked me this before, I told you about it.'

'I know.' Frank smiled. Field was hanging himself.

Butler knocked on the door and entered, carrying a slip of paper, and a holdall. Field swallowed hard. Tommy Butler picked up the questioning as soon as he sat down.

'Mister Field, how nice to meet you. I'm Detective Chief Superintendent Butler. I want to ask you about this hotel receipt.' Butler shoved the piece of paper under Field's nose on the desk. 'Feel free to have a look. Have you seen this before?'

'Where did you get this?'

'Please answer the question, Mister Field. Do you recognise it?' There was no escaping the evidence. A hotel receipt for the Pension Sonnenbichl, made out to Herr and Frau Field.

'Yes, that looks like our hotel.'

'I'm sure it is, Mister Field. Do you recognise this as being yours?'

'Yes, I suppose it must be. Why?' How they walked into these things, thought Frank, studying the Grey Fox, as he reeled in his prey.

'Do you recognise this bag, Mister Field?' Butler switched his attention to the holdall, which he held up for Field to see, then placed it on the table. Field looked scared to touch it.

'No.'

'You sure, Mister Field?'

'Quite sure, yes. I don't recognise it.'

'That's interesting, Mister Field,' Butler remarked, looking at Williams and sighing. 'Because inside this bag we found over fifteen thousand pounds. Along with this receipt in your name. The money was from the train robbery. The same train robbery you claim you know nothing about.'

'I don't know.'

Butler carried on. 'This piece of paper, along with the bag, have your fingerprints on them. Pretty conclusive, wouldn't you say, Mister Field?'

'I don't know.'

The man looked defeated. How well did he know the robbers? Would he name the rest of the gang? That would save the team some legwork. Maybe he was heavily involved in the organisation of the whole thing? Butler moved to the other area where COC3 had found evidence against Brian Field.

'Let's talk about Leatherslade Farm, shall we?' Field just nodded. 'What role did you play in the purchase of Leatherslade Farm?'

'I work for Mister Wheater. You'd better ask him.'

'Oh, we have, Mister Field. He says you did all the work.'

'That's not true,' Field barked. Turn the lawyers on each other, nice touch, thought Frank.

'You were seen taking a visitor to the farm,' Butler carried on. Field looked more alarmed by this than anything else, worse than having his fingerprints all over a bag containing stolen money. 'You took a potential buyer to the farm, didn't you?'

'Yes, I did. But that's all I did,' Field cracked. 'I didn't have anything to do with the robbery, not me. I'm not a thief.'

'So you say,' Butler chuckled. 'I'm going to bring somebody into the room in a minute, and I want you to tell me if this was the man you accompanied to view the farm. Who you bought the farm for.' Butler promptly stood and left the room, and Frank watched Field closely. He was sweating, the calm exterior abandoned.

When Butler returned, he had Lennie Field and DS Watson

with him. The other Field's name had appeared on the deeds as the new owner of the farm.

'Mister Field, I'm certain this man accompanied you to Leatherslade Farm, posing as a possible buyer. What do you say to that?'

The subject studied the face briefly, and then appeared to breathe a sigh of relief, as if he was expecting somebody else to be brought in. Despite this, he made no outright denial.

'It looks like him, but I can't say for certain it is him.'

'Have a good look, Mister Field.'

Williams smiled as both men looked confused. They knew Lennie Field was the stooge, the name on the paperwork. He and Butler had interviewed him earlier, and it was clear that he had no idea what was going on. Still, that was no excuse. Lennie would go down with the rest of the gang.

'It looks like him. But I don't think it is him.' The suspect looked confused. 'I'm not sure. Maybe.'

'What on earth do you mean?' Butler enquired, starting to lose his patience.

'I don't know. I just don't know.' Brian shook his head as he spoke.

'Thank you,' Butler said, and indicated for Watson to remove the other Field from the room. What an odd response, thought Frank. There were reliable witnesses not only to Brian and Lennie Field visiting the estate agents, but also the property back in July.

'Mister Field. You did visit the farm as you told us earlier with the purchaser, a Mister Leonard Field, didn't you?'

'Yes.'

'Did he not use that name on the visit?' Butler asked.

'I don't know. It might have been another name.'

'And he's no relation of yours?'

'No.'

'How did Mister Field, this other Mister Field, Leonard, hear about the farm?'

'I don't know, you'd have to ask Mister Wheater.'

'We have. He says you made first contact with Leonard Field.'

'I'm not saying any more,' Brian replied, and sat back in his chair, head in his hands. We've got him, thought Frank. When they clammed up, especially after talking a lot to begin with, they knew that they were up to their neck in it. He was in the legal profession, he should have known not to say a word from the start. Now he was done for.

'How involved were you in the purchase of the farm?' Butler pressed the suspect.

'I can't say any more.'

'And you must have realised, when the farm was in the newspapers a few weeks ago, that you were involved in its purchase?'

Field sat with his arms crossed, looking at the floor, ignoring Butler. The Grey Fox must have been sorely tempted to slap him one. Normally he hated it when they went quiet.

'You are aware that if you knew who bought the farm, you should have come forward and told the police?' Butler pressed. 'Straight away, you should have told us.'

Field continued to look impassive, resigned. Frank almost felt sorry for him. He wasn't a real criminal, just a greedy onlooker who thought he could easily line his pockets.

'Very well, Mister Field. I don't have time to ask you the same questions again and again. We're going to take you up to Aylesbury, where you'll be formally charged with robbery, and being an accessory to robbery.' Field made no reply. 'Let's go and talk to Wheater again, shall we?' Butler said to Frank, and the pair left the room, leaving Brian Field to stew in his own guilt. Frank had to congratulate DCI Mesher and his fraud boys; they had unravelled the paperwork pretty efficiently. Both Brian and Lennie Field would be added to the growing list of robbers and their accomplices behind bars.

Williams sat a short while later, eating a sandwich in the

canteen. He pulled his personal list of names from his jacket pocket and studied it. Cordrey, Boal, and three of their relatives up for receiving. Biggs, Hussey, Wisbey and Wilson were all going nowhere, along with the Fields. He reckoned they were probably about half way through reeling in the entire gang. None of them were going to talk, he knew that now, everybody was tight-lipped. The search for Edwards, White, Reynolds, Daly and James was on. There might have been a few more hangers-on, but these were the ringleaders, all still at large. Unlike these hapless Fields and the solicitor, they must have planned ahead. Looking to not only conceal their money well, but also use their network of friends to stay hidden. Frank was determined to track them down eventually.

He studied the other names that he and Watson had worked so diligently to draught. His new charge was relying on a combination of informants, he said. Frank thought about Smith, Pembroke and Welch. They would make a mistake sooner or later, and that was when his team would strike, so long as they were patient, and kept up the observation.

Goody was going to be a tougher nut to crack. He was smart and careful, wouldn't give them any help, unlike most of the others. Barclay wanted to meet up urgently, said he had something to help nail him. Whatever it was, he wanted to keep it quiet from Tommy Butler for now. The Chief didn't need to know how everything got done, just the results. Frank threw his crusts in the bin; there was no hair left to curl. Things were coming together steadily, and he was confident that the gang were falling apart.

57

19th September 1963: Beaford, Devon

'I'm just bloody sick of diggin' bloody holes, Bob, that's all.' Pembroke was sweating, as Welch leant on his own shovel, wiping his brow. Dan was younger than him, but utterly trustworthy. They had pulled a few stunts together before, and now they were inexorably linked, thanks to the robbery of the century. That was what they were calling it now.

It had taken them a week to bring the money to the cottage, following Barclay's tip-off about the place in The New Forest being rumbled. Bob tracked Danny down at an old friend's place as soon as he got off the phone, and they visited their farmhouse the next day. It was clear that somebody had been searching the property, furniture had been re-arranged, and there were even muddy footprints in the kitchen. Whoever it was, they hadn't been particularly careful, or successful. They were relieved to discover that the spot among the trees where their money was buried was undisturbed. However, all the evidence supported Barclay's claim that the farmhouse location was blown. After hiding out in a small hotel in Weymouth for a few days, they were forced to move their money down to Devon, and planned to use the property that the northerners said Lavery had paid for. Bob and Danny were digging again, this time in a new spot, at the base of a tree behind their second safe house, a place called Beaford Cottage.

They were also buoyed by the presence of two of their trusted friends, Charlie Lilley and Ron Harvey. The chest weighed a bloody ton when fully laden, and they were working together to get it buried as fast as possible. Charlie was also a central part of Bob's alibi. The plan was for all four to stay at the cottage while the fuss over the robbery died down, and keep an eye on their share.

With the money finally underground, the four men trudged back up to the house, and prepared to celebrate. Why steal that amount of money, and then sit on all of it? Sure, put a good proportion of it in a safe place, but what was money for, but to spend? They planned to head for the local town and a rather nice pub Bob had spotted on the way in. Nobody would be looking for them down there. The Flying Squad were experts in and around London, but wouldn't travel that far, not even chasing stolen money.

'Come on, drinks are on me,' Bob declared, as he just about managed to keep pace with the other three men. He was the oldest and most unfit of the group, but this heist seemed to have put some life back into his legs. Two weeks of celebration began there and then, eating into nearly a thousand pounds in pubs and hotels along the Devon coast. They were invisible, invincible, aided by Tommy Lavery and his inside information on the investigation. Butler and his men could stick their investigation where the sun didn't shine.

★ ★ ★

After putting his binoculars away, Jack Armstrong pulled steadily away in his stolen Ford Cortina. The cars he borrowed meant nothing to him, and the arrangement was always short-lived. Information had reached him through Barclay, that local officers were staking out the cottage, and that it had been placed under observation until the men moved away. Whilst they were in position, everything would be contained. The police were under instruction to follow the men, but didn't know exactly where the money was. Jack Armstrong had been watching as they buried it, and now he had it pinpointed. Making it look like somebody had been snooping around the previous safe house in the New Forest was all about forcing Welch and Pembroke to break cover, and head for Beaford. His instructions had been to take nothing; unless it was simply lying there on the kitchen table, just disturb things. Lavery wanted them down in Devon where they could be controlled.

He pulled up at a phone box and dialled the number.

'Mercury calling,' he began.

'I read you, Mercury. This is Venus. All is clear.' What the hell was all this nonsense? He had to play along, because Tommy loved this sort of fun and games.

'Good. They're here all right, they moved it.'

'Good. I love these boys, they're so bloody predictable.'

The voice at the other end boomed with pleasure. Armstrong had to admit that Lavery was adept at playing people, and wondered how much he too was being manipulated. Thinking about it was troubling, so he tried to dismiss it. The boss trusted him, and that was all he needed to know. There had been several opportunities for him to line his personal pocket in the past couple of months, and with the exception of that small bundle in Dorking, he had deferred. He knew where his priorities lay, in staying alive. There was no future in being a rich corpse.

'I know. There's a couple of hangers on as well,' he added.

'Don't worry about them.'

'I'm not. I'm just telling you, there's four of them here.'

'No problem. Listen, stay handy, but you don't need to watch twenty-four hours a day. I'll get word to you when they move on.'

'You don't want me to watch them?'

'I said, there's no need.' Tommy sounded impatient. 'The local law are doing that. It's covered.'

'Okay.'

'Talk to you soon. Venus saying goodbye.'

Armstrong hung up and headed back to the car. He would leave this one at a railway station, maybe Exeter this time. He had to keep the faith in Lavery, realised full well he was only one cog in the whole plan, and wondered again just how far Tommy reached. Any old regional police force, New Scotland Yard, Ireland, he was everywhere, and Jack was just one man. He knew his limitations, and was determined to stick to them.

58

26th September 1963: The Goat and Compasses pub,
Marylebone, London

Jack waited patiently for the lecture to finish. He had no interest in the technical details of spectrums and ranges of paint. All he and Tommy wanted to know was whether the evidence would be strong enough to land Gordon Goody in jail. He eyed this Doctor Stannard contemptuously. Lavery looked bored to tears.

'Look, just tell me straight, is it gonna be enough to convict him?' Tommy asked.

'I think it will,' Stannard replied.

'You *think* it will?' Jack watched as Lavery gave the scientist his deadly stare.

'I do, yes,' he replied nervously. 'We've got enough of that paint to match up with his shoes.'

'It will stand up,' Cliff Barclay added. 'Doctor Stannard here can be very persuasive in court.'

Lavery would have little choice but to believe the two men, this expert witness and one of his moles. They both knew the consequences if they didn't carry out his instructions. Barclay seemed solid so far, and Stannard, well they had a special hold over him. Everybody had a weakness; it was just a matter of working out what it was. In the case of this little bespectacled so-called expert, it happened to be young men. It was secrets that got you every time.

'We're going to use the paint idea on someone else as well, this Boal,' Stannard continued.

'Why?' Lavery asked.

'If we're playing with evidence, we might as well do it for two men,' Barclay argued. 'We've got more chance of it all being considered if the paint helps to convict another suspect as well. It's a sensible move if we don't want the judge to throw Goody's case out.' Jack thought that there did seem to be some logic to this.

'Who is this bloody Boal, anyway?' Lavery almost shouted. Jack had told him that he was an innocent bystander, went nowhere near the farm. His presence complicated matters.

'The Squad think he was in on it. This paint evidence will re-enforce what we want Butler to think,' Barclay added. 'We don't want him doing an about turn on the investigation, not even on an innocent man.'

'And they think he was there?' Lavery asked.

'Yep.'

'Fuckin' idiots.' Lavery's distaste for the law wasn't being helped by this Boal affair. Both he and Mickey had a particular interest in Boal, and his mate Cordrey. Thirty grand's worth of particular interest.

Jack looked at the two men sat opposite in the pub. Both were drinking lager, which told you everything you needed to know. The boss drew on his drink, a scotch with water. Lavery had taken to the shorts, hated the southern piss, he said. Jack had to agree. Tommy pointed his finger aggressively in Barclay's direction.

'We give you the bloody names; you barely use the information. Then you rope some other fool in for no good reason. If you're after innocent men, I'm surprised you haven't come looking for me,' Lavery laughed. Jack looked around *The Goat and Compasses* on the Edgware Road, which was empty apart from a man and a woman sitting at the bar. They were safe there.

'It's Hatherill and Butler. You should see them. They keep secrets from each other, it's hilarious,' Barclay grinned.

'Is it?' Lavery asked, angrily. 'How can we trust the police force today, eh? If you can't get basic stuff done?'

Jack eyed both Stannard and Barclay taking the criticism. He knew he should pity them, but they were the law after all. Strictly speaking, Stannard wasn't on the force; he was a forensic expert they pulled in for big cases. When they got the nod from Barclay that he was working the investigation, Parlane checked up on his background, found what they wanted. Now Butler and his team would have all the evidence they needed to bring in one of the ringleaders. Lavery seemed to want Gordon Goody sitting in a cell now that they had dug up Bob Corden's garden, and recovered most of his share. Corden was missing, had probably disappeared as soon as he realised that Goody's money had gone. There would be only one direction the finger would point.

Barclay looked at his watch. 'I've got to go; they're expecting me back at the Yard.'

'Well, mind how you go,' Lavery responded, looking bored. 'In fact, I think it's about time you started talking to somebody else on the team.'

'There's another?' Barclay looked surprised. Did he really think that he was the only inside contact Lavery had? He might have been on the force for fifteen years, but Cliff Barclay, or whatever he was calling himself now, still had plenty to learn. Everywhere Jack looked there were people being turned upside down.

'Go carefully. And don't give anything away, obviously. But it might be worth your while talking to one of the young sergeants on the Squad. You never know what mutual friends we might have.'

Barclay still looked incredulous. 'So, I'm not alone?'

'Look, I can't spend my entire time running about, passing information from one person to another. I want you to be the main point of contact from now on, understand?' Barclay nodded obediently. 'I've had enough pissing about. It's about time you two talked.'

Barclay rose from the table and downed his drink. 'You're not gonna tell me who it is?'

'You're the fuckin' detective, work it out. Jesus.'

Barclay put his hat on and walked quickly out of the door, leaving Jack and Tommy with Stannard.

'What you fuckin' still doing here? Piss off and do your job,' Lavery whispered, and Stannard also disappeared, knocking a couple of empty glasses over on the table as he went.

'Fuckin' idiots,' Tommy hissed under his breath, smiling at Jack.

'Yeah,' he agreed.

'Right. I need you to catch up with George again. He's got somebody for you to meet. We've found Harry Smith.'

59

Gordon Goody parked his Jaguar extremely carefully in the street, a two-minute walk away from the police station. It was not unknown for the owners of certain vehicles in their car park to return to 'accidentally' smashed headlights or dented wings. This visit was simply a requirement of his bail, nothing more than procedure. Before long they would lose interest in him, and he could get on with his future plans. Jack Armstrong had already promised to resolve the thorny problem of Stan, the driver. Dublin seemed a good place to spend his gains, and his thoughts had turned to investing in property and opening a restaurant over there.

As he walked in and approached the front desk, his heart sank. Butler and Vibart from the Flying Squad were waiting for him, which didn't look good.

'Gordon. Pleased to see you,' Butler said, sarcastically. He was a terrier; Goody gave him that. But he was sure they were chancing their arm again; there would be no evidence to link him to the farm or the train. His money would be safely undisturbed. He had carried on living a meagre existence, not even holding on to so much as a pound note from the robbery, just in case the story in the newspapers about the marked notes turned out to be true. It was probably a load of bull that Butler had spread to try to panic them.

'Can we have a quiet word? We've got a room set aside for us, out back,' Butler beamed. I bet you have, thought Gordon. Maybe they would try to beat it out of him.

'Sure. Don't I have to sign anything?' he said, remembering his bail conditions. He didn't want that weasel Vibart tricking him into a spell inside.

'We've taken care of that,' Vibart added. Gordon mistrusted Vibart more than most. At least Butler was straight about things. He could be nasty, tenacious, yell at you, but he wasn't snide like Vibart. He decided to ignore the DCI and only address his boss.

'I should sign my forms, all the same.'

Goody went up to the desk, and within two minutes had shown that he had been present at Putney station at the specified time. Butler led him inside the building proper, and Vibart followed behind. He kept his eyes on the sneaky one and tensed, waiting for a kick to come. Butler eventually led them into a small interview room, with a table and four chairs.

'Have a seat, Gordon, if you will.'

Butler was all smiles and courtesy. Vibart looked like he was going to explode. As soon as Gordon sat down, Butler produced a pair of shoes from within a polythene bag, and placed them on the table.

'Are these your shoes, Gordon?'

Goody studied them closely. They were definitely similar to a pair he owned.

'They look like mine.' What were they up to? He didn't wear any like that on the job; he had boots on the whole time.

'Have you ever lent them to anybody?' Butler enquired.

'No, of course not.' Gordon forced a smile, and Butler joined him. Vibart continued to scowl.

'You're sure you've never lent them to anybody?'

'Sure.'

'Right, you're nicked then.' Butler sat back jubilantly.

'What?'

'You're nicked, Gordon.'

'What for?' What were they playing at?

'Robbing the mail train,' Butler and Vibart added in unison, the latter with glee.

'What?'

'Yeah, Gordon. You robbed the train. What do you say to that?'

Gordon thought carefully. History was full of cases where the police had tried to goad people in to denying things, knowing they had firm evidence to trip them up later in court. All it meant was that the sentence would be longer. But they had nothing on him, so he decided to give Butler and Vibart the silent treatment.

'Gordon. We know you were involved in the mail train robbery in August. It's no use denying it,' Butler continued.

Goody wasn't going to play the game. 'I'd like to speak to my solicitor, please.'

'What, John Wheater? Or Brian Field, maybe?' Vibart asked, unable to hold back a laugh.

Gordon vaguely recognised the first name, felt the second one vibrate through him. What had Brian done? Grass on them all?

'I'm saying nothing until I've spoken to a brief.'

Gordon folded his arms and sat back in his chair. What were they playing at? Shoes? He knew he didn't wear those on the farm, or on the job. They were fitting him up. Everything came back to the Heathrow job. For three months they tried to nail him, he survived two trials, and he walked free. This was payback as far as the police were concerned, especially Vibart. That little worm had worked the case, been exasperated by Gordon wriggling through his fingers. He looked at the two men across the table. They both grinned, happy with their revenge.

60

10th October 1963: Shoreditch, London

Joe Watson had been busy on early morning raids of late, as well as pushing for more information on the streets of South London into the night. They were putting in ridiculous hours, and every day there were fresh warrants, places to search. They were regularly being dealt new names, known associates of the suspects, but most seemed to have nothing to do with the crime. Maybe the Met were having an influence, using the robbery as an opportunity to rattle a few cages. Things were apparently pretty quiet on the streets compared to before the heist; the police were watching everywhere. A few criminals were pretty pissed off with the train robbers, because this job had brought increased attention on everybody. He knew that for some, the quicker the gang were brought in, the better.

This time he was tagging along with DS Moore and DS Slipper, as they went in search of Harry Smith, who had eluded them for three weeks. Despite being thought of as a prominent member of the gang, no underground sources would tip off where he was. His house had been turned over twice, with no clues. The pubs he frequented in the East End were regularly visited, but there were no signs. Now they turned to his mother and father, who worked for a bookmaker in Shoreditch. This time they at least found something.

They showed their warrant to Mr and Mrs Smith, who

grudgingly let them in. An extensive search found piles of notes, along with postal orders, scattered about the home. Bookmakers were well known for laundering money, and often ran rackets exchanging large quantities of cash for postal orders. It looked like this was precisely what Smith's parents were up to. In all, they recovered nearly ten grand, piling it up on the kitchen table. Mrs Smith was comically concealing bundles of notes in her underwear, which made Slipper blush. A WPC had to be called in to complete the search.

Many of the notes they found were wet, and stuck together, and smelt as if they had been buried. They inspected the back garden, but found no obvious signs of recent digging. The couple claimed that they were merely drying out a significant marker that had been placed the day before, brought into the bookmakers by a 'big player.' The team's observations revealed that Danny Regan, a known associate of Harry Smith's, had visited the property. Everything seemed to fit. Either Regan was in on the job, and was using the Smith family to launder the money, or he was helping Harry directly. Whichever it was, they knew the observation had to continue.

'Didn't we raid Regan last week?' Slipper asked Moore. Watson knew the answer, because he had been on that one.

'It was two weeks ago. Regan's place in Aldersgate,' Watson filled the officers in. He knew that they only turned the place over because he was a neighbour of Jimmy White, one of the faces that had been in the newspapers and on the run.

'You were there?' Slipper asked.

'Yeah. Nothing,' Joe replied. 'Regan came into Cannon Row, but didn't say a word.'

'Bloody figures,' Slipper noted. 'So, this Regan knows Smith as well?'

'Yeah, he does. And White. He lived next door to Jimmy White's sandwich shop.'

'Like bloody refugees,' Slipper snorted.

The three men realised the Smiths were sitting listening to their conversation. Slipper told the couple they were to be taken down to New Scotland Yard, and charged with receiving stolen money from the mail train robbery. Neither said a word.

'Come on then, Joe, you're the bloody expert. Where's Harry Smith now?' Slipper asked. 'This lot ain't telling us.' They had moved out into the hall, careful not to be overheard.

'I dunno. We heard a few things last week, when he was shifting about a lot, then nothing.'

'Nothing?' asked Moore.

'No. He's completely slipped off the radar. Even the locals, you know, those in his boozer, they haven't seen him for days.'

'Maybe he's gone abroad?' Slipper asked.

'We don't even know for certain he was on the robbery,' Moore added. 'There's no fingerprints, no forensics on him.'

'Oh, he would have been there,' Slipper said. 'They bloody all were, every one of 'em on our wall. Just some of 'em was more careful than others.'

Watson wondered if this were true. Maybe it was simply a lottery which dictated who got pulled in, and who stayed free. Smith was a worry. Lavery had asked him to keep tabs on him, advise if he left London. There was no word through legitimate channels about where he was. As far as Frank Williams was concerned, there wasn't enough evidence to put out a public appeal for Smith, which was fortunate. The plan was to keep things away from Hatherill, especially as Butler was now in sole command of the Flying Squad. They had to focus on catching criminals, not worry about the politicians. Joe had additional considerations, and he needed to track down Harry Smith before Lavery realised he had dropped off his radar.

61

Harry Smith struggled against the twine that bound him to a chair. Jack Armstrong watched through a gap in the door of the warehouse, poised to strike. Mickey Griffin stood alongside him. They had been spying on the two men and their prisoner for about twenty minutes, and frankly time was up.

They marched into the vast room, shotguns waving in the air. 'Hello, lads. Nice to meet you,' Jack shouted. Smith looked petrified, stuck in his seat. The other two froze. 'You're good at tying knots, I'll give you that.' Armstrong carried on calmly, addressing the man standing closest to Smith. 'Drop the bat,' he instructed.

It fell to the floor with a clatter, and the man rolled it with his foot in the direction of Mickey Griffin, without being ordered to do so. The other put his hands up, a cigarette offering smoke up to the ceiling.

'Drop that as well,' Mickey shouted. What was he going to do, blind them with his fag?

The pair with their hands in the air looked like lucky chancers who had stumbled across a train robber, and decided to drag him off and beat out of him where his money was. Armstrong studied Smith in the chair, as they slowly advanced. There was blood pouring from the side of his head. Had they taken this task too seriously?

'Move. Over to the column,' Jack ordered, pointing his shotgun at the two men. Both scowled back, and shuffled their way to the middle of the room.

Jack went over to the chair, where Harry Smith sat, shivering. Jesus, he had pissed himself. Armstrong walked around to the back and studied the bonds holding Smith firm. The room stank of grease and urine. What did they do to him?

'Who the fuck are you?' Parlane asked. You know bloody well who we are, Jack thought, but kept up the pretence.

'No, who the fuck are you?' Jack responded, stepping in front of Smith and keeping his shotgun aimed at Parlane's head. There was no reply from the two men. The one with the cigarette stubbed it out on the floor of the warehouse. It would be best if Morgan said nothing at all.

'Keep your hands up, if you will?' Armstrong commanded. He wouldn't mind just a little bit of resistance, he was sure Griffin would be all for it. 'Do you know who you've got here?'

'Fuck off,' was all Parlane offered. Jesus, couldn't he come up with anything more original?

'This is a friend of ours. You all right, Harry?' Jack said, turning around.

'Yeah.' Harry tried to crack a smile, but winced. The cut looked to be pretty deep.

'You did this, did you?' Jack asked, turning back to the kidnappers.

He walked towards Parlane, waving his shotgun at him threateningly. Griffin stood motionless in the corner of the room. When was he going to bloody well join in?

'Have you been asking our friend where his money is?' Armstrong shouted at the men stood in the middle of the empty warehouse. He hoped Smith was buying it.

'Don't you want to know?' Parlane replied. Good one.

'We just want to know what he's told you.'

'Fuck all,' Parlane answered, looking at the floor. Don't start bloody laughing; you clown.

'He's told you nothing? About where his share of the money is?' Armstrong pushed again, pointing his empty shotgun at each man in turn. There was no need to take chances, and Smith wouldn't know from where he was sat if it was loaded or not.

'Nothing. I had to give him a reminder,' Parlane replied.

'This is a good friend of ours.' Jack looked across at Griffin. 'Mickey, what do you think we should do with this pair?'

'I dunno. Should we kill 'em?' Mickey suggested with a wicked grin. Parlane's face looked suitably shocked. There was no harm in going slightly off script. They had to make it look genuine, after all. Jack thought about being left alone in the caravan park in the dead of night, with bloodied knees and a potential killer dog on his tail. He could make Parlane pay.

'I dunno. Maybe.'

He turned his attention to the man in the chair again, putting his shotgun on the ground to untie him. The knots were tough to shift, so he used a knife from out of his back pocket. Smith rose gingerly to his feet, shaking his legs to get the circulation going. Fortunately for the effect of the drama they were acting out, he still looked groggy.

'You all right, Harry?' Jack asked.

Smith nodded. 'Yeah. What you doing here?'

'We're your bloody rescue party, your guardian angels, Harry.'

'Ah. Cheers.'

'No problem. You didn't tell 'em anything about your money, did you?'

'Nothing.'

'Or about anyone else who was on the job with you?'

'No, course not. They didn't ask me.'

'Didn't they?' Armstrong replied, turning to look at the two men at gunpoint, mouthing, 'tossers' at Parlane and Morgan. They were supposed to make this look like a genuine kidnapping.

'How long they had you?'

'I dunno. A few hours, I think.'

'Well, you're safe now, mate.'

Griffin handcuffed the two men to a steel column that rose up in the middle of the warehouse. Neither man argued. Jack didn't notice if Mickey slipped a key into one of their pockets, and hoped he had remembered that part of the plan. Parlane and Morgan would be pretty pissed off if they left them there unable to escape. Jack turned his attention to Smith, and what he needed to hear, as he addressed the two stranded men. Before he could do so, Griffin kicked Morgan in the back, making him slump against the column. Harry Smith grimaced. It certainly looked pretty convincing.

'No,' Parlane shouted, but too late. Mickey repeated the dose for him, and then whacked him across the shoulder with the butt of his shotgun for good measure. That was more like it, Jack thought. It was a fair return for what they did to poor Harry in the chair. Armstrong addressed the two kidnappers.

'Now, you greedy pair of fuckers. This never happened, all right? You never took our friend here anywhere. We never showed up. We never cuffed you. This is just a bad dream, understand?'

Both men nodded, Parlane vigorously, Morgan slowly. Where did Lavery find some of his men?

'Shall we call the police, when we're out of here?' Jack asked Griffin. 'Rather than kill 'em, I mean?'

'I dunno. Maybe we'll forget where we left 'em,' Mickey replied. 'They might starve to death.' That was better; he was really getting into the spirit of it.

'Yeah, maybe you're right. Come on, Harry, we're off before somebody misses these two.'

The three men walked out into the bright sunshine, and Jack's waiting car. Harry expressed his thanks many times during the drive to a new safe house; one that they told him was set up especially for him. Smith was so grateful it almost hurt. All right mate, we know, Jack thought. Just do as we say from now on, and all will be fine. Smith even offered to take them straight to the lock up where part of his money was, to give them something to say thank you.

Harry didn't ask how they worked out where he was being held, or even that he had been snatched in the first place. Maybe the excitement of being released from captivity had gone to his head. Smith was falling into line nicely. A nice problem was starting to emerge. They were going to need more safe places to put men and money.

62

15th October 1963: Aylesbury prison

'Morning, Charlie. How're you keeping?' Armstrong asked.

He was visiting under the name of Jack Haynes, but Charlie Wilson recognised him straight away. The prisoner even smiled, which was a pleasant surprise.

'Shit. I'm in here, ain't I? No thanks to you.' Wilson snuffled, wiping his nose on his sleeve. 'Sorry, I didn't mean that.' Charlie lowered his voice. 'I heard there was a problem.'

'Sore point, Charlie.' Word must have reached him about the thirty grand going missing. 'I've come to see how you're getting on.' Jack looked at Wilson, and thought he looked tired. That's what happened when you played for the wrong side.

'What d'you think?' Wilson replied. Jack looked into his eyes. Lavery needed Charlie to be sat where he was, at least for the time being. This had become an elaborate chess game, moving pieces around a board. Except that they couldn't control everyone, some were frustratingly out of reach. The police locking up half the gang was helping them to keep their eyes on some of the action.

'What's your lawyer like?' Jack asked. Charlie looked downcast, not surprising for a man looking at fifteen years, maybe more.

'He's fine.'

'He from Lessers?'

'Yeah, course. How'd you know?'

'Tommy knows a lot of things, remember?'

306

Wilson understood what he meant. 'I know a lot of people,' he said defiantly.

'I know you do, and I respect that. The problem is, you're sat here, and I'm out there.' Jack pointed to a window. 'There's much more you can do outside.'

Wilson's eyes lit up. He whispered, 'You gonna spring me?'

'Not from here. No chance. The whole country's watching you. You need to take your chances at trial first. Then, if things don't go to plan, we can look at something.' Guilty men were more desperate than those awaiting trial.

'Really?'

'Anything's possible Charlie, if you try hard enough.'

Wilson looked hopeful at first, but then frowned. 'What about when we're moving about, you know, from prison to the courtroom?'

'Again, it's not that we don't want to try. But there's television, papers, everywhere. When things die down, if things don't work out how we'd like them to, then we can look at it.'

'So, you'll only spring me if I'm found guilty?' Wilson asked.

'It's not just that, Charlie. Why go on the run if you might get off? You've been found not guilty before, remember the Heathrow trial?' Jack encouraged.

'This is different. Why've you come to see me, then? It's not hard to work out I'm pissed off, sitting in here. They got fingerprints, I'm screwed.'

'It doesn't look good, I know.'

'Unless you can talk to the forensics, do something about that?'

'I've checked. It's watertight.'

'Really?'

'Really. The farm was full of fingerprints.'

'It was supposed to be cleaned up,' Wilson raised his voice, and then dropped it to a heavy whisper. 'By you.' He pointed an accusing finger in Jack's face. 'You and that silent mate of yours.' Jack gestured for Charlie to calm down.

'You heard what happened. You said you knew there was a problem.'

'Yeah, I heard something. I just hoped it wasn't true.'

'One of your lot nicked our fuckin' money.'

Wilson just looked miserable. Jack knew that it was Roger who took his and Mickey's share. Barclay had given him the figures, and it added up. Charlie wasn't fingering anybody for stealing the thirty grand, so he carried on filling him in.

'We went back, all set to dump the vehicles and torch the place, and one of your pals fucked off with our fee. Would you do it, if that happened to you?'

Wilson sat in silence. Lavery wanted Jack to work on his sense of loyalty. Just wait until you hear the rest of the tale, he thought.

'I'm taking a risk coming here, Charlie, you know that. I want to talk to you about the future.'

'I don't have a future.'

'You do. You've got over a hundred thousand futures.'

'You're not having that.'

'It's not about money.'

'That's easy for you to say. Your boss has got half a fuckin' million in the bank,' Wilson said, staring Jack down. Lavery argued that Jack was ideally placed to break the news, and set the trap.

'No, he doesn't. He's got nothing.' It was actually climbing towards a full million.

'What d'you mean? You and that Paddy got half a million each?' Wilson whispered, looking around. Nobody seemed to flinch.

'The fucker nicked the lot, didn't he? Robbed us, and pissed off back to Ireland with the bloody lot.'

'No way?'

'Oh, yeah. Charlie, there was a bloody army of 'em waiting, we got ambushed, we was lucky to come out of it alive. They had machine guns, the lot. It was bloody embarrassing.' Jack stopped to check on Wilson's reaction, hoping he looked suitably humbled.

'We've been robbed, so we got a right to be pissed off too. We were robbed more than the bloody GPO, I tell you.'

'Can't you go after him? The Ulsterman?'

'What, in Ireland? He's a fuckin' terrorist, Charlie. Didn't you work that out?' Wilson looked dumbfounded. 'That lot with their armoury? We'd be dead in two minutes.'

Wilson looked confused. 'So, he was a conman?'

'I dunno about that. He was right about the train, wasn't he?'

'Yeah, he was that,' Wilson smiled.

'And my boss fronted up all the expenses, that hundred quid a week you all got, that was out of his pocket too.'

'Shit.'

'Yeah, shit. But Tommy is gonna sort that Irishman out in the long term, don't you worry about that.'

'I hope he does.' Wilson seemed to be buying it.

'Well, what I came to say was, this Lesser & Co, these solicitors, they got a few good people working there, you know? Some people very skilled at moving money about.'

'What d'you mean?'

'I mean, Charlie, the best thing for you to do, and the rest of you boys in here, is to talk to someone who can help you hide your money somewhere a bit safer than underground. Wash it away into the economy.'

'Wait a minute,' Charlie replied. He looked like he had been thinking about this already. 'I dunno about handing money over to a solicitor, bent or otherwise.'

'It doesn't have to be that way. You got people on the outside you trust, right?' Wilson nodded. 'Well, all you need is somebody to do the paperwork for your people out there, to flush it away, and bring it back nice and clean for you.'

'At a charge, I assume?'

'All these things attract a charge, you know that, Charlie.'

'And then this solicitor fucks off with my money.'

'No, he won't. We can ensure that doesn't happen. Your friends on the outside can ensure it doesn't happen. We've been robbed enough already, Charlie, all of us. My boss of his money, you of your liberty.'

'That's something I'd rather have, to be honest.' Wilson looked a sad figure, hunched over the table, pain in his eyes.

'What, freedom?'

'Yeah. I got a wife and kids. I wanna be with them.'

'Be patient, Charlie. I'm sure something will turn up, even if they send you down for a little stretch. I'll be there to sort you out, if you fancy going over the wall.'

Wilson eyed Armstrong, who returned the glare. I'm here to help you; Jack hoped his face said, while inside he was laughing, knowing they were going to turn him over.

'Have a word with your friends in here, will you? There's a George Stanley, at Lessers, comes highly recommended. He's good at making things disappear. He's helped my boss before.' There was a faint flicker of recognition at the name in Wilson's eyes. 'Have a think about it anyway. You never know, you might walk out of here one day.'

'Now that would be a miracle,' Wilson said.

'Just think about it, I ask no more.'

Jack shook Wilson's hand and left. He wasn't sure if he'd convinced Charlie about using Stanley and Lessers to launder his money, but he was only there to plant the seed. Maybe in time he could be brought around to the idea, with a little friendly persuasion.

63

25th October 1963: New Scotland Yard

In an interview room deep inside New Scotland Yard, Frank Williams sat passively observing Tommy Butler doing the hard work. The Grey Fox paced the room and eyed Bob Welch menacingly. It wouldn't scare Bob. He was pretty straight for a crook; one of the few Williams had a grudging respect for. Mind you, he had bloody well landed himself right in it. How did those stupid thieves manage to leave so many clues lying around? The fingerprint boys found Welch's dabs all over the place – sauce bottles, windowsills, salt pots, and worst of all, on the bank note wrappers, which had been dumped in the cellar. That was an elementary mistake, incontrovertible evidence.

Even picking him up had been easy that evening. He had returned from Devon to meet his brother by train, and they had been waiting for him outside London Bridge. Welch would be wondering who had grassed him up. They knew that Bob had hidden his money somewhere, they still weren't certain exactly where.

Butler started at the beginning, asking whether Welch had ever been to Cheddington, and to Leatherslade Farm before, the usual trap. Then he moved on to asking about his accomplices.

'I'm going to mention a few names to you now, Bob, if that's okay?' Welch indicated he should carry on, which Butler did. 'Bruce Reynolds, John Daly, Roy James, Ronald Edwards, James White. You know any of these men?'

'No, I dunno any of these people.' A strange reply, thought Frank. Everyone knew he had links with Edwards in the past. Why deny that?

'A number of people have been charged in this case. Do you know any of them?' Butler asked.

'I know Hussey, and Wisbey,' Welch admitted. At least that was something.

'How do you know them?'

'Through spieling, you know.'

'We made an appointment to meet you and a legal representative last month, on the 25th of September. Why didn't you show up?'

'I dunno what you mean.'

'You don't remember the appointment?'

'No.'

Butler tried another tack. 'When we talked to you before, you said you were with a Charles Lilley and James Kensit on the night of the seventh and eighth of August, is that correct?'

'I guess so.'

'Have you seen either of them since?' Don't deny it for God's sake, Frank thought. We've been watching you one way or another for weeks.

'No.'

'Neither of them?'

'No.'

Frank sighed. There was just no helping some people. Butler carried on the inquisition.

'And where have you been staying since we last interviewed you? You've not been at home, have you, Bob?'

They knew about the hideout in Devon, which the local police were still keeping under observation, but had no idea where his money was. Williams hoped to despatch a few of his men down there in the next couple of days to find out, now that they had Welch in custody.

'I been here and there.'

'Here and there?' Butler squared up to Welch, surprising him, hands pressed against the table, face up close. Welch remained calm.

'Yeah, here and there.'

'You need to tell us where.'

'I'm not saying any more.'

'We'll keep you overnight.'

'That's fine. I'll talk to a solicitor in the morning.'

'Yes, I guess you will,' Butler replied dryly. 'You have nothing more to add to your statement from last month, or about where you've been for the past five weeks?'

'No, nothing to say.'

'Okay, we're going to take you up to Aylesbury, where you'll be charged, just like all the others.'

'All right. I've got nothing to say.' Welch repeated.

Williams looked at the suspect, a defeated man. They knew for certain now that Welch had been involved in the robbery, so why keep up the charade? There was a mass of evidence to place him at the hideout, and he was a known associate of many of the others. Why persist with denying everything? What would he gain? Maybe he had already ushered his money abroad, hidden it in a Swiss bank account? That was what Frank would have done. To be honest, the case against many of the others was pretty flimsy, nothing more than hearsay and presence on an informant's list. He was the right man to dig for more concrete information from within the criminal community, together with Joe Watson. His young officer seemed to have an ability to persuade informers to talk. They would track down the rest of the gang, or at worst negotiate the return of some of the stolen money.

They left Welch in the room, ready for transporting to Aylesbury, and an appearance in front of a magistrate in the morning. Frank sought out Butler in the canteen.

'We need to go and search that place in Devon right now, Sir.' Frank almost pleaded with his boss, but the Chief looked at him darkly.

313

'No, not yet. I want to keep observing the place, just in case any of the men return. When word gets out we've lifted Welch, they might panic. Then we can catch them red-handed.'

'But isn't the retrieval of the money the priority? Without it, none of them can flee the country?' Williams asked. Surely Butler saw the logic in this?

'Look, Frank. We don't know for certain the money is there. They spent a few quid, so they tell us down there, but that doesn't mean they're sitting on the lot. Maybe they were just having a holiday?' Butler paused, starting on a stale cheese sandwich. He must have been living off them for weeks. 'We have a plan, Frank, and we shall stick to it. Nobody goes bursting in there until I give the word. Let the locals keep watching, and let's see who shows up before we go wading in with our size nines, shall we?'

Frank returned to the incident room, leaving his boss to finish off his meal. He thought about the man who was making their working lives a misery. The hours were killing morale, the team out on their feet after weeks of investigation. There were occasional bouts of celebration when a suspect was brought in, but mostly it was a hard slog. When he reached the hub of the investigation, he saw Moore, Watson and Barclay sitting at their desks, throwing paper cups about. This wasn't the time for frivolity; there were experienced thieves out there to catch. Screw the Grey Fox, they had to make another breakthrough, and Welch was the opportunity.

'Right. I don't care what Butler says about this. In fact we're not going to tell him.' Frank eyed Moore, who looked up eagerly. 'I want you to go to Devon, to the Welch place. We need to keep an extra eye on that cottage, search the place, and see if that money is there. If we wait for the locals to tell us if anyone shows up again, it might be too late. Moore, I want you to go down there first thing tomorrow, will you?'

'Yes, Guv.'

'What's down there again, Guv?' Watson asked.

'Welch's money. Possibly Pembroke's too, but we think he's

buggered off with his, when he left last week with Lilley. Those two could be bloody anywhere by now. Shows what happens when you let the locals run the show.' He paused for effect, and then delivered a jibe at the Grey Fox. 'Same if you're indecisive, things can drift. Watson, come with me, we've got a bit of rattling to do in our locals. It's early yet.'

64

26th October 1963: Beaford, Devon

'The Yard are on their way down in the morning. You've got to go and lift it now.'

More bloody demands, thought Armstrong, but then again, this was a significant amount of money they were talking about. Two full shares, buried near a certain tree, at the rear of the cottage, and this time he was determined to get there before any courting couples. Lavery's anger had barely dissipated after the escapade near Dorking. He was just about back on the level in terms of credit, thanks to their work with Harry Smith.

He asked to bring Parlane along for this one, rather than Griffin. He wasn't as strong, and therefore less useful for digging holes and removing suitcases full of money, but he was definitely a safer driver, there was no way George would be pulled over for speeding, he was far too careful. Overall, he was a slightly more professional operator. Lavery was insistent that they depart immediately.

'What about the local force, aren't they supposed to be watching the place?' Jack asked.

'They've slackened off, apparently. Big issues with resourcing, especially for cases that have got nothing to do with them. They only watch the place during the daytime. The shift doesn't clock on until seven o'clock these days.'

'In the morning?'

'Yeah, Jack, the morning. Better get moving, go there tonight, remove it before the Yard turns up tomorrow, which they will.'

Armstrong followed his orders. They set off in their van half an hour later, at eleven. A steady drive meant that they arrived at Beaford by about five in the morning, sharing the time behind the wheel in order to stay fresh. It took about an hour to find the correct burial site in the slowly improving light. He had gone back to mark the spot the week before, and prayed that they hadn't moved the money in the meantime. The adrenaline was still rushing through Jack's veins when he heard a 'thunk' from a shovel, followed by a loud 'fuck', from Parlane, as he hit something solid. Both men hurriedly dug at the earth until the lid of the trunk could be lifted.

'We're not fuckin' carrying that, are we?' Parlane asked.

'No, we're not. Open it up.'

There was no lock, and it took the strength of both men to raise the lid. They smelt the musty contents before they saw them. Everything reeked of mould and damp, and reminded Jack of dead bodies. What the hell else did they bury in there?

'Jesus, what a stink,' Parlane remarked. The standard of conversation didn't improve despite the fact he was working with George.

'Come on, let's get the cases out,' Jack ordered. They removed eight in all from the buried trunk, and laid them out on the grass.

'What do we do? Carry 'em?' Parlane asked.

'We can't drive in this deep to the trees, can we? It's too dense.' Just like you, Jack thought. Parlane or Griffin, which was the most stupid? It was still a toss up. 'Right, here's what we do,' he announced to his partner. 'We take two cases each on our first trip to the van, and then we nip straight back for the rest, okay? It's gonna be light any minute. I don't want to take any chances.' Memories of the Welsh coast and Dorking woods were coming back to Armstrong. Better to return with at least part of the money than none at all.

'They look fuckin' heavy,' Parlane complained.

'Of course they're fuckin' heavy. They're full of money. Come on.'

'Then we come back for the others?'

'I said, yeah. Come on.'

The first visit to their hidden van was a nightmare. They had to throw the suitcases over a high fence. It barely registered on the way in, but transporting objects back over it was no picnic. It took both men using all their strength to heave them one at a time over the obstacle. The cases were incredibly heavy, and all Armstrong wanted to do was lie down when they reached the vehicle. The improving light drove them on. Jack was sweating, and Parlane was panting desperately when they made it back to the trunk. It was easier to locate the second time around, but the coming sunrise would also help make them more visible, adding more urgency. They closed the trunk, and re-buried it as best they could, but they were in a hurry. If the men ever came back, they would know that they had been turned over immediately.

They struggled with the second set of suitcases even more than the first trip, and collapsed against the van when they closed the door for the final time.

'Come on, we've got to get the fuck out of here,' Armstrong ordered, obviously. They jumped in the van. 'But don't speed off, we can't afford to get lifted with this load in the back.' He knew that if he were working with Griffin, Mickey would have ignored him, and floored it all the way. They were heading for a storage facility in Bristol, a place Lavery had assured him things could be hidden for a couple of days, before moving the money north.

Armstrong wondered to himself what his chances would be if he did try to go it alone, maybe disappear with a couple of the suitcases. He briefly contemplated smashing Parlane over the head, and catching a ferry to Ireland. He knew the answer almost before the idea popped into his brain. Sooner or later, he would be found washed up on a beach, or buried in a wood just like the empty trunk that belonged to Bob Welch and Danny Pembroke. No amount of money was worth that risk.

65

10th November 1963: The A4 near Bath

Bruce Reynolds pulled his car into a lay-by, and waited. He was five minutes late, but there was no sign of John. He imagined he would probably have at least one of those bloodsuckers with him when he showed up.

Life was still a struggle. Little Nicholas was staying with Mary Manson, who was holding up well considering the police had dragged her in for receiving, before they surprisingly released her. They were probably watching Mary now, knowing she was already helping them, which made his son off limits. Bruce and Franny were holed up in Croydon, as close to home as they could safely hide. Word was out that they needed help, as did a few of the rest of the gang. His money was still secure in Lincoln; well protected by Jimmy Darwin, who had handed him John's share early that morning. After the trials of the men under arrest, which were due in the New Year, they would try to head abroad. One of Lavery's contacts at Lessers & Co had helped him to slip twenty grand into a Swiss bank account already. Even Lavery was under pressure, just like the gang, and told him that the double-crossing Ulsterman took his share of the first million. What a bastard. They were in on this together, trying to make the most of the situation.

A small van drew up, with the name of a Wembley plastering firm on the side, which was a strange thing to steal. It would stick out like a sore thumb in the West Country. Poor John was dealing with a bunch of amateurs, but he was a big boy now and Bruce was about to cut him free.

Daly stepped out of the passenger side, and walked up to Bruce's car.

'Good to see you, mate,' he said, sticking his hand through the open window and shaking.

'And you, mate.'

He looked to have lost a lot of weight. Bruce and Franny had been living well, helped by a friend who did the majority of their shopping, while they stayed hidden. It looked like John was on a starvation diet. Daly rubbed his hands together nervously, although it was far from cold.

'Have you got it?'

'Course I got it, John.'

'Good. Can I have it?'

'Who you got with you?' Bruce asked.

'Just Mickey and Bill.'

'Those two I saw in Belgravia?'

'Yeah, them.'

Bruce paused. He wasn't going to hold the money back from his brother-in-law. He just wanted John to be sure he was doing the right thing, dealing with those two. Daly beat him to it.

'You still don't trust 'em do you?'

'No, I don't.'

'I tell you, Bruce, they're solid.'

'Well, just you be careful, John. There are people out there who'd do anything to shop us, all of us.'

'Not Mickey and Bill.'

'So long as you're sure?' Bruce tried hard not to sound like a disapproving parent.

'Just give us me money, mate,' John pleaded.

'All right.'

Bruce got out and opened up the boot of his Zephyr. It was full of suitcases.

'Fuck me. It's a lot, ain't it?' John said, as he stared at the luggage.

'Yeah, it is mate. Just be careful with it.'

'We will.'

'You off to hide it, then?'

'Course.'

'Where?'

'Just Cornwall. Somewhere safe. Mickey knows somewhere.'

Bruce struggled to avoid a look of distaste. 'I bet he does.'

'Bruce, come off it.'

'Just be careful.'

'Anybody follow you?' John asked nervously.

'Course not. What d'you think I am?'

'Sorry, Bruce, just a bit edgy.'

'Did anyone follow you?' Bruce returned the question, pointing at the bizarre choice of van they had turned up in. It was easy to remember, as well as trace, if you wanted to. They were idiots, and John was probably heading for disaster with that pair.

'No, we're safe, Bruce, honest.'

Daly zipped open one of the suitcases, and Bruce kept watch up and down the deserted side road off the A4. John pulled out a bundle of notes and stuffed them into his coat pocket.

'Just for the lads. They deserve something for looking after me.'

'Be careful, John. You never know.'

'Leave it, Bruce, they're good.'

Reynolds studied the two men as they leapt out of their van and walked over. His instinct was to jump in his car and run. They could be setting him up, standing there in the middle of nowhere with over a hundred grand on display.

Mickey Black nodded to Reynolds. 'Morning, Bruce. How are you?'

'I'm fine. Just look after John, will you?' Like they would listen to him, with all that money close at hand.

'We will,' Bill Goodwin replied, smiling.

Both looked delighted to be that close to John's share at last.

Bruce watched the three men as they lifted a suitcase each and dropped them into the back of the van, then drive off without a goodbye. He won't have that money for long, Bruce thought. His own circle of friends was reliable, and close. He also had Lavery for back up, although he would prefer it if the Beast didn't seem to know where he was all the time. His mind flashed back to the night before the robbery, everyone gathered, listening. Lavery seemed to have the inside track on the investigation, which was extremely handy in his current predicament. They had moved once on Tommy's recommendation already, and Bruce discovered that the place they vacated got turned over the next morning. Dependable and well-informed friends would be invaluable over the next few months, if he was going to stay hidden and keep hold of his money.

66

23rd November 1963: Aylesbury Police Station

'I can't say it's any of them,' Wyatt said. 'He was taller, thinner.'

'Did he wear glasses?' Butler asked, probably hoping for more evidence against Bruce Reynolds.

'I don't remember.'

Tommy Butler sighed, and Frank Williams looked on, unsurprised. The idea of an identity parade was just a shot in the dark. They had no idea which of the gang had been seen by the farmer when he had visited Leatherslade Farm. He claimed to have met a man who said he was a decorator, the day before the mail train was hit. The descriptions he gave to the local police back in August were vague, and even showing him mug shots didn't help.

'Have another look, will you?'

Butler was insistent, indicating the man should walk down the line again. Charlie Wilson grinned, and Jimmy Hussey winked at Frank Williams after the farmer had passed him. They also drew a blank earlier, with a woman who claimed to have seen three men at the entrance to the farm track. Two separate parades, involving the eight men they had in custody, had delivered nothing except confusion. She had picked out a local constable out of uniform. The solicitors were rubbing their hands with glee. The fact that there was no reliable face-to-face witness to draw on for the court case gave both the senior squad officers concerns.

The investigation was running cold, even though they had

several of the gang behind bars and were keeping tabs on a few more suspects. Hatherill was losing patience, and the pressure was coming downwards, through Butler. This meant that they were called upon to work even longer hours, which most of the team thought was impossible, unless they slept at New Scotland Yard as well.

Williams left the room, and bumped into Joe Watson in the corridor. His young officer looked to be in shock.

'I can't believe it.'

'What's happened?' Had Vibart and his men found another suspect?

'Kennedy. He's dead.'

'Oh, that.' Frank struggled to hide his disappointment that it wasn't a breakthrough in the case. He was so focused on the robbery, nothing else had permeated, even the death of a President. 'Yeah, terrible. What are you doing up here in Aylesbury?'

'Sir, I've got something. Another tip-off. Something important.'

'Go on, what is it?'

They had spent the last three weeks running around London chasing lead after lead, and nothing new was emerging, so he didn't hold out much hope. The men they had in Aylesbury and Bedford were being committed to trial in January, but he wanted more of the gang. The problem was that they were hidden, deep in the undergrowth.

'Well, word is that one or two of them want to come in. At least thinking about it.'

'Who?' This was something different at least.

'Buster Edwards is looking to turn himself in, and so is Harry Smith.'

'Tell me more. Where d'you hear this?'

'One of my sources. It's reliable.'

Frank nodded to his junior officer. His information had proved invaluable so far. 'So, what did they say?'

'Only that they might return some money, if we then left them alone.'

'Really?'

This surprised Frank. If it had been him, he would wait and see what the sentences were for the convicted men, if he could stay hidden long enough. Maybe all their kicking-in doors and hassling criminals was getting through to the gang? They knew criminals were pissed off with the higher profile of policing and the continual raids in London. Perhaps there was a real danger of the rest being turned in?

'Yeah. If we do a deal, they might go for it.'

Frank pondered this, because he had already discussed with Butler the idea of offering a way out for those on the list, if they turned themselves in. The Chief had insisted that it was out of the question. No deals, not for this lot, that was a directive from the politicians. However, the gang weren't to know this.

'Look, can I meet your source?' Frank asked, hoping that Watson would relent. He was still intrigued as to who it was.

'I doubt he'd agree to that.'

'Can you at least ask him?' I'll follow Watson, that's the thing to do, Frank thought.

'I'll ask him. But I know he'll say no to it.'

'Just ask him, will you?'

'Right, Guv. So, what d'you want me to do about this offer?' Watson asked, changing the subject rather obviously. Protecting a source was understandable, however irritating it was.

'Push it forward. We need another arrest soon.' The momentum was falling away from the investigation, and it needed a kick-start.

'I'll see what I can do. They'll want assurances, you know, a deal. From you, personally.'

'Me?'

'Yeah. Word is they'd like to deal with you, nobody else.'

Williams knew his years of mixing with the criminal fraternity and their contacts would pay off, and maybe this was going to be it.

'Let them think it's on, a possibility. We'll see what Butler says.'

Frank wasn't going to ask him. He would handle things himself; the Chief would only say no.

'D'you need this sorted right away?' Watson asked.

'As quickly as you can, yes.'

'I'll get right on it,' Watson said, and he walked quickly down the corridor. What was he doing up in Aylesbury anyway, Frank wondered? The question slipped from his mind as Butler came out of the room they were using for the parade, and buttonholed him.

'Come on, this is a waste of time. Let's get back to the Yard. We'll let Fewtrell deal with anything else here. Bloody country locals,' he sighed.

Frank pondered on Butler's motives for dragging them out to Aylesbury. Did he really think that an identity parade would deliver? Would it really make any difference, given the forensic evidence they already had? He and his team were supposed to be out there on the streets of London, sniffing out the rest of the gang. If what Watson said was true, some of the stolen money might be on the table. The old adage applied in this case; if you followed the money, you would find the thieves.

67

3rd December 1963: Eaton Square, London

Frank and the team had caught a break at last. They had known for a week that Belgravia was the target area. The problem was pinpointing exactly where John Daly was hiding out, among the well-heeled flats. Now Watson had come up trumps. They had a definite address for their man, and had been watching the property in Eaton Square for two days. Following a meeting at New Scotland Yard, Butler decreed it was time to strike.

Butler and Williams parked up two streets away, supported by five other officers. They had significant inside information about the code being used by anybody accessing the property – two short rings followed by a longer one. Butler rang the bell of the basement flat, and they waited. Frank was anticipating a fight inside, thinking Daly might have two or three minders with him, so DS Moore and two others stood behind the senior officers. As it happened, Daly's wife opened the door with a short-lived smile.

Butler quickly barged into the flat, and Williams followed. They swept past the woman, and were met with the sight of Daly in a pair of pyjamas and dressing gown, rising from the sofa in the living room. There was no sign of anybody else, no protection at his side. Daly was trapped.

'John Daly?' Butler asked.

'My name's Paul Grant.'

Frank and the team had been told that Daly and his wife were renting the flat under the name. Daly looked like a changed man, had lost weight, and grown a closely cropped beard. The things they would do, hoping to stay hidden, Frank thought. He joined in the conversation.

'John Daly, we know it's you. Come on, you must remember me.'

Daly looked at him and sighed. 'Hello, Mister Williams. I guess you got me.'

'We have a warrant to search this flat,' Butler said. 'My officers will conduct the search, if that's all right?'

'I can't say no, can I?' Daly replied.

'No, you can't,' Butler smiled. 'Please sit down while we search the place.' The Grey Fox indicated to Moore to begin, and Daly sat down in a chair. Butler picked up the questioning again. 'Mister Daly, have you ever been to Cheddington?'

'No, never.'

'Have you ever been to Leatherslade Farm?'

'No, I've never been there.'

'That's interesting,' Butler continued. 'Because we have discovered several of your fingerprints there.' They had abandoned the approach of gradually revealing what they knew, interviewed suspects more directly now.

'You're wasting your time. I've never been to that farm. That's the truth.'

'Are you sure?' Butler pressed.

'Positive. I've never been there.' Frank thought again about why some criminals carried on lying in the face of incriminating evidence. They deserved to be caught.

'Okay, Mister Daly,' Butler continued. 'When this search has been completed, we're taking you to New Scotland Yard, and then to Aylesbury where you'll be charged with the mail train robbery. Is there anything else you want to say?'

'You're not taking her, are you?' he replied, pointing to his wife, who had sat down in an armchair, crying.

'Just you, John. Anything else you want to say?'

'Nothing for now, no.'

Frank left the room and joined Moore and the other officers in their search of the flat.

'Look at this, Sir,' Moore said as they met in the bedroom. He held up a drawer, showing the contents. There were a few letters, along with gun and driving licences. Williams picked these up and studied them. They were in the name of Michael Black. Not that Michael Black, surely? It was an alias Ronnie Clarke had used, back when he was conning businessmen. Maybe he was helping Daly out? The thieves were attracting all sorts of lowlife.

There was a commotion at the front door, and Williams ran out to see what was going on.

'Sir, look, we've got a visitor,' DS Nevill said, smiling.

Nevill and Slipper, who had been watching the rear entrance, had a man pinned against the wall. A bag of groceries lay spilt on the floor.

'Someone's been doing a bit of shopping for Mr and Mrs Daly, by the looks of it. He's got a key to the flat as well,' Nevill announced.

What an idiot, Frank thought, walking in just as they were checking the place over. How did he not see that the flat was occupied? The two officers turned him around, and Frank laughed out loud.

'William Goodwin. What are you doing here?'

'Hello, Mister Williams. Just visiting.'

'I bet you are. You're nicked.'

68

3rd December 1963: Thornton Heath, London

'I think we should check the briefcase,' Bruce Reynolds announced to his wife. The news of his brother-in-law's arrest had just come across on the radio, and he felt devastated. Slowly the gang were being rounded up, and it felt like the net was closing in. He was downstairs in the flat where they were being kept hidden by a friend. He opened another bottle of wine to share with Franny, as she went upstairs to check. The briefcase contained what he called 'movers' money, handy cash for getting about from place to place, while the rest was safe in the Midlands.

Franny broke his concentration as he played with the bottle opener, hissing as she walked back down the stairs. 'There's a policeman at the window.'

Bruce thought about the hidden money. If they had come to arrest him, he couldn't be caught in possession. Franny probably didn't get as far as the briefcase, to put it somewhere safe. Then he heard her voice at the door.

'No, nobody's here,' she said, calmly, loud enough for him to hear. 'No, I didn't report an intruder, no.' Intruder? It must be code, for his benefit. The voice of what must have been a police officer echoed down the stairs, into the flat.

'Well, there was a report of a ladder up to the window, at the back,' he said. Unless this was some sort of elaborate double bluff, they weren't there to arrest him. A ladder? Had someone been trying to break into their flat, chancing their arm? Was their cover blown?

'I don't know anything about it,' Franny replied, still sounding cool.

'Do you mind if we come in and take a look around?' he heard from outside the door.

Bruce acted quickly. The stunt might work again. He took his clothes off, and crouched naked behind the sofa, like a character in a West End farce. His wife walked into the room, followed by two uniformed policemen. Franny covered her mouth, and appeared suitably embarrassed. Bruce joined in the acting, standing up from his hiding place, covering his groin. Franny started the explanation.

'You see, my husband's away, and this is just a friend, who has come round to help,' she began. The two coppers struggled to look Bruce in the face, which was handy. He had been plastered all over the newspapers, and doubtless every police station wall, for weeks. Maybe they had grown too accustomed to his face and didn't realise who they had in the room? One of the uniforms looked at his wife.

'Sorry, madam. We didn't mean to...' The policeman paused, not sure what to say. 'We were just following up a report of a break-in.'

'I'm so embarrassed. Please, my husband is away,' she repeated.

The other officer questioned Bruce. 'Could I just have your name, Sir?'

'It's Bert Smith,' Bruce bluffed.

'And your address?'

'235 Battersea Park Road,' Reynolds replied. He knew it was a genuine address. One of the policemen noted down the details.

'Madam, you've not seen anything suspicious recently?'

'No. I was just, you know, busy, sort of thing.' She looked suitably sheepish, and Bruce made to retrieve his clothes, keeping his face in the shadow when he could.

The two uniforms soon left, making their apologies, and Bruce and Franny shared a chuckle. Those wide-eyed boys fell for it, although it was clear that they had to move on. All it would take was for one of those two lads to return to their local station and recognise his face on the bulletin board, and they would be straight back. They quickly packed a suitcase each, Bruce picked up his passport and the briefcase with the money, and they headed out into the street, jumping into their borrowed car that was parked in a square a short walk away. Every precaution had been taken to keep their identity a secret in this quiet corner of South London, but that was now blown. They headed straight for the only haven available, one they had planned to use after Christmas. Armstrong had told him about a mews flat in Kensington the previous week, saying it was available to them if they needed it in an emergency. Jack guaranteed that it was a safe place, and a minder would be available on hand if required. All they had to do was ring a particular number, and everything would be taken care of. He knew Buster was living the same way, somewhere out in the countryside. He and Franny were going to have a more upmarket address for a while.

69

'Just show us where the hell it is, and we'll let you go,' Armstrong demanded.

Black shook his head, and Parlane smacked him again, this time across the face. Black was tied up in a chair, unable to move. Parlane rung his hand, then shook it in the air, before holding it up ready to strike again.

'Look, we know it's hidden here; we're not stupid,' Jack sighed.

They were in the cellar of a cottage on the edge of the village of Boscastle. They had asked Black to lead them there, but that was just for show. Armstrong knew precisely where the hideout was, what they didn't know yet was where exactly the money was hidden at the property, and this was the subject of their interrogation.

'Go and have another look, will you?' Jack asked.

'You fuckin' go,' Parlane retorted.

Armstrong turned to Black. 'See what you're doing? You're making us argue. You don't want to make us angry, do you Mickey?' The man shook his head. 'Well bloody well tell us where you buried it.'

More head shaking came from the subject in the chair. Maybe tying him up and shoving him in the boot of the car for the whole journey had affected his memory? Armstrong decided to take a more subtle approach.

'Look, we'd just like to point out a few things to you. Daly's been taken in, he's fucked. They got him; he won't be out of prison for a few years now. He won't be coming after you, whatever you do.' Black said nothing, fear all over his face. He bloody well ought to be scared, Jack thought. 'Unless you're greedy, and you're thinking this money is rightfully yours, then you've got no right to it. We're here in John's best interests, we'll take care of it now.'

'I dunno who the hell you are,' Black replied, spitting on the floor. A small globule started to spread, forming a filthy pool.

'You know who we are, certainly what we are. We're friends of John Daly, we're here to look after his share. You know Goodwin got lifted too, didn't you?' Black looked genuinely surprised. 'Well, he did. So, that only leaves you free who knows where it's buried.'

'I want some of it. If I show you where it is, I want half of it.'

'Half? Are you mad? What d'you think John's gonna do when he hears you've taken half of his money?'

'How will he find out?' Black asked uncertainly.

'We'll make sure he finds out. Remember, we're friends of John's, just like you. Except we're looking after his interests, not our own.'

'I still want half.'

'You'll get fuckin' nothin' if you don't stop being so greedy,' Parlane interjected, kicking Black in the groin. He groaned, unable to move or protect himself other than closing his legs a little.

'Look, we haven't got all day. I've got another idea,' Armstrong said, turning to look at Parlane but really addressing the prisoner. 'Let's just accept that we go and dig up the whole bloody garden, fair enough. But when we're done, and we will find it eventually, we call the police and tell them there's a train robber sitting tied up in a certain cellar. We'll even leave some of the money lying around, with prints on it, so they've got a bit of evidence. What d'you think to that?'

'Sounds good,' Parlane smiled, playing along. 'Apart from the digging bit. I wonder what they'll do when they find him in here?'

'Arrest him. Take him to Aylesbury jail, like all the rest of 'em.

And Daly's in there too. Wait 'til he finds out his friend lost him his money, and then got nicked as well.'

'I thought you said you was looking after it for John?' Black groaned.

'We are. But if we have to go looking for it, we're dumping you in the shit. If you help us, we'll change our mind about that.'

Armstrong looked at the dishevelled mess that was Mickey Black, or whatever he was calling himself. They found no identification on him, but they knew who it was. Parlane was an expert in finding people.

'All right. I'll tell you.'

'You'll do more than that, you're gonna dig it up for us.'

'Oh, fuck off.'

'It's your choice, Mickey. Dig, or be left here for the police.' Black looked like he was going to cry. What a pathetic specimen, Jack thought. Where did Daly get this one?

'All right. I'll show you where it's buried. I still want some money.'

'How's about ten grand?' Armstrong offered, knowing full well he was going to end up with nothing. 'That's not a bad deal, considering.'

'Considering what?'

'Considering the alternative is us leaving you here and landing you in it.'

'All right. I'll show you, if you let me go. And give me ten grand.'

'No bloody running off, you bastard. You do, we know where you live, anyway.'

Black looked resigned. Parlane untied him, and he groaned some more, finally leading them up the cellar steps to the cottage. When they reached the garden, the prisoner pointed at the vegetable patch.

'It's under there.'

'Good. Get bloody digging.'

After ten minutes, Black unearthed three large suitcases, and dragged them out of the ground.

'Refill the earth, then,' Armstrong commanded.

'You're joking?' Black asked, defeated.

'No, we're not. Fill it in. Just in case anybody comes looking who shouldn't.'

Black set to work again and Armstrong and Parlane shared a look. Jack considered what to do with Black. They could just leave him there, but that might draw attention both to him and their visit. Two old ladies who lived next door had seen them arrive, and because they exchanged pleasantries, they might be remembered. Jack had told the nosey neighbours that they were going to undertake some roofing work for the owners. The meeting was unavoidable, but who would believe two old biddies anyway?

With the suitcases safely in the boot of their car there was no room for Black, so he travelled to Liskeard in the back seat. He looked dejected and utterly downtrodden, but this was nothing compared to the expression on his face when they stopped the car in a quiet street round the corner from the train station.

Armstrong passed a small bundle of five-pound notes to Black, and shook his hand.

'That's all you're getting. You should get home with that.'

'But you said ten grand,' Black pleaded.

'Did I? You must have misheard me. Now piss off, and steer away from John if you know what's good for you. We're gonna tell him you gave his money away.'

'You can't, you fuckers.'

'Look.' Jack leant through the gap in between the front seats to push his face right up to Black. 'We was on that job too, right.' He saw a look of surprise in the face. 'And we don't want little pricks like you taking John's money, all right?' Parlane just kept a lookout under the streetlights.

'But…' Black started to protest.

'Shut it. Don't make a scene, Mickey,' Armstrong said, staring deep into his eyes.

Black made one last plea. 'I want my money.'

'It's not your money, Mickey, it's John's. You're a fuckin' parasite, you are. We're gonna look after it for him. Now piss off.'

'I know a few people,' Black muttered.

'Yeah, and so do we, now get out of the car while you still can. You've been very lucky,' Armstrong said forcefully. 'Go on, piss off.'

Black fell out of the back seat in a crumpled mess, and Parlane sped off. Armstrong thought about John Daly on the long journey back to Manchester. He remembered a quiet man who tampered with the signals up the track, well out of his way. He didn't say a word to him or Mickey the entire time. He really did pick some losers to help him out, should have been more careful who his friends were.

70

The James raid was all about the planning. Their information was that the former racing driver had changed his appearance; grown a beard, and even had an escape route mapped out. The observation team had watched the flat on Ryder Terrace in St John's Wood before Butler gave the word to go in that evening. They had even studied plans of the building, in case he dug a tunnel. James was an adept cat burglar, so the rooftops were his most likely form of escape.

Two days were taken up with meetings and preparation. Over twenty officers would be engaged in the operation. This time the inside knowledge came through Frank's own contacts, rather than Watson. He was secretly pleased that he wasn't losing his touch on the London streets.

Whilst the preparations were being finalised, Frank received an urgent visit from DS Bradbury, who was an important link for processing leads, evidence and information, and ran the incident room at the Yard. Bradbury was breathless as he ran into Frank's office.

'Frank, we just got a message.'

'Go on, is it urgent? You know we're heading over to North London tonight?'

'I just got a call from a man who says they've got fifty thousand of the train robbery money, in sacks.'

Bradbury looked shocked. Williams tried to keep calm. He and Watson had been working on Harry Smith trading money for a guarantee of facing only receiving, rather than robbery charges. They knew there was no evidence against him, but Smith sounded nervous about fingerprints, according to Watson's sources. He didn't know they had nothing to pin on him. Negotiations were underway for fifty grand to be handed in, and the gesture wouldn't be forgotten when it came to trial. It was a right bugger that this was happening slap bang in the middle of the James raid.

'What did he say?' Williams asked.

'Just gave a street, and a telephone kiosk, and said we had to be there in five minutes. Gave your name, Sir.'

'Did he say who the man was who was going to give himself up?'

'No, just to be there in five minutes. Great Dover Street. Newington.'

'I know it. How much did he say?'

'Fifty thousand.'

It sounded like Smith. The new strategy to work on the insecurities of the other suspects might have been paying off. Williams ran to Tommy Butler's office, and charged in. He was looking at blueprints of the block where Roy James was staying in St John's Wood, and looked at peace with the world.

'Chief, we got a phone call. One of the robbers is handing in fifty grand.'

'What?' Butler looked stunned at first, and then cracked into a smile.

'We've got a call, fifty grand is being handed in.'

'Where?'

'Great Dover Street, it's not far from here. It'll take us two minutes.'

Butler appeared to mull it over, then looked down at the map again. 'It's a hoax.'

Frank knew that it was genuine. They had been working hard

on such an exchange, and this was the result of more of Watson's graft. Butler had shown no interest in the possibility of deals when Frank had mentioned them before.

'We've got five minutes to get there.'

'It's a bloody hoax, Frank, you know it is.' There had been a few false alarms of supposed robbers handing themselves in recently; it seemed to be a game half the underworld were playing, winding them up. Butler had lost heart with the idea.

'I'm sure this is real.'

'How d'you know?' Butler asked, looking up.

'Trust me, Sir, I know this one is real.'

Frank carried on pleading, until Butler relented. He was a copper who worked on instinct, the same way as the Grey Fox. The two men ran out to the Chief's car, and raced the five-minute journey to Great Dover Street. Frank Williams hoped that Smith didn't get cold feet. This would be a major breakthrough, and would also prove to their superiors that negotiating with the thieves, rather than splashing their faces all over the newspapers, was the correct approach to take.

71

Jack Armstrong sat and watched the street, before glancing to his right. One of his fellow train robbers, Harry Smith, the man the police had absolutely no evidence to convict, but who was certain himself that they did, was shaking beside him. In the front seat, Danny Regan and DS Watson from the Robbery Squad sat smoking. They could clearly see the telephone kiosk. Smith was getting increasingly nervous, as nobody had shown up yet. The call had been placed twelve minutes earlier, according to Jack's watch.

'They're not gonna show. They don't believe me,' Smith blurted out.

'Calm down, Harry. They'll come,' Armstrong replied, 'won't they, DS Watson?'

'Oh, they will,' Watson said quietly. He appeared to be distracted.

'You sure, DS Watson?' Jack delighted in referring to the insider by his rank and surname. It separated him from the rest of them. They were men of honour, and this was just a scumbag.

Before Watson could reply, they saw a Mini Cooper draw up outside the telephone kiosk. Two men appeared to be sitting inside, but didn't move. They would be police officers, and were also watching and waiting. Armstrong's car contained the men who were one step ahead. Smith fidgeted in his seat, and wiped condensation off his window in a small circle.

'Don't do that,' Armstrong barked, irritated that he wouldn't sit still. He trained his binoculars at the kiosk, fifty yards away. There were a few passers by, but he doubted they were plain-clothes police officers. There was no way they could have got there in time.

The two men eventually got out of the Mini, and opened up the kiosk. They dragged out two large potato sacks, which the car occupants knew contained robbery money, into the street.

'Open them up, go on,' Armstrong bated. The men didn't obey. Instead they hauled the sacks into the back seat of the car. 'I'd just love to see their faces when they see the money,' Jack added.

'They'll take it to the Yard, to the incident room,' Watson said.

'I bet you've got some lovely exhibits in that room?' Jack asked.

'A few.'

'You got any pictures of me, or Harry here?'

'None of you. We got a picture of Harry, yeah.' Smith shifted uneasily in his seat again. They turned their attention back to the Mini, which hadn't moved off.

'Who was it?' Armstrong asked.

'That was Tommy Butler and Frank Williams,' Watson said, failing to hide the pride in his voice.

'Oooh, we are honoured,' Jack countered sarcastically.

'What they doing?' Danny Regan asked, his first words since they parked up. Armstrong was warming to this quiet character. After a couple of visits from Mickey Griffin, Danny was now convinced that working with them on this project was the right thing to do. Regan was already investing Smith's money in properties when they rescued Harry. Lavery and Smith now jointly owned the company involved, but there was only one direction the returns were going to move in the future. Harry was a man on edge, after a three-way conversation with Jack and DS Watson that morning had convinced Smith to turn some of his money in, directly to Frank Williams.

Armstrong struggled to understand the point of it at first. Why give fifty grand back, just like that? It appeared to be a strange decision, a plan of Tommy's he could only partly follow. He talked about making the rest of the gang more willing to part with their cash in order to stay hidden. If they thought the evidence against them was damning, they would cling to any help they could find. Being under Lavery's protection was the safest place to be, with all the leeches of London fighting for their small, desperate slices of pies they didn't deserve to feed upon. 'It's about the big picture, Jack, don't you see?' his boss had insisted, but it still didn't make total sense.

'They're waiting to see if Harry here shows up,' Watson announced.

'I'm not going. I've changed my mind,' Smith said.

'Oh, don't worry, Harry, you weren't going anywhere,' Jack said forcefully, remembering his instructions.

'You what?'

'Why d'you want to give yourself up, you idiot?'

Smith looked perplexed, and then grew angry. 'Cos they was gonna let me off,' he said, staring Armstrong in the eyes. Jack calmly returned his gaze.

'Listen, they was never gonna let you off, they want the money,' Jack countered. 'Your pay off right there is your insurance, right? You don't need to actually give yourself up. Williams will leave you alone now, won't he, Watson?'

'He's right,' Joe added quietly. 'You gave up some money, so the heat is off. Frank Williams knows it was your money. Even if we catch up with you, you get a reduced sentence, just receiving.'

'But they've got evidence I was there, you said,' Smith was almost crying.

'Did I?' Armstrong asked. 'I don't remember saying that. Do you remember saying that, DS Watson?' The officer in the front sat in silence. 'Do you?' Jack repeated.

'Not that I recall,' Watson said, knowing the extent of his betrayal.

'But you said…' Smith started, and then sank back in his seat.

'It don't make any difference. You made an investment today. You put down a payment on your future, for when they catch up with you,' said Armstrong.

'They ain't gonna catch up with me,' Smith replied, 'are they Danny?'

'I hope not,' said Regan.

'We know where you live, Harry,' Watson began insistently. 'We picked up your mum and dad for receiving. We're watching Danny here, half the time,' Watson insisted.

'Are you?' Regan asked.

'We're watching every villain in South London. Course we're watching you. I'm watching you right now,' Watson smiled.

'Fuckin' hell, what chance we got?' Regan exhaled in resignation.

'Thing is, now you've made this sacrifice, you've earned the right to a fair warning, if anything's happening,' Armstrong said, before directing his words at Watson. 'Hasn't he?'

'Yeah. Now I can let you know if the investigation is about to swoop,' the Detective Sergeant agreed.

'So, it's money well spent,' Jack summarised. He turned his attention to the Mini Cooper. 'There they go,' he announced, 'let's just wait and see, in case it's a double bluff, see if anyone else shows up with their pointy hats on.' The Mini drove off; heading in the direction it came from, back to New Scotland Yard.

'We're busy tonight, another operation is on,' Watson said.

'Oh, anybody we know?' Jack casually enquired.

'Yeah, it is actually.'

'And?'

'Can't tell you that,' Watson said.

'Yeah, you fuckin' can,' Armstrong replied, pointing his gun at Watson's head. It had been safely hidden in his jacket pocket ever since they picked up Smith and Regan that afternoon, along with the money he and Parlane had dug up, just for the hand over.

'Roy James,' Watson replied quickly. 'I'm not on the raid tonight. You're my special project, Harry.' Smith didn't seem too impressed he was the subject of such dedicated attention.

Jack thought through Lavery's approach again. For fifty grand Smith was buying Frank Williams's confidence in DS Watson, his mole on the inside of the investigation. At the same time he was sending out a signal to the other robbers on the run, that he could broker leniency, and had the investigation under control from the inside. Were this Butler and Williams also on the payroll, and the humble DS Watson didn't know it?

Armstrong returned his attention to the bloke who thought he could drive a train, but was hopeless at stopping them. 'Roy James, eh? Ah well, he had a good run, didn't he?'

72

10th December 1963: St John's Wood, London

A WPC was sent out in front, while the rest of the officers remained hidden. Frank Williams watched from his vantage point, keen to get his hands on another of the gang. The escapade with Harry Smith, he was sure it was he that left the money in the sacks, had given him some fortitude. For now, they had to focus on James, who had eluded capture for three months. There was one near escape, back in October, when Vibart set off for Goodwood racetrack where he was supposed to be racing. Unfortunately, Roy must have got wind of their movements, and left the track an hour before Vibart arrived with two squad cars. The day after that, James's own car, a flash Jaguar, was found abandoned in Chiswick, and he disappeared completely.

They could hear music playing from inside the flat. Frank thought he saw the silhouette of a figure at the window, which then dipped out of sight. Although the WPC tried the door twice, there was no reply. He was buggered if they were going to mess about any longer, so he beckoned DS Moore to follow him over to a position underneath the window, which was one floor up. Moore climbed on to Williams's shoulders, and broke the glass, clambering in. DS Nevill then gave Frank a leg up as he followed Moore inside. He just managed to catch sight of a figure leaping up a spiral staircase, heading for what they knew was a skylight. They had the place totally surrounded.

He heard more officers bursting in through the front door, but they were too late. Moore shouted down that James was already running across the rooftops. Frank heard afterwards from his colleague that he ran full pelt in pursuit over the top of adjoining houses. James was heading straight into a trap. After throwing a holdall off the end of the roof, he jumped down and landed in the arms of a large PC called Matthews, exactly where Williams had placed him.

Back at New Scotland Yard, James was indignant when Williams and Butler sat him down to interview. He said nothing on the way in, looked like a sulking child. Maybe he was wondering who had grassed him up, Frank thought. The information originally came from a woman who was too scared to identify herself, and was passed on by a publican he had known for years. Butler took up the interrogation, which Frank had got used to.

'Roy, why did you run away when we knocked the door?'

James looked insulted by the question, and then laughed. 'Ha, I should think so. Just to get nicked?'

'Roy, can you tell us where you were on the night of the seventh and eighth of August this year?'

James feigned surprise this time; he was going through a whole range of fake emotions. 'Nobody can remember that far back.'

'Try to remember, Roy,' Butler asked, patiently.

'I wasn't at the farm I've read about.'

'Do you mean Leatherslade Farm?'

'Is that what it's called?' James replied. 'I didn't know. Anyway, I haven't been there before.'

'And this holdall we found on you, is this yours?' Butler asked, placing it on the table.

'Never seen it before,' James retorted.

'Sorry?'

'Never seen it before.'

'But we saw you with it, when you legged it,' Butler said. 'You

348

threw it down on the ground from the roof.' Frank had to admit James had a nerve, ridiculous as he sounded.

'No, it's not mine.'

Butler laughed this time. Frank Williams thought again about the stupidity of some criminals. They found bundles of wet, wrapped up notes in the holdall he had thrown off the roof. DS Nevill reckoned there was well over ten thousand inside it. He was caught red-handed, and still didn't have the decency to admit it. They had also found his fingerprints on a Pyrex dish and a bottle at the farm, so he was a certainty to go down. As Butler wrapped up the interview, informing James he was going to be taken to Aylesbury to be formally charged with the robbery, Frank left the room. Butler could do what he liked with James now, because he was safely wrapped up. He needed to focus on the rest of the gang who were on the loose, a slowly dwindling group.

As far as he could tell, none of the other suspects had left the country. Watson's informant had backed up this theory the day before. There were at least five men still at large, but now they had tabs on only one, Danny Pembroke. White, Reynolds and Edwards were out there somewhere, and he was desperately trying to reach them through his own contacts.

Smith was the bloody frustrating one. They came that close to nabbing him earlier, he was convinced he would be there by the kiosk with the money. Perhaps they had turned up too late, or frightened him off. According to Watson, Smith thought they had a mountain of evidence against him, but they had nothing. Nicking him for receiving was the best they could hope for. Butler seemed delighted to have recovered part of the money. The final count was apparently just under forty-eight grand. The look on the Grey Fox's face was priceless when he tipped the sacks out on to the table in the incident room; musty and damp notes bundled up, piles of them. They were starting to claw their way back at the gang.

73

Jack Armstrong strolled along the path towards the front door, and peered through the letterbox. He resisted the temptation to knock, knew that surprise would work in his favour. Through the open curtains of the living room he could see the back garden, and there was the figure, hammering something into what looked like a bird tray. He silently crept around the side gate, and cleared his throat as he approached.

'Hello, Stan. How are you?' The old man looked up, and dropped his hammer with a dull thump on the grass. 'Or should I say, Freddie?' Jack asked.

The man picked up his hammer, and held the implement out in front of him, as if it was a sword. Fat lot of use that would do him, Jack thought, feeling the gun against his chest.

'You recognise me, then?' Jack smiled.

'Of course I recognise you.'

Jack held his arms up in mock surrender. 'Good. Make us a cup of tea, would you? I'm bloody parched.'

The old man put the hammer down, and raised himself up to face Jack. He looked much older than Armstrong remembered him, the man who failed to shunt the mail train along that night. Parlane's intelligence was correct. There was no name to track him down with at first, other than the label of Stan, which nobody truly believed, because Ronnie Biggs always protected his identity. Even

350

a visit to Charmian, by Parlane, had apparently revealed nothing. But George knew how to find people, and had eventually given Jack his real name and address. The old man said nothing as he slid open a French window, and led Armstrong inside, to the small kitchen. He certainly wasn't living it up on his little share of the proceeds. Finally, Stan, or Freddie Johnson, as he was should have been known, faced him, and asked a vital question.

'Milk and sugar?'

'Yeah, and two, please,' Jack replied. There was no harm in being polite, even if he had been asked by Gordon Goody to kill the man in front of him.

Goody seemed to be in a panic when they had met up, before he was arrested the year before. He had explained how the gang were convinced that the police would be on to the old driver, and that he would rat on all of them. Without saying it directly, he intimated that they would look favourably on Stan disappearing forever. Lavery knew nothing of the request; this was just something between Great Train Robbers, although Parlane was happy to help for a secret fee. Gordon had also promised Jack ten grand back in September, on top of any money that the driver might have left from his share. It took Parlane two months to find him.

There was an uneasy silence as they waited for the kettle to boil. The old man interrupted this by visiting the toilet upstairs. Jack half expected him to return with a shotgun in his hands, but instead, when he emerged, all he carried was a hand towel. Back in the kitchen, the man poured water into a small teapot, and finally spoke up.

'Why are you here?'

'A few of the gang want to know how you are,' Jack replied softly. He was borrowing Lavery's trick, speaking quietly. It seemed to give you more of a threatening air. Freddie had nothing to say, and stirred the leaves carefully. He looked to be shaking. Jack had all day to carry out the task, was in no hurry. It was as if their confrontation was moving in slow motion. The man poured milk

351

into two mugs, and then added the tea from the pot, not leaving it in long enough to Jack's taste to allow it to brew properly.

'Here,' Freddie said, handing a chipped mug to Armstrong. It certainly didn't look like he was enjoying his ten grand. The two men sat down at the kitchen table, which was mostly covered with model soldiers, arranged in lines on pieces of old newspaper. This prompted Jack to ask a question. There was no harm in passing the time in a civilised manner.

'You been reading the papers?' Jack asked.

'Yeah.'

'What d'you think?' He would know he meant the trial.

'I think some of us were unlucky.' It sounded strange, this man referring to the gang as 'us'.

'How d'you mean?'

'With fingerprints.'

'You didn't wear any gloves, did you?' Jack asked.

'No.' The old man looked sheepish.

'Nobody's been to visit you?' Jack asked. Unless he had a record, they would have nothing to match his prints against. 'The law, I mean?'

'No, nobody.'

'That's good.' Jack eyed the man sat opposite him.

Freddie gulped the contents of his mug down quickly. 'I won't say a word,' he said.

'I intend to make sure that you don't.' As he said the words, Jack thought about the options in front of him. The gang certainly wanted him silenced. The man opposite sank into his chair. Jack studied a couple of family photographs on the kitchen windowsill.

'My late wife, Jean,' he said, before Jack could ask.

'Got any kids?'

'Yeah. Two girls. They're living in South Africa. Cape Town.' Freddie smiled, probably thinking of their new lives half way around the world. Nobody would miss this old bloke, Jack mused.

'You have much contact with them?' Armstrong quizzed.

'We exchange Christmas cards, that's about all.'

'I see.'

Jack drained the last of his insipid tea, and placed his mug carefully down on the kitchen table. The man probably deserved to die for that cuppa, as much as anything else. He remembered the desperate plea from Gordon Goody to eliminate the chances of the driver testifying against the gang in court. But what did he owe Gordon, or the rest of them, for that matter? They had worked on a job together, but that was about it. The scraping of a chair in front of him disturbed his concentration. He looked up to see the old man brandishing a kitchen knife in his direction. Jack stood to confront him.

'Put it down, Stan. I mean, Freddie.'

The man started waving the knife around. 'You've come to kill me, haven't you?'

Jack stepped back from his chair and pulled out his gun. I shall see your knife, and raise you one of these, he thought.

The man stood firm, brandishing his weapon, before his shoulders started to shake, and he broke into sobs.

'Please don't kill me,' he whispered through the tears. Don't pull that one on me, please, Jack thought. It had never worked before.

'Put the knife down, Freddie.'

'Don't kill me,' he begged.

'Put it down.' This time Jack shouted, raising his weapon, and pointing it at the man's head.

Freddie turned and dropped his knife in the sink, with a clatter, and sat back down in his chair, tears flowing.

'Stop crying,' Jack ordered. The man sniffed into his sleeve. 'Stop crying, and we can talk about this. Crying won't make any difference.' Countless men had cried in this sort of situation in front of him before, and it never changed his mind.

The man looked up at him, this time bravely staring down the barrel of the gun. At least he as showing more balls than some of Armstrong's previous victims.

'I'm not gonna kill you,' Jack announced.

In truth, he had made his mind up before he approached the old cottage. There was no need to murder this old bloke. He was so out of his depth, utterly petrified. He wouldn't volunteer information to the police, because they had no idea that he existed. The solution was not to kill him, but to hide him somewhere that meant he would never be asked any questions.

'I'm not gonna kill you,' Jack repeated.

'Really?' The man sniffed hopefully, his voice cracking.

'Yeah.'

'You can have my money. I've still got it.'

'Where?'

Freddie stood, and led Jack into the living room, still at gunpoint. The old man searched underneath his sofa, and pulled out a briefcase. What an amazing hiding place, Jack thought.

'It's all in there. I haven't touched any of it. Have it.'

'I didn't come for the money,' Jack replied.

'No, you came here to kill me,' he said, defiantly.

'I'm not gonna kill you, for God's sake.'

Jack had to admit that he deserved the ten grand more than the miserable specimen in front of him. The bloke was volunteering it; he would be a fool to refuse. Maybe he was going soft, but this was a decision he could take with a clear conscience for a change. Freddie handed him the briefcase, and Jack laid it down on the carpet in front of him. He opened up the clasp and studied the bundled notes inside. It looked like they had remained untouched since the day of the robbery. He pulled a handful of bills out, fivers and tenners, thrusting them into the old man's hand.

'You ever been to South Africa?' Jack asked.

'No.'

'Right. Today's your lucky day. Get yourself a brochure, and pack yourself a suitcase. You're going on holiday. For good.'

74

14th February 1964: Boscastle, Cornwall

'Just what did you expect?' Armstrong asked.

'I expected my bloody money to still be here. That's what I expected.' John Daly looked furious. He had led Jack straight to the vegetable patch in the garden, and swore repeatedly when he failed to find anything under the earth.

Jack tried to ignore the obscenities. 'Well, you know, nobody's seen Michael Black for months,' Jack hinted, hoping that John would start to put two and two together.

'He didn't come and visit me, I know that.'

'No, he didn't,' Armstrong replied, knowing that he was one of the few who did make the effort, all to ensure Daly would accept his fate. They just weren't expecting him to be out so quickly. Jack had sat watching in court; saw with his own eyes the shock on John's face when the judge dismissed his case at the trial, two days earlier. Ten other men were lined up in the dock, all looking like they were going to go down for years. Daly's brief had successfully argued that the fingerprints that formed the entire case against him were inadmissible, because they could have been made on the Monopoly cards at any point in time. The biggest surprise was that this decision did not influence the situations of any of the others, where the evidence was being allowed. As far as Jack was concerned, Daly was a lucky man. The money would have been a bonus for John, but that was missing, along with the last man Daly thought had seen it, Mickey Black. Both were hidden where Tommy Lavery wanted them.

'Does anyone know where the hell he's gone?' Daly asked, collapsing on to a metal chair in the cottage garden.

'He's hiding, as far as we know. Do you want us to look for him?'

'You think you can find him?'

'That won't be a problem,' Jack answered honestly.

'I've got nothing to pay you with,' Daly laughed, and Armstrong joined in. At least he was greeting being ripped off with a sense of humour.

'Don't worry. You're part of the firm, we look after each other. We'll find him. What do you want us to do with him?'

Armstrong knew exactly where Michael Black, or Terry Swift, as he was currently pretending to be, was.

'Do you know who grassed me up? In Belgravia?' Daly asked.

'I think you can probably work that one out for yourself, can't you?'

'It weren't Billy.'

He meant Goodwin. It was a pity that he had showed up at the flat, just as the police swooped for Daly, otherwise he could have been implicated in the tip-off as well, and removed from the equation. They had separate plans for Billy Goodwin.

'Maybe not. Nobody's seen him either. The police let him go.'

'Bastards. You dunno who to trust.' Daly cut a sad and forlorn figure, with his head in his hands.

'No, you bloody don't,' Armstrong agreed. 'There's a bond you get from being on a job together, isn't there?'

'Yeah, there is. Do you know where Bruce is?'

'I don't personally, but I know someone whose job it is to look after him.'

'I'd like to meet him.' John looked to be brightening up at the prospect of catching up with his brother-in-law.

'I'm not sure if that's possible.'

'I'd like to, all the same.'

'I'll have a word, see if we can arrange it.'

'He's still in the country, then?'

'I don't really know.'

Armstrong was under instructions to be careful with John Daly, and kept his replies guarded. The way he had wriggled out of the charges made everybody suspicious. He was either extremely lucky, or working for the other side in some way. There was a definite suspicion that he had provided the police with information, in order to get a deal done with the judge. None of the others on trial had the same leverage for some reason. There was certainly no need to tell him more than was necessary.

'We buried it here, under the vegetable patch,' Daly said.

'Did you? Very ingenious,' Jack replied, trying to sound as if this was the first time he had heard the news. He pictured Michael Black, fear making his body rigid, digging the suitcases up at that very spot. 'You wouldn't suspect anything would you, a place that gets dug regularly. Good thinking.'

'That was the idea,' Daly replied, smiling and looking pleased with himself. You poor fool, Jack thought. They had a story ready for him.

'Look, there's not much more we can do. But Tommy Lavery has got a token of thanks for you, for all your efforts on the job, knowing you were robbed of your share.'

'How did you know it was missing?'

Armstrong was prepared for the revelation. 'We kept an eye on Black. He was sniffing around somebody else's money as well, someone who's still on the run.'

'Bruce?' John asked. Jack nodded in reply, enough to tease him.

'What a bastard. He warned me about Mickey, you know?'

'Did he?' Jack said, trying to look surprised. Good old Bruce.

'Yeah. Warned me off him, and Billy Goodwin.'

'Ah, well, maybe Bruce is a good judge of character,' Jack replied.

Daly went quiet, looked like he was thinking something through. Armstrong dropped the bait in front of him.

'Look, like I said, we've got five grand for you, it's not a massive amount, but we know you've been turned over. We don't want anybody on the crew going light.'

'Five grand?' Daly looked disappointed.

Don't get greedy, Jack mused. 'Look, you can take it or leave it. It's a gesture of thanks. Tommy doesn't want anybody going without, after all the effort you put in, and all the shit you've had to put up with.' With the suspicions over his release, they wanted John Daly out of the way, and grateful for it.

Daly didn't take long to weigh up his options. 'I'll take it. And please, thank Tommy.'

'I will. Wait here.'

Jack went back to his car, which was parked on the driveway of the cottage, retrieving a battered briefcase from the boot. He thought it was a sensible idea, had suggested it to his boss. After a brief argument, which made him slightly uneasy, he managed to persuade Lavery. Even five grand should make Daly content, not go shooting his mouth off. Revenge on Black would be a different thing, and they would be happy to appear to help him out there.

'We don't want you to go empty handed. Here.' Armstrong offered the briefcase to Daly, back in the garden. John opened it up, and peered inside. 'It's not even money from the robbery, it's clean,' Jack added.

Daly smiled. 'Thanks, Jack, I mean it.'

'Don't worry. Now, what do you want to do about Michael Black?'

'I want to fuckin' kill him, is what I want to do.'

'We can arrange that if you'd like.' Armstrong had to provide one word of caution. 'Don't forget, if anything does happen to Black, the police will come knocking on your door. So, we need to plan things properly, should he, say, have an unfortunate accident.' He ought to get the inference from that.

'Let me think about it. You sure I can't meet up with Bruce? I'd love to see how he's getting on.'

'I'll find out for you, I can't say any more than that.' Daly simply nodded in reply. Jack tried to finish off the discussion, as he had work to do. 'Best of luck, John. It's been a strange ride, hasn't it?' Jack offered Daly a handshake. John remained seated, looking up at his old ally.

'It has. Cheers, Jack.'

The plan originally was to leave Daly behind at the cottage. He kept saying he wanted some privacy, to get away from all the publicity that was dogging him. Now John appeared to change his mind.

'Tell you what, Jack. Can I have a lift back to London?'

'I'm not heading there, I'm afraid; I've got other business to attend to, for Tommy. I can give you a lift to the nearest train station, if you'd like?'

'Cheers, thanks, yeah.'

'Maybe you can buy that boat you were talking about?'

'Maybe, yeah.' Daly looked a defeated man; despite the five grand he had just received. John was either a tremendously gifted actor, or really had no idea how or why he had been released.

The two men walked round to the front of the cottage, and climbed into Armstrong's car. Jack looked across again at John Daly, who was a pale shadow of the jovial man he had met on the job. He would get by with his money, he was certain of it. What was the alternative? Judging by how badly the trial was going for the rest of them, a long stretch. Daly was one of the lucky ones in the crew; and he shouldn't forget that. There were far worse places to be. Like in the shoes of Mickey Black.

75

'Guilty.'

The words echoed around the chamber like bullets in a barrel, repeated after each man's name was read out.

Douglas Gordon Goody, Roy John James, Robert Welch, James Hussey, Charles Frederick Wilson, Thomas William Wisbey, William Boal and Roger Cordrey.

All were guilty of robbing Frank Dewhurst, a GPO official, and also of conspiracy to rob. Brian Arthur Field and Leonard Denis Field were only found guilty of the lesser conspiracy charge, along with the solicitor, John Wheater, the most respectable looking man on trial.

Jack Armstrong sat alongside Tommy Lavery in the courthouse as the verdicts were read out, studying the resigned faces of the men in the dock. They were there to show support, and the gang had all clocked them at some point in the trial, sitting among the journalists. Jack knew his boss's biggest concern was all that stuff about Gordon Goody's shoes. There were no fingerprints for him, but Stannard's evidence came across strongly, he thought. The expert argued that it was a million to one chance that the paint on the soles of his shoes didn't match the squashed paint tin that was retrieved from Leatherslade Farm.

Jack sat impassively studying each man as they faced their fate. He had sweated hard with every one of them, yet there he was, sitting in safety. The whisper among the press was that the gang were looking at huge sentences. News of that would come another day, and Biggs was still awaiting his own trial. An idiot copper mentioned in his testimony that Ronnie had done time before, which meant he sat all this out in Aylesbury jail, waiting to be tried separately. His time would come, and he was bound to meet the same verdict.

There was a buzz where they sat as the journalists took their notes, preparing to file their stories. He overheard a few wondering who had masterminded the whole operation, whether it was Reynolds or Edwards, two men still on the run. Jack tried to stop himself from studying Lavery whenever they discussed this. He knew his boss would simply smile in that dark, malevolent way of his. A face that told you how proud he was of his achievements, but forbade you from uttering a word about it to anyone.

Judge Davies tried to calm down the hubbub in the court, after the verdicts were read out. He had already instructed that nobody could leave until proceedings were completed. Jack watched this strange representation of the establishment, of a forgotten time. The world was moving on, and relics like him, as well as the politicians, were going to be swept aside by men of business. The landscape of the country was going to change, and men like his boss were trampling all over the law. The figures in the dock were in the vanguard of challenging privilege and the establishment, although they wouldn't feel like it at that moment. They were labelled 'Robin Hoods', were popular, famous, and openly praised for their bravery. What good is all that, thought Jack, if you are banged up inside?

The judge thanked and then dismissed the jury, before giving permission for those present to leave. Jack and Tommy sat in their seats and watched the guilty men being taken down, before moving on. Word was that the police were asking for at least twenty years, perhaps more. The longer, the better, as far as his boss was concerned. The more those men thought that they were distanced from their rewards, the more likely they would be to seek their help. That was where George Stanley from Lessers & Co, a firm of solicitors many of the guilty men were using, came in. Jack, and men like Parlane and Griffin, would also help those still on the run to understand how to invest what was left of their shares.

They knew that both Reynolds and Edwards wanted out of the country, and hearing the verdicts would drive them closer to the brink. If the sentences were severe, they might ask for the next plane to Switzerland or Mexico. Jimmy White was a lost cause, most of his money already gone, his caravan cleaned out. Word was that he had changed his identity, and was farming somewhere up north. There was no need to bother him any more. Lavery lost interest in the robbers when they ran out of money.

As they left the courtroom, filing out alongside a few of the other reporters, one asked Tommy a question.

'Who you working for? Seen you here a few days, only I never worked out which paper you worked on.'

'We're freelance,' Lavery smiled, looking right through the journalist and marching off in the direction of the car park.

Jack followed, and pondered the value of freedom. Those men in the dock would surely rate it extremely highly. They reckoned there were four prime escape candidates, including Goody and Wilson. He and Parlane were to start planning immediately, Lavery told him. Watching those members of the gang he had worked with, trudge down to the cells, had set his mind thinking. Was he destined to always be a lackey, a hatchet man? Would he ever be free enough to make his own decisions? He supposed that he had exercised a degree of choice over the fate of the old train driver. He knew, deep down, that while Lavery ruled the roost, he would be following orders. To be viewed as the Beast's right-hand man carried a degree of kudos, but maybe there was more to life than that? The problem was working out how to break free, and where to get help.

76

7th April 1964: Wraysbury, Buckinghamshire

Bruce Reynolds walked up the gravel drive, looking for a familiar face at the window. In the darkness he thought he could make out a shape, but these days the world was full of shadows that made him nervous. The sentences had determined that the only course of action was to stay on the run. Thirty years? It was bloody ridiculous. They might as well have gone in tooled up; they couldn't be given any more for armed robbery. He had been thinking about handing himself in, along with part of his money, if the sentences had been light, but the judge's decision took that possibility out of the equation.

The reassurances were there from both his new contact, and Tommy Lavery. It appeared that the same man who was keeping him and Franny safe, was doing likewise for Buster. He could scarcely believe it; he was going to meet up with his old friend for the first time in months. Bruce looked back down the drive to where the car had dropped him off, and the Corsair had already vanished. They had been transported from Kensington to a safe house in Cambridge, where he and his wife were currently living. And now here he was, back in rural Buckinghamshire, this time at the other end of the sprawling county from the robbery that had blighted their lives.

When he reached the front door it was ajar, and the suspicions returned. Was it a set up? Word was that Roy James was brought in because of one, and now there were only five of the team on the run, if you forgot the northerners. There was no news on Harry Smith, or Danny Pembroke, not even Jimmy White. He had every confidence that the old paratrooper would keep himself hidden; he knew every trick in the book. If he had to place a bet, it would be that Jimmy White still had all his money intact, and would be lying on a beach somewhere. To be honest, he didn't care what happened to Smith or Pembroke. Apparently, the police had lifted both of them a few times, and didn't have enough evidence to take it any further. This just added to the suspicion that they had talked, although it appeared no reference was made to them at the trial. Mary Manson was still keeping them abreast of proceedings from afar, as she was still looking after Nicholas. Jack Armstrong was always there when he needed him, along with Geordie. At least Lavery had kept his word in terms of protection.

He peered inside, and nervously placed a foot on the threshold of the front door.

'Gotcha!' a voice shouted, and a hand slapped Bruce on the shoulder, pulling him inside. Buster Edwards shut the door behind them, laughing, and they shook hands warmly. He looked a changed man; slimmer, leaner, much thinner in the face. He was dressed in pyjamas and slippers, and led Reynolds into his living room. Bruce felt his own appearance hadn't altered much, and although he had toyed a couple of times with growing a beard, he just couldn't get on with it. His plan was simply to stay hidden until they could move abroad. This was one of the things he wanted to discuss with his old friend, along with the events at the trial.

'How the hell are you, mate?' Buster asked, sitting down. The curtains were drawn, and his old friend caught him looking at them. 'Always like that. Got no choice.'

'Me too. Nightmare, ain't it?'

'Yeah,' Buster sighed.

He looked a defeated man, not what Bruce had wanted to see. He hoped to lift his own spirits by seeing Buster again, but this sight just made him more depressed. Was this going to be their lot for the rest of their lives? He would rather walk into Brixton nick and surrender.

They chatted about the trial for a few minutes, and it was clear that Buster had also been following it very closely, and came to the same conclusions as him. Giving up was no longer on the cards. They felt for their fallen comrades, obviously, but Buster appeared to be settled with his lot.

'I can't complain too much. June's on eggshells every day. She thinks she saw someone in the village here that used to know her sister. Amazing, ain't it?'

Bruce had to admit that it was worse for their wives. The men were used to having to lie low, keep off the radar and avoid their usual haunts, at least for a short while. Now he was missing their old life, dodging and ducking trouble, spending evenings in Soho clubs, talking to birds, being the big man. That would never happen again, at least not in England; they had seen to that. This job had been too big, that was the problem. There was no point in stealing a bloody fortune if you couldn't spend it. Buster looked miserable.

'You not gonna make a run for it, you know, France or something?' Bruce asked. They couldn't go together, but it would be fun if they could meet up again.

'Nah, not yet. We're safe here, I think.'

'They bleeding you dry?' Bruce asked. His anonymity was costing him a hundred and twenty quid a week, making a serious dent in his money. He had already paid one visit to Lincoln and Jimmy Darwin to remove thirty grand, and was due another. The next trip was to secure his future abroad.

'A bit. But we can't spend it at the moment, can we?'

Bruce was forced to agree. 'Nah, maybe we need to get out the country?'

'I've thought about it, but June, I'm not sure she wants to leave England,' Buster said sadly. Poor bastard, Bruce thought. Franny was desperate to flee. It was just a matter of ensuring they could also be re-united with Nicholas.

'We're going,' Bruce threw in. Buster looked shocked, but then smiled.

'Good luck to you, mate. Here, what about your boy?'

'He's still staying with Mary. When we find somewhere, she'll bring him out.'

'They might follow him?'

'We'll find a way. Franny misses him so much.'

'He won't know who you are.'

'Don't I know it?' If he was totally honest with himself, Bruce wasn't one for the domestic life. He preferred the good times, and small children didn't really fit in with that.

'Where you thinking of going?' Buster asked.

'France. Or Mexico, one or the other.'

'Nice,' Buster replied, nodding. Bruce couldn't imagine his friend in either of those two countries. Maybe America, a place where they at least spoke English. 'Why Mexico?'

'They don't have an extradition agreement with us, do they?'

'Ah, yeah, I see.'

'You're not looking to get out?' Bruce asked.

'We'll see. Maybe the appeals will change things,' Buster suggested. Some of the convicted men were planning to challenge their sentences, because thirty years was unprecedented. Bruce thought he could handle serving seven or eight, but not much more, especially with that amount of money sitting, waiting, for him.

'Nah, we're leaving.' Bruce and Franny had made their minds up.

'What about your money?' Buster asked.

'Oh, it's going with us,' Bruce laughed. Why would he leave that behind?

'Lavery can help you, you know, get it into Switzerland,' Buster suggested.

'I know.' He could do many things, that Tommy.

'He's already deposited a bit for us. About a third of mine is already there.'

'Well, why don't you go to Switzerland, then?' Bruce asked.

'It's up to June, really.'

Bruce was hardly surprised. Buster did wear the trousers, but when you were on the run, the balance in a relationship had to change. There was no more sleeping around for him any more. Maybe he needed to have another conversation with Lavery about moving money out of the country. He tried to imagine being ripped off to the tune of half a million pounds. It was staggering.

'You should ask Geordie,' Buster suggested. 'He's changed our identity once. He'll help you leave the country.'

'Who are you, then?' Bruce asked, laughing.

'We were Mr and Mrs Green. Now we're Mr and Mrs Forrest.'

'How very horticultural.'

Joking aside, Bruce thought that it might be worth pursuing new identities at the same time as going abroad.

'Geordie can do passports, I should think,' Buster said, with a serious look on his face.

'Yeah, I expect he can,' Bruce agreed. It seemed that Geordie could arrange most things, so long as it was for money. Maybe he would ask Jack Armstrong instead. The bonds of being on a massive job together always counted for something.

Their conversation slipped into old times, as they reminisced about their days running around the West End, back when Buster ran a nightclub and Bruce was his biggest customer. He thought that they sounded like a pair of old criminals in retirement. Maybe that was what they had become. Two old stagers, with their best days behind them, on the run from the law. At least they had a nice little nest egg to keep their wives happy for a while. Mexico, Bruce thought, rather than the South of France. The beaches of St Tropez would be the first place Tommy Butler would go looking for him. Maybe he would try to learn Spanish, it would give him something to do while the flit was being arranged.

77

7th May 1964: New Scotland Yard

Joe Watson walked into the courtyard at New Scotland Yard for a crafty cigarette, and bumped into Cliff Barclay. He hadn't seen him for a few months, not since before the trial in January.

'All right, Joe?' Barclay offered Watson a light, which he accepted.

'All right,' Joe replied coldly. Frank Williams had warned him about Barclay, that he was not to be trusted; his cards were marked from on high. If he wanted to progress in the force, Frank advised, he should follow his boss, rather than the likes of the man alongside him.

'Bit of a fuck up, eh?' Barclay said, smiling.

They had just gone through the humiliation of another failed identity parade with Harry Smith. Joe thought back to that night in the car with one of Lavery's men. Harry had bought protection, handing over half of his money.

'Looks like it, yeah.'

'We just can't seem to get him, can we?' Barclay mused.

'No.' Joe drew on his cigarette, wondering why Barclay was so interested in Smith.

'Still, we got the rest of them, didn't we? Apart from those on the run.' Barclay sniffed annoyingly, and then blew his nose on a handkerchief.

'There's a few of them still,' Joe replied. The three men they were most actively pursuing were Reynolds, White and Edwards, but they were probably out of the country.

'I know. Maybe Smith wasn't involved.'

'Oh, he was involved all right,' Joe said.

Barclay stared straight into his eyes, and deep into his soul. 'How d'you know for certain? What, were you there that night?' Joe froze and Barclay pressed him. 'On the robbery?'

Watson tried to relax. 'I just know, all right?'

Barclay dug a tissue out of his pocket, and coughed something up into it. His mere presence made Joe uneasy.

'You know why he's getting away with it? Our friend Smith?' Barclay looked around. Two uniformed officers appeared in the far corner of the courtyard. 'Come on; let's go for a walk, Joe. I'd like a chat.'

Although he was technically outranked, Watson was reluctant, especially with the suspicions about Barclay. You heard stories about colleagues who were on the take, or who had inside knowledge of what solicitors were up to, so he wondered what Barclay's angle was. There was only one way to find out. Joe followed him out into the street, and they talked as they walked.

'Now, DS Watson, what do you know about Harry Smith?'

'Nothing different to you. Known associate of many of the gang, Reynolds, Edwards, Goody, all of them.'

'True. But what else do you know?'

'Not much else.'

'Really?' Barclay turned to face Joe as they passed a group of early evening revellers, as he carried on walking down Dacre Street.

'Yeah.'

Just what was Barclay getting at? There was word of people on the force rooting out corruption. He had to tread carefully. Maybe Cliff Barclay was working on the Squad for Hatherill or Butler, looking for the wrong 'uns on the team.

'Have you ever spoken to Smith before?' Barclay asked.

'Yeah.'

'Outside of an interview room?'

'What d'you mean?' Joe's mind went back to that evening outside the telephone kiosk.

'I mean, DS Watson, have you had any other contact with our friend, Harry Smith?'

'No.' Joe tried to avoid eye contact, and stared straight ahead

'Follow me, Watson.'

They walked in silence for a couple of minutes, Barclay leading the way. They crossed Birdcage Walk and entered St James's Park. Nothing was said until Barclay settled on a bench. Joe sat beside him, wary of being watched. Was Barclay setting a trap?

'Listen, Watson, I know, all right. You've got nothing to worry about.' Barclay stared across at him as Joe tried to focus on passers by. 'In situations like this, you've got to take courage.'

The words paralysed him. It was the same phrase that both Lavery and Bob Welch had used. But Welch still went down for the robbery. He was confused, and felt like the world was spinning around him.

'What's that?'

'You heard me. I know, Joe.' Barclay sighed deeply, and wrinkled his scrawny face. 'We work for the same man. We've been working for the same man for a long time.'

Watson cast his mind back. It was nearly three years now. Three long years since Tommy Lavery recruited him, groomed him, and placed him exactly where he wanted him. And Cliff Barclay was on the same side, so he said.

'You mean?'

'Don't say any names, Joe. There's no need. I'm actually quite relieved it's you, Joe.'

Watson pulled his coat around him, trying to protect himself against the truth.

'How did he recruit you, then?' Joe asked.

'It doesn't matter. Listen, the thing is this, Harry Smith is being protected.'

'I know.'

'You were there, weren't you, that night he handed over half his money?' Barclay enquired. Joe just nodded. 'So was I, only you didn't spot me.'

'Why were you there?'

'I was watching you, Joe. And Armstrong. I had to make sure you both handed the cash over, and that Smith didn't turn himself in.'

'That was never the plan. Armstrong saw to that.' Joe remembered the gun pointed at a scared Harry Smith in the back of the car.

'I know. Everything was under control. It was a message to the rest of the gang, about who was in charge. That even though there was no evidence, Smith needed protecting. Still needs protecting, as you saw today.'

'So, you got to the witnesses?'

'I didn't personally, no. I don't know, maybe somebody else did, maybe Smith just has one of those faces you forget. Either way, he thinks he's being protected, and that's the key thing.'

Joe thought about Barclay, and how deeply he might have been involved in the robbery itself. Maybe he was there, and the earlier question was a bluff? He pulled himself up from the bench rather shakily, and started to walk back towards the Yard. Barclay set off after him.

'Joe, don't worry about it. It was meant to be this way. It also made sure that Frank Williams was confident in you and your abilities.' Barclay tugged at his sleeve. 'And your information.'

Joe hoped that some of the credit he had received was largely down to him working informants in the pubs and clubs, rather than simply being a puppet of Tommy Lavery. Maybe he had over-estimated his own abilities. He was a total fraud as a police officer. A cloud of despair hung over him, as he trudged his way back along the street towards the entrance to New Scotland Yard. Barclay had pricked his self-belief, blown apart the last vestiges he had of pride and esteem. Lavery had him totally by the balls, as always, but now it felt like he had stolen his life. He wondered if he would ever be released, break free of the shackles that bound him to lies and deceit. Joe looked back at Cliff Barclay, trailing in his wake, and wondered whether this was how it was for all police officers, one way or another.

78

4th June 1964: Elstree Aerodrome

Bruce lifted his second suitcase on to the light aircraft. He'd never been one to admire planes, was a car man to his bones, but this Cessna looked pretty smart. It was just an eight-seater, but he and Jack Armstrong were the only two passengers. His old accomplice from the robbery had insisted on escorting him from their safe house in Cambridge, where he and Franny had been staying for a few months.

'I'm coming with you,' Armstrong said. 'Not to Belgium, but to Gatwick.'

'Gatwick?'

'Yeah. We're taking a quick hop down there, and then the pilot will clear the flight to Ostend. I'm getting off before we leave the country. I've got work to do.'

'I'm sure you have,' Bruce replied absent-mindedly. Then he thought again about exactly what it was that Jack was employed to do. It was clear he was a money minder. It had really pissed him off when it emerged that he had been carrying on the job, but Jack Armstrong put in a solid shift moving those mailbags, apparently worked well in the engine too, persuading the driver to shunt along those precious hundreds of yards, after somebody hit him. Jack Mills was now painted as a hero; the picture of his bandaged head didn't do the boys any favours in the trial when it came to the sentences.

'It'll save me going through London,' Armstrong said. 'I'm heading for the South coast, you don't mind if I cadge a lift?'

'Be my guest,' Bruce said.

It was hardly up to him. Jack was far from what Bruce imagined an ideal travel companion to be, rarely said a word, but he was trustworthy. He knew now that people you could have faith in were few and far between. His stash in Lincoln had been raided, according to Jimmy Darwin. There was only fifty grand of his share left. Jimmy hid that much in his loft, in a fake boiler casing. They still got away with thirty thousand, but he had to be thankful. Geordie then set up a hurried meeting with Armstrong, which led to the balance being transferred into a Swiss bank account within a week. Now he felt his money was safe. Mind you, he did have to pass some of it on, in order to make his escape. Privately chartered aircraft flying off the official radar to Belgium didn't come cheap, and neither did flights to Central America with a false passport in the name of Miller. He was booked with Sabena Airlines from Brussels to Mexico City two days later.

Armstrong had no luggage, and offered to carry Bruce's overnight bag for him, but he declined. Reynolds had seven grand in cash in a briefcase, along with his two suitcases. Once inside the aircraft, they waited for what seemed like an age on the tarmac while the pilot made lengthy preparations. Bruce couldn't help feeling vulnerable, kept looking outside for police cars to come haring down the runaway. Armstrong spent this time flicking through a magazine, ignoring him. When they finally took off, Jack broke the silence, and asked him about the robbery.

'Do you regret the job, Bruce?' It was a fair question.

'No, not really.'

'You sure?' Armstrong sounded largely disinterested in his view, was just making conversation.

'No. We were big, we're famous.'

'Yeah, but you're on the run.'

'I know. But still, it's what we went into the life for.'

He wouldn't have swapped the last twelve months for anything in the world, even though at times it had been miserable. The rush of the job, the excitement of thieving so much money, the impact it had on the establishment. They had really put the politicians' noses out of joint, and the police were livid. It was ten times better than the Heathrow blag. There was a buzz from giving Tommy Butler and his mob the run-around.

Armstrong lapsed back into his magazine. Bruce decided to use the short time he had to probe a little. He wouldn't have this chance again to find out more about the background to the robbery.

'Jack, do you know who the insider was? Who originally gave the tip-off to the Ulsterman?'

'The what?'

'The Ulsterman. It's what Gordon christened the Irish bloke who came to us with the job in the first place.'

'The Ulsterman, hmm.' Armstrong seemed to be weighing up the name. 'No, sorry can't help you there. You know who I work for, and it's not any bloody Mick.'

'So, you didn't know any of their lot? Anyone who worked with him?'

'No,' Jack replied coldly.

'And you don't know what his real identity was? Whether he worked for the GPO, or something like that?'

'No, no idea.'

Armstrong looked out of the window, now apparently fascinated by cloud formations. Bruce had formed the idea that Lavery was behind the whole thing, fixed everything up, and then got double-crossed by the Ulsterman. Whoever the hell he really was.

'You don't know who this guy was, then?' Bruce tried again.

'No. Or any of his lot.' Jack turned to look at him, fixing him a stare. 'All I do know, is he fuckin' robbed us blind. He did that.'

'How did he rob you?' Bruce found it difficult to believe somebody as professional as Jack Armstrong could be turned over so easily.

'Don't ask me about it, please. It's too painful.' Jack looked like he wanted to jump out of the plane without a parachute.

'I bet your boss was pleased?'

'I said, don't ask.' Armstrong scowled at him.

'I'm wondering, that's all. How a man as powerful, as obviously influential as your boss, gets ripped off by a bunch of Paddies.'

'Don't fuckin' ask, I said.' Jack reached across from his seat and grabbed Bruce by the lapels, and then quickly let go. 'Sorry.'

Bruce tried to relax. He would certainly think twice about robbing Jack. He knew nothing about Irish criminals, hadn't come across too many in London. Maybe they were a coming force in England? Well, if they were, he wasn't going to be around to find out. He planned to be on the other side of the world in a few days time, oblivious to the in fighting of Lavery and his partner.

'Don't forget one thing,' Armstrong turned and said.

'Go on.'

'We don't exist. Me, my boss, Geordie, Mickey Griffin, we don't exist. Never have. Same even goes for this Ulster bloke, right?' Bruce nodded. 'If anybody asks you about any of this, remember, we're ghosts, phantoms. We never existed. You lot came up with this caper all by yourselves, okay?'

'Got it.'

Bruce was happy to take the credit for such a famous heist. He settled back into his seat for the rest of the short flight, thinking about all the planning and execution he oversaw. He deserved to be remembered, was the brain behind the whole thing. Bruce Reynolds might not have provided the initial finance, or the original inside information, but he was the man that made it all happen. He was going to go down in history as a criminal mastermind.

79

12th August 1964: Winson Green Prison, Birmingham

'You're coming out.'

'No fuckin' way.'

'Shut up, or we'll all be in the shit,' Jack Armstrong demanded. This was another of his robbery related missions, and unquestionably the riskiest and most stupid of them all. Breaking Charlie Wilson out of prison. The idiot didn't want to go, who the hell did he think he was?

Parlane threw some clothes on the floor. 'Get dressed, will ya?'

Mickey Griffin pulled out a gun and waved it in Wilson's direction.

'There's no need for that, is there Charlie? You're coming with us.' Jack tried to smooth the atmosphere, and pulled his mask aside, seeing a flicker of recognition in Wilson's eyes. 'Yeah, it's us, come on.'

Charlie smiled for the first time. 'Hello, Jack. Good to see ya.'

'And you, Charlie. You forgotten Mickey here?'

'Cheers, Mickey.'

Griffin grunted, probably put out that Wilson didn't clock him. That might not be a bad thing a year after the robbery. Jack had been pretty busy, but Mickey had been stood down on a few matters, according to Lavery, concentrating on local work back in Manchester. Except for this job, where they needed a number of hands, so Griffin was back on the team.

Wilson accepted his fate and quickly pulled on a pair of black trousers, a dark sweater, and a balaclava, so that he was dressed the same way as the three visitors. Armstrong led them past the bound figure of an unconscious guard outside. Wilson still had the honour of a high security cell, but these things could be circumvented if you had the contacts. Down the stairs and out of C Wing they went, and Parlane took over in front, leading through a series of locked doors, keys jangling quietly in his hands. After a careful couple of minutes, inching their way along the most exposed stretch, a long corridor leading to the bathhouse, they emerged into the prison yard and a still night. Outside, Parlane wrapped the keys in a cloth bag to keep the noise to a minimum, something he was supposed to have done earlier.

'This way,' Armstrong whispered, now back in charge. Parlane had insisted on looking after the keys after he smashed the guard on the head, like a prize for his efforts. Jack led everyone to a yellow chalk mark in the wall, easy to spot in the torchlight. He checked his watch; it was a quarter past three, so they should have been ready. Jack made a coarse 'cuckoo' sound in the still night air, and heard this repeated back at him from over the wall. After an anxious wait, a rope ladder appeared in front of them. He could imagine the scene now if the boys on the other side failed to do their job. Four blokes, including three unlicensed visitors, stuck in the prison yard, with their proverbial dicks hanging out.

Everyone climbed the rope ladder, Armstrong going last. When he reached the other side, all he saw was Parlane. He looked around the builders' yard, which adjoined the prison.

'Where are they?' Jack asked, already frustrated with his old colleague, Griffin.

'Mickey's away with him already. Just to make sure,' Parlane replied breathlessly.

'They were supposed to wait for us.' What the hell was he up to? 'Come on, hurry,' he insisted.

Armstrong and Parlane sprinted through the yard, which

emptied out on to a canal towpath. Jack spotted two figures running ahead to his right, and they followed. He was in better shape than his colleague, who wheezed and panted behind him, and despite considerable verbal encouragement, Parlane struggled to keep up. Fuck him. He accelerated away, desperate to stay in touch with Wilson and Griffin. Mickey looked in good shape, and Wilson appeared to be lean and fit in his cell, too. Jack followed them as they turned right, now only twenty yards behind, and emerged into a car park. Griffin and Wilson were getting into the back of a Rover, and he saw Morgan behind the wheel of another similar car parked immediately behind it. He turned to look back; there was no sign of Parlane yet. What the hell was keeping him?

'You ready?' Morgan asked, sticking his head out of the car window. 'Where's George?'

Armstrong jumped in the back seat as the other car sped off. 'Just fuckin' go, will ya?'

Morgan revved the engine and started to move off just as Parlane appeared around the corner, arms flailing. Jack re-opened the back door and Parlane flung himself into the back seat, landing on top of him in a nasty, sweaty heap.

'Get off me, you tit,' Jack shouted, as Morgan span the wheel and turned left on to a main road.

'Sorry,' Parlane panted.

'Anyone follow you?' Jack asked.

Parlane righted himself in the back seat. 'No.'

'No? And you dived on me like that?'

'So? We're in a hurry aren't we?'

'Suppose we are.'

Jack thought about their timetable for the evening, and looked at his watch again. In ten minutes they needed to be at an address in Edgbaston. From there, Wilson was being moved by van to a safe house in the country. Armstrong was detailed to go every step of the way with him, which was why Mickey Griffin legging it really pissed him off. Lavery had cautioned that Charlie knew some dangerous people, and that if he got a whiff of a rescue, a few of them might show up, just for old time's sake. They didn't want an audience when they took Wilson to recover his fee for breaking him out. Twenty grand in cash, Lavery said, payable in full within two days of his escape. If Charlie didn't come up with the money in time, he would go back to Winson Green with a beating and an increased sentence.

As their car sped across Birmingham, Jack wondered how many more men he might be asked to spring from prison. They would be on red alert now, and Lavery would know this, so there had to be a reason that Wilson took priority, although he couldn't fathom it. Occasionally he had visited some of the gang, just to be sociable. He would also pass on messages about the availability of George Stanley and his laundering facilities for his boss. Wilson looked particularly glum the last time he visited. He didn't even bother turning up for his appeal. But that evening in the prison yard, Charlie appeared to be revitalised by escape.

They pulled up outside an end terrace house and both cars emptied quietly. Griffin led them inside, and Jack noticed that Parlane was jangling something conspicuously.

'What's that?' he asked.

Parlane shrugged and emptied a massive ring of prison keys into his hand.

'Why didn't you chuck 'em in the canal?' Jack demanded.

'Dunno. I like 'em,' Parlane replied.

Jack took a deep breath. 'Go outside, go a long way away, and chuck 'em down a drain,' he exploded. As Parlane walked away, he finished off under his breath, 'and don't fuckin' come back.' He was still surrounded by bloody amateurs.

80

Buster Edwards wriggled on his crate and turned over another three of a kind. He was beating Geordie hands down, and taking him for a few quid in the process. Not that he needed the money; he knew he was one of the few in the gang with both his freedom and his share intact. Most of his cash was safe, but staying hidden for nearly a year and a half was an expensive business. Now he was going abroad, and the pit of his stomach rolled at the thought of leaving his homeland behind, not just because of the pitching of the trawler.

'At least try, Geordie,' he pleaded.

'I am trying, you're too good.'

Playing nine-card brag for three hours would test anybody's patience, and he was bored, despite being about twenty quid up. His life had dropped down so many gears it was unrecognisable to how it was before the robbery. If you had asked the Buster Edwards that jumped into the HVP coach what he would be doing by 1965, it wouldn't have been hiding in the depths of a freezing cold fishing boat. Those dreams of living it up in America, with June and his daughter Nicky, evaporated as soon as he went into hiding. Now he was trying to start again, on his own to begin with. Geordie had organised plastic surgery for him, in Germany. All at a price, of course, along with a new identity, courtesy of an anonymous boat trip to Belgium. He searched around in his holdall and fished out the folded letter. It was in Bruce's unmistakably neat handwriting, received the month before, and delivered via Geordie, his new best friend. Join us in Mexico, it pleaded, which was all the encouragement Buster needed. His opponent stubbed out his cigarette and made to light another.

'How long?' Buster asked.

Geordie looked at his watch. 'About an hour, no more, so long as we're on time.'

Zeebrugge was their destination, and Buster looked at his meagre possessions. Both he and Geordie were dressed like merchant seamen, donkey jackets and all the gear. His basic travel items were stuffed inside the small holdall, along with a couple of changes of clothes. Then there were the two suitcases full of the remains of his train robbery money, inside the crate. The twenty thousand pound fee for escape had already been collected by Jack Armstrong, at Tilbury docks, on his departure. No money, no secret passage across The Channel, he insisted. Armstrong shook him warmly by the hand when they said goodbye. He seemed to be one of the good guys; he and Geordie didn't fleece him, despite the temptation that must have been there; they took nothing other than the pre-arranged weekly fee. He feared that when they were shepherded into Wraysbury, Lavery and his associates would rob him of everything, but it didn't pan out that way. He and June got by for a while, but in the end they were fed up with continually looking over their shoulders. The pull of a new life and identities to match became too much, and Jack and Geordie said they could facilitate everything. He was heading for Cologne, where the plastic surgeon was lined up. 'Even June won't recognise you,' Geordie had joked. Then the plan was to join Bruce in Mexico.

Buster opened up his fake passport in the name of Jack Miller. The photo would have to do, and a contact of Geordie's in Germany was going to arrange for a new one when the surgery was finished. All for a price once more, but Buster wanted a future where he no longer had to hide every time the doorbell rang.

Armstrong promised they would smuggle June and Nicky out of the country at a later date.

The rest of the journey passed with Geordie rushing about, making preparations, going up to the deck and returning at regular intervals. Eventually, he sat down in front of Buster, to give him his final instructions.

'We're gonna pull into the container port in a minute. You'll have to sit tight for a couple of hours before you get the signal to move.'

'What's the signal?' Buster asked.

Geordie looked confused. 'Didn't Jack tell you the signal before we left?'

'No.'

'Oh well, I think it'll be obvious. Someone will come and ask if your name is Jack Miller. Just go with him.'

'Aren't you coming with me?' Buster pleaded hopefully. He and June had become so reliant on Geordie, he felt like he needed permission to piss first.

'No, Buster, I'm not coming. I've got work to do back in England.'

A thought occurred to Buster. 'Have you been looking after other people too? Other members of the gang?'

'You're my last one. There was only you and Bruce. When we dock, my time with you is up.'

'Do you work for Lavery?' Buster asked.

'I work for a lot of people. Besides, you shouldn't ask a question like that.'

'Won't you come with me, stay and help me? I'll pay you.' Buster pointed at the crate. 'I can afford it, you know that.'

Geordie shook his head. 'Thanks for the offer, but I can't. Besides, I've still got to make sure your wife and daughter get out to meet you.'

Once he had reached Mexico, the priority would be to get the girls out. Charlie Wilson had been sprung the year before, and was rumoured to be there, as well as Bruce. That would be some party, the three of them drinking and reminiscing about old times and the train robbery. They were famous men. He could imagine their life stories in print or on film.

'Well, I thought I might ask,' Buster lamented. 'No harm in asking, is there?'

'Suppose not, but I can't. Good luck.' Geordie went up on deck, and Buster heard nothing from him again.

They docked about half an hour later, and hearing nothing on deck, Buster finally lost patience hiding, and headed up the stairs. He peeked out and saw that their boat was moored at the end of a long jetty. He nervously waited to see if anybody approached, and after a while gave up and stepped out on to the gangway. The port looked to be deserted in the dim light, just after sunset. It felt like he had been abandoned in the middle of nowhere, rather than at a gateway to the European continent. He jumped out of his skin when he heard the quiet tones to his left.

'Good evening, Mister Miller. Nice to see you.'

Buster looked round to find two men leaning against a fishing vessel tied up next-door, smoking cigarettes. One pushed off from the boat and headed towards him, tossing his butt into the dock. The voice sounded familiar, a London accent.

'I said, good evening, Mister Miller. You need to get used to the name now, Buster.'

He didn't recognise the face. Was he being set up? This could have been two of Butler's boys, ready to pounce.

'Who are you?' he asked nervously.

'This is my colleague, Karl. He's gonna take you to Cologne tonight. He will help prepare you for the operation.' Buster swallowed. Plastic surgery sounded exciting, because it meant a new life. But this close to it, he wondered about the pain and the disfigurement that you heard about. Would he have second thoughts just as he was about to go under the knife?

'And who are you?' he asked.

'You call me Cliff. Don't worry, I'm on your side, I'm a friend of Tommy Lavery's. I'm here to look after you from now on.'

81

25th April 1965: Wandsworth Prison, London

'You know we sprung Charlie, don't you?'

'Yeah, but at a pretty price, I heard,' Ronnie Biggs mumbled, looking like he had just heard his mother died. He was a right miserable bastard. Jack Armstrong sighed. There was just no pleasing some people.

'What would you pay for freedom, Ronnie?' Jack eyed Biggs across the table in the visiting room. 'How much do you value seeing your wife and kids in the next what, thirty years? How's your wife gonna cope without you all that time, Ronnie? How are you gonna cope without Charmian?'

'How'd you know her name?'

'Come on, Ron. We knew everything about you, remember?'

'But I didn't get one of those sheets of paper?' Biggs cut a forlorn figure opposite Jack.

'So what? We know all about you now.'

Jack smiled, and Biggs scratched his head. Was there really anything going on inside there, Armstrong wondered. Sometimes he doubted it. Ronnie was an unlikely ally of Bruce Reynolds, and it was still a mystery why they let him in on the job. He had more respect for the old train driver, but Biggs was about to get lucky.

'You don't know where my money is.' Biggs looked like he was going to burst with animosity.

'That's not our business, Ronnie. You earned that money, you put a full shift in, just like the rest of us.'

Jack smiled through the lies, but he knew many of the other gang members were resentful. The whispers at the farm were that Biggs was too small-time. Jack didn't really care what they thought. His focus was on where Ronnie had squirrelled his share away, because he was one of the men where they had lost the trail. Even the police had found no signs of his money back then. Parlane had followed Biggs's wife for two weeks before the visit, and there appeared to be nothing suspicious going on, no strange men sniffing around her. She seemed to be living a quite ordinary suburban existence; you wouldn't have guessed that her husband was sitting on over a hundred grand. Lavery decided that they would open him up with the promise of a new life.

'Anyway,' Jack continued. 'Thing is, we've got Charlie out the country; the same goes for Buster and Bruce. Now it's your turn, if you want, Ronnie.' He smiled as he delivered what he hoped would be a clincher, doused with a helping of reality. 'They got out with the vast majority of their money intact.'

'Vast majority?' Biggs interrupted, leaning forward in his chair.

'Yeah. You don't think these things are free? You think a fake passport is an easy or cheap thing to get hold of, do you? Spare me,' Jack said, trying to stay calm. They were right. Biggs was hard work to get through to.

'I suppose not.'

'No, well, they're not. Anyway, just think about it. You could be sitting on a beach with Bruce in a couple of months.'

'Really?' Biggs looked like he might believe the flannel at last.

'Yeah, really. They all got out the country. We got Charlie out of Winson Green, it's much tighter than here. We can make it happen, Ronnie.'

'I'll think about it,' Biggs said as he leant forward again. There was a short pause and then Ronnie smiled at last. 'I've thought about it, I'm in. I mean out.' He laughed and Jack joined in. You had to play the game with the comedians.

'Good. We need information about your block.'

'No problem. How will you do it?'

'Let me look after the details. We just need to know who's in the cells around you. We need to make sure nobody gets excited at the wrong time. We don't want anybody saying, "Can I come too?" just as we're about to go over the wall.'

Biggs sat in silence for a few seconds. Armstrong wondered what he was pondering, and soon found out.

'I want someone to come with me.'

'No.'

'Tom Flower, he's gotta come as well. He's my cellmate.'

'I don't care if he's your fuckin' prison wife. He's not coming.'

'No Tom, no me.'

'Fine.'

Jack sat back and eyed Biggs. His arms were folded, head bowed. He was so out of his depth, it wasn't true. There was a huge amount of preparation needed for a break out, even from a lax prison like Wandsworth. The authorities must have reasoned that Biggs was low risk, because the others were constantly being shuffled about. Jimmy Hussey had been Lavery's main priority for escape, because they had no idea where his money had gone. But he was about to be moved again to Norwich, so the word was, and unless they struck while he was being transported, preparations wouldn't be easy. You had to establish relationships with warders well in advance of an escape. Biggs was the number two target, because his money was also unaccounted for.

'All right. Here's how it can work. Just like we did for Charlie. Maybe we can persuade him to send you a postcard; to convince you it'll work. That you're better off out there than stuck in here for thirty years.'

'I might only do fifteen,' Biggs replied with a grin.

It was time for Jack to give him a reality check. 'So, even if you only did that, that would be what, another thirteen years from now, Ronnie? Is Charmian gonna be waiting for you? Are your kids gonna even recognise you, let alone care who you are? Think about it.'

Biggs resembled a small child, hunched up in his plastic chair. His face was screwed up, and it looked like he was going to cry. Not in here, man, not the visiting room. Your life would be a misery if you did.

'All right. How much?' Biggs relented.

'Thirty grand. That's to get you and your mate out, if you insist on him coming.' Biggs nodded. 'Well, once he's out, he's on his own,' Jack added.

'Fine. He won't mind.'

'Good. Then we take you abroad, along with your money, if you want.'

'I keep my money. Only I know where it is. There's no use asking Charmian, she don't know.'

Armstrong had already thought about it. If he had a wife, he wouldn't tell her where his hundred grand was either, not if he was going to be locked up for thirty years.

'Where d'you want to go?' Armstrong asked, hoping to improve Biggs's mood.

Ronnie thought for a moment, and then grinned. 'Down Under.'

'What, Australia?'

'Yeah. Oz. I like the sound of that.'

'You sure? It's a long way from home.'

'Nothing wrong with that. At least they speak English.'

Jack had to admit Biggs had a point. He knew Reynolds, Edwards and Wilson had all found their way to Mexico at some point. He didn't fancy speaking Spanish. The Costa Brava was different; there were English places out there where you could hide and not have to speak a word of the local lingo.

'All right. Now we're on to something. You'll need a new identity as well.'

'Can I pick the name?' Biggs asked.

'No you fuckin' can't,' Jack replied, almost losing his temper. Who did he think he was? 'It all depends on what passports we can get our hands on.' Biggs nodded, obviously no idea how it worked. 'You get what we can find for you.'

'So, thirty grand?'

'Thirty, plus whatever the cost is to get your new identity. That might be another five.'

'Don't rip me off, Jack. We worked together, remember?' Biggs pleaded.

'Yeah. But you're in here and I'm out there. And I'm trying to get you out there too, remember.'

Biggs nodded, then asked, 'How come they didn't catch you then, Jack?'

'I wore my gloves, didn't I?'

It was a cheap shot, but Jack felt that he was justified in delivering it. Biggs took his off to play Monopoly, and they also found his prints on loads of other items, including plates and sauce bottles. He was a fool. Biggs rocked in his chair and folded his arms again.

Jack pressed on. 'Look. You'll get a visit from a man who works for Lessers, you know, your solicitors.'

'Oh, them.'

'Yeah, them. His name's George Stanley. He'll arrange the money transfer with you. He deals with that side of things.'

'So, I deal with him now?'

'Yeah. I'm sure you can find a way to get the money from wherever it is now, into his account.' Biggs still looked a desperate man. Jack was offering him the chance of a lifetime; freedom to enjoy what was left of his money, what was wrong with him? He issued a reminder. 'You managed it to pay for your solicitor.'

Biggs nodded. 'I can arrange it.'

'Good. When we get word he has the payment, then we spring you.'

'You'd better not fuck me over, Jack,' Biggs threatened, although it didn't feel convincing.

'We won't. Remember, we've all got something in common. We've got this bond, haven't we? This thing that'll keep us together. We don't abandon our own, nobody does in this game, Ronnie.'

Jack shook hands with Biggs and left the room. As he exited, he took a sneaky look back, and saw Biggs with his head in his hands. It looked like he was going to cry. Were they tears of shame? Jack reasoned that his time on the outside would be short-lived. Even if they broke him out of Wandsworth, Ronnie Biggs would be one of the forgotten men of the robbery.

82

14th September 1967: Como Golf Club, Hudson, Quebec, Canada

'Afternoon, Mister Alloway.'

'Jesus wept,' was all Charlie Wilson could offer in reply.

'It is Mister Alloway, isn't it?' Jack Armstrong asked. It had bloody well better be, after traipsing halfway across the world. Wilson peered at him, and rubbed his eyes.

'No.' Charlie stood to walk away.

'Don't make a scene, Mister Alloway,' Jack whispered, grabbing Wilson's arm. Charlie sat down again in one of the plush clubhouse chairs. The Como was a select establishment, you didn't get to be a member unless you were a respected part of the local community, and had a few dollars behind you.

'What d'you want?' Wilson hissed. 'What you doing here?'

'I've come to see you. Brought you a present.'

'Oh yeah?' Wilson threatened. A couple of members turned and stared, and Charlie smiled in their direction, tipping an imaginary cap on his head. The men looked away.

'Yeah. I got something for you.'

'Let's go outside.'

'Fine by me, Mister Alloway.'

'And you can cut that shit out for a start,' Charlie hissed again.

Armstrong followed Wilson out to the putting green, where two men who must have been in their seventies, were trickling balls towards tiny flags, stuck into a large lawn. Jack didn't see the point of the stupid game, but it took all sorts. He knew Tommy played, it was a part of his lifestyle now, mixing with judges and politicians and the like. His flight to Montreal had been uncomfortable because Lavery wouldn't stump up for a first class seat. The hotel was lousy, and his taxi journey over the Ottowa River had used up most of the flimsy Canadian dollars he had brought along. He was looking forward to a good drink, but he had work to take care of first.

They walked past the green and over to a bench underneath a pine tree, where Charlie sat down and rolled a cigarette. Jack had given up the rollies because he got sick of trying to make them on the move, and fished a Marlboro out of his own packet.

'Come on, then. It must be something, if you've come all this way to see me.'

'It's good news, Charlie.'

'I bet it is.'

'No, honest.' Jack was carrying a small holdall and a leather briefcase. He picked the latter up, and placed it on the bench. 'Here's the interest on your latest investment.'

Wilson looked at him quizzically. 'What?'

'It's the interest on your latest investment. You gone deaf or something?'

'No. How much?' Charlie asked.

'It's in Bahamian dollars.' Wilson raised an eyebrow. 'Don't ask,' Jack muttered. He was buggered if he knew why the money was being transported in foreign currency. What was wrong with good old-fashioned pound notes? They were happy enough to steal them.

'I see,' Wilson said. 'How much?' He sounded calm, less annoyed than when he was buttonholed in the bar.

'I'm told it's over ten grand, English money, in this funny currency you ordered.'

'Ordered?' Wilson looked bemused.

Jack shrugged. 'I'm just doing what I'm told.' For God's sake, didn't he know?

'What's all this about?' Wilson asked.

Armstrong realised that he needed to repeat the explanation Lavery had given him. This was all rather tiresome. 'Tommy says this is the interest you've earned, based on your investments with him over the past two years. I assume that makes sense to you?'

Wilson nodded, and opened the clasp on the briefcase, peering inside at the strange bank notes. Monopoly money, Jack wanted to say, but that would have been in poor taste.

'This is just my interest, then?'

'That's what I said, yeah.'

'Where's my real money? My original money?'

'Ah, I assume that is still safe. This is extra, this here. I've also got a message from my employer.'

Wilson closed the briefcase and looked around. Apart from Jack and Charlie on the bench, there didn't appear to be anybody under the age of sixty in the entire club. Why spend your time there if you were a rich man like Wilson? What a waste of a life.

'I don't get it. This is mine, yeah?' Charlie asked.

'Yeah.'

'But it's not my original money?'

'No, that's safe.' This was hard work. Maybe Charlie's brain had switched off now he was living a quiet life. Jack continued. 'Tommy says that you need to invest more into the fund, and that it's going to produce even more returns, better than this.' Jack hoped he was remembering the words correctly. The aim was to get Wilson to unearth the rest of his money, because thirty grand was still hidden somewhere. This was an incentive for Charlie to give Lavery access; the ten thousand in funny money was a hook to grab his attention.

'I don't get it.'

'He told me you would understand.'

'I'm not sure I do.'

Right, Jack thought. I will have to explain this in simple terms. 'Look. You invested money together, you and Tommy, while you was inside.' Wilson nodded slowly. 'Well, this is your payout from that. But there is an obligation that goes with this nice little payout. You've got to invest more in the same company.'

Jack opened up his holdall and pulled out a small brochure. 'Glory Estates', it announced.

He continued, handing the leaflet to Charlie. 'This is the company you now own shares in, along with Tommy. It's a property investment company; most of it is based in Spain. A lot of Brits want to buy expensive villas over there these days, you know. And your company is in there, riding the crest of a wave. The one which delivered this money here.' Jack pointed at the cash lying in the briefcase. Charlie still looked confused. 'Look, Charlie, you're a rich man now; thanks to the money you invested with Tommy. He's offering to make you even richer. It's a case of adding more, to make more. That's how property investment works.'

Wilson looked through the brochure for a few seconds, and then peeked again at the dollars in the briefcase. Surely he would get it, Jack thought. He must realise that this was his big chance to make an even bigger fortune. Legitimately.

'So, if I put more money into this Glory whatever it is, Tommy will make more money?'

'You'll both make more money. You're equal partners. As you arranged two years ago.'

'Did we?' Charlie look surprised.

Jack sighed. This was proving to be harder work than he had expected. 'Yeah. That's where this cash came from.'

'Ah,' Charlie said. Was he getting it? 'Tommy wants more of my money invested in our company?'

Bingo. 'You got it.'

'Why doesn't Tommy invest in it himself?'

'He will. You both have to, you're partners.'

Wilson weighed the brochure in his hand and stared into space, back towards the clubhouse.

'What if I say "no"? What if I say, "Piss off Tommy, I'm happy with my dollars here?"'

Jack was prepared for the challenge. 'Well, that is entirely your decision.'

'Good.'

'Only, if you don't invest some more, then the partnership may have to be dissolved.'

'Dissolved?'

'Yeah.'

'What does that mean?' Charlie asked. Jack thought he was starting to look nervous.

'Well, Charlie.' Jack paused to remember how his boss had described the possible situation. 'Firstly, the original money you invested would be forfeited. Lost.' Wilson still looked confused. 'And secondly, it might mean that some other services that Tommy has been providing for the past few years, may also be dissolved.'

'Meaning?'

'You work it out, Charlie. If you don't want to play ball, somebody might find out where you are.'

'Fuck off.'

'Think about it, Charlie.'

'I have. Tell Lavery from me, he can fuck off.'

'Are you sure that's the message I should take back?'

Wilson hesitated, looking uncertain. 'Let me think about it. How much does he want me to invest, exactly?'

'Thirty thousands pounds should cover it.'

Wilson laughed. 'Can I think about it?'

'You've got two days. Ring me at this hotel,' Armstrong replied, standing up and snatching the briefcase back. 'You get this back if you say yes.' He handed Wilson a slip of headed paper from The Four Seasons Hotel in Montreal, and scribbled his room number on it. 'If you decide not to continue the investment, I go home, it's that simple.'

'Do I have a choice?' Charlie asked.

'You know you've always got a choice,' Jack answered as sincerely as he could. 'Just make sure you make the right one, Charlie.'

★ ★ ★

Armstrong answered the phone in a daze. What bloody time was it? He turned the bedside light on, and saw from the clock that it was half past nine in the morning.

'Is that Jack?'

'Yeah.'

'Hey, Jack, it's Charlie.'

'Ah, good.'

Armstrong tried to sit upright in bed, but struggled to co-ordinate his body. Maybe it was all that scotch he had consumed the night before. There had to be a few perks for this lousy bloody job from time to time.

'You're not gonna like it.'

Bugger. He desperately hoped that Charlie would play along. Of all the crew, he respected Wilson the most. You knew where you were with him, and he was pretty smart. Not smart enough to understand the right decision to take, though.

'Charlie,' he started to plead.

'No, don't. I've had enough, Jack. I've got a nice, quiet life, my wife and kids are settled, they love it out here. I just want to be left alone.'

'I don't remember that being an option.'

'You said it was.' Jack listened to the desperate voice at the other end of the line, making a poor decision. 'You said I had a choice to make.'

'Yeah, but you know what I was really saying. You should invest the rest of your money in this company.'

There was a slight pause at the other end of the line. 'How d'you know thirty grand is all I got left?'

Jack tried to crank his brain into gear. This wasn't a fair fight. Wilson was awake, and his own body was six hours ahead, or behind, or whatever it was supposed to be.

'Just a lucky guess.'

'No, I'll take my chances,' Charlie said. 'Please can you respectfully tell Tommy Lavery, I'd rather not take him up on his generous offer, and he can keep his strange dollars, too.'

'Are you sure? Remember who you're dealing with here.'

'The same goes for me. I'm a fuckin' great train robber you know.'

'I know. So am I,' Jack replied, although nobody was ever going to find out about his involvement.

Charlie shouted down the telephone, lost his temper. 'Look, you can tell Lavery to stick his investment up his arse. I want to stay here. Tell him to leave me alone.'

Such bravado. At least Jack had the heart to take the expletive out, and re-phrase the decline of the request when he reported back to his boss. That probably saved his life, even if it did nothing to guarantee his freedom.

83

28th January 1968: BOAC flight from Montreal to Heathrow

Frank Williams was handcuffed to Charlie Wilson, halfway across the Atlantic from Montreal to London. The Grey Fox didn't fancy being attached to a criminal like Wilson for such a long flight, so Frank got the job, and he was determined to spend the time constructively. The Home Office were even paying for them to travel in Business Class, and he was becoming accustomed to drinking beer with his free hand. Wilson did likewise. Despite where he was sat, Charlie looked utterly defeated. His wife and kids were still in Canada, desperate to fight deportation.

Frank thought back to the bitter cold of the small town of Rigaud, less than an hour from Montreal, and the snow falling everywhere. Half the road signs were in French, what was all that about? He had taken his gloves off for about five seconds, and nearly got frostbite. The Mounties had lent him and Tommy Butler special clothing to fight off the weather, and arrived in force behind the pair of them when they pulled up outside the target address. The Grey Fox got the pleasure of knocking on Charlie Wilson's door, and asking if he was in. The look on Pat's face was priceless.

Their information was that the entire Wilson family were living under the name of Alloway. Barclay was the man who came up with the tip-off, dragged out of a source down on the South coast. The same officer had also revealed that Jimmy White was hiding out in Nottinghamshire, and negotiated the return of Buster Edwards.

Maybe Frank was losing his touch, what with Watson and then Cliff Barclay beating him to the punch with the train robbers. Still, he was cuffed to one of the three remaining suspects on the run, in an ideal position to learn more. Reynolds was still out there somewhere, and Biggs had been sprung from jail eighteen months before, but Wilson was the one that Butler had been obsessing about.

So far it had all been small talk, but now Butler had fallen asleep across the aisle.

'Charlie. I'm sorry it's come to this.' Frank genuinely had respect for Wilson, more than most villains he came across, even if he was too stupid to stay hidden.

'Are you? Are you really, Mister Williams?'

'I am. I can't believe you got caught up in this one.'

'Neither can I.' Wilson laughed to himself. 'I can't believe a lot of what's happened.'

'Tell me, Charlie, how did it get started?'

'I can't tell you that, Mister Williams.'

'No?'

Wilson smiled at him, raising his glass with his free hand. 'You know I won't say anything, so you're wasting your breath asking me.'

'Really?'

'Yeah, really. Nobody's talked on this whole job, have they?'

Frank thought about what Wilson said. The imprisoned gang had revealed nothing about who else took part. The squad had given up on Smith and Pembroke – there was never going to be any evidence to make it stick with them. He was convinced that Harry Smith had been at the trackside that night. Why else would he give up the fifty grand? They were only going to focus on Reynolds and Biggs once they got Wilson back to Parkhurst, on the Isle of Wight, where all the high profile robbers were now being held amid tight security. Butler was in semi-retirement, working just this one case. He wouldn't give up until the last two were locked up.

'You lot have been tight, I'll give you that,' Frank admitted.

'Yeah, well, it was a good crew. In the end.'

'In the end? What do you mean?' Frank asked.

'Ah, nothing. The ones that lasted the longest, apart from Ronnie, we were the main men, and you know that. It's sort of just, really.'

Frank pondered this criminal logic. Did those who masterminded the robbery deserve to be free for the longest? Or were they all simply a gang of thieves who made a load of mistakes, just some got luckier than others? He preferred the latter explanation.

'So, who was in charge? You know, Charlie, I mean, really in charge?'

Wilson looked him in the eye. 'We all were.'

'Come off it, Charlie, this is me you're talking to.'

'I know, Mister Williams. And I know what you're asking me about. And you're getting nothing.'

'I think someone was the boss, someone we don't know about.'

'Why d'you think that?' Wilson asked, smiling.

'I can't figure out how you got all the inside information. And got to pull together such a big crew. All without any help.'

'Maybe we're just bloody good thieves?'

'Not good enough to avoid getting caught,' Frank replied.

'Maybe. You'll just have to go on wondering then, won't you?'

Frank thought about how much of this might be a cover story, this idea that there was a criminal mastermind behind it all. If the police and the press assumed that the men they had been hunting down were mere pawns in a massive game, they might get a lighter sentence. Well, if that was the idea, it certainly didn't work. Thirty years would deter gangs in the future. There had been a few extraordinary stories in the press about who was behind it all. God knew where they came from, certainly not his team. Theories ranged from Nazis and American white supremacists, all the way to the Russians, and many places in between. If they had made a run for it, they might have been successful. But as he always said, deep down criminals were basically stupid. They made mistakes, and Leatherslade Farm, and the state they left it in, was a critical one.

He tried one last time to find out more from Wilson, while he had the chance.

'What happened to all the money, Charlie? You knew if the money came back you'd all have got shorter sentences?'

'No chance for me. I escaped.'

'All right, maybe not for you, but for the others.'

'What's the point? I bet nobody's got any money left, either those on the run, or those inside.'

'Why d'you say that?' Frank asked.

'I just think nobody's really been a big winner out of all this. None of us really got what we thought we would.' Wilson stared into the distance, casting about for the eye of a flight attendant.

'You mean there was less than you expected on the train?'

'Nah, I don't mean that.'

The attendant appeared and Wilson asked for another scotch, a double this time. He really was milking this for all he could. Why not, Frank thought, Charlie was heading for a few years inside as soon as they touched down. There would be no court appearance for him, he was an escapee, he was going straight back to prison.

'What, then?' Frank asked.

'Look,' Wilson turned to face him, swilling his whisky in a tumbler, 'none of us got rich on the back of this job. It was just too big to get away with. None of us are gonna be living it up in the South of France, are we?'

'Reynolds probably is.'

Wilson looked to be thinking about his old schoolboy friend, and smiled. 'Yeah, maybe Bruce'll do all right out of it.'

'You're not jealous that he's still free?'

'Nah, good luck to him.'

Charlie looked to genuinely believe it. In Frank's experience, villains who were caught were usually envious of those who got away. From all the times he had visited the men in prison on this one over the previous two years, angling for more information, it seemed that they were pleased for those still on the run. The numbers were dwindling now.

'Well, Charlie, I don't reckon you'll be free to spend any of your money for a long time.'

'I know, Mister Williams. But I bet I've got a lot less to spend than you think.'

'Where's all your money gone, then?' Williams asked.

'Now that's a long story,' Charlie replied sadly. 'A long story.'

84

'What you doing in here? It's hardly the best place to hide, is it?'

Bruce looked up to see who was annoying him, and saw a familiar face. It was Jack Armstrong. What was he doing in Maxine's at two o'clock in the morning? He hadn't seen the man for a couple of years, but he still had that same serious expression.

'How are you, Jack? You alone?' Bruce asked.

'I'm always alone these days.'

'What, no Mickey?'

'He's banged up. Armed robbery, would you believe?' Reynolds spluttered, unable to hold back a laugh. Armstrong continued. 'What brings you to these parts, Bruce?'

'Life.'

Bruce shrugged, and sipped his whisky. What did it matter if Jack saw him there? He had been living a strange existence ever since they returned to the capital, earlier in the summer. Following two wild years in Mexico, both he and Franny had yearned to live somewhere that they spoke English again, which would also help Nicholas. They had tried Quebec, where Charlie Wilson was hiding out, but that was too cold. They bounced around southern France for a few months, but London was where they yearned to be. In August, the three of them had moved into a mews flat in Kensington with the help of Geordie Adams. Bruce even took to hanging about in a few of his old haunts, and that was why he was propping up a bar in Soho at that hour.

'You hear about me from Geordie?' he asked.

'Yeah, in a roundabout way. Bruce, what the hell are you doing?' Armstrong pleaded.

'I'm having a drink. Care to join me?' Bruce pointed at the empty chair beside him.

'No, thanks. I'm busy.'

'Oh yeah, doing what?'

'Looking after you, Bruce. That's part of my job.'

'You don't need to look after me, Jack. I'm a big boy. Haven't you heard? I'm bloody famous.' Reynolds raised his glass and downed the contents. It no longer burned his throat as it went down.

'Too famous, Bruce.'

'I haven't got any money left, if that's what you're after. Well, not much, anyway.'

'No?'

'Nah. It costs to live abroad, didn't anyone tell you that?'

Bruce was resentful about the fact that nothing came cheap, especially if you wanted to live a little. You try keeping Franny happy on a dwindling pile of cash, he thought.

'I'm not after your money, Bruce.' Armstrong had that fierce look on his face again. 'Look, come with me, you don't want to be seen hanging round places like this. Someone might clock you.'

'So?' Bruce didn't care who saw him.

'You got some sort of death wish? You trying to give yourself up?'

Maybe I am, Bruce thought to himself. Perhaps I want to get caught, let people know who I am, what I planned and what we did. He wondered how he would react if Tommy Butler walked in at that moment, with ten coppers in tow. He wouldn't run for it, he was tired of all that.

'Look. They've not got you yet. It don't matter how much money you've got left, you're still free,' Jack pleaded. 'You know how long the others got, don't you?'

Thirty years, Bruce thought. That was forever; no way he could even do fifteen. By the time he came out he would be an old man. Franny would have left him, and Nicholas would have grown up. No, getting caught wouldn't do him any favours.

'I'm running out of options, Jack,' Bruce said. In truth, that had happened a long time ago.

Armstrong looked anxious. 'Look, let's get out of here, for a start. Come on, Bruce, we need to go some place quieter.'

Bruce staggered to his feet. He had been drinking into the small hours again, and Franny would be angry. Every time he rolled in late she had a word for him. They were still living as Mr and Mrs Miller, but they saw Geordie only once a month now, when they paid the rent. His minder appeared to own the place they were staying at. To all intents and purposes, they were self sufficient, as much as you could be, with only seven grand left.

The fresh air of Compton Street hit him as he walked outside, and he tried to add up where all his money had gone. Ten grand as a keeper's fee to Jimmy Darwin; that was fair enough, he took a few risks for him, and hid both his and John's money, with no advance warning. Thirty of it went missing when Jimmy got raided. It cost him another twenty grand to leave the country, paid to Geordie, from his Swiss bank account. Maybe another five paid to the minder over the course of a year, for looking after them in various parts of England before that. Again, that was acceptable. The rest was frittered away on cars and the high life in Mexico.

He might have to start again. Surely people would want to work with one of the infamous train robbers? It would be an honour to be on a crew led by Bruce Reynolds, scourge of the establishment and the law. That evening he had been turning over how feasible it might be to hit the mail train that ran from the West Country up to Waterloo. Security would be tighter now, but he knew how easy it was to tamper with signals. That Roger Cordrey, what a con artist. Knowing how to cover a bulb with a glove had netted him over a hundred grand; he did bugger all else on the job. Then he got caught with the money, and by the sounds of it, Jack and Mickey Griffin's share too. He wondered if Lavery's boys had been able to get to Roger on the inside yet. God help him if they did.

Thoughts of future capers spun around in his head until he realised Jack Armstrong had led him to a parked car in the dimly lit street. Bruce studied it, a smart Bentley, exactly the sort that he should have been driving. The back seat window wound down, and he peered inside, leaning against the door, unsteady on his feet.

'Evening, Bruce.' Tommy Lavery smiled at him. 'It's really good to see you.'

'Likewise,' was all Reynolds could muster, as memories of the briefing the night before the robbery hit him. This man knew so much, but his men had kept him safe for three years. Would it stay the same now that his money was running out?

'Jack tells me he found you drinking in public.'

'Yeah, what of it?' Bruce was comfortable being a little prickly with him. They had too much in common for there to be a public falling out.

'Nothing. That's your business. I just wanted to say hello.' The window wound up again and the car pulled off. Bruce stared in confusion as the motor took a left, and disappeared from view. Did that really happen? Maybe Jack was right; he had been drinking too much.

'Come on, Bruce,' Armstrong implored. 'I've got a place you can go where all of you can stay hidden. London's too busy, too many criminals hanging about, you know what I mean?'

Reynolds nodded. Jack was right; he was on a suicide mission, visiting drinking clubs from his past. Was he desperate to be caught, to claim his rightful notoriety? He should have been lying low. Tommy Butler and Frank Williams would be sniffing around, listening, hearing the word that Bruce Reynolds was back.

Armstrong's next words tapped into his desperation. 'I know somewhere that nobody will find you.'

85

Villa Cap Martin overlooked Torbay harbour, standing proud amid the town of Torquay. Its white and blue wooden frame appeared increasingly weather-beaten after a week of hard winds and rain. An unmarked police car approached in the gloom of early morning, and Joe Watson stepped out alongside the Grey Fox. This was the one that had vexed Butler for four years, and now they were poised to swoop. They were accompanied in the distance by three squad cars from the local force, but Butler instructed everybody to keep back. This was his collar.

The former leader of the Squad walked up to the front door of the villa, and knocked politely. It was six in the morning, the ideal time to rouse train robbers from their sleep. Franny Reynolds answered the door, rubbing her eyes. Butler was all politeness.

'Mrs Reynolds, I need to see your husband.'

The woman ran inside and headed up the stairs, Butler and Watson following her. Word was that Reynolds was unarmed, had little money left, and was a sitting duck. All they had to do was find a way in and arrest him. Joe had been told that his protection had been called off; as soon as he was located, he would be easy to take.

Joe got to come on the hush-hush trip to Devon because he had been central to locating Reynolds. Frank Williams was working in vice now, attempting to clear up the fleshpots of the West End. Most of the rest of the team from the Robbery Squad had been dispersed.

Some had retired, notably Cliff Barclay, and nobody had a clue where he had gone, although he had been central in brokering the surrender of Buster Edwards two years earlier. Tommy Butler stayed on, working part-time, still obsessed with tracking down the rest of the gang. This pull would almost complete the task. The taking of Charlie Wilson had been a strange one by all accounts; how anybody worked out that he was in a small town in Quebec was beyond Joe. Jimmy White had been living a quiet life in Mansfield when they tracked him down in 1966, and all his money had gone. None of the gang seemed to have profited from the robbery, as far as he could tell. The one exception might have been Biggs, and they were convinced that he was hiding in Australia, the last man standing after Reynolds.

'Hello, Bruce, it's been a long time,' Butler said, as they walked into the bedroom. The suspect was sitting on his bed, smoking, wearing a dressing gown.

'Ah, well, Mister Butler, c'est la vie.'

Reynolds looked completely resigned to his fate. After four years on the run, it was all coming to a rather tame end in a small villa in Devon. Joe had a more glamorous vision of the conclusion in his head, maybe a shootout in a warehouse. This seemed so subdued, and unworthy of the glamour of the crime.

'You know you've got to come with us,' Butler announced.

'I know.'

The official line that Joe was forced to give, was that one of his now legendary informers had dropped the wink about this place in the West Country, and that Reynolds and his wife were hiding there. Lavery was extremely forceful in pressing home how much he wanted Bruce behind bars at last.

Butler had already talked about doing a deal with Reynolds to retrieve the rest of his money on the way down in the car. He thought he was harbouring a huge sum, given the small amounts they had turned up over the years. His belief was that somebody had to have the lion's share, and Reynolds was clearly one of the ringleaders. Logic, according to Butler, would then decree that Bruce still had a significant amount of money hidden away.

Joe Watson could hazard a guess where most of the missing money had gone, but revealing anything would be the last thing he did. His own career had progressed rapidly after the majority of the gang were locked up, and he was now a Detective Inspector in the Met. His Flying Squad days were thankfully over, and his next regional move had been confirmed. The Kent coast was calling him. Getting out of the capital would help him to finally escape Lavery's clutches. If he were solving minor break-ins and petty crime in the backwater of Dover, Tommy would lose interest in him. There would be many benefits – the air was cleaner, and doubtless it wouldn't be full of prostitutes and lunatics. A few quiet years by the seaside might prove very beneficial for his health.

He watched as Butler marched Reynolds out to his car. The Grey Fox appeared to be delighted, as he brought in the last of the ringleaders. Joe had neither the heart, nor the inclination, to correct the detective at the forefront of the train robbery investigation. Nobody needed to know the dark truth, and now he could start to make amends in his own quiet way.

86

Dressed in his expensive suit, and sporting a perennially deep suntan, brought on by spending most of the previous five years aboard his yacht in the Mediterranean, the passenger dropped into the rear seat of the Bentley, outside a hotel on Manchester's Piccadilly. His driver closed the door and assumed his position at the wheel. It was eight o'clock in the morning, and they were heading for a business meeting in Liverpool, as they had done at the same time for the previous two days. He was close to finishing the deal, tying up cocaine shipments from Turkey and Iran. The passenger smiled to himself, absent-mindedly studying his reflection in the mirror in front of him. He poured himself a tonic from the copiously stocked drinks cabinet. It was the little touches that made his life worthwhile, no expense spared. His head still throbbed from the night before, although the rest of his body pulsed, remembering the two women who had shared his bed in the Penthouse suite.

He opened up his copy of *The Times*, and scanned the pages, impatiently waiting for his driver to head off. Property investment, and then drug trafficking, had served him well. The whole world was at his fingertips, he could do anything he wished, go wherever he wanted, and have any woman he chose. Those dark days on the back streets of Manchester, wife and children weighing down his ambition, were long forgotten, a distant memory. He was a force of nature, untouchable.

'Won't be a minute, boss,' the driver said; as he stepped out of the car, and propped open the bonnet. He disappeared from view, and the passenger sighed, going back to his newspaper, annoyed at the shortage of sporting news. He wondered about the consequences of being late for his meeting. Kamran would just have to bloody well wait, that was how things worked. He sipped at his drink, and pondered the day ahead. He was booked on the golf course at one, hoped he would have time for a nice spot of lunch beforehand.

The five-pound bomb attached to the chassis was triggered by remote control from a nearby square. It ripped through the underside of the Bentley, blasting upwards and outwards. Metal debris and body parts were scattered along the street, and decimated shop windows. The front door of the hotel, which the car had been parked immediately outside, was destroyed; such was the force of the explosion.

After walking from his place of nearby safety, the bomber rounded the corner, and quickly surveyed the scene. There were bodies strewn along the pavement, and glass everywhere. Alarm bells rang out, and women screamed. What remained of the Bentley had turned into a fireball. The devastation was fitting, because the target had been obliterated. He nodded to a suited figure as it passed, recognising the expressionless face. He reversed his steps, moving back towards the square, and dropped the device into a rubbish bin. He calmly strode over to a phone box, and rang the number he had been given.

'It looks like a success,' he whispered into the receiver.

'The job is done?' The voice at the other end of the line questioned.

'Absolutely. No doubt. The target is dead.'

'Good man.' The steely voice in his ear was now focused on action. 'Right, you know we have one more thing to do.'

'Aye. See you, then.'

'See you.'

87

9th March 1974: The Manchester to London line

Jack Armstrong read the newspaper report of the blast again, confirming that Lavery was dead. He returned to gazing out of the train window, taking in the passing countryside. He would definitely sneak a look when they passed through Leighton Buzzard station, seek out the part of the track where they had become famous. Most of the crew were still inside. Ronnie Biggs was on the run, rumours ranging from Australia to Mexico to Brazil. Danny Pembroke and Harry Smith had avoided arrest, and he had no idea where they were. Tommy had given up on that pair as soon as he had their money. Mickey Griffin got caught up in a nasty drugs business with a few nutters from Leeds, and was doing fifteen years in Durham prison. John Daly disappeared. Brian Field died in a car crash the year before, not long after he was released. He knew too much, and Lavery had lost patience with a loose end that Jack was forced to tidy up.

The printed words lifted his soul, represented a brighter future. There was going to be considerable chaos in the North West as a result of this, and he was on his way to London to keep out of trouble. Perhaps the protection that he had enjoyed over the previous few years might evaporate now that the Beast was dead. His life was bound to change. He didn't know exactly how high up Tommy had reached, but he wondered if there were mass celebrations going on in New Scotland Yard at that very moment.

The links to the men he controlled would be instantly cut, Tommy had no succession plan.

Jack's mind turned to Spain. That would be the place to go. He would retire when everything had died down. Perhaps he could visit George Stanley, talk to him about where the money had gone from the fake property investments, and the re-directed Swiss bank accounts. A nice little visit to Lesser & Co might provide him with a handy retirement fund.

Two men walked into his empty first class compartment as he returned to his newspaper, and sat down opposite him.

'Hello, Jack.'

Armstrong looked up and stared into the eyes of Eddie Maloney. He must have been wearing a wig; either that or his hair had miraculously grown back, because he didn't recognise him at first.

'Jesus. You startled me,' Jack said, analysing the situation quickly. Had they come to congratulate him on the accuracy of his information? Tommy left the hotel at exactly eight in the morning the day before, as he had promised. Jack just managed to get out of range of the explosion in time.

'Are you happy, Jack?'

'You mean in life generally, or right now?'

'Both.'

Armstrong held up the newspaper. 'The world's changing. Things are gonna be different now. I have no ties any more.'

'I know, it's good, isn't it?'

'I suppose.'

'Nobody to answer to?'

'No.' Jack tried to smile, but felt weary. They didn't mention a personal thank you afterwards.

'Your information was excellent. He was an easy target. Now we can all be happy.' Maloney smiled as he addressed him. 'We're very grateful to you for co-operating with us.'

Maloney's companion shifted uneasily in his seat. Jack

wondered what to do, started to weigh up his options. His gun was in his jacket pocket, above him on the luggage rack.

Eddie seemed to catch where his mind was going. 'Relax, Jack. You have nothing to worry about, here in public.' He laughed, but this didn't fill Armstrong with any confidence.

'I helped you. You wanted to get at Tommy, and I helped you.'

'I know, and we're very pleased with the result, Jack.' The man's accent seemed to have changed considerably. Now it was clear he was from Ireland, whereas every time Armstrong had met him back in the days of the robbery, he sounded like he was a well-educated Englishman.

'I'm not asking for anything in return. I know you wanted rid of Tommy,' Jack said.

'I know. But you also know why.'

'He pissed you off. After the robbery.' Armstrong wondered how widely the rumours had spread about the Irish being the ones who did the double-crossing.

'He certainly did that. He pissed off a whole bloody organisation, Jack. That's not a wise thing to do.' Maloney sounded determined, and looked out of the window at the passing countryside.

Jack relaxed a little. 'Well, he's paid for it now, hasn't he?' he said, knowing that justice had been served.

'I guess. But he had a bloody good run, didn't he?' Maloney said.

Jack had to admit that Lavery lived well on the proceeds of the robbery. When he stopped to work it out, he reckoned his boss got his hands on well over half of the take. Not a bad achievement for a man who didn't lift a finger on the job. He had done all the bloody legwork, as far as he was concerned, and look where it had got him. He was lucky enough to buy a first class ticket, but little more. There was no high life for Jack Armstrong on the back of the robbery.

'I suppose he did.' Jack agreed. He wanted to live comfortably, no more. He wasn't greedy, like Tommy.

Maloney stood and opened the window, pulling it halfway down. He poked his head out and breathed in dramatically.

'How's your mate, Mickey?'

'Mickey? He's all right. Doing a stretch now, as it happens.'

'Yes, I know. Durham, right?'

'Right.' The sense of unease returned.

'Is he doing okay there? You know, he's not having any trouble with some of the other inmates?' Maloney asked, leaning back against the partially open window, staring at Jack.

'I wouldn't know.'

Jack had lost all contact with Griffin after one visit, as Lavery ordered. Griffin knew the score. You did the time, and you kept your mouth shut.

'We want to thank you for helping us get to Lavery. He was an enemy of our organisation. An enemy of the Free State of Ireland. As such, he was a justifiable target.'

'An enemy?'

'Yes, an enemy. He stole from us.'

'I didn't know.'

'Didn't you? That's not what Mickey Griffin said.'

Maloney put a finger to his lips, and then Jack noticed movement opposite him. The other carriage occupant was pointing a gun, fitted with a silencer, at his head. It felt like a complete circle, tables turned on that misty night on the Welsh coast. So, Mickey Griffin had turned on him.

'Jack, we are truly grateful you brought us to Tommy. But we have unfinished business, too.'

'But…'

Maloney held his hand up, and then put his finger back to his lips.

'Shush now, Jack. We know. We know it was you.' Maloney sounded like he was telling him a bedtime story. 'Their names, if you're interested, were Mick Fitzgerald and Brian Beard. They were soldiers, just like you, doing their jobs, just like you. I know how it is when you work for someone like Tommy Lavery. Our organisation is the same. You follow an order, that's what makes you a soldier. That's what makes you live and die by the code.'

Armstrong's mind raced. How could he persuade Maloney to let him go? Could he offer him money? How could he fight his way out of this corner? Surely they wouldn't pull the trigger on him in such a public place? They were terrorists, but they weren't idiots.

'Please,' Armstrong begged. 'Tell me what you want.'

History would never record the fact that he was one of the Great Train Robbers. He wasn't going to be remembered as one of those glamorous thieves, worshipped in the pubs and clubs, spoken of in awe by the man in the street. In the future, he would be a forgotten smudge in the margin of an infamous crime. Jack Armstrong looked down the barrel of the gun, and prayed for atonement.

Appendix

The sentences given to the gang:

30 years: Ronnie Biggs, Gordon Goody, Jim Hussey, Roy James, Bob Welch, Charlie Wilson, Tommy Wisbey

25 years: Bruce Reynolds

25 years, reduced to 5 years on appeal: Brian Field, Lennie Field

21 years, reduced to 14 years on appeal: Bill Boal

20 years, reduced to 14 years on appeal: Roger Cordrey

18 years: Jimmy White

15 years: Ronald Edwards

3 years: John Wheater

Found not guilty on direction of the judge: John Daly

Never charged: Danny Pembroke, Harry Smith, Jack Armstrong, Mickey Griffin

Source material

Although this story is fictional, it is built around the real facts of The Great Train Robbery of 1963, many of which are accessible in archives at the British Library. The characters that comprise the men who robbed the robbers in this version are purely fictional, although there are many reports of a mysterious 'Ulsterman' in some factual accounts. The most intriguing thing about all of these sources is their frequently contradictory nature.

The following publications played a significant role in researching 'The Men Who Robbed The Great Train Robbers':

Peta Fordham, 'The Robbers' Tale' (Hodder & Stroughton, 1965)

George Hatherill, 'A Detective's Story' (McGraw-Hill, 1971)

Frank Williams, 'No Fixed Address: The Great Train Robbers On The Run' (W.H. Allen, 1973)

Piers Paul Read, 'The Train Robbers' (W.H. Allen, 1978)

Bruce Reynolds, 'Crossing The Line: The Autobiography of a Thief' (Virgin, 2003)

Tim Coates, 'Moments of History: The Great British Train Robbery, 1963' (Tim Coates, 2003)

Wensley Clarkson, 'Killing Charlie' (Mainstream Publishing, 2006)

Peter Guttridge, 'The Great Train Robbery; Crime Archive' (The National Archives, 2008)

Nick Russell-Pavier & Stewart Richards, 'The Great Train Robbery: Crime of the century' (Weidenfeld & Nicholson, 2012)

Andrew Cook, 'The Great Train Robbery: The Untold Story from the Closed Investigation Files' (The History Press, 2013)

Acknowledgements

The following people have played an invaluable part in bringing this book to life:

Gretchen Smith, for her painstaking eye for detail, and amazing editorial input. Sam Jorbison, for early guidance on focus. Without him, this book would be unpalatable. I am also indebted to the team at Matador, for their great support in bringing this story to the page. Most of all, I have to thank Jackie and Peggy for their extraordinary patience, putting up with this intrusion in their lives for so long.

Lightning Source UK Ltd.
Milton Keynes UK
UKHW020931150822
407319UK00011B/2172

9 781783 062